PRIZED

FARSEEN CHRONICLES BOOK 7

N. R. TUCKER

Two Becomes Five

5009 – 4989 BCE

Chapter 1 – 5009 BCE

Rayna ran full out, jumping the ditch and running in a straight line for the Forest Lord's home, but the river dragons continued to close in. Her wolf form had attracted their attention, and her attempt to elude them had failed. Her breath came in rapid bursts, and her leg muscles ached from the effort.

There was no time to shift, and Rayna was unsure if the dragons would care which skin she wore: wolf or humanoid. She did not know their eating habits. Unlike the traditional dragons Rayna had fought, the smaller river dragons appeared as huge snakes with four short legs and a pronounced head with two horns. She was beginning to realize that Ellwood assumed she knew more about the Farseen than she did.

Since arriving here, Rayna spent most of her time learning about the Farseen and the odd Fae rules of court that were now her life. It had been too long since she had changed forms, and she had planned a relaxing run.

The largest of the dragons swiped at her back and took some fur. Outrunning them was no longer an option. She called fire and burned the dragon nearest to her, killing him. The others slowed their approach, but since Ellwood arrived at that moment, Rayna was unsure which event halted the chase.

"Cease. You dare attack one under my protection?" Lord Ellwood, Forest Lord of the Northern Realm, standing nearly seven feet tall, appeared between the dragons and Rayna. Panting, Rayna shifted to her human form and moved to stand by Ellwood. As she changed, the clothes she had been wearing when she first took her wolf form molded around her body.

1

Prized

"Had we known a shifter from the Seen resided therein, we would not have considered her prey." Nodding to Rayna, the dragon added, "She is well able to defend herself, but I will spread the word of her visit."

"Not visit. Lady Rayna is here to stay. We are exchanging vows."

Bowing, the dragon didn't remove her eyes from Rayna. "May the waters of your journey together move at a pace you can both survive."

The dragons returned to the river.

At Rayna's confused look, Ellwood laughed. "The dragon wished us luck."

Rayna raised her eyebrows. "A blessing or a curse?"

"It was both." Ellwood pulled Rayna into his arms and placed a gentle kiss on her forehead. "I gave orders to announce your arrival to the lesser fae. The one who failed me shall be punished. Perhaps you should stay within the residence until I verify those orders have been carried out to my satisfaction."

"Seems wise. Will the dragons seek revenge? I killed one of them."

"No, my love. They attacked first. You defended yourself."

Rayna nodded that she understood, but she didn't agree. Rules of conduct could be broken or at least bent enough to allow for revenge if one was careful.

A week later, Rayna sat on a rock by the Kaveri River, watching the merfolk and river dragons play. She had learned much since her fight with the dragons. She knew that the merfolk before her were called river merfolk and were smaller than their ocean cousins. To survive in the river, they had lost their long tail fin and acquired two legs. Their feet and hands looked more frog-like than humanoid, and they retained their scales. Gills allowed them to breathe in and out of the water. After their rocky introduction, the river dragons had accepted Rayna, and she enjoyed sitting by the river away from the court. In fact, she found the lesser fae to be friendly and forthright, more so than the ruling fae.

The ruling fae hid behind ritual, selecting words carefully to mask their true intention. It was confusing, mostly because there were many fae Rayna couldn't read. A skill she had depended on back home in the Seen. Rayna could tap into the mind, which wasn't as helpful as one might think. While she could pick up surface thoughts, most minds were cluttered with outlandish thoughts and responses never spoken. It was confusing. Rayna's real gift was sensing emotions. In the Seen, she always knew what others felt, and thus Rayna could help resolve conflicts. That didn't work so well in the Farseen. Even Ellwood's mind was closed to her. On some level, she suspected that was one of the things she loved about him.

*****

"I vow to address your needs, cherish your heart, and honor you in my court so long as we choose to stay together." Ellwood, one of the five realm lords, looked into his chosen mate's eyes as he spoke. Rayna's enthusiasm and approval had both surprised and pleased him. He decided to exchange vows with her because of a prophecy. Ellwood had not expected to care about her. Introducing his bride to his world, seeing it through her eyes, had changed him. It had been years since he noticed the beauty of his realm.

"I vow to attend to your needs, shield your heart from harm, and honor you so long as we choose to stay together." Rayna, daughter of the Shifter Sovereign, smiled tentatively.

Ellwood's smile lit his eyes. Her vow was a good one. In the Seen, a servant of whatever gods were worshiped, would read established vows for the couple to exchange. Here in the Farseen, vows were specific promises, exchanged in private, no witnesses, save the stone.

As the couple spoke their vows, the words carved into the stone Ellwood had placed at the falls earlier in the day. The stone was spelled to carve mating vows. Since fae did not lie, the carving stood as a reminder of what the couple had promised to contribute to the union. The vows were a magical contract no one could break, unless the couple, standing together, broke the stone holding their vows. If one of them died, the stone shattered on its own. Such was the nature of the spell. Fae always chose their words carefully.

From this day forward, Lady Rayna was the wife of one of the five realm lords of the Farseen. Her life would change drastically in ways she was as yet unaware. Ellwood pulled his wife into his arms and kissed her.

Hours later, Lord Ellwood stood on the deck of the treehouse he had built for his mate and their future progeny. He watched river merfolk playing tag with the glowing, multi-colored jellyfish of the Kaveri River. He was pleased with his new bride and with the vows she chose. To shield his heart from harm, she would have to choose him over her shifter family. He had placed the vow stone at the entrance to the private family area of the Northern Realm residence.

Prized

Many fae thought he was tainting the purity of the species by taking a non-fae to wife, although none would say so to his face. Ellwood knew better. On the night of Rayna's birth, a formidable seer visited him. The conversation was etched in his memory.

"You dare enter my bedchamber, witch?" Ellwood jumped out of bed and grabbed his sword. He didn't have to tell his companion for the evening to leave. Using an intelligence Ellwood didn't know she had, she ran from the room.

"Your bedchamber has hosted so many, I thought you would not mind."

Ellwood eyed the fae witch. She was a black-haired beauty, but he frequently observed that beauty appearing without warning usually wanted something, and he didn't grant favors. He also didn't relax his stance. "What brings you here?"

"I bring news of an important birth in the Seen."

"The Seen?" Ellwood rubbed his chin. The only thing the Seen was good for was hunting. Humans and shifters made excellent prey, as did some of the other creatures there.

"Yes, the Shifter Sovereign has given birth to twins, a boy and girl. The girl will be a great power and will gift you two sets of triplets. Two of those off-spring, one from each set, will become powers and will be known throughout the dimensions."

Ellwood grinned at the thought of powerful children who obeyed his every command. He could subjugate the five realms of the Farseen or rule the Seen, perhaps both. Assuming the children were strong enough and bowed to his rule.

The seer clicked her teeth together. "Before you descend further into your plot, the child needs to come to adulthood in the Seen. Only then should she exchange vows with you and move here."

"Vows?" Ellwood's face lit up in surprise. Having children with a shifter was one thing. Crossbreeding preternatural species frequently resulted in powerful children. But vows? That was a commitment.

"Everything hinges on you exchanging vows with the shifter and convincing her to live here in your realm." With those words, the seer opened a way and was gone.

Ellwood never saw the witch again, though he did search for her. Since many fae had the ability to glamour, to change their outward appearance, he was not surprised that the witch had taken another form to visit him. Ellwood took her words to heart, and became a

4

regular visitor to the Seen, hunting game, not humans, on the isles where the Shifter Sovereign lived. Eventually, Ellwood introduced himself to the sovereign's clan, the Alpha Clan, and occasionally gifted his kill to them. His plan, for all its simplicity, worked. The Alpha Clan welcomed his visits, the only naysayer being Kyan, Rayna's twin. Kyan had a deep dislike of the Forest Lord, but that was okay. Ellwood didn't like Kyan either. It was impossible to trust someone whose mind was completely closed.

Ellwood was drawn from his memory by a voice.

"Why are you out here, husband mine?" Rayna had thrown on a robe made of material so thin it accentuated, rather than concealed, her body.

He smiled in appreciation of a body as near perfect as any Ellwood had ever seen. And he had seen a lot of bodies in his nearly two thousand years of life. Ellwood swept her into his arms and twirled her around before setting her down. "I was thanking the five realms for my good fortune in finding you, my love."

Rayna grinned and, walking backward, pulled Ellwood toward their bed.

*****

Kyan stalked his prey for hours. His black hair, braided in rows to keep the long locks out of his way, made no sound as he scanned the horizon. The beads had been covered in leather to prevent any noise, a critical need when on the hunt. He fingered one of the beads. Rayna had covered them herself. She called it her going away present. Just the thought of his sister with that fae made his teeth clench. Kyan's time in the woods had done much to improve his temper, but the mere thought of Ellwood returned a sneer to his lips.

Kyan had been sent home early from the Farseen because, according to his mother, threatening a fae at his own vow announcement was not polite. His sneer deepened into a scowl. It wasn't so much a threat as a promise. All Kyan did was describe how Ellwood, Forest Lord of the Northern Realm, would die if he caused Rayna any pain. Perfectly acceptable brotherly response in the Seen, but apparently the fae weren't willing to discuss such things in public. Oh well, he never aspired to curry favor with the fae anyway. Kyan still didn't understand why his mother was so enthusiastic about Rayna's choice for a mate.

Prized

His prey stepped out of the tree line. With a grin, Kyan raised his bow and took aim at the brown bear. The animal was rare in the northern isles, and he was pleased to have tracked it. This one would feed the clan, and he could use some new leathers. He released his arrow too late, for the bear was already running. Kyan looked up and frowned. A green dragon flew through a way that opened high in the sky. Based on her size, which was huge, she was an old dragon.

The green landed in the open field where the bear had been. "Fare thee well, shifter?"

"I would fare better had you waited until after I killed my prey." Kyan walked out of the trees. Better to find out what the dragon wanted. It was rare that a dragon left their home dimension and entered the Seen. Dragons made humans nervous, which proved humans were intelligent about some things. Dragons made everyone nervous.

The green was a traditional dragon and the largest he had ever seen. It could have easily killed the bear Kyan had tracked. The wingspan alone was impressive. The neck and tail appeared to be about the same length, while the arms, legs, and torso were all muscle. The green scales glittered in the sunlight with the color ranging from pale lime to dark ivy. If humans saw the creature, there would be panic.

"I am Tulvir, Green Dragon Supreme Matriarch. You and I shall be friends."

"You don't know me."

Tulvir lowered her neck until she was eye to eye with Kyan. "Think you that I lie?"

"No," Kyan replied with his usual sharpness before he thought better of it. A supreme matriarch was the strongest and most deadly of her dragon tribe, and no creature from the Farseen lied. Withhold information, yes. Divert attention from a subject, absolutely. Tell a direct lie, no. It was a waste of time, as most fae could discern a lie when spoken aloud. "But I think you may have the wrong shifter."

The green laughed, sending smoke out her nostrils. "The ruling fae and the shifters call you the Sovereign's Assassin. Is that not enough of a title? If not, then perhaps I should call you Kyan of the Alpha Clan, though only other members of the clan know you as such."

Frowning that she named him true, Kyan placed his bow on his back. A well-placed arrow might anger the matriarch, but it wouldn't cause her great harm unless he hit one of two specific points on her body, which were currently protected. Shifting into his wolf would simply make him a desirable snack. "Why would you desire my friendship?"

"You hid in plain sight. You do what is right because it is right and not for personal gain. That is rare among those who walk on two legs." Tulvir sat and closed her wings behind her back. "A war is coming. Your sister's marriage, and the two sets of triplets she will birth, have changed things in such a way that war cannot be prevented. It is a war that will destroy the Seen... unless you and I work together."

"Why would you help the Seen? And more to the point, why do you offer to help a shifter?" Kyan raised an eyebrow. Dragons were known for seeing the future, and, unlike humanoid seers, dragons rarely missed important details.

"Why wouldn't I? I know what will happen if the fae rules over the Seen, and it is not to be allowed. Together, we shall weave defenses into your clan. Come to my lair three days hence." Tulvir stood and spoke directly into Kyan's mind as she flew into the way she had left open in the sky. *Do not speak of this with your family. Your twin is too enamored with the Forest Lord to keep anything from him, and your mother cannot hide her thoughts from Rayna.*

Kyan laughed as the way closed. He always suspected Rayna was a stronger telepath than she admitted. If the green was to be believed, now he had proof. Good thing his mind had always been closed to everyone, except dragons apparently.

*****

On the appointed day, Kyan opened a way to the Farseen, about a mile from the entrance to Tulvir's lair. It had taken some time to find the location of the dragon's lair. He succeeded but now owed a debt to a fae. As he approached, he wondered if it was smart of him to be here without telling his clan where he was. Forget that, he knew it wasn't smart. He approached the cave entrance as two adult dragons uncoiled and looked down at him.

The dragon on the left said, "Enter in peace. Congregate in peace. Leave in peace."

Kyan finished the quote, saying the words all dragons exchanged before a formal meeting. "Or make the blood price so high, your enemies will desire peace."

The dragon on the right laughed. "Indeed, young shifter. It has been an age since I've enjoyed a high blood price. While I would find it amusing, my matriarch awaits you." Both dragons turned sideways, signaling for Kyan to pass.

Kyan nodded and entered the cave. Only a dragon would address a shifter in his twenties as young. Humans, and most shifters, considered him too old to be without a wife. His mother, the sovereign, had given up trying to force him to marry and produce children. At the first fork, he was pleased to see a small, whelp-sized dragon standing in front of one of the lava tubes. The whelp pointed to the other tube, sending Kyan higher into the mountain. Whelp-sized dragons guarded every fork. Kyan tried to keep track but feared he had lost count of the twists and turns. If the whelps were not there when he left, he would be in the cave for a while searching for an exit. He continued to count his steps after each turn and hoped he counted true.

The lava cave was cool and dry. The tube was smooth, nothing like the caves where Kyan grew up. Assuming a dragon would not nest in an active volcano, Kyan continued to walk. Two hundred and seventeen paces past the last fork, the tube opened into a large cavern.

Tulvir, resting in the far corner, raised her head. "Welcome to my nest, Kyan."

Kyan bowed. "I am pleased to be here."

"Your pleasure does not concern me. The safety of our two dimensions does." Tulvir uncoiled and waved one of her claws, causing a rock to disappear.

Kyan looked on in shock as a rock shaped to serve as a table was revealed. Atop it lay jewels and small rods of gold and silver as well as materials that could be used for creating rings, bracelets, and necklaces. "What's this? If you want to create baubles, you should have approached Adair."

Kyan would have no idea what the materials were if not for his friend. Adair made jewels for the rulers of human settlements as well as shifter clans and witches. Even the fae traveled from the Farseen to trade with him. Kyan spent many hours watching Adair work. There was a comfort to be had in watching something created for its beauty. Kyan only made weapons, which he supposed had their own kind of beauty in the feel and precision of the tool.

Tulvir laughed, expelling smoke. "I have no need of baubles. These will be weapons, crafted by you, to protect the Alpha Clan. Rayna's wedding, and the two sets of triplets she shall birth, have made this necessary."

"You can't stab someone with a ruby." Kyan picked up one of the stones and tossed it in the air.

Tulvir reached out and snatched it before Kyan caught it. "Are you a child? So sure that all you see is exactly as presented? Dragons have long spelled objects, and those objects have become powers to be wielded only by the stout of heart and sharp of mind."

Kyan raised an eyebrow. He had heard of dragon spelled objects, but to his knowledge had never seen one. Most of those objects did indeed have great power, but they also carried great responsibility and frequently a huge downside. "Then why am I of use to you? Create the objects, cast your spells, and give them to my sisters."

"Am I your slave? Shall I do your work for you?" Tulvir flicked her tail, rolling a boulder across the cave floor, shaking the ground.

Kyan stood up straight and faced the dragon. "No disrespect was intended. I have limited powers to cast simple spells, and the only wearable objects I've ever created are weapons."

"I will spell the objects. No creature other than a dragon could cast the proper spell. But you, Assassin, will make beautiful baubles."

*****

"Why do that?" Kyan looked over Adair's shoulder.

Adair's hand slipped, but he managed to save the gem. He looked up from the delicate work of cutting the stone to get the correct sparkle and growled, "Don't do that."

Kyan tilted his head in surprise. "Do what?"

"Ask questions or sneak up behind me when I'm cutting a gem or stone. The wizard who commissioned this piece gave me this stone from her collection. I can't replace it and doubt I would like the curse she would place on me if I were to fail her." Adair placed the stone on the table and stretched. He needed a break anyway.

"But why cut it at all?"

"When did you become interested in jewelry work?"

"I've always watched you work."

"No, you've always napped while I worked and then joined me for a mug when I finished. Now you watch everything I do. You planning to create your own jewelry?"

Apparently. Kyan picked up a tool he couldn't determine a use for and laid it back down on the table. "Just interested. So why cut it?"

Prized

Adair eyed his friend but didn't speak.

Kyan sighed. He couldn't discuss the dragon's vision, but his friend deserved some type of answer. "The sovereign's business. I really do need to know anything you can teach me about cutting stones."

Appeased by the answer, for no shifter could disobey the sovereign, Adair picked up an uncut, colorless crystal. "You should have said so. This is an easy to find gem, although most are not of good quality for cutting. For any crystal, you want balance, brilliance, and clarity. The cut complements the stone, not the other way around."

Adair continued his monologue for the rest of the day. He explained the types of cuts he preferred and how to achieve them. He showed Kyan what the tools were for and demonstrated how to cut gems and polish stones. At sunset, Adair said, "It might be easier if I created the pieces for the sovereign."

"It would, but the task was given to me." Kyan shrugged.

"Then, my friend, we will work daily when you are available. Tools I can loan you for a time, but you'll have to bring your own gems and stones."

Kyan grinned, "I have what is needed. Come, the ale awaits."

"Excellent." Adair put up his work and released his dogs. The village knew his home contained valuables, but no one would enter his tent while his dogs patrolled.

*****

Kyan approached Tulvir's cave, and the guards waved him through. Kyan had been to visit the green supreme matriarch monthly. He finally learned his way through the maze of lava tubes, but whelps still stood guard over the path he was not to take. Kyan was beginning to think they always stood guard.

The bag of jewels was a weight on his shoulders. Not because it was heavy, but because he had failed. His jewelry looked nothing like the craftsmanship of Adair. He did not think Tulvir would be pleased.

Kyan walked into Tulvir's nest. She wasn't there, but the rock was removed from his work area, so he went straight to work. Knowing he was not devoting enough attention to this task and unhappy with his progress, Kyan muttered, "This is unfit for a human, much less the sovereign."

"On that, we can agree."

Kyan jumped. He had been so engrossed in his work he didn't notice when Tulvir came to stand behind him. Such a lapse could be his death.

"I am not pleased." Tulvir swept the table clean and waved a claw. New uncut jewels appeared in front of Kyan. "Start over. This time don't cut these stones until you have practiced on others."

"If Adair could cut the stones, I could mount them." Kyan made the same offer he had made repeatedly over the past year. He was surprised when she responded this time.

"Know you nothing of higher magic?" Tulvir curved her neck down until she was eye level with Kyan, which Kyan had learned meant she was displeased. Smoke came out Tulvir's nose as she said, "The spell is tied to the person who cuts the stone and their biological family. If Adair cuts the stone, his family will be protected by the spell, not yours."

Good to know. Why hadn't she mentioned that before?

Tulvir flicked her tail, sending boulders flying. "You do remember that I know what is in your mind, don't you?"

Kyan gritted his teeth. He was too accustomed to no one being able to enter his mind. "Yes, supreme matriarch."

"Perhaps we have rushed too much. We have time. We will meet twice a year — when all three moons are full — to review your progress. Cut no more of my stones until you are truly ready."

Chapter 2 – 4989 BCE

"Aiyeeee!"

The scream reverberated through the treehouse. Ellwood paced. While he looked forward to the prophesied birth of his first set of triplets, his worry for Rayna was a surprise. Ten years ago, they exchanged private vows at the waterfall, where many Northern Realm fae performed the task of carving their vows into a stone tablet. Afterward, he held a formal repast at the court to introduce his wife. And while Ellwood found Rayna to be an acceptable companion in every way that mattered, he had not expected to genuinely care about her.

The seer had prophesied two sets of triplets from Rayna. She would survive. She had to. Did all women experience pain with the birth of their young? Ellwood had never felt the need to gather such information, nor had he ever been near a woman during the actual birthing process. His pace increased when Rayna screamed again.

Ellwood's eyes cut to Kyan, who had made one of his thankfully rare trips to the Farseen for the birth. Kyan appeared calm, and that angered the Forest Lord. "Is that normal?"

"What?" Kyan looked up from studying the map of the Farseen.

Watching the shifter had, at first, amused the fae lord. Since they were waiting in the Northern Realm war room for news of the birth, Kyan had used the time to gather what data he could. Ellwood's map was a treasure trove of locations, including where lesser fae could be found. Even dragon lairs and elemental sanctums were marked.

Another scream, and Kyan nodded his understanding. "The few times I have been near a woman in childbirth, screams were normal." Kyan refocused on the map. No way would he admit to the fool his sister married that he knew Rayna would have two sets of triplets. Since this was the first set, Rayna and her children should be fine.

"Men know nothing of the birthing process." Lady Zylina lounged on a massive overstuffed pillow that could easily hold seven adults who didn't like each other. As always, she was dressed for travel and not as a lady of the court. Without the natural curves of her body, she would look more male than female in her tight leggings and tunic.

"Did you scream on your birthing bed?" Ellwood snarled at his sister.

The animosity between Ellwood and his twin was the subject of many bard songs. Lady Z flickered in and out of the realm, always traveling with her elemental friends. These last few years, Lady Z and Rayna had developed a friendship Ellwood was not pleased with.

Lady Z laughed. "I don't remember, but I daresay I did. The ability to birth children is what makes women so strong, Lord Ellwood."

Ellwood's lip curled at the term of respect. Lady Z respected no one.

A short time later, the healer's assistant hurried into the war room. "My Lord, Lady Rayna has gifted you a strong son and two beautiful daughters."

Ellwood smiled. All thoughts of Lady Z and Kyan left him as he followed. He had a son. A son who would be the power prophesied from this set of triplets.

*****

Watching her brother leave the room, Lady Z shrugged. "I will present a gift to each child, and then it's time for me to go."

"What?" Kyan looked up from the map. She was the only fae in the Northern Realm he trusted to protect Rayna and the babies.

Lady Z laughed. "You could not have expected me to stay."

"Why not?"

"My brother and I would fight if I remained too long. It would be disastrous for the realm."

"Defeat him and rule." Kyan observed everything. He knew Lady Z was stronger than Ellwood.

"You fool. I would be a worse ruler than Ellwood. If you worry so for your sister, you stay."

"Then she would lose either a brother or a husband."

"The solution reveals itself. Lady Rayna will have to take care of herself. I believe her to be capable in that regard." Lady Z followed her brother to see the triplets.

Kyan called wind but dissipated it before he turned the war room into shambles. Such a display of temper would be a waste of effort. He gritted his teeth and joined Lady Z to welcome his nieces and nephew to the world. In the birthing chamber, Rayna leaned back on pillows holding two babies, one with the traditional white hair of the ruling fae and one with jet-black hair like Rayna. Ellwood held the third whose white hair had a hint of shifter blonde.

Ellwood raised his bundle in the air. "My son. What shall he be called, my love?"

Rayna beamed at her mate, "Valiant, for he shall be courageous and gallant." She cooed at her daughters. Holding the child in her left arm high, Rayna said, "Tempest, our firstborn shall be called, for she will always hold a violent storm within her." Dropping Tempest whose hair was white with no hint of blonde back to her shoulder, Rayna held up the other girl, whose hair was as dark as Tempest's was fair. "Temperance, our third born will answer to, for she shall be moderation itself. Holding herself to a higher standard than others."

Regretting the fae tradition that the female who gives birth names the child, Ellwood asked, "How did these unusual names come to you?" Most fae, at least in the Northern Realm, had names based in nature, not virtues.

Rayna blushed, but said, "I have dreamed of these names for weeks. Two nights ago, I had a different dream, a conversation with the supreme matriarch of the reds. Ralliner said I should use the names from my dreams. When I awoke, I checked with the scribes and read the fae scrolls myself. To disregard the advice of a supreme matriarch is discouraged, even if the advice comes in a dream. The more I thought on the names, the better they appealed to me."

Lady Z placed a hand on her brother's shoulder and tickled Valiant's chin. "You are fortunate, Lord Ellwood. A supreme matriarch has shown interest in your progeny. Surely, the triplets will be a powerful force for your reign."

A slow smile spread over Ellwood's face. He released Valiant to Lady Z and turned to the record keepers. "You have heard my mate. Tempest, Valiant, and Temperance by order of birth are the names of our young. Announce to the five realms that they will be in court five days hence to begin their life in the Northern Realm."

"So soon?" Kyan said.

Lady Z, holding Valiant, looked up from whispering to the child and winked at Kyan. "It has ever been so. Children born into a realm appear in court after five days to receive gifts and show how strong they are."

Kyan shook his head. He would never understand the fae.

Once the announcement was made, Lord Ellwood handed off his son, kissed his mate, and left. Lady Z bowed and left, taking the rest of the ruling fae with her. The nannies placed the babies in their wee little beds and closed the door between the nursery and Rayna's birthing bed.

"That's a lot of attendants for a simple naming," Kyan said.

"The fae like their formalities," Rayna said.

Kyan handed her a small item wrapped in cloth.

Opening the gift, she exclaimed, "How pretty." Looking closer at the two bracelets, she raised her eyes to Kyan. "This one was made by Adair. The other one has a bit of magic in it."

"Yes, Adair made your mother's bracelet. I made the other." Kyan puffed up his chest.

"You? You made a bracelet of protection. When did you become interested in stone lore? And how did you work the magic?"

"Reasonable questions and an amusing tale, if you are interested?"

Rayna grinned. "I'm very interested."

Five days later, Kyan was still in the Farseen. He had decided to remain for the first court appearance of the triplets. He couldn't wait to return home. It had taken a lot of self-control to not attack Ellwood in his home, although he suspected the forest lord felt the same way. Kyan had been assigned a room near the Hall of Battles, which depicted various skirmishes the current and previous Forest Lords had won. Kyan had to walk through the hall to go anywhere in the residence. Kyan assumed Ellwood had done that to remind him that Ellwood was a strong warrior. Not that Kyan cared.

When Kyan made his way through the Hall of Battles, a female in a revealing dress stepped out from one of the pillars. Other than admire her physical attributes, he ignored her. Kyan's eyes didn't travel above her shoulders. A few fae women had approached him thus, but Kyan knew they weren't interested in him but in his uniqueness. Since most couldn't open a way, shifters rarely visited the Farseen. He had no intention of being a conquest, or worse, a consort if he wasn't careful.

As Kyan walked by, she said, "Don't you recognize me?"

Kyan stopped and turned to look in the direction of the voice he knew well. His eyes rose to her face, and he didn't stop the laugh that bubbled up inside him. Not that he wanted to. "Lady Z. I don't believe I've ever seen you without your traveling clothes. Have you returned?" He hoped so. If she remained, Kyan would feel confident leaving his sister and her children.

"I returned for this evening only." She motioned to her clothes and added, "I have found that if I dress for court upon occasion, it keeps everyone off balance."

"I do like the way you think." Kyan held out his arm, Lady Z slid her hand into place, and they continued toward the feasting hall. When they arrived at the top of the stairs, Kyan's mouth dropped open, and he stopped moving.

The entire hall was decorated in shades of green and brown, the Northern Realm's colors. Garlands, sparkling like the gems Kyan was still learning to cut, hung from the ceiling. He suspected they were gems and spelled to remain in place. The triplets resided in three carved wooden bassinettes with their personal symbol engraved on the headboard. Two guards stood beside each child. The number of gifts in front of the bassinettes nearly blocked a view of the children.

Not knowing which subject to bring up first, Kyan finally asked, "Are those real gems?"

"Yes, most ostentatious, but do not give Ellwood the pleasure of knowing he awed you." Lady Z placed pressure on Kyan's arm, and they continued down the steps into the room. She angled Kyan toward Ridge.

Watching everyone, Ridge, Advisor to the Northern Realm, stood to the side of the bassinettes. He bowed when Lady Z and Kyan approached. "Lady Zylina, you have returned. Does the staff know you are joining the repast tonight?"

"I told them when I arrived. You have nothing to fear except that you called me by that horrendous name."

Ridge grinned. "I have never feared seating arrangements, and you can't take offense when addressed by the name your mother gave you."

"I can and do… as you well know. If you were anyone else, I would blast you." Lady Z walked off in a huff.

"If I were anyone else, I wouldn't use your given name," Ridge said to her back as she walked away. Turning to Kyan, he asked, "How do you find our welcoming repast?"

"Aha, is that what this is?" Kyan waved his hand to encompass the hall.

"Indeed."

"I think my gift of welcome will be overshadowed by the sheer quantity that the triplets have already received."

Ridge said, "No, most of the gifts here will be used by the nannies and guards protecting the triplets. Later the family will present their gifts of welcome."

"Interesting." Kyan nodded and followed Lady Z.

Once the evening repast concluded, private congratulations were extended to Ellwood and Rayna, while respects were paid to the triplets. Kyan watched the proceedings with irritation. The formality of the realm courts made him long to kill something.

"You should learn to play the long game."

Kyan raised an eyebrow at Ridge. "What is the long game?"

"It is well known in court that you dislike Lord Ellwood, and he returns the feeling. Consider confusing everyone." Ridge walked away without waiting for an answer.

Kyan smiled. The advice was sound. While the court was still crowded with well-wishers, Kyan approached Lord Ellwood and performed a bow. "Lord Ellwood, your wife has gifted you three strong children. I can return to the Seen with the knowledge that you will protect my sister, nieces, and nephew to the full extent of your impressive powers." Kyan turned and joined Lady Z.

Lady Z whispered, "A threat worthy of the fae."

"How so?" Kyan raised an eyebrow. He had meant the words as a compliment.

Ridge said through gritted teeth. "You just told Lord Ellwood that if any harm comes to his family, it will be due to his ineptitude."

"I did?"

"Shifter, next time I offer you unsolicited advice, I shall use smaller words." Ridge walked away to join Ellwood.

Lady Z's laughter could be heard throughout the court.

Prized

Kyan shrugged. He learned something else that night. Ridge might be an ally. Perhaps he could be counted on to watch Rayna and the kids.

Before leaving the Northern Realm, Kyan visited Tulvir's cave, exchanged greetings with the dragon guards, walked through the labyrinth to Tulvir's nest, and continued his training with the supreme matriarch. Kyan's ability to set or wrap the gems improved each year, which was why he was able to make the bracelet for Rayna. Even Adair commented favorably on Kyan's settings. While Kyan was able to convert rocks into acceptable jewelry, his cutting of gemstones was subpar. This cycle of training repeated itself while the triplets grew.

A Farseen Childhood

4983 BCE – 4972 BCE

Prized

Chapter 3 – 4983 BCE

Standing between a large flowering bush and a fruit tree next to the herb garden, Valiant watched Tempest practice control of wind. Of the three, only Tempest had shown the fae ability to master an element. While control was iffy at best, fae could wield power over the elements almost before they could walk. Shape shifter abilities would not appear until puberty. Rumor in the court was that Valiant and Temperance would be shifters, and Tempest would be a fae. He wasn't sure how he felt about that.

Not that his feelings on the subject mattered. Whatever abilities they had would manifest as they wished. The triplets had no control over the process and could only wait to see what happened. With one fae parent and one shifter parent, the triplets would have some combination of talents, although half-breeds tended to have a more dominant half.

Valiant reached out and grabbed a tree limb to remain standing when a strong gust of wind would have knocked him over. He watched Tempest – caught in the wind – fly through the air and hit the same tree he held. She slid to the ground with a groan. As the gust dissipated, Valiant looked at the garden. Small, uprooted trees were flung every which way, and the flowering plants Lady Rayna had brought from the Seen were tossed about in heaps, uprooted. Mother would be furious. The chef wouldn't be happy either. He frequently used small cuttings from the herbs in the food he prepared.

"What happened?" Tempest ignored Valiant's hand and stood on her own.

"You called more wind than you could control." Ridge stepped out from behind a large tree with Ciam at his side.

"You were spying," Tempest accused.

Prized

"Nae, little one. I am here to inform you that the Forest Lord demands your attendance in the receiving room."

"Don't call me little one." Tempest's eyes flashed.

Smirking, Ridge bowed to the six-year-old. "As you desire, Mistress Tempest. I will escort you to the Forest Lord."

"I don't need an escort. I'll go to the receiving room when I decide." Tempest would have stormed away, but Ridge stopped her.

"That attitude is exactly why I'm here to escort you. Mistress Temperance can be relied upon to obey. Valiant will occasionally obey, but not you. Never you." Ridge gently took her arm and walked toward the residence.

Valiant smiled at their backs. Tempest tugged on Ridge's arm, but her actions appeared to bother Ridge not at all. No one ever got the better of Ridge, especially not a six-year-old. Not even Tempest.

"Valiant, 'tis time for weapons practice." Ciam turned and walked toward the practice field.

Valiant followed quickly, pleased that Ciam would be his teacher this day. Of all of the warriors in the Northern Realm, he always performed better under his cousin's amiable eye. Ciam corrected without making Valiant feel like a failure. They arrived at the practice field where, as expected, Valiant was ignored, though many spoke to Ciam. Valiant raised his bow and cocked an arrow.

"Wait. We must move the target closer." Ciam motioned to a pixie who moved the target.

Valiant gritted his teeth while he waited. He knew targets were moved closer for one his age, but still, it felt like a failure. When he was on the practice field with Lord Ellwood, the targets were never moved closer. Father repeatedly told Valiant that — as his son — there would be no special treatment. In fact, anytime the phrase *as his son* was used by Ellwood, Valiant knew that any concession made for others his age would not apply to him.

When Ciam nodded to Valiant, he cocked an arrow and let it fly. He sent more arrows toward the target in rapid succession.

"You've been practicing." Ciam watched Valiant retrieve his arrows and returned to the mark. Every arrow had landed on the target, over half in the bullseye.

Valiant blushed at the rare praise. Excluding Ciam, no one in court offered encouragement, just critique. Repeating the comment he heard most often, Valiant said, "But not all landed true, in the center."

"You are young, such accuracy takes time and practice. Again. This time use your non-dominate hand."

"How fares my son this day?" Lord Ellwood stopped beside Ciam.

Nervous, Valiant let loose another round of three. Only one hit the center target, but since it was with his non-dominate hand, Valiant thought he had done well. He turned, hopeful for some small word of encouragement from his father, which he didn't get.

Lord Ellwood appeared not to notice Valiant's efforts as he watched Tempest take the field and let loose three arrows for her weapons training as well. Ignoring Valiant, he proclaimed, "See my firstborn. Her aim is impressive."

Valiant bit his lip to keep from speaking. Tempest had only hit the center target once as well, using her dominant hand, but she received their father's praise.

While the warriors praised Tempest and ignored Valiant, Lord Ellwood turned to Ciam. "Walk with me."

"Another round with the arrows, then switch to the spear. I'll return if I can," Ciam said.

Valiant bowed. "Your instruction has been enlightening."

Ciam clapped him on the shoulder and left, following Ellwood to where Tempest practiced.

Focused on his target once again, Valiant let the arrows fly until his quiver emptied. Valiant dropped his bow and picked up his spear. Taking aim, he threw the spear at the target. It fell short.

"Valiant, you might want to step closer to the target. Your shifter blood appears to hamper your ability to control your weapon."

Valiant didn't look to see which warrior made the comment, though he suspected Barric. They all laughed. All of his arrows landed true after his father left, but not one word of acknowledgment was uttered. He misses the target with his spear, everyone notices. Valiant trudged over to collect his spear and return to his mark. Once again, he took aim and threw the spear. This time it landed near the center of the target, but no one commented or even appeared to notice. He wasn't surprised. The warriors simply followed the lead of their realm lord.

Angry, even though he had expected their reaction, Valiant grabbed his spear, took aim, let loose his weapon, and missed the target completely.

Prized

"I had hoped to see some small improvement in your aim, my son."

Valiant twirled around to face his father, surprised he had returned so soon, and alone. Out of the corner of his eye, Valiant saw that Ciam remained with Tempest, instructing her. Without warning, a blunt fighting stick flew through the air and hit Valiant squarely in the stomach. He roared in pain.

A mammoth hand closed around Valiant's dominant arm, and Ellwood hissed, "Never cry out. You are my son. You will take the pain, embrace it, and never show it."

"Yes, Lord Ellwood." Valiant stood as tall as he could, but he was still partly bent over, breathing heavily. No way that stick hit him on accident.

Barric, not much older than Valiant and the son of Joren, the Northern Realm Representative on the High Council, picked up the stick and smirked at Valiant where Ellwood couldn't see. Turning to the Forest Lord, Barric bowed, "We were sparring adjacent to Valiant. And the stick flew when I blocked it."

Ellwood laughed. "Of course. Valiant will be more aware of his surroundings in the future, won't you?"

"Yes, Lord Ellwood." Valiant glared at Barric, but they both knew Valiant could say nothing without incurring Ellwood's wrath.

"Come, Valiant. Mother desires your attendance." Temperance called from the edge of the training field. When she realized their father stood beside Valiant, she stepped back.

"It appears your mother has saved you from practice yet again. Go." Ellwood turned and spoke to his warriors, ignoring his son.

Valiant gathered up his weapons and followed his sister.

"You don't seem happy."

Valiant snorted. "Happy? Should I be happy that Barric made a fool of me and father supported him? I don't enjoy being laughed at. Never does anyone notice my successes."

"Do not concern yourself with them. One day you will lead the warriors. Then they will respect you."

Valiant didn't reply but, as young as he was, he knew they would not respect him unless something changed. And nothing would change until the lord of the realm showed Valiant a sliver of respect. His status as a half-breed was not what the warriors objected to, although they used that excuse often enough when his mother wasn't around. Valiant knew that their objection to him was that his father objected to him. Everything Valiant did, no matter how good, wasn't good enough for Lord Ellwood.

*****

It was a beautiful spring day, yet Valiant had spent the afternoon attending to history studies. What a waste of a perfectly good day. He didn't understand why anyone thought the songs of past battles would prepare him for adult life. He spent more time evaluating the tune and format of the songs than absorbing the meaning of the words. And to make it worse, both of his sisters were missing. One of the three would frequently be pulled from academic lessons to study fighting and other, more physical, subjects, but rarely was one of them left alone in the study rooms.

He looked up when the doors swung open, and Tempest walked in. "Where have you been all afternoon? You missed history." Valiant's hands tightened into fists.

Tempest smiled. "Advisor Ridge is teaching me to control wind."

"What?"

"Yes, Father said if I insisted on tearing up the garden, I should at least learn the correct way to command the element." Tempest took her seat but didn't open the history scroll. "Ridge is a wonderful teacher."

Why was it when Tempest broke the rules, or destroyed something, she was rewarded? Before the morning repast, she had ruined part of the herb garden, again. The chef was not happy, but Father punished her with training under Ridge's watchful eye. Not that he wanted Ridge to train him, but still. Had Valiant destroyed the chef's garden, Lord Ellwood would have beaten him. Valiant gripped the quill too hard and broke it. He tossed the useless writing implement to the side and picked up a new one.

"And what were you doing?" Valiant asked when Temperance walked in.

Temperance hopped from foot to foot, smiling. "I can manipulate all four of the elements. Not well mind you, but Lady Z said I show promise. Cousin Ciam has been assigned to train me."

"All four came to you at once?" Anger flashed across Tempest's features.

Valiant hid his chuckle behind a cough. Tempest had expected to be the first to call all four elements. She had said so often enough. It had been a while since she first called wind, and it was still the only element that answered her call.

Temperance didn't notice her sister's mood, and said, "Yes. I'm grateful Lady Z was with me in the garden. She took my water, put out the fire before it spread, and then she stilled the wind and the ground. I have so much to learn."

"How nice for you." Valiant tossed his scroll on the desk and headed for the door to family treehouses.

"Where are you going?" Tempest asked.

"Nowhere," Valiant muttered. "Nowhere at all."

Valiant shuffled down the hall. Now, both of his sisters called at least one element. He looked forward to the day he could control the elements and had expected Ciam, Lady Z's only child, to be his trainer. Ciam was as close to a friend as Valiant had. Aside from his sisters, everyone else in court was old. Ciam was an adult and probably old, but he was Valiant's biggest supporter. An accomplished warrior, Ciam was kind, showing Valiant how to hold a bow and arrow, correcting his fighting stances, and teaching him survival skills. Ciam never scolded, as Ridge did, or belittled Valiant's attempts, as Father did.

Valiant left the residence and walked with no clear direction in mind. On a whim, he grabbed one of his spears as he passed the training center. Anger bubbled up, and he threw it as hard as he could at a tree.

"What possible reason could you have for throwing a spear at that tree?" Ash, Master-At-Arms for the Northern Realm, asked.

Valiant retrieved his spear and walked back to his mark before he answered. "Improving my accuracy. Isn't that what I'm supposed to do?"

"There are many targets on the practice fields. Why this tree?"

"No reason." When Ash didn't say anything else, Valiant muttered, "Here I can mess up alone."

Ash nodded. "Come. You may practice in my private gardens any time you wish. Don't attack any more innocent trees. You might stab a treeman, and that would anger the trees and Lord Ellwood. Would your anger be a result of your sisters commanding the elements?"

Valiant struggled to keep up with Ash, and his answer came out in a huff. "It matters not."

"It matters greatly. Hide your jealousy, or a bard will write a song about your battered ego. I doubt you would enjoy that, especially if it became popular."

Valiant's eyes grew large as Corentin, the largest of the Farseen's three moons. He had always assumed songs written about him would depict his great deeds, not make him look like a court jester. Ash was right. He had to be more careful.

Practicing in Ash's secluded training center turned out to be all Valiant could hope for. It was an unusual design, a garden with targets spread throughout. The only people he ever saw there were Ash or his children, and his young left as soon as they saw Valiant. He wasn't sure if they had been ordered to do so or if they left because they didn't like him, but truthfully, he didn't care. Without insults whittling away at his self-esteem, Valiant found his accuracy improved significantly. He even looked forward to the next exhibition, expecting to show off before his father and the entire realm.

Valiant didn't miss a day practicing in Ash's garden. He frequently arrived as the sun rose, thinking he would practice and leave before the family wanted the use of their garden. Today he was late. As Valiant took aim with his bow, Harden, the eldest male of Ash's young, walked into the garden with his weapons. When he saw Valiant, he started to backtrack.

"You don't have to leave unless you want to," Valiant said. If Valiant remembered correctly, Harden was about his age.

"Father said we were to give you privacy. I thought you weren't coming today as it is past the time you normally arrive." Harden adjusted his weapons in his arms but remained where he was.

"You can remain. Perhaps we could have a contest."

"Why? You never miss. I could never beat you." Harden looked Valiant over. "I don't know why you practice so much. Even father and his particular friends say you have the best eye and truest aim of anyone our age."

Valiant's mouth dropped open. "If you heard the warriors speak on our realm lord's practice field, you would know that isn't true."

"Do you say my father lies?" Harden's throwing hand tightened around his spear.

"No." Valiant shrugged at Harden's anger and the threat of attack it implied. "It's just that no one ever tells me I'm good enough."

"What?"

Prized

"My father doesn't believe I'm living up to his standards as his son, and the court behaves accordingly." Valiant would have clapped a hand over his mouth if the action would have taken the words back. He hadn't intended to say that.

"Oh." Harden's grip loosened. "Well, all I hear at morning repast is, 'Why don't you practice like Valiant?' 'Did you see Valiant continue to practice after a perfect throw? That's the difference between good and great.'"

Valiant tilted his head. "Do you mock me?"

"Why would I admit something so annoying?"

"Maybe someone asked you to."

Harden laughed. "Name one person you trust."

"Tempest and Temperance." The names tumbled out before he considered how it would sound.

"You trust your sisters?"

"Don't you?"

"Not my sisters. They run to Father for everything."

"We would never run to Lord Ellwood."

Neither boy spoke for a moment, then Harden asked, "Would you show me your stance for spear throwing?"

"Huh?"

Blushing, Harden admitted, "I've been watching you, trying to learn it, because you get more power from your throw, but I'm doing something wrong."

Valiant grinned. Ciam had helped him modify his stance just to get more power. "Okay."

The boys practiced stances for a while before Harden took aim at the target and scored a hit.

"Woohoo!" Harden jumped excitedly. "I've never before hit the target at this distance."

Valiant grinned, pleased that he had been able to help someone. It was the first time he had ever instructed someone else, and he liked the feeling. When he noticed Ash walking their way, the grin faded.

Harden didn't notice Valiant's change in mood, and yelled, "Did you see that, Father?"

"Indeed. It was kind of Valiant to offer instruction." Ash turned to Valiant. "I understand you are wanted back at the residence."

Valiant nodded. While storing his equipment, he said to Harden, "I'll be back tomorrow after the noon repast. Join me if you wish."

Harden grinned, but didn't answer. Instead, he turned to his father. "Is it permissible?"

"As long as Valiant desires your company, you may."

"I'll be here."

Valiant left Ash's residence pleased with himself. Not only did he discover that some adults thought well of him, but he might also have made a friend, his first. Wiping the sweat from his brow, contemplating a cool down swim in the river, he didn't pay attention to his surroundings. Valiant failed to notice his path was blocked until he nearly ran into Ridge.

"You would do well to pay better attention to your surroundings." Ridge's trademark smirk covered his face. "Lord Ellwood wants you to walk the Dark Woods."

"Now? Why?"

"Of course, now. As for why, I didn't ask the Forest Lord why he would send his young son to inspect his holdings. He has commanded you to do so before."

"Only when I've angered him," Valiant muttered. The land was surveyed daily by the groundskeeper's staff. They checked the land for sickness in the forest and kept an eye out for unaligned fae. There was no real reason for Valiant to do so except as a punishment.

"Then, you have your answer." Ridge continued down the path toward the residence and said, "Perhaps you should pay particular attention to the western edge."

Valiant snorted and headed east through the Dark Woods, ignoring Ridge's suggestion. He didn't have a clue what he had done to anger Father. Mayhap Lord Ellwood was simply bored.

Later that afternoon, Valiant coaxed his sisters down the nearly overgrown path he had found. "Come. It's worth the walk."

"We could get in trouble. If Lady Adaryn catches us playing when we should be identifying herbs in the garden, she might tell Lord Ellwood," Temperance said.

"No, she won't. As long as we can answer her questions tomorrow, she will be pleased." Tempest picked up the pace. "What have you found?"

"It's just off the trail near the river."

"I wouldn't call this a trail." Temperance pushed a bush to the side and jumped some vines.

Valiant grinned and pointed to a cave entrance.

Prized

"You've found a cave. How nice," Temperance curled her lip.

"Excellent." Tempest peeked inside. "It's perfect."

"I thought so," Valiant said, pleased by Tempest's reaction.

"Perfect for what?" Temperance asked as she brushed dirt from her clothing.

"A lair." Valiant and Tempest replied in concert. Tempest added, "A place no one but us knows about. Somewhere we can be away from court and prying eyes. Freedom."

Temperance rolled her eyes. "It's a bit musty."

"It's a cave, but we can clean it up. I'll bet we can get some pixies to keep it clean enough that even you will be happy." Tempest moved confidently into the cave. "It'll be great."

Ridge watched the triplets for a few minutes and smiled. He knew Valiant would go east just because he had recommended west. The cave was at the edge of land Ridge hoped to win from the Forest Lord, and it was far away from the route most travelers took. The forest nymph coterie in this section of the Dark Woods was loyal to Ridge and would watch over the kids while they used the cave as an escape, allowing them to be safe at the same time. Ridge backed away and moved silently through the woods. The kids never saw him.

Chapter 4 – 4981 BCE

"I'm tired of history scrolls. I want excitement," Valiant said. The triplets walked together on the living bridge toward the feasting hall and the noon repast. The morning had been spent in the library, reading scrolls.

"You always want excitement," Temperance retorted.

"As do I," Tempest said. "Scrolls are not nearly as interesting as fighting and hunting."

"Even searching for plants is better than reading scrolls," Valiant agreed.

"Scrolls have their place," Lord Ellwood said from behind them.

All three children stopped and turned their eyes on their father. Concern twisted Valiant's stomach, as if he had eaten something bad. His sisters turned expectantly toward their father. They were rarely punished for no reason. Lord Ellwood's smile was amused, as opposed to irritated, so Valiant asked, "Are you dining with us today, Father?"

"No. I have a small token for Tempest and Temperance." He handed each girl a stone.

Valiant stepped back. Tempest shot him a look of pity, which only served to fuel his anger. She didn't notice as she refocused on the stone in her hand and asked, "Are these communication stones?"

"Yes." Lord Ellwood beamed at his eldest. "With these, the two of you can talk whenever or wherever you are."

"These will work between the dimensions, right Father?" Temperance asked.

Prized

"Yes, clever girl. They will." Ellwood kissed each daughter on the forehead. Temperance blushed with pleasure. Tempest didn't. The Forest Lord walked away without acknowledging Valiant at all.

Temperance would have spoken, but Tempest caught her eye and shook her head. Valiant shrugged. He was used to it. "Enjoy your stones. Tell Mother I'm taking a walk instead of joining the noon repast." Valiant walked away. Once again, he was left out. It was so common an occurrence that he wondered why it still bothered him. There was no denying Valiant felt hurt, which was ridiculous. Father would never change, and Valiant needed to accept that truth.

He moved through the woods at a fast clip but still noticed a nymph following him. Valiant rounded some boulders, climbed a tree, and waited. When she walked underneath, he dropped from the tree and blocked her path. "You thought I didn't notice."

"You don't usually," Seda, leader of the forest nymph coterie, admitted.

"Why are you watching me?" At first, Valiant had assumed the coterie lived nearby, but he had begun to notice he was followed on the path more often than not.

"Who says I am?"

"I do." His eyes narrowed on the nymph. "Who has your allegiance?" When she didn't respond, he asked, "Is it the Forest Lord?"

"No."

"Lady Rayna?"

"No."

Valiant crossed his arms over his chest. "Must I name every member of the realm?"

Seda sighed. "I gave my word. We only watch to protect you and your sisters when in these woods. If any harm were to befall you, we would alert the realm."

Valiant shook his head. "It's either Ridge or Ash. I suspect Ridge."

Seda smiled. "He will be surprised that you were the first to discover his scheme. He's been waiting for Mistress Tempest to find him out and yell at him."

Valiant grinned. "You may tell him I know but will not speak of it."

"You don't mind?"

"I mind, but this way I know my sisters are safe." Valiant turned and ran deeper into the forest, toward the cave.

Seda sighed and motioned for someone else to follow him. She had to inform Ridge of this development.

*****

"How much trouble am I in?" Dressed for evening repast, Valiant and his sisters walked down the living bridge toward the public halls of the residence. In addition to lunch, he skipped his afternoon lessons.

"Why would you be? Mother sent word to Lady Adaryn that you were on a task for her." Tempest raised an eyebrow. "What task?"

"Nothing exciting," Valiant said, pleased Mother had covered for him. She always seemed to know when Lord Ellwood had ignored him while heaping attention and presents on his sisters. He led his sisters down the living bridge toward the evening repast. Most fathers doted on their sons. Valiant still didn't know what he had done to lose his father's respect, if he had ever had it. Lord Ellwood barely tolerated his only son. Taking a deep breath, Valiant asked, "Have you practiced with the stones yet?"

"Some," Temperance admitted reluctantly.

He grinned. "Don't worry. I won't cry like a baby just because Father ignored me again."

"What happened?" Tempest asked.

When she narrowed her gaze on him, Valiant gently pushed her back. "Stay out of my head."

"What?"

Temperance shook her head. "Don't deny it. You always get the same look on your face when you're mind walking."

Tempest chewed on her bottom lip.

"Did you really think we couldn't tell?" Valiant asked. When she didn't immediately respond, he laughed.

"I'll get better." The words were spoken as a vow.

"Don't be mad. You'll master it eventually, and then no one will know what you're doing," Temperance said.

"I have trouble mind walking in Valiant's head," Tempest admitted.

Valiant's mouth dropped open. "What? You never said."

"Why would I admit a weakness? You know how Father is."

"Is it just Valiant?" Temperance asked, hopefully.

"Yes. Now hush. We're too near the Hall of Battles." Tempest moved quickly down the hall.

Valiant nodded as he and Temperance rushed to catch up. He and Tempest were much more attune to Father, and his spies, than Temperance. She was the most trusting of the trio. Temperance was also the most obedient and had the least to hide. Valiant peeked into the feasting hall and grinned. Harden waved at him from a table full of their peers. "Look. Do we get our own table tonight?"

"Of course not. You are to sit in your proper seats at the head table with Lord Ellwood and Lady Rayna," Lady Adaryn said as she walked by. "That table is for other young of the realm who were invited to join the repast this night."

Valiant sighed. The table, all kids near their age, no adults, looked like fun. He and his sisters went to the head table and sat. He noticed his sisters also watched the rowdy table. Both looked as envious as he.

After the repast, as the adults moved to the dancing hall, Harden joined the triplets. "Valiant, must you remain for dancing, or will you join us? Lady Adaryn has prepared games on the balcony."

Valiant looked over and noticed the other kids were watching. He turned to Temperance. "You ask. Father is much more likely to agree if he thinks it's your idea."

Tempest eyed Harden and gave her sister a little shove. "Yes, go."

When Temperance walked away, Tempest dug her elbow into Valiant's side. "Are you going to introduce us?"

Valiant blushed and searched his brain to recall the proper phrase. "Er, Mistress Tempest, I present Harden, son of Ash."

Tempest held out her hand. Harden's eyes widened. He glanced at Valiant, who leaned over and whispered, "Repasts are formal. You must kiss her hand and say hello."

Harden frowned, but leaned forward and touched his lips to the hand Tempest extended. When he was slow to speak, Valiant cleared his throat.

"Oh, right, hello?" Harden's voice raised in question as he said the last word.

"It's nice to meet you," Valiant whispered.

"Nice to meet you," Harden repeated.

Valiant grinned. Glad, for once, he knew the rules of court life.

"Is that all? Did I do it right?" Harden asked.

"Very well done, indeed." Lady Adaryn said. "Come to the balcony, unless you wish to join in the festivities on the dance floor."

"Us too?" Tempest asked.

"Yes, Mistress Tempest. The Forest Lord thinks the evening air will be good for all three of you."

Temperance joined them with a grin. "It should be grand fun." She cocked her head to one side and looked at Valiant. He rolled his eyes. "Mistress Temperance, I present Harden, son of Ash."

Harden quickly kissed Temperance's hand and said all that was proper before following Valiant outside.

Elm approached and asked, "Do we do the hand kiss now?"

"No," Valiant said. "Only inside the formal halls."

"That's a relief."

Tempest raised a single eyebrow and glared at him.

"I didn't mean... I just... Oh, starless night. I've never kissed a hand. I didn't want to do it wrong." Elm admitted.

While the others laughed, Tempest said, "Ask Harden for pointers. He did very well."

Harden blushed at the praise and introduced the triplets to the children who didn't live in the residence.

Outside, amid games, the triplets made friends with children who didn't live inside the residence for the first time.

*****

"Valiant, perhaps no one told you, but the purpose of throwing the spear is to hit the target." Barric maintained a stoic expression, but his eyes danced with laughter. The other young fae standing behind him laughed.

Valiant retrieved his spear but didn't speak. Barric was now in a position of authority over a small squad of young males who were not quite adults, and still he enjoyed belittling Valiant. He was beyond tired of thinly veiled insults from the warriors. Barric was nothing but a bully, hurling insults at someone younger than himself. Valiant had promised Cian, who had once again been called by the Forest Lord, that he would throw the spear twelve times, but he was done with the warriors and their comments. Even with his daily practice in Ash's private training center, Valiant missed the center mark twice in ten throws. Naturally, the warriors, and other trainees, commented on the two near misses rather than the eight perfect throws. Gathering the rest of his gear, Valiant left the practice field. His goal had been to sneak into the nursery, where he and his sisters would live until age twelve when they would be considered adults. He hated the nursery and the childhood it represented.

He returned his weapons to their storage location, grabbed his lute, and went outside. Relieved that all went according to plan, Valiant thought to sit at the river's edge, but the herb garden was unoccupied for once, so he sat there. Neither location was frequented by Lord Ellwood. Thankful to be alone, Valiant sat down and tuned his instrument, which did much to relax him. The stringed instrument was new, acquired from a bard from the Southern Realm, and it had cost him dearly in trade. Hopefully, his father would never find out. Before Valiant could sing his first song, he was interrupted.

"How fair thee, nephew?" Lady Z's voice pulled Valiant out of his relaxed state and back to being angry.

"I didn't know you were back."

Lady Z raised an eyebrow. "Is etiquette no longer a desirable skill in my brother's court?"

Schooling his features, Valiant answered her original question. "Well enough, Lady Z. Will you be with us for long?"

"Much better. And no, only for a few days." Z pointed to the lute. "Which bard is your sponsor?"

"I don't have one."

"Does Lord Ellwood not encourage your musical talent?"

Valiant rolled his eyes. "Tell him I spent my time thus, and you can judge his reaction for yourself." Picking up his lute, Valiant moved toward the path the triplets had created between the garden and the nursery.

Lady Z called after him. "Are you so sure that everyone runs to Lord Ellwood to report on you?"

Valiant stopped and shrugged. "Most do."

"I am not most. I approve of your interest in music. You have the talent for it, and talent should always be encouraged."

"That's not Father's view," Valiant said over his shoulder as he walked away. He ended up in the library, knowing that if Lord Ellwood learned Valiant was singing, this would be one of the last places Father would think to look. It wouldn't prevent his punishment, but it would delay it.

A short time later, Valiant didn't look up when someone entered the family library. He kept his nose in the scrolls. If it was father, he would yell his objection to the lute. If someone else had entered the room, Valiant didn't care. He took a shallow breath and recognized his mother's scent.

"Studying during free time?" Lady Rayna entered the room without a sound. She rarely made noise when walking, and Valiant wondered if it was a trait all full-blooded shifters shared or if it could be learned. Though he tried, his footfalls were never so silent.

"What has Lord Ellwood objected to this time, Mother?"

"Nothing that I know of, my son."

Valiant waited. If Rayna was in the library, there was a reason.

Rayna moved around the room. "Your temper needs tending. Since moving to the Farseen, I found that writing my thoughts and feelings down helps me to understand them and soothes my temper."

"You think I should keep a journal? Does Father approve of this use of my time?" Valiant didn't bother to hide his disbelief. Besides, his mother had a temper to be feared. If writing things down improved it, he didn't think it was by much.

Rayna handed Valiant a small bundle of blank parchment. "Not all activities need to be discussed with your father."

Valiant looked at the parchment and raised his eyes to his mother's retreating form. Probably wouldn't hurt, unless the Forest Lord found the evidence. If he did this, a suitable hiding place must be a top priority. Besides, Valiant could record the ballads he had begun writing. He would almost be following his mother's instruction.

Chapter 5 – 4979 BCE

"I can't wait to get there." Valiant picked up the pace as the triplets approached the Hall of Battles, where the carvings of battles won by the current and previous forest lords adorned the columns. Every time Valiant passed the carved columns, he longed for the day when his adventures would grace the hall. Even though birthright was not how realm lords were chosen, his ten-year-old self fully expected that he would be the next Forest Lord of the Northern Realm and more pillars would have to be built to display his prowess on the battlefield. When the triplets reached their destination, waiting patiently was beyond Valiant's ability. He noticed Tempest looked bored. "What's the matter, sister mine?"

Tempest shrugged. "I don't share your eagerness for this journey. I doubt they will teach us anything of value."

"Why must we go?" Temperance asked. "And why can't Mother go with us?"

"Mother has duties here. We're going to the Seen to meet the Alpha Clan and begin our training in case we shift. No reason for her to attend us," Tempest said.

"Quite right, daughter mine." Ellwood joined his children. "Upon your return, I expect to hear tales of your deeds in the Seen."

"I'm sure I will have stories worthy of your son, Father." Valiant stood tall, hoping for praise, but doubting he would receive any.

"I expect anything is possible," Ellwood responded absently without taking his eyes off Tempest. "Try not to accidentally set fire to the Alpha Clan, my child. But if you do, what until a way is opened so you can escape."

Tempest rolled her eyes, and Valiant's eyes danced. Last week, when she called fire for the first time, Tempest destroyed the gardener's favorite roses, transplanted from the Seen. He still hadn't forgiven her, probably because a song was written about the chef's mirth that, for once, Mistress Tempest left his cooking herbs alone. Valiant knew Tempest intended to find replacement roses on this trip in the hopes the gardener would stop growling when he saw her.

Valiant placed a bored expression on his face. After Master-At-Arms Ash pointed out that showing jealousy toward his sister's accomplishments made him look ridiculous, he had tried to imitate Ridge's smirk. Once Tempest laughed at him for that, Valiant decided boredom would be the guise to cover his true feelings. He had spent much time looking at his reflection, creating the perfect countenance that said he was attentive but bored. He could now summon that look regardless of how he truly felt.

When a way opened on the receiving platform, Valiant straightened his back. They had yet to meet any member of their shifter family, although he knew some of them had attended the birth and first-year celebrations. Valiant grinned when a tall, dark-haired man exited the way. This must be Kyan, Rayna's twin. Although Kyan was a few inches shorter than the nearly two meters tall Forest Lord, the shifter managed to look just as imposing.

Tempest tilted her head and appeared to be confused.

Before Valiant could ask what was wrong, Kyan bowed slightly toward Ellwood. "Forest Lord, I see no one has killed you yet."

Ellwood held out his hands in a look-at-me pose, apparently unconcerned by the insult. "A few have tried. As you can see, they failed."

"Pity," Kyan retorted.

Valiant's eyes widened. No one ever spoke thus to Lord Ellwood. Kyan might be just a shifter, but if he could talk to the Forest Lord like that, perhaps he was formidable.

"Brother mine, you look well." Rayna walked into the room, and all eyes turned to her. When she wished it, she commanded attention. Valiant believed she did it on purpose to stop Father's temper from exploding. Rayna hugged Kyan and kissed his cheek before drawing him towards the triplets. "Come and see how my young have grown."

Prized

"Indeed, they look hardy." Kyan looked them over, eyeing their clothes. He kissed the hand of each girl and bowed to Valiant. "Cwenhild, shifter sovereign, awaits the arrival of her grandchildren."

Valiant, pleased to be greeted with a bow, responded in kind. "We are content to visit with the shifter sovereign." Glancing out the side of his eye, Valiant saw Rayna smile and knew he had responded correctly. Had Valiant called the sovereign his grandmother, Father might have taken offense, as he frequently did when the shifter side of their heritage was mentioned. Valiant still didn't understand why. Lord Ellwood had repeatedly told his children that shifting would give them an advantage as long as they chose a proper form. Although, Father had yet to identify what shape he would find acceptable.

Rayna hugged each of her children, whispering last-minute instructions based on their personalities. To Tempest, she said, "Behave. No practicing element control without approval. Humans don't know about us." To Valiant, Rayna said, "Listen to Temperance. She is wise beyond her years." To Temperance, she simply said, "Try to enjoy yourself."

Rayna stood back, and the triplets followed Kyan through the way into the dimension of the Seen.

When they reached the other side, Valiant looked around, disappointed. The forest of the Seen looked very much like any forest in the Northern Realm.

Kyan gave Valiant a knowing smile. "Don't worry, there are differences, and I will show you a few over the coming weeks. But first, you must change." He pulled out the clothes he had stashed in case the triplets were not dressed appropriately.

"We are well dressed for traveling," Temperance objected.

Valiant grinned. He had watched as she picked her clothing with care. Every item she wore identified her as one of Lord Ellwood's daughters. In the Farseen, the apparel was a warning to stay away. He suspected it gave her comfort in this strange land. Temperance was the shyest of the trio.

"You are dressed for traveling in the Farseen. The clothing you wear will bring you unwanted attention in the Seen. We must blend in, not stand out."

"If we must," Tempest grabbed the bag Kyan had placed in front of her and changed behind a large boulder. She returned while her siblings were still eyeing the clothing. "It looks odd but is strangely comfortable."

Valiant pressed his hands into leathers as smooth as those of the Farseen, although not as decorated. There were no stones for decoration or protection. He suspected that was the point. Valiant grabbed the leathers and stepped behind a rock to change. Temperance did the same.

When they rejoined Kyan and Tempest, Temperance repacked Valiant's clothes into his pack so that the flap would close. She giggled and said, "You're so messy."

Valiant shrugged. He hadn't bothered to pack properly because he knew Temperance would check it anyway. She was precise with all things, even those that didn't matter.

"Now come, we have a half-day journey to the Alpha Clan." Kyan led them down a well-worn path through the woods.

"Why so far?" Valiant asked.

Tempest huffed. "If a fae fighting force had come through the way instead of us, it would have taken time to get to the clan. I suspect hidden guards, who shift into birds or swift-moving animals, would have rushed to report the invasion."

Kyan grinned. "Indeed, Tempest."

"She is Mistress Tempest to you, and you will show respect." Valiant's reaction to a near-stranger, family or not, showing such familiarity to his sister surprised even him.

Kyan stopped walking. "You are in the Seen now. Such titles are unnecessary and, if heard by the humans, deadly. While here, you will be addressed as Tempest, Valiant, and Temperance. Here in the Seen, we must blend in with the humans."

"You are stronger. Why not rule humans?" Valiant asked. It was a question he had wondered about when the Seen had been discussed in his studies.

"Shifters have no desire to rule humans. We prefer to work with them."

Valiant didn't respond, but he found it odd. Although the ruling fae didn't control the lesser fae, the lesser fae certainly knew about them. Why wouldn't shifters do the same with humans?

They traveled in relative silence for a while. When the triplets topped a hill and could see a crossroad, they saw their first people of the Seen.

Prized

Valiant looked at Tempest when she slowed down. "What?"

"They're humans," Tempest whispered.

Valiant rolled his eyes. "What? You didn't think we would meet any?"

"Of course, I just didn't expect them to be normal." Tempest's smile was one of satisfaction. "They think the same way we do.

"Humans are quite intelligent," Kyan explained. "But they can't call magic, and many consider magic to be evil."

The quartet continued down the road. Finally, they passed a grouping of structures, each with thatched roofs and rectangular walls of woven willow rods. Valiant stared at the buildings, surprised that the buildings were not built of stone, as they were in the Farseen.

Kyan slowed as they neared the crossing. "The trail to the west goes to a shifter settlement. The trail to the east takes you to humans. Beyond the human settlement, a colony of blood-sucking demons lives in temporary tents and a series of caves. Never travel east alone." He eyed Tempest, "The bloodsuckers are like nothing in the Farseen. They can and will enthrall you, and your actions will no longer serve you, but them."

Tempest looked east but didn't speak.

"What's to the North?" Valiant asked. He had heard tales of human-looking demons in the Seen who existed on blood. It was said the blood was drained from a body by two long sharp teeth. These demons rarely entered the Farseen because the sun there harmed them. Tempest had suggested, and Valiant agreed with her, that these demons were made up creatures to keep young fae with the gift of opening a way from entering the Seen without approval.

"North will take you to the Alpha Clan, and Cwenhild, our sovereign." Kyan resumed his steps.

"And south? What would we have found had we traveled south from the point where we arrived?" Tempest asked.

Kyan nodded in approval. "To the south are many more human settlements and two settlements of witches. Witches aren't as powerful as the witches of the Farseen, and they tend to have one or two spells that they focus on. We also have wizards, but wizards normally work alone and in secret. Most wizards match witches of the Farseen in power."

Tempest stared at her uncle. She hadn't heard of casters in the Seen who weren't shifters. "Are they allies?"

"Depends on the day. Sometimes." Kyan motioned for Temperance to catch up.

Tempest frowned and took the lead.

Kyan joined her in five long steps. "You have Rayna's talent, I see. No matter how hard you try, you will find that my mind is not open to you. I am mind-blind. If Rayna knows of your talent, she should have warned you."

Tempest shook her head. "Had she told me I still would have tried for myself. Now I know what someone who is mind-blind feels like, or rather doesn't feel like, in my head. I wouldn't have felt it so clearly if I had been expecting it."

Kyan pursed his lips together. Tempest was wise beyond her years, probably a result of her mind walking skills. Rayna had been that way. She was able to defuse issues before they became issues thanks to her knowledge. Although, it appeared that Tempest wasn't as interested in helping others as she was in acquiring knowledge.

"Mind-blind. Does that mean Mother and Tempest see nothing from your mind?" Valiant asked.

"Yes."

"Perhaps I will get that ability when I shift and have powers to call," Valiant said wistfully.

Kyan ruffled Valiant's hair. "I doubt it. I was born this way. From birth, none have been able to enter my mind."

"Not even the demons who enthrall their victims?" Tempest asked.

"Not even the demons," Kyan agreed. He didn't admit that a dragon could enter his mind. They might be his nieces and nephew, but they were the children of the Forest Lord. No reason to give them information that they might use against him one day.

Approaching their destination, they saw more shifters. They passed a man working at a table under the shade of a tree. Three dogs sat around him. The dogs moved only their heads, following the approach of three new young in their territory. Their master was unconcerned, and they followed his lead.

Tempest stopped, looking over the stones. "This is cut in the same manner as Mother's necklace." She cut her eyes to Kyan. "Mother said you gave her the stone as a present when we were born."

Prized

Kyan and the man shook hands. Turning to the kids, Kyan said, "This is Adair, the best maker of baubles in any dimension. Adair, meet Rayna's triplets, Tempest, Valiant, and Temperance."

As Kyan said their name, each child inclined their heads to Adair. Valiant noticed a girl, about his age, peeking around a large tree. She smiled, and he grinned back.

"Carwen, come meet more of the sovereign's family." Adair introduced his daughter to the triplets and picked up the stone Tempest had looked at. "You have a good eye. I did use this exact cut on a necklace your uncle commissioned."

Tempest picked up a set of bracelets and was surprised when they made noise when they touched. "How does one fight while wearing such a thing?"

Valiant eyed the bracelets Tempest held. The jangling, though a pleasant sound, would alert the enemy to the position of the wearer. He agreed with Tempest. Useless.

"Not all activities involve fighting," Adair said.

Tempest raised a single eyebrow. "Most do. One should always be prepared to fight. These trinkets would make noise and give your position away. I see no use for them."

"Then perhaps a single bracelet would better serve you."

"I have no need for anything that doesn't help me fight," Tempest replied firmly.

Adair looked over at Kyan. "A niece who shares your views."

Kyan nodded. "Come, Cwenhild awaits."

They arrived at the Alpha Clan's holdings just as the sun dipped below the horizon. The triplets watched as a shifter female, who looked about the same age as Rayna, stepped out of a hut. "Welcome. It is good that you are finally home."

"We aren't home. We are visiting because Mother demanded it." Tempest looked into her grandmother's eyes.

Cwenhild smiled, and the next thing Tempest knew she was on the ground. Valiant and Temperance ran to their sister. Tempest glared at Cwenhild.

Cwenhild reached down and pulled Tempest to a standing position, whispering loud enough for all three to hear but no louder. "You have not fully controlled your mind powers. If you attempt to enter my mind again without permission, your ability to reason might

44

suffer." Louder, she added, "Kyan, once they are fed, bring them to the circle to meet the rest of the family."

"Yes, Cwenhild." Kyan bowed.

Cwenhild turned and entered the hut she had just left.

"Why do you not call her Mother?" Temperance asked.

"We look to be the same age. The humans would have questions."

Confusion flitted across Tempest's face, and she asked, "How is that important?"

"We move as each new generation begins to reproduce. It keeps humans from finding out we don't age after adulthood. Titles, such as Mother or Father, would not be helpful."

"There is much to learn about this land," Tempest said.

Kyan ushered them into the hut the triplets would share during their visit. "On that, we can agree. Settle in quickly and meet me outside. Food awaits."

While the triplets unpacked their small packs, Temperance said, "There is a strange buzzing in this dimension."

"Yes, but it's no worse than in the Farseen." Valiant tossed his pack next to a roll. "I'm going to miss my sleeping hammock."

"We can make our own hammocks while we're here," Tempest said absently.

"What are you thinking, sister mine?" Temperance asked.

Tempest shook her head. "I thought Cwenhild would be kinder than Ellwood. I believe I was wrong."

"I couldn't believe she tossed you. I only saw the call of wind after it happened. I thought shifters were less able to control the elements than the fae. Cwenhild seemed very capable to me." Valiant's smirk was as good as Ridge's at that moment. "What did you see?"

"Nothing. Perhaps Cwenhild's like Kyan, mind-blind. I've never met anyone who could hide their mind completely from me. If she did, she's strong." Tempest rubbed her shoulder where it slammed into the ground. "There are at least two people here whose actions I can't predict. I'm not sure being here is a good idea."

"You mean you're worried because you aren't in control," Valiant said. "So now you're like the rest of us. You have to hear words and watch movements to prepare for any action you might need to take. You will have to pay attention to people now."

"I don't like it." Tempest pursed her lips and opened her mind to see how many she could read. She immediately fell to the ground under the onslaught of so many thoughts. In court, only at repasts were the children with so many. Tempest groaned and locked her mind down. The elementals in this dimension didn't like her either.

"Are you ill?" Valiant, with Temperance's help, moved Tempest to the bedroll by the entrance. The one Tempest had tossed her pack on.

"I'm fine." Tempest shrugged off their help and stood up.

At the same time, Temperance fell to the ground.

"What is wrong with you two?" Valiant helped Temperance sit up.

"I... don't know," Temperance replied. "Something is in my mind."

Tempest leaned over her sister. "Close your mind. Build a barrier around your mind, like Mother taught us."

A few seconds later, Temperance sat up. "Better. What was that?"

Tempest whispered, "Elementals."

"What? They've never bothered me."

"Not in the Farseen, but we're in the Seen now. Grandmother Niamh taught me to guard against them in the Farseen since I'm the only one they actively dislike. I had hoped elementals in the Seen would ignore me the way the ones in the Farseen ignore you and Valiant, but it doesn't appear to be the case." Tempest turned to Valiant. "How about you?"

"So far, nothing. I hope they don't attack in front of anyone. I'll look weak," Valiant said.

"Close your mind to keep everyone out."

Tempest's recommendation irritated him, and his response came out as a growl. "You know I can't keep you out."

"No, but you can keep Mother out and perhaps the elementals," she retorted.

Valiant nodded. She had a point.

Kyan tapped the hut flap causing it to billow. "What is taking so long?"

"Sorry." Tempest opened the flap before the others could answer. "I was talking about the things we would learn while here."

"Less talking, more walking. The meal is getting cold."

"Meal?" Tempest asked.

"Meal... repast. Didn't Rayna teach you anything about the Seen?"

Valiant shook his head. "No, just a few stories at bedtime."

Kyan pushed the children toward the evening meal.

The evening meal was not as formal as the triplets were used to, and they enjoyed eating as the sun set, and the single moon rose.

"What are you looking at?" Temperance asked Valiant.

"I suspect, like me, he's looking at what isn't there," Tempest said.

"Exactly," Valiant agreed. "There's only one small moon up there. It's nearly full, but it shines very little light down upon us."

"It's quite bright this evening," Carwen said. She sat with the triplets while her father talked with Kyan.

"We have three moons. One is huge. When it's nearly full, it's almost as bright as the sun," Valiant explained.

"It's not that bright," Tempest disagreed. "But it is much bigger and brighter than that tiny moon. I doubt this moon is as large as Odol. What do you call your moon?"

Carwen giggled. "Moon. We only have one."

After dinner, Carwen introduced the triplets to the other kids in the clan.

"Do you play games in the Farseen?" Taren asked.

"Of course." Valiant glared at the other boy.

"How about a game of chase?"

"What are the rules?" Tempest asked.

"One person is the hunter. The hunter counts out loud to twenty while the others hide. At twenty, the hunter looks for anyone and chases. As soon as he touches someone, that person becomes the hunter and counts to twenty."

"Simple enough. Let's play."

Taren grinned. "I'll be the hunter first." He closed his eyes and counted while the others scattered.

Valiant hid in an exceptionally thick bush, thinking the small light from the moon should conceal him well. Valiant positioned himself so he could see Taren. He frowned at Tempest, who hadn't moved. She stood right beside Taren. As soon as he said *twenty* and opened his eyes, he lunged at Tempest.

She used wind to rise above him. Out of his reach, she laughed.

Anger moved across Taren's face, but then he smirked. "I forgot to tell you no powers. How is it you have elemental powers already?"

Looking at him from her position hovering over his head, Tempest said, "Fae can wield elemental powers almost as soon as they can walk."

"Must be nice to control wind." Taren sounded wistful.

Prized

"Not just wind," Tempest explained. "I can call earth, fire, and water, too."

"Really?"

"Sure. So can Temperance."

"And Valiant?"

"No, not yet." Tempest lowered herself to the ground while they had been talking.

Taren grinned and tapped her on the shoulder and ran full out. "You're the hunter," he called over his shoulder.

Tempest snarled at her mistake, but then she laughed, closed her eyes, and began her count while the others searched for new hiding places.

Valiant found a new hiding place, still fuming that Tempest told Taren he didn't have command of the elements. If asked, he would have admitted it himself, but Tempest shouldn't have volunteered such information.

*****

"What's this?" Carwen, Adair's daughter, asked as she touched the instrument.

Valiant blushed. He was always followed, never allowed to be alone, although normally adults followed him. He thought he had moved far enough away from the camp to not be heard. When he looked up, he realized how wrong he had been. With Carwen were most of the young their age, including Taren. Valiant didn't like Taren any more than Taren liked Valiant. The boys had a rivalry going over every aspect of living — hunting, working in the fields, carrying water — both wanted to be first no matter what the task.

"Is that what was making the noise?" Taren asked.

"'Twas a lovely sound." Carwen shot Taren an amused look.

When others agreed, Taren scoffed. "Yeah, but what is it? It has strings, so it's not a flute. Who was singing?"

Valiant's blush deepened. "I was singing. Have you never seen a lute before?" When the others shook their heads, he held up the stringed instrument. "Want to hear?"

"That's why we're here." Taren sat on the ground, leaned against a tree, and closed his eyes. The others also got comfortable.

Valiant grinned and began to play. He stuck with the most popular songs the fae bards had given him permission to sing in public, and he was gratified by the reception he received.

48

Temperance entered the clearing and passed Valiant an exasperated look. "This is where everyone has hidden."

Taren opened his eyes and sat up at the interruption. "We've done our chores. We were going to play a game and heard Valiant playing his lute. Decided to listen for a while. His fingers are nimble, and his voice is surprisingly pleasant."

"Pleasant?" Carwen glared at Taren. "It's enchanting."

Temperance folded her arms in front of her chest. "Yes, Valiant has a lovely singing voice, and his playing is the best in all the realms, maybe even in the Seen, but Kyan wants help in the fields."

Grumbling, the kids went to help Kyan.

Valiant did as well. He grinned all the way to the settlement. Carwen thought his voice enchanting.

*****

The morning was crisp, and the sunrise vibrant as Kyan walked past the triplets. "After you finish eating, grab your packs, and meet me at the circle. We're going further north."

Valiant and his sisters grinned and wolfed down first meal. They had been in the Seen for over a week and had yet to leave the village. So far, their training included mundane tasks, like cooking and gardening in the Seen, how to interact with humans, and a small amount of shifter specific training.

Valiant was excited to finally explore the area and perhaps hunt in the Seen. He would enjoy taking down a predator or perhaps a large herd animal to feed the clan. Either would be a worthy story to tell his father and might even result in a bard song that would be sung in court. A tribute to Valiant's first brave deed.

In short order, the triplets grabbed their packs and returned to the stones, laid out to allow eating in groups, where the Alpha Clan ate meals together. It was also the primary meeting area. All three had observed the elder clan members ignored them if the mouth was shut, and a task, such as knife cleaning, was in process. They had learned much sitting quietly off to the side.

"Let's see what's in your pack," Kyan said.

"You want to inspect our packs. You think we don't know how to travel?" Valiant held his pack tight, but Tempest and Temperance laid them on the rock beside Kyan.

"We know how to pack for the Farseen. Mayhap the Seen requires different tools," Temperance said.

Prized

Valiant sighed in disgust and tossed his pack on the rock.

Kyan looked through the packs. "Acceptable, except that you have no food."

"We gather on the way." Valiant's tone was scornful.

Kyan pegged him with a hard stare. "And how will you identify edible plants?"

Telyn, Cwenhild's sister and a healer, handed the triplets some dried meat. "They will have this, and you will point out acceptable plants on the journey."

Valiant accepted the food with a blush. He hadn't considered that edible plants would be different in the Seen. The plants in the gardens were similar enough.

They walked for a good bit stopping only for plant identification. The ground was fertile, and edible plants were in good supply.

"What is that ring?" Temperance pointed to the oval ring on Kyan's left hand.

"It's the enforcer's ring, isn't it?" Tempest asked. "Rayna said it's a symbol of your authority when traveling for the sovereign."

Kyan looked down at his hand and nodded.

"Is it a ring of power?" Temperance asked.

Tempest huffed. "Spelling objects requires special abilities in the casting arts. Kyan can't do that."

"Tempest." Valiant glared at his sister.

"It's a fact. Few can spell objects. It's no slight to Kyan."

"You may try to remove the ring if you wish." Kyan held out his hand.

Tempest pulled on the ring. Nothing happened. She growled and tugged hard in an attempt to twist it off. "Why won't it come off?"

"It's spelled. It can only be removed when the sovereign selects a new enforcer. I can't remove it either."

Tempest crossed her arms and blocked Kyan's path. "How?"

"Perhaps I'll tell you when you're older." Kyan stepped around Tempest and continued on the trail.

Valiant followed his uncle, holding his smile until he was past Tempest.

"Why does Kavi live so far from the rest of the clan?" Valiant pushed a small tree limb out of the way and held it as his sisters passed. The trail was not well worn, and he suspected Kavi did not have many visitors.

"Her ability to mind talk is depilating. Being around others hurts her." Kyan's eyes cut to Tempest. "Close your minds as tight as you can. That will help her."

Tempest pursed her lips and asked, "Why doesn't she close her mind tighter?"

"Must you question everything?" Kyan asked.

"She reminds me of Rayna. So sure she knows the answer and always questioning anyway." A tall, thin woman with pale skin, yellow-blonde hair, and ice blue eyes stood in the trail before them. She was dressed in the style of a farm laborer, but her clothes were clean and well-mended.

"Kavi, meet Tempest, Valiant, and Temperance. Rayna's triplets."

"Well met, progeny of Lady Rayna and the Forest Lord." Kavi bowed as well as any member of the realm.

"Well met." The triplets responded in sync.

Tempest eyed Kavi. "You pulled the memory of a proper fae greeting from our minds, didn't you?"

"I see you are also as quick to judge as your mother," Kavi said. "There was no need. I spent time in the Southern Realm long before your mother was born. I know how to conduct myself in a court, and I doubt the rules have changed."

The kids grinned. According to the elder fae, rules of court conduct had not changed in the recorded history of the Farseen, thousands of years.

Valiant reached out his hand to shake Kavi's, as Kyan had taught him. Tempest pulled his hand back. Before he could argue with her, Tempest whispered, "If she has trouble blocking a mind, touching will make it worse."

"Your sister is right. I do not touch anyone."

"Are our minds closed tight enough to be of use?" Temperance asked.

Kavi said, "Valiant's is."

Valiant grinned at the praise.

Tempest rolled her eyes and said, "He might as well be mind-blind like Kyan for no one but me can read him."

Valiant frowned at his sister. Would it hurt her to let him be the best at something for once?

"You are wrong," Kavi replied. "Valiant is not mind-blind. The gift he has that allows him to block all from his mind will grow and be a powerful weapon."

Valiant stood up straight from the praise. Something he rarely received.

Kavi handed Valiant the basket of herbs she had picked. "You may carry this to my cave, and I will tell you something of your gift. Not since Kyan's father, have I felt the like."

"His gifts haven't manifested yet," Tempest argued.

"That doesn't mean he doesn't have them. It simply means Valiant will develop them later. If you paid attention to the signs, you would know what his gifts are." Kavi moved down the trail.

The triplets ran to catch up, throwing questions at Kavi.

Kyan followed at a slower pace, grinning. He had expected the children to be impressed by Kavi's knowledge of things. Anyone granted an audience with her was.

*****

"That's not the right place to cut." Tempest leaned over Kyan to watch as he copied Adair's cut of the clear gem. She watched Kyan's lessons because the activity soothed her. Besides, Valiant was working in the fields, and Temperance was cooking. Tempest saw no reason to waste time in such pursuits.

"Don't talk when I'm cutting," Kyan growled.

Accustomed to their bickering, Adair looked over at the table to see what Kyan was doing. "She's right. Don't cut there. It will shatter."

Ignoring his friend and his niece, Kyan cut the stone as he planned. It shattered. "Don't say a word."

Adair tapped Tempest on the shoulder. "Come to my table. I'll let you cut your own stone. Let's see if you're as good at finding the proper place to cut when you're the one to make the incision."

To spare Kyan's feelings, Tempest hid her smile and followed Adair. Though she couldn't hear Kyan's thoughts, she would be angry if she had been proven wrong and thought Kyan would as well. Tempest had never cared about anyone's feelings before, but now that she was around a few people she couldn't read, Tempest watched people more closely and noticed that sometimes her words, though true, hurt others. It reminded her too much of how Lord Ellwood treated his subjects, and Tempest didn't want to be like him.

Most of the Alpha Clan seemed to have great control over their minds. With luck, Tempest would learn their ways. She might become more powerful than Lord Ellwood.

*****

Valiant strummed his lute. He had known a moment's concern when he realized no such instrument existed in the Seen. Still, the entire clan enjoyed his concerts, and he thought he was safe sharing the knowledge of a stringed instrument. At first, he had been reluctant to play for the clan. But, unlike his father, and therefore the entire Northern Realm, his shifter family enjoyed the songs he sang. The stringed instrument, with its long neck and rounded belly, was odd to the shifters. They were accustomed to a musician playing the flute or a bard singing songs. When Valiant sang while playing his lute, all the nearby shifters gathered to listen. It was gratifying. So far, he only played songs written by the fae bards. He planned to sing one of his own songs this evening. He looked around to make sure no one was watching. It was a habit that saved him from trouble back home. Lord Ellwood thought singing was a waste of time for his only son. Valiant smiled, for Carwen was the only one nearby.

"Are you going to play?" Carwen, Adair's daughter, called from where she prepped herbs, either for a meal or a spell. "I enjoy listening to your songs while I work. It makes the time go faster."

Valiant nodded and resumed playing.

"Only when you strum your lute do you appear at peace. You will make a wonderful bard." Cwenhild gathered her leathers and sat beside her grandson.

"No. I'll lead warriors." Valiant held his lute carefully in his hands. "This is just something to pass the time."

"It is something you love. Do not give up on your interest lightly."

"This will not be my life. Father will not stand for it." Valiant returned to his strumming. He was surprised when Cwenhild stayed and listened for a while. For the first time, he was able to study his powerful grandmother. She had her eyes closed as she listened to his music. He was stunned to find that his mother felt more powerful to him. So far, he had never felt the compulsion to follow his mother's orders, at least not in a shifter way. Like all children, he knew the desire to obey when she was angry. Tempest had expressed the same lack of pressure to follow their Mother. They decided amongst themselves that it was because they were more fae than shifter but didn't bother to ask an adult for confirmation. He hadn't asked Temperance, and as far as he knew, Tempest hadn't either. Temperance seemed weaker than either of them, even though she was the first to call all four elements, and Valiant had yet to call a single element. Valiant sometimes felt guilty because he and Tempest tended to ignore Temperance's abilities much of the time.

Cwenhild stood, and Valiant stopped playing. "Continue child. I have tasks to attend to, but your songs soothed me. You have a talent that should be encouraged. While in my camp, if you have no tasks waiting for you, you may play whenever and wherever you desire."

Valiant continued to strum the lute as she left.

"Now that we're alone, play something fun. I have roots and herbs to prepare for the evening meal. It's boring work," Carwen said.

Grinning, Valiant sang a lively tune about three Billy goats and a troll. By the end of the song, the younger children had gathered around, begging for more songs like that one.

*****

"Kyan said we shouldn't go east," Temperance called after Tempest, running to catch up.

"Kyan says a lot of things." After a few weeks with the shifters, Tempest moved with purpose. While Valiant trained with Kyan, the girls were expected to cook. Tempest's lip curled. She didn't cook, sew, or harvest crops. The shifters didn't understand that she was destined to be a warrior. She had no time for training in mundane tasks. "You can head back and help with evening meal. I want to see a blood-sucking demon."

"And when they enthrall you?"

"They won't. How could they? My mind is too powerful." Tempest stopped when a tall, dark-skinned man stepped from behind a tree. His skin wasn't the deep brown many fae, and humans, had but quite reddish in color. His clothes would be acceptable in a realm court. He was covered with jewels. Just the type of clothing Kyan had said not to wear in the Seen. Tempest had never encountered anyone like him before. He looked almost like a ruling fae with his lack of facial hair. Fae males didn't have facial hair until they were hundreds of years old. She watched as he approached and opened her mind to determine his intentions.

How generous you are to invite me in, little one.

Tempest set her mental shield, but it was too late. The stranger was inside her mind.

My, you are a powerful one, aren't you? You will make an excellent thrall. Pick up a rock and throw it at your sister. His words were not spoken aloud but played in her head.

Tempest watched through her eyes as her right hand followed the instructions. She was unable to stop her hand, use her voice, or change her facial expression.

"Tempest, what are you doing?" Not fully understanding, but knowing something was wrong, Temperance turned to run and bumped into a solid mass of muscle.

Kyan pushed her toward Valiant. "Stand with your brother." He didn't watch to make sure Temperance obeyed him before focusing on the blood-sucking demon. "Cimil, release my niece." Kyan's voice was firm.

Valiant, dagger already in his fighting hand, looked about and noticed enthralled, or perhaps other demons, waiting in the shadows of the trees. He drew Temperance in closer to his side.

Cimil's smile was unconcerned. "I would have thought you would guard such a prize better. Tempest will make an excellent addition to my family."

"You will have no family when I gift you the final death."

"You lack the skill to kill me. If you could, you would have done so long ago. I cannot enthrall you, but how will you stop your niece from killing you without harming her?" Cimil looked back at Tempest and said, "Kill Kyan."

Tempest moved forward, pulled the daggers she kept in her left and right boots, and ran at Kyan.

Kyan dropped into a fighting stance thankful Tempest lived in the Farseen. Their sparring sessions had shown him her biggest weakness. She had not been trained to battle intelligent animals. It was a common flaw in fae training. When a shifter took animal form, like most fae, Tempest tried to fight the animal as if the opponent were just an animal.

When Tempest jumped at her uncle, he shifted to his wolf and leaped to the side. Her arc resulted in Tempest hitting the ground with her head. Kyan jumped on her back and used his paws to knock her daggers away.

Valiant collected both daggers and handed one to Temperance. Young though they were, they were as well trained at combat. Both took up fighting stances, back-to-back, ready for any attack from the woods.

Kyan, still in wolf form, ran at Cimil. Cimil laughed, turned to mist, and disappeared. His followers in the woods ran, heading east to their master's home. Kyan shifted and walked over to an unconscious Tempest and picked her up. "Come. We must return home."

Valiant and Temperance said nothing, but each kept a dagger in hand, ready for another attack.

Six hours later, Valiant and Temperance stood watch over the still unconscious form of their sister. When the flap to their tent opened, both turned to face the entrance with weapons drawn.

"I am alone," Healer Telyn, Cwenhild's sister and third in the Alpha clan, said. She closed the flap and walked over to Tempest. "Worry not that she is still asleep. The longer she sleeps, the better she will fight the call of the demon."

"What makes you think we're worried?" Valiant asked. Could all shifters read minds or just the Alpha Clan?

"'Tis only natural that you would be concerned."

Valiant eyed the healer with distrust. "You can read our minds, can't you?"

"Temperance, yes," Telyn admitted. "I believe your mind is closed to all but Tempest."

"I wish that were so, but I've received orders from many in your clan," Valiant muttered.

"Yes, you have. Many can send you a message mind-to-mind, but none of the clan can hear your thoughts. Not even Cwenhild."

"He didn't need to know that." Kyan walked into the tent.

Valiant pursed his lips together. Tempest was right. The clan had been keeping secrets from them.

Telyn smiled at Kyan. "Proper training means the child must have full knowledge of his abilities. That none can enter his mind is an advantage, but there is a cost. None, save Tempest, will know if he is in danger. And she keeps her mind closed most of the time. Valiant must understand why he is so closely guarded."

So that's why he was always watched. He assumed it was because he was a fool, as his father so often told him. Valiant looked back and forth between the two adults. Bowing to Telyn, he said, "Your words have been received and will be used wisely."

Confused by the odd statement coming from a child, Telyn smiled tentatively.

Kyan grinned. "To thank someone in the Farseen is to owe that person a favor. Valiant's words are high praise to you."

"Once Tempest awakens, call me if I'm needed." Telyn left.

"You should have told me." Valiant glared at Kyan.

"The question is, what else haven't they told us?" Tempest didn't open her eyes when she spoke.

Irritation that Tempest didn't immediately tell them she was awake battled with relief that she was finally awake. Irritation won. Valiant growled, "Starless night, how long have you been awake?"

"Only just. I woke as Telyn entered the hut." Tempest attempted to sit up but was so dizzy she laid back on the bedroll.

Kyan said, "It's good you awoke."

Valiant stepped between Kyan and Tempest. "She asked you a question. What else haven't you told us?"

"Many things," Kyan responded, and amusement lit his face. "You are the children of the Forest Lord of the Northern Realm. Your loyalty to the Shifter Sovereign is not assured. Can you say you have kept no secrets?"

Temperance smiled and patted Valiant on the shoulder. "He has a point. We are related by blood but have no knowledge of each other. Mother sent us here to learn. Perhaps we should."

"Temperance is right. Teach us, Uncle Kyan." Tempest used the human title as the shifters had taught her. She spun off the bedroll, tucked her feet underneath her, and stood. She scowled when dizziness threatened to overcome her, but she remained upright.

"The first thing you should learn is you almost died. Sit before you fall."

Tempest crossed her arms in front of her chest, refusing to sit. "I would have broken his hold over my mind."

"No, you wouldn't. The only way the demon could have gotten control of you was if you opened your mind to read him or stared straight into his eyes. Either way, Cimil was your master. Cwenhild had to shield your mind from him until you awoke. The dreams you had of Cwenhild fighting Cimil were not dreams. They were fighting in the dream world for control of your mind."

Prized

As the room started to sway, Tempest sat down and chewed her bottom lip. She had opened her mind and looked into the demon's eyes, a tactic that normally worked for her, providing insight into her enemy. Perhaps she needed to listen more. The dreams Kyan spoke of were vivid and unlike anything Tempest had ever experienced. "What makes you think I dreamed? I thought you were mind-blind."

"Cwenhild dropped to unconsciousness when Cimil enthralled you. She can only attack that demon in dreams."

"Not just demons. Cwenhild knocked me out." Tempest's accusation hung in the air.

Kyan shook his head. "Did you try to fight her?"

"She was in my head."

"Then she had to stop you before you interfered with the battle for your mind," Kyan said matter of factually.

"She's as bad as Father," Tempest muttered.

Kyan's eyebrows rose in shock. "Cwenhild is nothing like Ellwood."

"Grandmother does as she sees fit, as does Father. She explains nothing, just like father. She expects obedience above all, just like father. Tell me, Uncle, how is Cwenhild different from Ellwood?"

Kyan barked a laugh. "I guess I never thought about it. They are very much alike. The difference is I trust Cwenhild to do what is best for our people. I don't trust Ellwood."

"That's the first smart thing you've said. I don't trust Father either, but Cwenhild has yet to prove herself to me. I trust no one blindly." Tempest raised an eyebrow, waiting to see what Kyan would do.

"Only you can decide whom you will trust. Once Cwenhild has rested, she will need to talk to you. For now, rest. Evening meal will be brought to you." Kyan left, closing the flap behind him.

Valiant turned on Tempest. "What really happened? What dreams? What did Cwenhild do?"

"Cwenhild arrived in my dreams and told me to hide while she and Cimil fought. I hide from no one. When I told her that, she threw me into a tree. When I woke still in the dream, I was frozen in place. All I could do was watch."

"Perhaps Kyan was right, and you were still enthralled to the demon," Valiant suggested.

Tempest scoffed but didn't reply. There was a chance he was right.

*****

58

After evening meal, Tempest approached Cwenhild's tent alone, as instructed. She could hear Valiant and Temperance playing with the shifter children and longed to be with them. Playing with other young was rare, and one of the few times Tempest felt at peace. Unlike the children of the Farseen, the shifter kids weren't concerned that she was the first-born of the Forest Lord or the granddaughter of their sovereign.

Tempest tapped on the tent.

"Come in, Tempest."

Tempest opened the flap and entered, surprised that Cwenhild knew it was her.

"Of course, it's you, child. I sent for you."

"Stay out of my mind," Tempest said.

"I see. It's okay for you to enter minds, but you feel no one should do the same to you." Cwenhild leaned back on her pillows. "You are not the strongest mind walker here, and I doubt you are the strongest in the Farseen."

"I know that," Tempest said. She had never before considered that entering another's mind was a violation of sorts, but now that she was on the receiving end, it did feel like one. Perhaps that was why Valiant hated it so.

"After the encounter with the demon, I suspect you do." Cwenhild tucked her furs around her.

Tempest rolled her eyes.

"Child, you are strong, but you must learn control. To that end, you will spend the next week with Kavi."

"You're banishing me?" Shock etched her face. No matter what Tempest did in the Farseen, she was never banished.

"No, not banishing. I'm sending you to Kavi so that you can learn from her."

"Learn? She can't block anyone." Tempest scoffed at the idea.

"Minds are not open or closed. There are layers. Kavi can teach you to dive deep into a mind, to learn that which someone might wish to keep hidden from others or something they have forgotten. She can also teach you to not broadcast your intentions."

That gave Tempest pause. When she was angry, she frequently lost control and sent her feelings to others. And if she could pull any information from another, she would be the most powerful. Only then would she not be a slave to the Forest Lord's whims.

Prized

"You might find she has other knowledge to share." Cwenhild kept her smile to herself.

*****

Kyan shifted and picked up the spear Valiant had thrown. Luckily the boy had missed his target. Harshly, Kyan shoved the spear into Valiant's hands. "Pay attention. Many shifters run in their other forms near the camp. It is a preferred way to travel. Make sure the animal is an animal before you try to spear it."

Valiant blushed but responded in kind. "You were running as a wolf and too near the young of the camp. I was protecting them."

"You were trying to be the hero." Kyan's voice softened. "I understand what it's like to have a powerful sister. You are no more in competition with Tempest than I was with Rayna."

"Not a hero, a warrior," Valiant muttered. "Had you been a real wolf, it would have been my fault had any of them been hurt."

"Is that what Ellwood would have said?"

"Of course. I'm the son of the Forest Lord of the Northern Realm. I must be the best."

Kyan sighed. He had known Ellwood was a harsh father. Valiant was still a child himself, younger than some he had tried to protect, yet he thought he was responsible for their safety. "Does he treat your sisters such?"

Valiant sneered at the foolish question. "They will be warriors but only until they become mothers. Then they will only fight to protect their kith and kin."

"You are sure they will remain in the Farseen?"

"Of course, they are daughters of the court. Where else would they live?"

"All three of you are children of the sovereign's line. The Seen would welcome you, and you could make a home in the Alpha Clan's camp."

Valiant didn't respond, but he didn't believe it was that easy.

"Come. I'm going to Kavi's to escort Tempest back to our camp."

"Why?" Valiant looked over in surprise. Tempest didn't need a guard, and they all knew the way. The fae had an excellent sense of direction. After traveling a path once, the fae had no trouble recreating their steps. The triplet half breeds were no different in that respect.

Kyan walked toward the path. "Your sister has a tendency to forget her duties when she wants to explore.

Valiant grinned. It was rare anyone noticed Tempest's flaws. Back home, Ridge was the only adult who seemed to, and mostly Ridge was amused by her antics rather than irritated.

*****

"What did you learn from Kavi?" Valiant looked up from his scroll when Tempest entered. When they returned to the clan, Tempest had been sent immediately to talk with Cwenhild. While he waited for her return, Valiant put the finishing touches on a new ballad about Tempest and Cimil. He never expected it to be heard by anyone, but his entire journal was written as bard songs.

"A lot. Kavi is much smarter than I thought. I look forward to additional trips to the Seen and visits with Kavi."

"You think you will move here?"

Tempest looked startled. "I hadn't thought of that. Why do you ask?"

"Kyan mentioned that all three of us would be welcome in the Alpha Clan."

"In the clan or in their camp?" Tempest's eyebrow rose in what was fast becoming her facial expression of choice.

Valiant tilted his head to one side and considered the question. "The camp. Is there a difference?"

"Yes," Temperance replied. "I've been watching. The Alpha Clan appears to be only Cwenhild's siblings and daughters, plus Kyan. The others are not in attendance at meetings, although they are assigned tasks."

Valiant frowned. "They want us for servants?"

"Not sure." Temperance shrugged.

"According to Kavi, at some point, Cwenhild's siblings can retire from active participation in the Alpha Clan, and her children become the clan." Tempest finished organizing and turned back to her siblings.

"When?"

Tempest shrugged. "Not sure. Sounds like Cwenhild needs enough children to run the clan."

Temperance raised an eyebrow in a fair imitation of Tempest's favorite expression. "That's senseless."

"That's the Seen."

*****

"I have something for you."

Prized

When the triplets looked up from their respective tasks, Kyan added, "I've noticed that all three of you have problems with elementals."

"That shouldn't be a surprise," Tempest said.

Valiant watched as she dumped the vegetables she had prepped into the stew. Tempest still loathed cooking, but she found the task of chopping vegetables to be soothing, so she did that without argument. Which meant Valiant and Temperance were assigned the other cooking chores, mostly because those in charge of cooking tired of arguing with Tempest.

"It's not, but Kavi suggested I address the issue." Kyan laid three carnelian daggers on the table. "One for each of you."

Tempest picked up the dagger that had her symbol carved into the handle. "The carnelian dagger is pretty but not very useful."

"On the contrary, it's very useful." Kyan's eye's twinkled. "Do you know what carnelian does?"

Tempest rolled her eyes at the teaching question. "Of course. It repels elementals, but only with the proper spells. You are not powerful enough to cast those types of spells. Very few are."

"Tempest," Temperance exclaimed.

Valiant shook his head. Tempest needed to learn to hold her tongue.

"Perhaps I'm not, but have you noticed anything since you picked up the dagger?" Kyan asked.

Reluctantly Tempest replied, "The elementals have backed away."

Valiant laughed and picked up his dagger. Sure enough, he immediately felt the elementals retreat. While they didn't attack him as they did his sisters, elementals hovered near his mind in the Seen. "I like this."

Tempest still didn't look happy. "Will it work in the Farseen as well?"

"It should," Kyan replied.

Valiant shook his head. Kyan shouldn't leave an opening that Tempest could pounce on.

Tempest said, "Should? You didn't test it?"

"Well, now, I'm not born of two dimensions, am I? Elementals don't consider me to be unnatural."

"How did you do this?"

Temperance picked up the dagger with her symbol and sighed in relief. "Can't you just be glad that he did?"

"I must understand." Tempest's face hardened.

"And one day, you shall, but now is the time for weapons training, not explaining." Kyan turned and left, careful to keep his smile hidden from view.

Following Kyan, Valiant was pleased to have another song to write in his journal. Valiant could already hear the melody, though the words would need some work. At this rate, he would have many songs of his travels in the Seen. Valiant wondered if he would ever sing them for anyone.

Chapter 6 – 4978 BCE

"If you go into the woods without a guard, Father will be angry," Temperance spoke with no expectation of being listened to.

"Father is always angry," Tempest said over her shoulder as she snuck through the bushes and into the woods.

"Perhaps he wouldn't be if you occasionally obeyed him," Temperance whispered to herself. She picked up the scroll and continued her reading.

Valiant laughed at Temperance and followed Tempest. He ran through the woods, dreaming of the day he would be able to shift. Perhaps he would be able to take multiple forms. Only the strongest of the Alpha shifters could do so. A moment of doubt crept into his thoughts. With a fae father, it was possible he would not shift. He pushed that thought away and followed his sister. "Where are we going?"

Tempest didn't slow down, so Valiant ran full out to catch her. "Slow down. There's no one chasing us."

"You're chasing me," Tempest retorted.

Valiant bit back his remark but didn't guard his thoughts.

"I am not a tyrant," Tempest said.

"Thought you kept your mind closed all the time now."

"I do. You're hard to block."

Valiant pushed out with his anger. He had developed a habit of pushing anger at Tempest when she irritated him. She didn't know and couldn't read the thoughts he pushed at her, so it seemed like an easy way to release his resentment. Mother had told him not to keep his anger bottled up, but he was pretty sure she didn't know how he was releasing it.

"That hurts." Tempest rubbed her forehead and turned on Valiant. "Did you do that?"

"Do what?"

"Did you push anger at me? I felt the emotion as my own."

"I can't do that."

"Then who did?" Tempest studied him for a moment. "Try again. Try to push an emotion at me but make it less annoying."

Even though it was a waste of time, Valiant closed his eyes and thought about the joy he would feel when he called wind for the first time. He focused that joy and pushed it at Tempest.

She smiled. "I didn't know you were jealous of me because I called the elements first."

"That's not what I sent you. Stay out of my mind."

"I didn't enter your mind. You pushed the joy you would feel when you successfully called an element. That joy included relief that you could call an element."

"Stay out of my head," Valiant repeated.

"I wasn't trying to get in your head. I was trying to get away from everyone. That includes you!" Tempest yelled.

"What ails thee? Father always punishes us when we don't follow his orders. You didn't kill the enemy when he said to."

Tempest stopped running and turned on Valiant. "They weren't the enemy. It was a stupid training exercise. I ended the battle without killing any warriors. They were his warriors."

"Exactly. Northern Realm warriors. They were born and raised to fight at their lord's pleasure. Their greatest honor is to die for their realm lord."

"Just like our greatest honor is to follow our father, without a thought of our own. Why would he kill them all because I didn't follow his orders?"

"Because…" Valiant crossed his arms in front of his chest drawing out the word. "You. Didn't. Follow his orders. He is Lord Ellwood and is to be obeyed. Always."

"I obey no one blindly. Father has done nothing to earn such devotion. Don't follow me." Tempest sped up and disappeared in the dark woods.

Prized

Valiant watched her run, hurt by his sister's words. How was it that Father doted on her and ignored him? He knew the answer. Even at eleven-years-old Tempest was always the victor in training, and she commanded respect. As young as they were, Tempest was the triplet to get the most attention and respect from the court. While Ellwood seemed incapable of showing respect to his offspring, he did seem to admire Tempest, especially her spirit. Any time Valiant had displayed a small amount of spirit, Father had been quick to ridicule him. Still unable to call the elements, Valiant was just as good as Tempest in all other aspects of training. But he had to admit, if only to himself, Tempest had a point. Did the warriors, like him, fulfill a function they didn't truly want? He took his time returning to the garden considering the possibility that the warriors didn't consider dying for the Forest Lord a high honor. He knew he wouldn't. As Valiant pushed through the bushes, a massive hand grabbed him by the neck and lifted him off the ground.

"Where is she?"

Valiant winced. Advisor Ridge was a hard taskmaster. Quick to point out any flaw in the way a weapon was held or wielded, Ridge was also the only one in the realm to never lose at hand-to-hand with Ellwood. Valiant saw Temperance sitting beneath the pink blooms of a tree. Her cheeks matched the blossoms meaning Ridge had already reprimanded her, even though no one thought Tempest would listen to Temperance. Valiant open his mouth to speak, and Ridge shook him.

Ridge narrowed his eyes on Valiant. "If you ask me whom I'm referring to, you will not like my response."

Valiant shrugged. It was what he had intended to say, so he didn't speak.

At the sound of others approaching, Ridge dropped Valiant to the ground. "Go sit with your sister. The one not wandering in the woods alone."

Usually, Valiant would argue with Ridge just because, as the son of the Forest Lord, he could. One look at Ridge's face had Valiant joining his sister on the bench.

"Where is Mistress Tempest?" Ash asked.

Ridge gritted his teeth. "In the dark woods. What is she late for this time?"

"Lord Ellwood told her to attend him in the receiving room." Ash sounded almost apologetic.

"That child will be the death of us all," Ridge muttered.

Yet, you accommodate her every whim. Valiant couldn't keep the thought out of his mind.

"Go back and tell Lord Ellwood I will find her." Ridge turned to enter the woods.

Ash glared at Ridge, "Perhaps you, as his advisor, should tell Lord Ellwood that his first-born is in the dark woods alone, and I, his Master-At-Arms, should attend to the search."

Ridge smiled at his friend. "Sorry, I claim the right of the search."

Ash walked off, muttering something Valiant didn't understand. He thought the Master-At-Arms had said the words afraid and Ridge, but that wasn't possible. Valiant had never seen Ridge afraid of anything.

Valiant stood up as Ridge passed. "I will go with you to search."

"Had you stayed with your sister, you would know where she went. No, stay with Temperance and make sure she doesn't run into the woods."

"But Temperance never disobeys," Valiant called to Ridge's back.

"At least one of you listen," Ridge retorted before disappearing into the underbrush of the Dark Woods.

"Come," Temperance pulled on Valiant's sleeve. "If we return to our rooms and finish our studies, perhaps Father will be pleased."

"Father is never pleased." Valiant allowed her to pull him toward their study rooms. He might sit there with her, but he would not study.

True to his intentions, Valiant didn't study. He composed a song in his head about his anger. One that would never be heard or even written down. He had no intention of putting his failures out there for all the world to see or hear. He stared out the window hoping to see Tempest and Ridge return. A short time later, he saw birds fly out of the trees and looked down. Valiant's mouth dropped open as Ridge walked out of the woods alone. It had not occurred to him that Ridge would not find Tempest.

Ignoring the teacher, Valiant opened the windows and yelled, "Where is she?"

Ridge looked up and snarled, "By evening repast, you will have your assignments completed to the satisfaction of Lady Adaryn."

Prized

Valiant rushed back to his seat and attended to his studies. Ridge would ask Lady Adaryn in front of Father, resulting in trouble for Valiant if she didn't give a glowing response.

While Lady Adaryn searched for a manuscript among the stacks, Temperance adjusted her scroll so that Valiant could read it. He smiled and copied her work, mixing up a couple of the herbs. Valiant knew from experience that if he scored perfect in herbs Lady Adaryn would realize he had copied. It was his worst area of study.

Late in the afternoon, Tempest trudged into the room with torn clothes and red dirt spread liberally on her face and hands.

Lady Adaryn looked up from grading the work of Valiant and Temperance. "Mistress Tempest! Are you harmed?"

"No, Lady Adaryn." Tempest was subdued. "Lord Ellwood said to tell you I will attend to my studies tomorrow, but for today it is time for the three of us to prepare for the evening repast."

"Then I shall see all of you tomorrow, if not at the evening repast." Lady Adaryn rose and adjusted her skirts. "Ridge will receive a satisfactory response to any questions he might ask this evening about today's studies."

"Good day, Lady Adaryn." Valiant smiled in relief. Lady Adaryn was tough but fair.

After Lady Adaryn left the study rooms, Temperance asked, "What happened?"

Valiant looked his sister over and said, "Did you fight a gorkong?"

"No. I was chased by a gorkong. I killed a werewolf."

"You would be dead if you were chased by a gorkong or fought a werewolf." Valiant raked an unbelieving eye over her battered appearance. Fighting either would result in more injuries than she sported. It was doubtful she would be walking after such an experience.

"Believe what you will." Tempest opened the doors that were a shortcut to the treehouses where Ellwood's family lived. As always, Valiant and Temperance followed.

Once properly attired, Valiant walked with his sisters to the evening repast. They were young to attend formal meals, but they had been doing so for years. Father was insistent that his offspring attend whenever the attendees were only Northern Realm subjects. As they approached the pillars depicting battles fought by the past and current Forest Lord, Valiant noticed the whispering was louder than usual.

"What did you do? The whole court is pointing," Valiant said. It wasn't true. No one in a realm court would do something so low as point, but they whispered until the triplets were within earshot and then stopped.

Tempest rolled her eyes, "I told you."

"Fine." Valiant broke ranks with his sisters and went to stand by Ciam, who would tell him the truth.

Ciam turned a broad smile on Valiant and clapped him on the back. "You must be proud of Mistress Tempest. Killing a werewolf with only her knife. The bards have already written a song and they will sing it tonight. I hear Lord Ellwood is satisfied with her first kill."

Valiant smiled at his cousin, but inside his head, he screamed. Tempest goes off in a huff, kills a werewolf, and returns victorious. The bards even wrote a song about her. Valiant expected to be the first of the triplets the bards would honor with a song of brave deeds.

He looked over at Tempest, and she shrugged. He then felt her in his mind. *I told you so.*

Valiant shook his head. He hated when she spoke into his mind and pushed his anger at Tempest. She stumbled, and he closed his mind. He had forgotten he could do that now.

Tempest turned and glared at him.

He mouthed the word "Sorry".

"What amuses you?" Ciam asked when a grinning Valiant sat down at the table.

"Nothing, just thinking," Valiant replied. If he could push feelings at Tempest, perhaps one day he would be able to send her a message. He was pleased that Ciam had invited him to sit with the warriors. None would pick on him with Ciam beside him and it had the added benefit of irritating Tempest. Ellwood's daughters would not be allowed to sit away from the family table until they were adults.

Remembering the good that had happened, Valiant kept a smile on his face a few hours later when a bard sat on one of the balconies and sang "Better an Angry Gorkong Than a Sleeping Werewolf". The first song ever written about Tempest.

As Mistress Tempest went out to play,
She forgot the rules and went astray.
She left her brother and sister too,
To search for adventure under skies so blue.

Prized

She played with the pixies, nymphs, and merfolk,
But eventually got hungry and it was no joke.
She headed for home thinking of food,
But what she found was a gorkong in a mood.

She had no worries, no concerns, no fear,
She pulled her dagger, the brave little dear.
The gorkong growled low and summoned his band.
Mistress Tempest stood ready, her dagger in hand.

It was then she saw out the side of her eye,
A small gorkong baby was what she did spy.
The gorkongs weren't angry. They feared for their young.
Mistress Tempest thought fast and headed off at a run.

One gorkong gave chase, which was not what she wanted.
She picked up her speed. She would not be daunted.
The gorkong was bigger and faster, it's true,
With powers still growing, she was feeling quite blue.

She stopped at a cave. She was too tired to trot.
At least in the dark she could hide, could she not?
She crawled up a rock and heard heavy breathing.
The gorkong had found her. She should be leaving.

She snuck toward the entrance at a fast crawl,
But in the opening the gorkong was standing quite tall.
Her eyesight adjusted and she turned to see,
A lone werewolf sleeping relaxed as could be.

The gorkong beat his chest and gave out a yell.
The werewolf jumped up as if he heard a bell.
He spied in his cave a young tasty treat.
The treat growled too. She would not be beat.

She raised her sword, a carnelian dagger.
A gift from her uncle, to keep up her swagger.
She faced the werewolf, all else forgotten.

If she got out alive, that would not be rotten.

One foe at a time, so her father always said.
She crouched and vowed the wolf would be dead.
The werewolf pounced, and her dagger hand rose,
Blood covered the young warrior, the color of a rose.

She then faced the gorkong her first kill complete
If he wanted to fight, she was ready to compete.
They stared at each other, the gorkong and child,
Then he left in peace, no longer very riled.

When you walk in the woods have your sword at the ready.
Be aware of your surroundings and keep things steady.
If you upset a gorkong, don't get in too deep.
Don't take refuge in a cave where a werewolf is asleep.

Valiant finally realized what he had missed. Tempest hadn't been covered in red clay. She had been bathed in the blood of a werewolf.

*****

"Why are you the one to open the way?" Valiant groused with no expectation of being listened to. Tempest demanded to be first to do anything, as if being the first-born by mere minutes made her the de facto leader.

"Because I'm the oldest." Tempest concentrated and opened the way. This was the first time they had been allowed to visit the Seen without Kyan coming to the Farseen to travel with them. Although after that first visit, Kyan had opened a way much closer to the Sovereign's camp.

Tempest walked through without waiting for the others.

Valiant and Temperance shook their heads and followed.

The triplets now made yearly trips to the Seen to visit their shifter relatives. It was something of a surprise to Valiant that Ellwood allowed the trips to continue, but he encouraged them.

Valiant smiled when he exited the way and saw they were in the open field at the edge of the Sovereign's woods. Carwen was alone, bent over in the center of the pasture, picking herbs. She was his best friend of all the shifters. He would even go so far as to say she was his best friend. Only Tempest was closer to him. "Go ahead, I'll help Carwen carry her load."

Temperance smiled, and Tempest laughed, but they went on ahead without comment.

"I don't need help," Carwen said when he stopped by her side. "Although the humans didn't know about us, they considered these woods to be haunted by ferrous beasts and never came near here. Taren's father takes the form of a Gorkong, and whenever humans come too close, the humans find themselves being chased by a huge hairy beast on two legs."

When she saw Valiant's pout, she smiled. "I would be happy for the company, though."

"I am here to serve. What can I collect for you?"

"Do you know what sorrel is?"

"Of course," Valiant scoffed. It was an easily picked herb that could be added to stews or salads.

"I could use a bundle."

Valiant smiled and went in search of sorrel. In no time, he returned with a nice sized bunch. In contrast to her earlier comment, Carwen did not object when Valiant carried the basket. They strolled through the woods. Valiant was at peace, glad he had at least one friend who didn't make him feel less than Tempest.

"Is it true? Did Tempest kill a werewolf and fight a gorkong?"

Valiant stopped and stared at her. How did she know?

"The whole village is talking about it. A fae bard came to see Father about a commission and sang the song after evening meal. Cwenhild said we were not to mention it in front of Tempest. You must be proud of her." Carwen smiled.

"Yes, I must." Valiant dropped the basket in disgust.

"Did I say something wrong?" Carwen's smile faded, and she became angry. "I thought you were different. Not like other boys. But you are. Mad that your sister did something first."

"I'm not mad about that. It's just… Tempest is the perfect child in the Farseen. Everything she does is without fault. Even when she runs off in a huff, she's rewarded with a song of her deeds. Just once, I would like to be acknowledged as a person in my own right. Not the son of the Forest Lord and most definitely not the brother of Tempest."

"Oh." Carwen dropped to the ground to pick up the plants that had fallen out of the basket.

Valiant sighed. "I'll pick up the mess. It was not my intention to ruin your basket."

"It's okay."

"No, it's not. Why are you suddenly so sad?" He knelt down, relieved that he didn't break the basket, and refilled the contents.

"I'm not sad."

Valiant stared at his friend.

Carwen gave a small sigh. "I shifted during the last full moon. The ones that didn't, especially Taren, are ignoring me. It hurts to be treated like I'm not there."

"You shifted. That's great. What form did you take?"

Pleased that Valiant was happy for her, Carwen replied, "Wolf."

"When will you shift for me?"

Carwen grinned. "Maybe after evening meal."

Valiant helped Carwen across the stream. He enjoyed looking out for her. Neither of his sisters appreciated assistance of any kind. At least not from him.

As they approached the village, Taren called out, "Valiant, have the bards written any songs of your great deeds?"

Valiant's lip curled up, but he had expected such a taunt when he learned the clan knew of the song. "The bards write as they see fit. If you like, I can sing the song written about my eldest sister's first kill. It's been very well received."

Tempest looked over in surprise. It was no secret among the triplets that Valiant was unhappy that she had been so honored first. When Valiant winked at her, she grinned and said, "In truth, the song sounds as if a great warrior did the deed instead of me, terrified in the moment. I suspect that many songs are full of exaggerations. But we have more exciting things to discuss than my walk in the woods. Carwen, how was your first shift? I want to hear all about it." Tempest slid her arm into Carwen's and pulled her away from the boys. Temperance left with them.

Normally, Valiant would have been irritated by an interruption in his time with Carwen, but not today. He turned to Taren and smiled, showing all of his teeth.

*****

73

Prized

Temperance took one look at Valiant when he entered their hut and grabbed the medicinal herbs from her pouch to tend his wounds.

"Stop it." Valiant batted away her hands.

Tempest shook her head. "Sit still, brother mine. Temperance will not be satisfied until she has tended your wounds. I trust Taren is in worse shape than you."

Valiant sat down and let Temperance do as she pleased. Tempest was right. It was the easiest way to deal with Temperance when she wanted to tend someone. "He is. Did you listen in my head the whole time?"

"No. We watched from the trees." Tempest grinned.

"You watched?" Valiant winced when Temperance applied a salve to his split lip. "Carwen too?"

"Yes." Temperance put away her herbs. "She seemed pleased that you won the day. Why did you fight?"

"Don't you know?"

"Tempest refused to tell me. Said it was your business, and while she couldn't block you, she wouldn't tell tales."

Valiant looked over at Tempest. When she shrugged, he smiled and said, "Taren and I had a disagreement."

Kyan opened their tent flap and entered without knocking. A breach of protocol within both the fae and shifter communities. "A disagreement that is over."

Valiant nodded. "As far as I'm concerned, yes. I believe he understands me now."

"The sovereign wants to hear nothing about a trivial fight between two boys who have not yet shifted. Do not speak of this in her hearing, or all involved will suffer." Kyan opened the flap and said over his shoulder, "Adair seems to favor you, nephew. You have been invited to sit with him at the evening meal."

When the flap closed, Valiant muttered, "Starless night."

"Are you not pleased?" Temperance asked.

"I had hoped to sit with Carwen this evening."

Tempest laughed. "Don't you think Carwen will sit with her father? By nightfall, the entire village will hear how you beat Taren to defend her honor. Sitting with Adair will show the village that he approves of your actions and you."

Valiant grinned. This visit had begun well.

*****

74

"What is your interest in this root?" Valiant held up an odd-looking plant by its root. The stem was nearly as tall as he was with a yellow flower larger than his fist. The petals of the flower were as thin as a blade of grass. The root smelled sweet. Valiant licked the root and made a face. It left a bitter taste in his mouth.

Carwen smiled. "Telyn needs it for her medicinal stores. I promised to gather some of the herbs that are best picked now."

Valiant nodded but hadn't really cared why they were gathering. Any time he spent with Carwen was time well spent. After a morning of herb gathering, they returned to the village and added their plants to the pile. They had not been the only ones scavenging for Telyn.

"Tempest, this is not the place to practice your fire control. Go nearer the river." Cwenhild turned to speak to a clan member and didn't notice Tempest's eyes narrowing on her.

Valiant shook his head. Cwenhild needed to take another tone with Tempest. His sister didn't respond well to orders of that nature. For that matter, neither would he. Father was the only person who barked orders back home, and they were unaccustomed to bowing to the will of anyone else.

Tempest, fire in her left hand surrounded by water controlled by her right hand, walked away from the camp. Some of the camp children were playing a chasing game, and one bumped into Tempest. The water dissipated, and her fire wobbled wildly and touched a basket. The basket of newly picked herbs went up in flames. Tempest used the water to douse the fire, but the damage had been done.

Cwenhild, face contorted in anger, turned on Tempest.

"I will replace the herbs," Tempest said quickly. Not because she was afraid of her grandmother, but because she had no tolerance for reprimands.

"Yes, you will." Cwenhild stormed off.

Tempest glared at Cwenhild's back.

"If I had done that, she would still be screaming in my face." Taren stopped by Tempest's side. "What makes you so special?"

Tempest turned her eyes, black as night, on Taren, and he backed up. Tempest walked away.

"Shouldn't someone follow her?" Carwen asked.

"No." The response, in unison, came from Valiant and Temperance.

*****

Prized

"Why are we gathering herbs in the east?" Valiant picked yarrow, placing some in the basket and some in his pouch. He would gift the herb to Temperance to make up for what she used after he got in fights. Fights that were not his fault. He never started them. Well, almost never. Taren had been begging for a beating. Didn't matter if Valiant was in the Seen or the Farseen. Someone always picked a fight.

"Why not in the east? This valley is rarely scavenged." Tempest dug up elfwort using small ground movements. The root was prized but could be difficult to harvest. It could be used topically for wounds and Telyn made a hard candy from it that was helpful for coughs and sore throats. Tempest was hoping to soothe the healer with the offering. Telyn had identified what needed to be replaced after Tempest accidentally set fire to the large basket of herbs. Tempest had listened last night when Telyn was talking. The triplets left the village before anyone else was awake.

"That's because this valley is what separates us from the blood-sucking demons." Temperance didn't look up from her search.

"Oh," Valiant said. "In addition to helping Tempest replace what she destroyed, we're disobeying orders to stay away from Cimil and his thralls. You remember how powerful he is, right?"

A wolf rose from behind some bushes and shifted. Kyan shook his head. "At least one of you understands, although I'm surprised it's Valiant."

"I'm not a fool," Valiant said.

"No, you aren't. But you allow Tempest to take you on adventures even when you know it's forbidden." Kyan turned to Temperance. "And you?"

Temperance blushed. "I had planned to run for help."

Kyan laughed.

"Aren't you going to ask me?" Tempest stood, her eyes darkening.

"You are here because this is where you have been told not to go. You planned to use the excuse that you couldn't find some of the herbs you burned any place else. Complete your task. We are guarding."

"We?" Tempest growled. "Who else is here?"

Kyan shifted and stretched out, pointedly ignoring her.

Four more wolf heads raised above the tall grass and cocked their heads in Tempest's direction. Valiant laughed. Tempest returned to her task and ignored everyone for the rest of the morning. Back in camp, they unloaded their herbs.

Telyn looked over the offerings and smiled. "You've replenished everything, and I see you found elfwort. Very good."

Valiant looked up in surprise. Telyn didn't berate Tempest for the fire, just thanked her for restoring what was destroyed. Few would be so gracious.

One of the children of the camp tugged on Valiant's sleeve. "Can you sing us a song?"

Valiant shook his head. "Not today. I'm to help in the fields."

Taren overheard and said, "If you watch the young, I'll work in the fields in your stead."

"Are you to watch them today?"

"Yes, but they would rather hear your songs."

"Yes." "Please." The kids who answered raised pleading eyes to Valiant.

Taren leaned in a little closer and spoke so softly, only Valiant could hear. "Your voice soothes the sovereign. We'll all be happier if she gets over her anger at the fire."

Valiant eyed Taren. He wasn't being mean at Tempest's expense. He genuinely wanted to help. Valiant nodded. "Okay, kids. If everyone's chores are done, I'll teach you a new song." By the time he had returned with his lute, most of the children had verified that they had no other chores to do. Cadel, who had extra tasks to make up for a prank he played, trudged toward the river with two buckets. Valiant tuned his lute with unusual precision. Cadel delivered the water to the community pot for dinner and joined the group just as Valiant struck the first chord.

After Valiant played a few songs the young were partial to, he slowed the tempo and sang a couple of ballads he knew the sovereign liked.

Prized

Coming of Age

4977 BCE – 4972 BCE

Prized

Chapter 7 – 4977 BCE

"Goodbye, nursery." Valiant bowed to the room as if it were alive.

Tempest laughed. "Tonight, we each sleep in our own treehouse."

"The nursery has been nice." Temperance grimaced.

"But we're adults now. Today is our day. Gifts all day and private quarters." Valiant hugged Temperance, knowing she wasn't fond of change. He, on the other hand, loved change. He had plans for this evening that most definitely didn't include his sisters.

"Watch yourself. The court is filled with females who will try to ensnare you. They want the power that the position as your companion will give them. That doesn't mean they want you." Tempest emphasized the last word.

"You worry too much." Valiant walked out of the nursery for the last time, his sisters followed. They arrived at the feasting hall to discover it had been decorated for their coming-of-age day. Valiant smiled, "Brilliant."

"Lady Tempest. Lady Temperance. Valiant. May today be marked with joy as you start your adult life." Ridge bowed.

Both ladies curtsied, and Valiant returned the bow.

As Ridge walked away, Tempest spoke into Valiant's mind. *I can think of no better greeting.*

Valiant huffed. Tempest needed to get over her obsession with Ridge. He was a great warrior, but the five realms had many great fighters... and Ridge had beaten them all, which was the problem. Tempest saw Ridge as the best, and she would only settle for the best. Good thing Lord Ellwood would have to approve any male wishing to address his daughters.

Prized

Lord Ellwood entered the hall with three of his personal guards, each carrying a box. Ellwood clapped his hands. "A glorious day. My children are adults, proper members of my court. I bring to each of you a gift." He waved his hands, and the three guards stepped forward.

Following fae custom, Tempest, as the eldest, moved in front of the others and accepted the box that was offered. She opened the box and smirked as she pulled out a scroll. "Father, you surprise me. Have you suddenly developed a love of study? You have only praised my fighting skills, never my mind."

"I have noticed your interest in the cutting of jewels. I thought you might benefit from proper training by Fennel."

Tempest raised an eyebrow. She thought she had been sly in hiding her jewelry and her interest. Perhaps a spell to bind jewelry to a specific person was needed. She had become interested in the subject in the Seen and had continued to hone her skills when she returned home. Tempest turned and inclined her head toward Fennel, who curtsied.

Valiant stepped forward, sure that he would get weapons befitting the son of the Forest Lord. He pulled out his own scroll and glanced at the title. At least it would be useful training. "And who shall train me?"

"I have that honor." Ridge bowed.

Valiant returned the bow, but he wasn't happy. Nothing he did on the training field pleased the Realm Advisor. His mood improved when he saw the expression on Tempest's face. For once, she was not hiding her emotions. She was jealous that Valiant would be training to lead warriors in battle while she learned to make jewelry.

Temperance stepped forward to stand in front of the remaining box before Tempest displayed her temper, a temper that was already the subject of many ballads sung by the bards. Songs that were never sung within the hearing of Lord Ellwood or Lady Rayna. Temperance pulled out her scroll, glanced at the title, and turned to Joren, the Northern Realm's representative to the High Council. "Will you be my trainer?"

Joren bowed. "Indeed, there is much to learn about the inner workings of the High Council and other governing bodies."

Following a morning of studies with their new mentors, the triplets returned to the feasting hall for the mid-day repast.

"Wonder what we'll get now?" Temperance asked.

Tempest snorted. "It can't be worse than what we got at first repast."

"You're the only one not happy with your gift." Valiant focused on his sisters, ignoring the number of females trying to catch his eye. He was beginning to think Tempest had been right about the reason ladies of the court would be interested in him, and he had no intention of getting entangled.

The Forest Lord did not put in an appearance, but the triplets found notes to check their new quarters. They ate with haste and rushed to the family treehouses. The triplets had been denied access beyond the nursery while their rooms were made ready. Each treehouse contained its own cluster of turrets in a single, large tree. Access between the trees consisted of a living bridge, where tree branches were woven together into a hallway with floor, walls, and ceiling. There were clear coverings over the windows, made by magical castings, providing breathtaking views while keeping inhabitants protected from the elements and intruders. They each ran into the room marked with their personal symbol.

"Perfect." Temperance twirled around her living area, which consisted of soothing shades of green with pops of yellow. Her balcony and windows overlooked the Home Woods of the residence. Perfect. Temperance ran to Tempest's rooms and swung open the door. "Oh my."

Tempest stood in the middle of a royal room. Decked out in the browns and greens that represented the Forest Lord's colors, she had a balcony that overlooked the Kaveri River and past it to the Dark Woods in the north. The treehouse was at least three times larger than Temperance's, but it lacked any semblance of warmth.

Valiant walked in, looked around, and grinned. "Today it pleases me to not be Father's favorite. You could hold court in here."

"I could hold beheadings in here." Tempest waved her hands around the room. "What was Father thinking?"

"That this ostentatious display would anger you." Temperance walked over to stand by Tempest. "You must not show your displeasure."

Tempest's mouth tightened for a second. Then she looked at Temperance and changed her expression to a single raised eyebrow. "How kind of you to point out the obvious."

Prized

"When faced with this," Temperance waved her hands around the room, "you could almost be forgiven for forgetting."

"Who would forgive me? Certainly not Father." Tempest sat down and laughed. "It's so bizarre, I almost like it."

"Now that's the proper attitude," Temperance agreed with a smile, pleased Tempest wasn't going to let her temper ruin the day.

"Come, show me your rooms." Tempest gathered her siblings, and they left.

Valiant opened the door to his treehouse and bowed his sisters into the living area.

"Lovely. Brown, with just a touch of green. You will be happy here," Temperance said.

"Happy, probably not, but I shall be content."

"I would think so. A properly sized room with weapons on the wall. This is a proper room." Tempest removed one of the weapons from the wall. "Not made by Father, but well balanced with expert scrollwork. I would be well pleased with such a room."

"Yeah, but we'll still have to hold all beheadings in your room, sister mine." Valiant picked up his lire and strummed. "I find myself surprised that Father allowed my lire to be moved to my adult quarters."

"Perhaps Father has mellowed and wants you to be happy," Temperance said.

The triplets burst out laughing. Whatever Lord Ellwood had hoped to affect by giving Tempest quarters that dwarfed those he gave Temperance and Valiant, the triplets were sure it wasn't to please any of them. All three were prepared when they received their final gift from Ellwood before the evening repast.

Valiant had no trouble showing pleasure as weapons, made by the Forest Lord's own hands, were unwrapped to go with his fighting leathers.

Tempest and Temperance received fighting leathers, but no weapons.

"My daughters are capable warriors, able to lead my fighters into battle, but it's time their thoughts turned to more domestic tasks. Each will be running their own residence one day."

No matter what, Tempest vowed to herself, she would have weapons made by the Forest Lord before the seasons changed. Tempest smiled and bowed to her father as a warrior. "I fear that unless the male in that household can hold my attention, my thoughts might turn to battle on the home front."

Many in the feasting hall tried to hide their amusement. Ridge wasn't one of them. Laughing, he bowed to the Forest Lord. "I believe I have victory, Lord Ellwood."

"Indeed, and you didn't have to raise a sword." Ellwood turned to one of his attendants, "The land east of the Kaveri River, at the edge of the wastelands, now belongs to Ridge. He tells me he desires to set up a residence there."

Valiant's mouth fell open, wondering what victory Ridge won. That was a very generous landholding Ridge just acquired.

"For whom are you building a residence?" Lady Briar asked.

Ridge laughed. "Perhaps you, Lady Briar."

Briar's warm laughter spread throughout the hall. "We are ill-suited, as you well know." Taking her escort's arm, she spoke loud enough for all to hear, "Farver, I am ready to sit at your table."

Farver bowed. "Yes, my lady." Everyone knew Lord Ellwood had given him permission to court Lady Briar. Still, she had not, until this very moment, accepted his advances.

Valiant had watched the playful exchange with interest. He didn't like Ridge, but the man flirted without getting entangled. Something Valiant needed to learn. He caught Tempest's expression out of the corner of his eye. She didn't look pleased that Ridge was building a residence for someone. *Don't let Father see your interest in Ridge.*

Tempest looked over in surprise. *Did you just speak into my mind?*

You heard that?

Yes, and I heard that as well. Tempest grinned. We can speak mind to mind. How wonderful.

Temperance walked over and grabbed her siblings by the arms, hissing, "Stop whatever you're doing. Father is watching."

Valiant glanced over and quickly ducked his head. The last thing he wanted was for Lord Ellwood to become angry with him, again. He turned and helped Temperance move Tempest to the table. Tempest never worried overmuch about Father's temper. Sometimes he thought she enjoyed fighting as much as Father. His sisters stayed close to Lord Ellwood this evening. Only with Father's permission would they be allowed on the dance floor. Temperance had stressed over anyone asking for a dance. Tempest hadn't worried at all. Valiant had a different type of stress.

Prized

He walked away from his family to secure dance partners for after the repast. It wasn't as hard as he had thought. Listening to Elm and Harden, his particular friends, he thought it would be difficult to ask fathers for permission to dance with their daughters. Both had recently reached their majority and grumbled about the rules. So far, everyone was very kind to Valiant.

"Harden, I believe our friend has become popular." Elm clapped Valiant on the shoulder. "Never have I seen anyone secure dance partners so easily."

"Indeed," Harden replied in a fair imitation of Ridge. "It's almost as if being the son of the Forest Lord gives him an edge. Who have you selected for the first dance?"

"You can wait and see like everyone else."

"I told you who I selected." Harden placed his hand over his heart as if Valiant had hurt him.

Elm laughed. "You told everyone."

"If you had led Lady Cayenne out for your first dance, you would have told everyone too," Harden retorted.

Valiant nodded. "He has a point. Lady Cayenne is deadly in a fight, and she is the most beautiful lady in our court."

"I would give Lady Temperance the title of most beautiful," Elm said.

"Not Lady Tempest?" Harden asked. "Of course, except for hair color, they look very similar."

"Lady Temperance is easier to talk to."

"Stop. No discussing my sisters as partners, dancing or otherwise."

Elm wiggled his eyebrows. "You do know your sisters will be dancing after the repast."

Valiant's blank stare greeted that comment.

"Didn't you think about that? While you were out securing dances, many approached the Forest Lord for permission."

"Of course, I thought about it. But why would anyone want to dance with them?"

"Your sisters are beautiful, and the daughters of the Realm Lord. Half the court is hoping to impress one of them." Harden turned as Tempest approached.

"Come." Tempest pulled Valiant's arm. "We finally have our own table. Harden, Elm, you are with us as well."

Valiant allowed himself to be pulled toward the table Tempest and Temperance had selected as their own. Valiant hadn't cared where they sat as long as they weren't at the head table with Lord Ellwood anymore. His eyes lit up when he saw their table was near a balcony, far away from their parents. "Nice."

Throughout the repast, the new adults tried to behave, knowing the Forest Lord wouldn't allow a rowdy table like the ones the triplets had heard some of the other realms allowed.

Afterwards, Lord Ellwood led Tempest onto the dance floor, as was custom. The lord of the realm opened an evening of dancing with his eldest daughter.

"I'm glad she's the eldest." Temperance kept her voice low, and only Valiant heard her.

At the appropriate time, Valiant walked over and bowed to Lady Zelkova, Harden's twin sister. He had selected her as a way to keep the gossips at bay. As the Master-At-Arms' daughter, she was an appropriate choice for the first dance of the son of the Forest Lord. She was also his friend, and he felt comfortable with her. She wouldn't read anything into his selection of her.

Before the song ended, he looked for Tempest and Temperance. Tempest's first dance after the opening with their father was with Elm, and Temperance was with Harden. The three friends looked at each other and smiled.

*****

Valiant walked into the stands of the Northern Realm Killing Field. Every realm had one. It was the place competitions were held so that all could observe. It was also the place where punishments were handed out. But today it was the place where Tempest had challenged the Forest Lord. Not for power or wealth, but to prove she was worthy of weapons forged by the Forest Lord himself. Valiant absently laid a hand on the hilt of his sword. It was the first time he attained anything before Tempest. A part of him suspected that was the reason Ellwood gifted him the weapons. It certainly wasn't a father's love for his son.

Tempest stood in the center of the field, calm and relaxed. Sorbus, Quercus, and Salix surrounded her.

"What is he doing out there?" Temperance, hands on hips, glared at the field.

Valiant followed her gaze. Sorbus and Quercus were experienced fighters, but Salix was barely older than the triplets. "Maybe father wants Salix to die?" Valiant whispered.

"It's not a to-the-death fight," Temperance retorted.

Valiant shrugged. Accidents happened.

Tempest bowed to each of the men, before turning to the Forest Lord and bowing.

Lord Ellwood returned the bow and sat down. "Begin."

All three men waited for her to attack. Tempest smiled... and disappeared. One second, she stood surrounded by the trio, and the next, she appeared behind Salix, hitting him over the head with the hilt of her sai. He dropped to the ground.

"When did she acquire the ability to teleport?" Valiant didn't bother to hide his irritation. Tempest had a new ability. One she hadn't mentioned and had control over. What else was she hiding?

"I don't know. Since you growl when a new ability comes to Tempest, she quit telling either of us," Temperance said. "Look."

Valiant followed Temperance's gaze and gritted his teeth. Finally! Tempest decided to focus on the most dangerous opponent before her. She should have used her new power to take out Sorbus while the surprise was fresh.

Tempest swung her twin sais at Sorbus. As soon as she had teleported behind Salix, Sorbus and Quercus moved to stand back to back. No matter how Tempest twisted and turned, one of the men always faced her. The dance continued for a few minutes until she deflected Sorbus's walking stick with one sai. She swung the other sai to disarm him. That failed, and the walking stick remained in his arms. He twirled the staff and moved quickly to keep her focus while Quercus remained still. As soon as Tempest was forced to turn her back to Quercus, he charged. At the last second, Tempest disappeared again, and Sorbus had to disarm Quercus to prevent injury. It didn't matter that the warriors were working together. As soon as someone was disarmed, they were out. Quercus bowed, signaling his defeat. He gathered up the abandoned weapons, helped a now conscious Salix to his feet, and they left the field.

Tempest appeared behind where Sorbus had been, but he was gone. Tempest tightened her hold on her sais and moved in a circle. He had that most rare fae gift of being unseen. He wasn't invisible, not really, but he was able to blend in with his surroundings. While it was uncommon for fae, it was a more common gift among the shifters. Tempest smiled and opened her shifter eyes, which saw movement better than her fae eyes and searched. When she found him, Tempest forced her eyes to move past as if she were continuing to look for him. When she had her back to the warrior, she heard him approaching, even though he was stealthy. Stealthy for a fae, but shifters had better senses. At the last second, Tempest turned and sliced his walking stick in half. The impact caused Sorbus to appear to all eyes.

Sorbus kept his grip on the two halves and used them as short clubs, batting away her sais. They continued this way for some time. No elements were used as this was a display of her ability to wield a weapon.

Ellwood's voice boomed across the field. "Enough. Well played, daughter mine. You shall have weapons, forged by my hands, before the winter solstice. Come, walk with me."

Bowing to Sorbus, Tempest returned her weapons to their sheaths and jogged over to her father's side.

Valiant was happy for her, but a small part of him was jealous as well. He had never heard Father utter the words, "Well played, my son." He doubted he ever would.

*****

The squadron of warriors lay flat on their backs. Most were unconscious. Tempest and Valiant had disabled the squad without loss of life. Ridge approved but was unsure how they managed it.

Ellwood was not nearly as pleased. "How?"

"I don't know." But I will find out. Ridge walked toward the duo.

Ridge stopped beside Lady Tempest. "There's something different about your fighting style."

"What?" Sheathing the weapons her father made her, Tempest looked at Ridge in surprise. "You taught us." Tempest exchanged a smile with her brother. Only Temperance knew that they could speak mind to mind between themselves. It was a rare talent and one they kept hidden from their father.

"Individually. When you and Valiant team up, no one can beat you. It is almost as if you speak to each other during the fight."

"That is not a gift Mother's people possess, and few fae are so blessed."

Ridge leaned down and whispered, "Your father knows something is different. Do not give him cause to doubt either of you." Standing straight, Ridge turned to Valiant. "You sparred well today, but more stealth will improve your successes."

Valiant glared at Ridge's back as he walked away. "If he ever gave me praise not tempered by criticism, the shock would be too great to bear."

"You would know you had accomplished a great feat." Tempest also watched Ridge walk away. He moved like the predator he was.

"If you two don't stop, Father will learn your secret," Temperance said.

"What secret, my child?" Ellwood stopped beside the triplets.

Temperance withdrew into herself, and Valiant scowled. Tempest smiled brightly and said, "Valiant and I have been working on hand singles. To communicate when fighting."

"Not very useful, unless you are side by side." Ellwood's disbelief was available for all to hear.

"True, but in close-quarter fighting, like this," Tempest waved her arms around, "the benefit is obvious." Tempest watched Lord Ellwood leave. Her eyes fell on Ridge, and her smile warmed.

Valiant's teeth clenched as he walked away. He wasn't going to have another argument with Tempest about her obsession with Ridge. Nothing changed. Instead of following the others into the residence, Valiant walked toward the river. He would enter the private gardens of the Forest Lord and use the back steps to enter the living bridge of the family treehouses.

Before he reached the arch that separated the private gardens, he saw Lady Zelkova sitting by the river. "Are you here alone?"

Zelkova brushed her hand over her face and smiled at Valiant. "I wanted some quiet to think."

Valiant wasn't fooled. She had been crying. Dropping to the ground beside her, he asked, "Is there anything I can do for you? Who made you cry? Is there anyone I might kill for you, Zel?"

As he had hoped, she laughed.

"There's no one to kill. I'm being foolish."

"Tell me, or I will have to search for the person who made you cry. And I will dole out an appropriate punishment."

Zelkova shook her head. "It truly is silly."

"Tell me."

"Pinus. I've told him I'm not interested. I've threatened to tell Father, and even said I would tell Lord Ellwood, but he keeps following me." Exhaling loudly, she said, "You won't tell Father or Harden, will you? I don't want Pinus injured, just gone."

Valiant raised her hand to his lips. "I will be pleased to address this concern for you."

"No. I don't want you — "

"Fear not, Lady Zelkova. All will be well. I won't have my friends harassed in court." Valiant reached out his hand to help Zelkova stand. "Zel, we're friends. Never be afraid to come to me."

A few hours later, Valiant escorted his sisters to the evening repast where some of their friends waited.

"Have you heard?" Harden asked. When Tempest shook her head, he said, "Someone beat Pinus."

"Someone?" Temperance asked.

"No one is sure who. Pinus has made himself obnoxious, chasing after ladies of the court. So many had complained to Father, he and Ridge are having trouble determining which family line did it."

"Ridge and Father are being vocal about this not turning into a feud," Harden said.

Valiant cringed. He hadn't thought of anything other than telling Pinus to stay away from Zel. He hadn't expected to fight, but Pinus had begged for it with his obnoxious attitude.

"Valiant, Ash is looking for you." Elm joined the crowd. When he saw Valiant's expression, he added, "Ridge and Ash are questioning every adult male about Pinus."

Valiant nodded and walked away. He found Ash on one of the balconies. "I hear you wanted to see me."

"Do you know what happened to Pinus?"

"I heard someone beat him up for making advances toward a female in their family."

"Pinus is awake now." Ridge stopped in front of Valiant. "Why did you do it?"

Rather than lie, Valiant said, "I simply told him to leave, er…"

Ridge relaxed. "Which of the Forest Lord's daughters did Pinus approach without leave?"

"Neither."

"Then why did you beat him?"

Valiant glanced at Ash and asked Ridge, "Could we speak alone?"

"No. Answer me."

Not willing to face Ash, he stared at Ridge. "It was Lady Zelkova."

Prized

"What?" Ash's voice carried, and those nearby turned to look at the trio.

"She was crying. I confronted Pinus but didn't expect to fight. I was surprised when he threw the first punch. My training kicked in, and you know he's not that good of a fighter. The kick would never have landed on either of you but hit him perfectly in the chest. I didn't mean to break ribs."

"I see." Ridge laid a hand on Ash's shoulder when Ash pressed his thumb and middle finger on either side of his nose and sighed. "I think it's safe to say that Pinus has made a fool of himself with over half of the ladies in court. Nearly every male questioned said they would like to take credit for it."

"What will we do?" Ash asked.

"I believe the court will be best served by saying Valiant and Pinus had a simple disagreement, and Valiant's temper got away from him," Ridge said.

"My temper didn't get away from me. Pinus stepped into the kick instead of away from it. How is that my fault?"

"The other alternative is that we tell everyone you rushed to defend Lady Zelkova's honor," Ridge said, although his tone was kind.

Valiant's mouth closed. If that got around, the gossips would hound him and Zel for details of their affection for each other. And Lord Ellwood would become unbearable on the subject.

"This is not fair to you, but I find myself desirous of keeping my daughter's name out of it," Ash said.

"Fine. I lost my temper, but can you point out that Pinus's pathetic fighting skills are the real reason he is hurt so bad?"

Ash clapped Valiant on the shoulder. "Fear not. Anyone who's ever sparred with him will know that to be the truth."

*****

"All three moons are full tonight." Temperance pitched her voice so that none, save her sister, would hear her. They were not alone in the garden.

"So?" Tempest didn't lower her voice or look up from her task. Focusing her fire to dance in a circle around a ball of water, without the water turning to steam, required concentration.

"We might shift." Temperance wasn't sure she wanted to shift. What if the animal took over? The bards had been singing songs of shifters going mad and the Alpha Clan putting them down.

Temperance was sure the songs were meant to scare the triplets. It certainly had that effect on her.

"We'll shift when we shift."

"You sure?"

"Of course. Shifters shift during their first year as an adult."

"But we're half fae. We might not."

"Must you agonize over every possible outcome?" Tempest snapped and immediately winced. She released the elements back to where they came from and sat down by Temperance. "I feel like I don't belong in my skin anymore. Everything irritates me, and everyone is talking too loud."

"Yes," Valiant agreed. He had entered the courtyard and joined his sisters. "And the smells. What's with the smells?"

"The clan said hearing and sense of smell would improve right before we shift. Perhaps this is our time." Tempest grinned at her brother.

"I need a snack. Let's see if the kitchen staff will part with some food." Valiant grabbed Tempest by the arm, and they walked away, talking excitedly about the prospect of their first shift.

Temperance remained seated, absently stitching a pattern on the cloth. She learned long ago that if others thought she was occupied, they left her alone. If Tempest had opened her mind, even a tiny bit, she would have known that Temperance was afraid. Not of the shift, but of the fact that she didn't think she would shift. Valiant and Tempest had both become exceedingly angry and were eating twice what they normally did. Both were signs they would shift soon. Temperance felt none of that. She also wasn't able to talk mind to mind to Valiant, like Tempest could. Since they had discovered that ability, Temperance felt even more left out. She didn't have improved hearing either, but Temperance had noticed smells were stronger. Her only shifter talent would probably be an improved sense of smell. Useless. Temperance scowled at the uneven pattern she had stitched on her cloth. She sighed and pulled out the stitches to start over.

*****

A few hours later, Valiant escorted his sisters into the feasting hall. He was ever watchful because he didn't like the way some of the males in the court eyed his sisters. For some reason Valiant didn't understand, his otherwise intelligent sisters seemed pleased with the attention. Even Tempest would flirt with males Valiant knew she despised. If all females did that, how was a male to discern if one was sincerely interested? As always, on the night of a full moon, the court watched the triplets intently to see if they would shift. Tonight, he found that it irritated him.

"Hello, Valiant."

"Evening, Lady Talmai." Valiant slowed and smiled but kept walking. He wouldn't mind getting to know her a little better, and tonight her brothers were not standing watch, but he had sisters of his own to watch.

Tempest laughed. "You could go back and talk to her. We don't require an escort."

"Yes, you do." Ridge leaned on a pillar depicting one of Ellwood's battles. "Conversations outside the feasting hall are not as closely monitored as you might think."

"Exactly." Valiant frowned. It's come to this. Ridge was his ally.

"Fine, then Ridge can escort us." Tempest moved with purpose and attached herself to Ridge's side.

Ridge motioned for Temperance to join them. "By all means. Come, ladies, the evening repast awaits." Over his shoulder, Ridge called, "Enjoy your evening, Valiant."

Valiant stood with his hands on his hips and glared at Ridge. No matter what anyone said, Ridge was not to be trusted with his sisters, especially not Tempest.

He moved to join them, but only got two steps before he doubled over. Valiant bit his lip to keep from crying out. No matter the cause, the son of the Forest Lord did not cry out. That lesson had been beaten into him early in life. Valiant noticed Tempest was also doubled over.

They locked eyes and spoke mind-to-mind, saying the same word. *Wolf.* In the next second, where Lady Tempest and Valiant had stood, now crouched two wolves. They had agreed months before that their form would be the larger wolf from the massive landmass to the west of the islands where the Alpha Clan lived in the Seen. The same wolf form Kavi took.

Lord Ellwood appeared beside Temperance. "An excellent choice for your shifter form. Excellent indeed. Bring meat for my children."

"No." Lady Rayna had never said that word to Lord Ellwood in public before, and he turned in surprise. His surprise turned to anger when he saw Kyan was in attendance.

"My husband, for their first shift they must hunt. Kyan and I shall go with them." Before she shifted, she asked Temperance, "Do you feel the call of the moon?"

"No."

"Then stay with Lord Ellwood. Do not look for us before sunrise." Lady Rayna shifted to her wolf form. Like Kyan, she had taken the shape of the smaller wolf found on the isles where she had been raised. Lady Rayna, Kyan, Lady Tempest, and Valiant ran out into the forest.

Ellwood watched, excited that Tempest was growing in her power. He had already determined she was the power from the first set of triplets the witch mentioned years before. As an afterthought, he turned to his other daughter and asked, "Tell me, daughter mine. Do you feel anything?"

"No, Father." Temperance hung her head and watched them leave, feeling less like her siblings than ever before.

"Perhaps next month you will try harder."

Schooling her face into a mask, Temperance said, "Yes, Lord Ellwood."

"Come Lady Temperance, the repast awaits." Ridge's voice was kind as he ushered her to the table the triplets had claimed as their own when they became adults. Even though she had suspected as much, Temperance was not at peace. For the first time in her life, sitting with her particular friends, Temperance felt utterly alone.

*****

Valiant felt free for the first time. No court rules. No shifter sovereign telling him what to do. No posturing. Just running. Hearing, sight, and scent were all superior to when he was in human form. Wondering why anyone would ever shift back to human, he glanced in Tempest's direction. She was a beautiful gray wolf, just like him, only a bit darker. *How about a game of tag?*

Yes, let's. Tempest grinned, showing her sharp, white teeth.

While the kids indulged in play, Rayna and Kyan looked on in amusement. It was rare that the Forest Lord's children were allowed to play so freely.

At first, the four wolves stayed together, but eventually, Tempest headed west toward the falls that separated the Northern and Western Realms. Valiant headed north, further into the Dark Woods.

A tangy scent reached his nose. He liked it. A lagohair shot across the path. Valiant's mouth lolled open, and he gave chase. It was fun for a while, running through the forest. At one point, he thought he had lost the trail, but he sniffed around and caught it again. He saw the lagohair hop over a downed tree. Focused on his dinner, Valiant sailed over the tree and caught the creature in his teeth. He crushed the neck and dropped to the ground to enjoy his meal. He didn't notice Kyan had paced him until he saw his uncle approach. Valiant growled.

Kyan, still in wolf form, stopped and snarled, his lip turning up even with his catch in his mouth. Kyan dropped to the ground to eat his own lagohair.

Pleased that he wouldn't have to share, Valiant returned to his meal. Once done, he relaxed and took in his new abilities. He could hear prey scurrying in the woods. And it was prey. He also felt a powerful presence watching him. Not prey. Not ruling fae either. He was pretty sure it was a dragon. Under no illusions that his wolf would be a match for a dragon, adult or otherwise, Valiant ignored the presence, and it moved on. Even with the remains of a fresh kill in front of him, he could smell the wet leaves from the rain earlier in the day, and hear baby birds chirping in the trees. Valiant could hear the river, though it was a mile away. It was amazing how many details he missed in human form. It was odd to see in shades of gray, but he could see better in the night than his fae eyes could.

Tempest and Rayna topped the hill and joined the men. Tempest bumped Valiant, and they trotted deeper into the Dark Woods. Rayna and Kyan followed, allowing the kids to explore their new gifts.

*****

"How was your first shift?" Temperance didn't look up from her studies.

Valiant dropped into the chair but didn't look at his scrolls. They returned to the residence at sunrise and had slept in, missing most of the day's lessons. "Great. It's amazing how much better my senses are in wolf form."

"Did you feel anything?" Tempest asked.

Temperance forced a laugh. "If you mean, did I feel the moon's call? No."

Valiant leaned toward his sister. "Did Father say anything about our shift or our chosen forms?"

"Lord Ellwood," Temperance drew out the title, "is pleased that two of his children shifted. He expects me to try harder next month."

Valiant laughed. "Try harder? How? Shifting is a biological response to the moon. You either have the predisposition, or you don't."

"Perhaps Lord Ellwood will listen when you tell him that. My opinion isn't worth much at this time." Temperance threw her quill and ink across the room and stormed out.

"A little tact would not go amiss." Tempest glared at her brother before running after Temperance.

"What did I do?" Valiant called after his sisters, but he didn't move to follow. Remembering the freedom of running the night before, he smiled to himself. Finally, he felt like Tempest's equal. In wolf form, in the woods, their mind to mind communication was more straightforward. Life was easier. It was as if the concerns he faced as a fae or shifter weren't important.

When his sisters didn't return, Valiant walked out of the family treehouses and down through the courtyard, entering the garden the triplets called their playground. He thought about the elements. Even if he couldn't call elements as a fae, most shapeshifters could call at least one element after their first shift. Although shifters were typically weaker in element control, it would be nice to have some power. Temperance could already control all four elements. Tempest's control of water and earth was impressive, but she was still learning to master her wind and fire. Both elements rushed to her whenever she lost her temper.

Valiant dropped to the grass and looked up at the sky, hoping for any response he called wind. A small breeze touched his face, but it could have been a normal wind. He called water, then fire, with nothing to show for his efforts. Disgusted with himself, he called ground and was buried underneath the rubble. He had managed to save a pocket of air so he could breathe, but Valiant had no idea how he accomplished that.

Thinking that he couldn't be that far underground, he tried to dig his way up. He clawed the ground above his head, and dirt dropped down on him, filling up his little pocket of air. He tilted his head down as best he could and coughed. Suddenly, the weight of the ground lifted off him, and he was grabbed. Valiant looked up into Ridge's eyes.

"Where are your sisters?"

"They weren't with me."

Ridge breathed a sigh of relief and released Valiant. "What were you thinking? You need someone experienced with the elements in attendance when you first manipulate them."

"Well, this is the first time it's worked. I thought I couldn't." Valiant gasped when he realized what he said and to whom he said it. He hadn't admitted that out loud to anyone, not even his sisters, although he was sure Tempest knew.

Ridge shook his head. "You either have too much courage or not enough. With you, there is no in-between. It is doubtful that, with your parents, you won't control all four elements. It is not uncommon for males to come into their powers later than females."

"Why didn't someone tell me?" Valiant asked, shocked at this turn of events.

"I assumed someone did."

Valiant glared at Ridge correctly interpreting that sentence. Fathers usually told their sons. Just like fathers prepare their sons for encounters with females and other essential information. Ellwood had never taken much interest in Valiant, except to reprimand him for failures.

Ridge rubbed the bridge of his nose. "Let's go for a walk."

"Why?"

"Because it's time you were told a few things, and I don't think you want your sisters showing up while we're talking."

It was late when Valiant finally returned to the residence.

"Where have you been?" Rayna stood before Valiant with her hands on her hips.

"Sorry, Mother. I was with Ridge."

Her eyes narrowed on her only son. "I checked the training fields and the library."

"We were at his residence."

"You should tell me before –"

"No. I'm no longer a child who should tell his mother everything." Valiant moved around his mother and continued down the hall.

"Valiant. This conversation is not over."

"Yes, it is," he called over his shoulder. Not for the first time, Valiant was pleased that his mother couldn't order him. He thought it might be because he was more fae than shifter, but regardless of the reason, he liked it. He passed Temperance's treehouse and had almost reached his own when Temperance threw open Tempest's door and blocked his path.

"Where were you all afternoon? Tempest was angry that you weren't here, and Mother was frantic." Temperance crossed her arms over her chest.

"I already told Mother. I was with Ridge at his residence. It'll be nice when he's finished with it. It will be a fortress to compare with any in the realm."

Tempest walked out of her treehouse and narrowed her eyes on Valiant. "Why would Ridge take you there?"

Valiant turned and pushed anger at her.

"Hey, that hurt." Tempest rubbed her temples.

"Stay out of my mind. You don't need to know everything."

Tempest glared at him as he walked by. He could block her when he concentrated, but he couldn't keep it up forever. She would find out what was going on.

"Stop. We all want to hide something sometimes." Temperance tapped Tempest on the shoulder. "Come on. It's time for our element practice."

Tempest allowed her sister to drag her toward the fields where they practiced daily. She had promised herself she would not enter minds without cause. But it was so easy to check what someone thought that Tempest forgot how intrusive it had felt when someone did it to her back in the Seen. She needed to lock her mind down tighter.

*****

"Clear your mind. In your case, anger makes your powers do weird things," Tempest said.

"I know," Valiant growled.

"Then do something about it." Tempest nodded at Temperance, and they attacked in unison. Tempest sent fire at Valiant while Temperance sent water. Both headed straight for him.

At the last second, Tempest's fire curved toward Temperance and Temperance's water curved toward Tempest. Temperance set a shield to protect herself, and Tempest got soaked.

"What did you do?" Tempest asked in wonder.

"Nothing."

"You did something." Temperance lowered her shield as the fire faded.

Prized

Valiant raised his hands in a stop motion. He didn't know what he had done. He simply hadn't wanted to push away both fire and water at the same time. He had a vague plan to use the water to put out the fire but didn't know how to make that happen. Controlling the elements wasn't as easy as he had first thought.

A few weeks later, he still didn't know how it worked, and he was still having the same issues controlling whatever element he tried to use.

Valiant pushed wind at Tempest. Tempest caught the wind and held it in place. Valiant snarled, "How do you do that?"

Tempest rolled her eyes. "By not giving in to my anger."

"Then you must not have much anger."

Tempest released the wind and let it uproot the small bushes near the river.

"Why did you do that? If I don't have this under control before Father finds out, I'm in trouble."

"Then listen."

"Stop," Temperance said. "Tempest, do you not remember how we lost control when we first got our powers? And Father wasn't trying to goad us into losing control." Tempest opened her mouth to argue, but Temperance turned from her and focused on Valiant. "You must find your center of calm. No matter what happens around you, you must keep calm."

"Wrap the anger in a bubble," Tempest suggested. When her siblings looked askance at her, she said, "It works for me."

"That's how you maintain control? You wrap the anger in a bubble?" Valiant didn't bother to hide his disbelief.

"Yes. Kavi suggested I cloak the anger like I cloak my mind to keep others out."

Blowing out air, Valiant created a bubble in his mind and stuffed the anger inside. He called wind again, and it remained under his control. In his excitement, he forgot about the bubble, and it opened, blowing his sisters into the river.

Tempest shot out of the water and pushed her hair out of her eyes. She ignored the water that caused her clothes to stick to her and the puddles at her feet. "Your bubble needs work."

Temperance walked out of the river and nodded her agreement. "For now, make sure one of us is with you everywhere you go. We can help you contain the elements."

Valiant sighed. He finally had powers, and now he needed babysitters.

*****

Valiant shifted to his wolf form and jumped over Temperance's head. Changing back to human in mid jump, he caught the ball and rolled on the ground, coming to a stop with one knee still on the ground. Laughing, Temperance tried to take the ball from him. She couldn't get a grip, so Valiant let the ball slip. Temperance grabbed her prize and ran in the other direction.

Grinning, Valiant stood and saw Ridge exit the Dark Woods. The smile dropped from Valiant's face. It wouldn't bode well for him if his father discovered he had allowed Temperance to win. "Why are you here?"

Ridge raised an eyebrow. "Merely to tell you that you are wanted on the training field."

"Hurry back and tell Father what you saw."

"Why would I…" Anger flashed in Ridge's eyes. Walking away, he said over his shoulder, "Fool. You're old enough to know who your defenders are."

Valiant stared after Ridge. He had never considered Ridge someone he could trust. Only one other time had Ridge helped him, and Valiant had assumed that help was to keep his sisters safe. It had, however, been a very informative afternoon.

"What did you do to send Ridge away?"

Tempest's anger pulled Valiant out of his thoughts. "I didn't do anything."

"Apparently, you did." Tempest glared at him.

"Hush. We were having a perfectly lovely time. Now you're both angry. Valiant didn't do anything to send Ridge away." Temperance threw the ball back to Valiant.

"Then why did he leave?" Tempest watched the path Ridge had taken even though he was gone from sight.

"He returned to the training fields after delivering a message, as is his duty." Valiant tossed the ball to Tempest. "And I'm going there myself. Father demands it."

"Just you."

Prized

"Yes, just me. As usual, you and Temperance have done nothing to anger him. I better go find out what I did this time." Valiant walked away.

Cutting through the courtyard, Valiant saw a large number of fae, mostly warriors, but many of the court, awaited his father's pleasure this day. Today was to be a public humiliation day. Valiant stopped in front of him. "You sent for me, Lord Ellwood."

"Pinus has informed me that he saw you wielding all four elements yesterday. I am pleased."

Valiant glared at Pinus, who smiled in return. Valiant had hoped for time to become more proficient with the elements before telling his father. "I can call all four elements, but I'm still honing my skills."

"We will make allowances. Let's see a demonstration of your gifts." Ellwood pointed to the open area that the fae made.

Valiant walked to the center of the field, knowing allowances would not be made. Ellwood was bored and decided his son would be the afternoon's entertainment. Valiant's anger at the injustice of it all fueled his call of wind. So strong was the call, the fae were tossed around like leaves. Next, Valiant called water and doused them all before sending fire, which could find no home because everything was soaked. Finally, he pulled the ground and made a wall of earth between him and the rest of the fae.

As he turned to leave, Valiant saw Ridge leaning on a tree.

"While I understand your desire to make them look the fool, you would have done better to leave Lord Ellwood untouched. He will be angry."

"He's always angry."

"Perhaps. Might I suggest you make yourself scarce for a couple of days."

"Such wisdom. Is that why you stand as Father's advisor?" Valiant opened a way and left to the sounds of Ridge laughing. At least someone was having a good day. Ridge always did like a good jab, even if it was aimed at him.

Valiant exited the way into the Seen. He shifted to his wolf and ran through the woods toward the Alpha Clan. Perhaps Kyan would be able to help him control his powers. He caught a scent he loved above all others and angled toward Carwen. He watched her pick herbs for a few minutes, enjoying the sight. Finally, he made some noise so he wouldn't scare her and stepped out of the woods.

Turning toward the sound, Carwen smiled. The smile dropped from her face when she didn't recognize the wolf. She smelled Valiant's scent, but she didn't see him.

Realizing that she wouldn't know him, Valiant shifted. "I forgot you hadn't seen my form. I meant no harm."

"Of course, you didn't. 'Tis a beautiful wolf. I didn't know you were visiting."

"I hadn't planned to. Could you ask Kyan to meet me away from camp?"

"Is there a problem?"

"No, but I could use his advice, and I would prefer no one else know I'm here."

Carwen nodded. "I should be able to do that." She pulled some dried meat from her pouch. "You can eat this while you wait."

Valiant grinned. "You are a good person."

It didn't take long for Kyan to return, alone. "Carwen said there wasn't a problem. Is that true?"

"Well, I lost my temper and used all four elements on Lord Ellwood and a number of his court."

Kyan laughed. "I can't wait to hear the song a bard will write of that."

"I can," Valiant muttered. He would be a laughingstock.

"Tell me exactly what happened." When Valiant finished his tale, Kyan shrugged. "I can understand why you gave into temptation, but I doubt it was the best move you could have made. Your temper needs taming."

"That seems to be the general opinion."

"We shall go traveling." Kyan walked northwest away from the clan and most other humans.

"We shall?" Valiant rushed to catch up. When they stopped, he dropped to the ground, thinking he would rest.

Kyan took that moment to throw fire. Before Valiant could respond, the flames careened away from him.

"I could have responded." Valiant, incensed that Kyan didn't trust him to deal with a single attack, got in Kyan's face. Tempest and Temperance had been doing the same thing.

Kyan tipped his head to the side and laughed. "No wonder you're having problems.

"What?"

Prized

"You have my father's gift."

Valiant stilled. He had never heard anyone mention Kyan and Rayna's father. He and Tempest had assumed there was a great story behind that, but they had yet to discover it. "What gift?"

"You are immune to the elements when they are used against you. They simply don't react properly around you. I'll bet spells have trouble finding you as well."

"No one has tried to spell me, at least not to my knowledge. Does that mean I'm immune to becoming a vampire's thrall as well?"

"I'm not sure. As far as I know, father never fought a vampire." Kyan headed over a hill into some woods, and they continued their travels.

They traveled with no supplies, hunting mostly in wolf form. Kyan was strict in his training, but not unkind. Under the instruction of his uncle, Valiant found he could control his powers. He also discovered his ability to sidestep elements sent in his direction was a huge benefit. The movement was subtle, and he hoped to keep it a secret.

Valiant returned to the residence when the new moon cycle started. He found his mother and both sisters waiting for him in his rooms. Judging by the look on Rayna's face, he wasn't so sure he wouldn't rather face his father's wrath. Wondering how long they had waited thus, he asked, "Have my private rooms moved?"

"You're lucky you still have private rooms," Rayna said. "I don't want to hear where you've been. I don't want to know what you were doing. And I certainly don't want to know who you were with. The only thing I want to know is how you will explain your absence to Lord Ellwood."

Valiant had already thought of that, and said, "Following Ridge's advice."

Rayna sputtered. Before she regained her voice, Temperance said, "Well, that will certainly appease Father. Valiant is finally listening to the Realm Advisor."

"And why didn't Ridge tell us about this advice he gave?" Rayna narrowed her eyes on her only son.

"In truth," Temperance said, "I doubt anyone asked him. And I, like everyone else, was careful not to garner Father's attention by asking such a question in his presence."

"Do not be late for this evening's repast." Rayna left.

Valiant watched his mother leave. He didn't know how, but he was sure she knew he had been with Kyan.

"Mother may not want to know where, what, or who, but I do." Tempest patted the pillows she and Tempest were relaxing on. "Come, brother mine, tell us of your grand adventure."

Chapter 8 – 4976 BCE

"Is that what you're wearing?" Valiant looked Tempest up and down. "Our first trip as adults outside of the Northern Realm, and you're not even wearing the realm's colors?" He was dressed in dark green and browns, as befitted the son of the Forest Lord. Tempest was not.

Her silk dress was the color of the eggplant gourd found in the Seen. The stitching was gold, as was the design stitched over the bodice. An overlay of lace ran from her waist to the floor. The sleeves tied at the upper arm, leaving her shoulders bare. The ends of the strings used to tie everything in place glowed and sparkled like a sprite. Her white-blonde hair was long enough that she could sit on it. For this evening, the hair she normally braided and wrapped around her head had been left down.

"Is there a law that I don't know of?" Tempest struck a pose that Valiant knew she wanted him to react to, so he didn't allow the growl to escape his lips.

"Not a law, but it is tradition." Temperance shut the door to her treehouse and joined her siblings. Dressed in dark green and gold-tinted brown, she looked like the perfect daughter of the Northern Realm court.

"Traditions don't interest me, but you look lovely, sister mine," Tempest said.

Valiant shook his head. Tempest was pleased. Temperance was dressed in a demure ensemble that clashed perfectly with the revealing nature of the dress Tempest wore. He wondered if Tempest had somehow told Temperance what to wear.

"Let's go." Valiant escorted his sisters toward the platform where ways were opened within the residence. *I better not get blamed for your attire.*

Tempest grinned and squeezed his arm but otherwise didn't acknowledge Valiant's mind-to-mind comment. When they arrived at the landing pad where ways should be opened within the residence, Valiant was surprised Tempest broadcasted her feelings to him, something she rarely did anymore. Tempest was disappointed that Lord Ellwood wasn't there to see them off. Still, she was more disappointed in Ridge's response or rather lack thereof. He didn't seem to notice her at all.

You surely didn't expect Ridge to react. Valiant grinned when Tempest snarled at him. She led the procession into the way and stopped, causing Valiant to bump into her. They stood next to a rock shaped like a mushroom facing a mountain that didn't form a peak but was strangely flat-topped. At the base was a cave entrance guarded by the Southern Realm warriors. The breeze coming off the sea was pleasant.

"Look at the trees. Aren't they magnificent?" Temperance pointed toward a grouping between the mound they stood on and the water.

Valiant turned to see something he had never seen before. Trees with one huge trunk hosting palm fronds on the very top of the tree. He had seen drawings, of course, but never had he seen the like.

After greeting the Southern Realm guards, Ridge led the triplets into the main cavern.

"Stunning," Tempest said. "Do the glowing rocks allow the plants to grow?"

Valiant agreed. It was stunning. The cave, full of glowing rocks and vegetation, looked like any village on a cloudy day. The plants appeared to be the same as they saw outside. It wasn't possible to see the cave walls, but he suspected it had been designed that way.

"Indeed, Lady Tempest. I would be pleased to provide a tour of the receiving area for both you and Lady Temperance. With Valiant's permission, of course," Rock said.

Everyone turned to look at Valiant. Eyes wide, he realized as the eldest adult male of the family line in attendance, the males of the Southern Realm would have to approach him for permission to dance with, or spend time with, his sisters. Out of the side of his eye, Valiant saw Ridge's very slight nod. Perhaps touring the receiving area in the Southern Realm was the same as walking the Hall of Battles in the

Northern Realm. Hoping he wasn't making a mistake, Valiant said, "If my sisters desire to see more of the public area in this hidden gem, how could I refuse?"

Tempest smiled in approval and took one of Rock's proffered arms as Temperance took the other. The trio walked away with Rock pointing out points of interest to the first-time visitors.

"Well done."

Valiant wasn't sure he heard Ridge correctly, or even if he had spoken. Before he could question the advisor, they were joined by Lord Elros's younger sister, Lady Maeve.

"Valiant, will you play for us this evening? I've heard you are accomplished on the lute."

He should have expected this. His singing and playing angered Lord Ellwood, but the rest of the realms seemed to enjoy his songs, and he frequently sang when traveling with his mother before he attained his majority. He had assumed no one would ask now that he was an adult. Bowing to hide his embarrassment, Valiant said, "I did not bring my lute with me."

"I would be pleased to loan you my instrument for the evening," a man dressed as a bard said.

It mattered not what he did. If he played, his father would be irritated that he entertained the Southern Realm. If he didn't play, his father would be incensed that he turned down a request from the Cavern Lord's sister. Remembering something he had been told, Valiant said, "I will play and sing, but only if you accompany me, Lady Maeve. Tales of your voice's attributes have reached the Northern Realm."

Lady Maeve blushed prettily. "I would be pleased to do so."

And that is how Valiant spent an enjoyable evening playing the lute and singing with Lady Maeve.

When the triplets were back in the Northern Realm, walking down the living bridge, Tempest leaned up and kissed her brother on the cheek. "My dress might have been the talk of the evening if you and Lady Maeve hadn't provided such a lovely concert. I forgive you for upstaging me only because it was grand to see you so happy."

"It was a wonderful evening." Temperance also kissed Valiant's cheek before the girls entered their treehouses.

Valiant entered his own treehouse and went to stand on his balcony overlooking the Dark Woods. His sisters were right. It had been a wonderful evening. Probably the best evening of his adult life in the Farseen. It was almost as good as being in the Seen, with Carwen.

The next morning Valiant was not surprised to find his father in the family library.

Lord Ellwood looked up from the scroll Valiant was sure he wasn't reading. "Did you enjoy yourself in the Southern Realm?"

"Indeed. Lady Maeve requested a song, and we performed a duet. Her voice is quite pleasing."

"As I heard it, you performed all evening. Perhaps your interest in music is not a waste, after all. A coupling with the Southern Realm might please me." Ellwood clapped his son on the shoulder and left.

Valiant glared at his father's retreating figure. The first time Lord Ellwood had come close to approving his actions, and it was because there might be a benefit to the Northern Realm.

*****

Frowning, Ridge walked toward the Hall of Battles. He knew better. There was no logical reason for him to meet her, except he gave his word. Ridge wouldn't break his word, not even to save himself some trouble. Lady Tempest might be an adult in the eyes of the fae and shifters, but Tempest was still young. She was also impulsive and sure she knew more than anyone else. Sometimes Ridge thought she did. Tempest had an interesting way of seeing beyond the obvious. Lady Tempest was also the most interesting female he had ever met. Like everyone else, Lord Ellwood took the wrong approach with his eldest. He issued orders and expected blind obedience. That might work with Lady Temperance, but Lady Tempest had to understand why. She followed no one. It was one of the things Ridge liked about her.

He passed some males and followed their eyes. Ridge shook his head. "Pinus, you will never garner Lady Tempest's attention by swaggering like a unicorn."

"I am not swaggering."

Sorbus, one of the guards, said, "You always swagger. It's ridiculous."

Pinus stood to his full height, but Ridge still towered over him. "If you are so wise when it comes to Lady Tempest, why don't you approach her?"

"Not me," Sorbus said. "She used her carnelian dagger to cut the last person who approached without an invitation. "

Prized

"The challenge was to Ridge."

Ridge cocked his head. "What is the prize for this wager?" Ridge watched Pinus's expression change from challenge to concern. Obviously, Pinus hadn't expected him to accept. "I'm waiting."

"You must convince Lady Tempest to stay with you until evening repast. If you can't, you must entertain us with a ballad I select before tomorrow's repast, here, in the Hall of Battles."

Ridge smirked. Pinus was a fool who didn't know how easy that would be. "And if I win, you will sing a ballad I select."

Pinus frowned but nodded his agreement.

"Either way, everyone else suffers. Hopefully, Ridge will lose. He's not a bard, but his singing won't hurt our ears, unlike Pinus's voice," Sorbus said.

"Challenge accepted." Ridge walked away from the men. As he approached, Lady Tempest stood riveted to the drawings on one of the pillars. "Your father's first major victory. A worthy piece to be sure."

Tempest glanced around him and asked, "Why didn't you make them leave?"

"I don't have that power. Pinus challenged me, and they await the outcome."

Tempest narrowed her eyes on Ridge. "Does this challenge have anything to do with me?"

"Yes, but Pinus issued the challenge, not me."

"What is it?"

"If I told you, it would invalidate the challenge. Shall we stroll through the pillars and admire Lord Ellwood's prowess on the battlefield?" Ridge held out his arm. He could keep her in the hall, where there would be observers until time to eat. Someone had to look out for Lady Tempest. She certainly didn't.

Tempest eyed the arm, and Ridge smothered his smile. He knew she wanted to walk with him, but she didn't like that a challenge over her decision had been issued. Ridge was sure her shifter hearing had allowed her to hear the entire conversation. He became concerned when a sweet smile lit her face.

"Wouldn't you rather swagger?" she asked as she slid her arm into his.

110

Ridge burst out laughing. He was right. She had heard the entire conversation. "Only with you on my arm, Lady Tempest. Only with you."

*****

The next evening, Tempest pushed Valiant and Temperance down the living bridge from their treehouses toward the Hall of Battles.

"What's your hurry?" Temperance asked. She was still tying her sash as they moved.

"I don't want to miss this."

"Why? Surely the bards will write a song about it." When Temperance slowed, Tempest took her sister by the arm and rushed her along.

The triplets rounded the corner to find a crowd milling around the pillars.

Pinus stood forlornly in front of Ridge. "No bard will play for me, and I can't play an instrument."

"What difference does that make? You can't sing, either." Sorbus leaned on one of the pillars, laughing with the others.

"What's this?" Valiant looked around and realized he was the only one who didn't know what was going on. He had been thinking of his evening plans and had ignored his sisters and their quarrel.

Sorbus grinned. "Pinus lost a challenge to Ridge, and he has to sing *Better an Angry Gorkong Than a Sleeping Werewolf*, before the repast. He can't find a bard to play for him."

Valiant called out. "I'll play for you, Pinus, if I can have use of a lute."

"I offer mine." One of the bards handed his lute to Valiant. "You understand. I don't wish to be blamed for the racket. I have my livelihood to think of."

Nodding, Valiant strummed the instrument and verified it was tuned before looking at Pinus. "You ready?"

"No, but let's get this over with."

Pinus managed to start at the right beat, but that was the best Valiant could say. Apparently, Pinus decided to yell the words. His tactic had the desired effect. Excluding the few who wished to see the spectacle firsthand, the onlookers left in all due haste.

Wincing from Pinus's not so dulcet tones, Valiant continued to play until the last line of the ballad was belted out.

Prized

"Never have I heard such a racket. Why are you assaulting everyone's ears?" Lord Ellwood stopped before Valiant as the crowd dissipated. At Valiant's signal, Pinus inched away with the others. Valiant saw no reason to include anyone else in what was sure to be his punishment.

Tempest and Temperance had giggled through the entire song. Tempest said, "I believe Valiant's playing was not the cause of the assault on your ears, Father mine."

Ellwood ignored his daughters. "Since you have free time enough to waste playing the lute, I have a job for you." Calling out to his master-of-arms, Ellwood said, "Ash, you have no need to travel to the Central Realm this evening. Valiant has volunteered to make the journey for you."

Valiant ground his teeth together but remained silent. This was a lesson he had learned the hard way. Nothing he said would lessen his father's wrath, especially since he was still angry over the concert at the Southern Realm. For once, Lord Ellwood wasn't mad that Valiant played, but rather that Ellwood hadn't been consulted. Valiant handed the lute to Temperance, who would make sure it got back to the bard and waited for instructions.

Ash looked between Lord Ellwood and Valiant and shot Valiant an apologetic smile before handing him the pouch. "The Sky Lord awaits your arrival."

Valiant hid his frown. He knew the Sky Lord's residence was high in the sky, held in place above an active volcano by some magic he didn't understand. He had yet to visit there and didn't know how to gain access to the residence.

Tempest approached Lord Ellwood. "How exciting for Valiant. I've longed to visit. I hear it's beautiful, but I lack the knowledge to gain entry. Tell me, Lord Ellwood, how does one access the Sky Lord's residence?"

"I'm sure Valiant will regale you with that knowledge when he returns." Lord Ellwood walked away.

Valiant glared at Lord Ellwood's retreating form. Once again, he was placed in the role of jester. Sure, no one was laughing now, but it was only a matter of time. Valiant turned and left the feasting hall. With no clear idea as to how he would enter the residence, he could at least get to the nearby volcano by opening a way. That he knew how to do.

Opening a way, he ignored Ridge calling out to him and Tempest yelling in his head.

*****

Valiant exited the way into the valley of the Central Realm. The largest herd of unicorns he had ever seen pranced in the fields. Unlike Ridge's comment that had resulted in the bet, the unicorns didn't swagger so much as prance. Valiant didn't notice he was humming the song a bard had shared with him earlier in the day. It was the song of the bet between Pinus and Ridge, missing only the last verse which the bard was probably finishing up now. The first bard to sing a song publicly got the credit for the song, and there was a rush-to-sing mentality. Even so, many bards had taken to presenting their songs to Valiant before singing them in public. He had a knack for suggesting small changes that made the song better. Everyone was careful to make sure Ellwood did not know of this activity.

Valiant looked east to the volcano and then up. And up some more. The Central Realm floated high above. Made sense. It hovered over an active volcano. How in the world would he ever get up there?

There were specific procedures to enter any realm residence. In the Northern Realm, visitors entered by way of the floating stairs. To attempt any other entrance resulted in death. Valiant suspected the same would be true if he opened a way to the edge of the Central Realm's platform where he could make out a landing pad. As the son of the Forest Lord, he might not be killed, but he would become a joke. He was already a joke in the Northern Realm. He had no desire to become a joke in any of the other realms. Dropping the pouch into one of the pockets of his cape, Valiant placed his hands on his hips. Who was he kidding? He was a joke.

"Fairly met, Valiant of the Northern Realm."

Valiant whipped his head around. The speaker was a boy a couple of years his junior. "Fairly met. You have the advantage of me. Who are you?"

"I am Cloud, son of Obi." He bowed.

Valiant returned the bow. "How do you know me?"

"You're a bard. Your songs of the Seen are interesting. My brother is apprenticed to Bard Kanti. He sings songs to me at night. I like yours the best."

Valiant had not met Kanti, but he knew her songs. She was the only female bard currently living, and her voice was said to sooth all who heard her sing. "I am pleased you like my songs, but it doesn't explain how you know my name is Valiant."

"My eldest sister, Lady Lekan. She drew your likeness after she met you in the Northern Realm feasting hall. I asked who she drew. She said you were the bard whose songs I enjoyed."

Valiant nodded. He vaguely remembered a raven-haired beauty from the Central Realm. Perhaps this could work in his favor. "Do you think your sister would meet me here?"

"Father would not approve."

Smart kid. Valiant smiled. "Perhaps I could talk to your father."

"Wait with me. I'm meeting Father here to dine at the residence tonight." Cloud's face fell. "But if you are visiting, I will be sent home."

Surprised at Cloud's disappointment that he wouldn't attend the feasting hall tonight, Valiant said, "Don't worry. I'm here to present documents to Lord Sky. I won't be staying for dinner."

Cloud looked Valiant over and shook his head. "You're dressed for the feasting hall."

"I was dressed for the Northern Realm's feasting hall when Lord Ellwood gave me this small task."

Cloud would have argued, but instead, he turned at his father's approach. Valiant turned as well. Obi, Central Realm High Council representative, stood even in height to Valiant, although Valiant was still growing.

"Well met, Valiant. Are you dining with the Sky Lord this evening?"

Valiant bowed. "Obi, 'tis pleasant to see you again. I have come only to provide a small service to Lord Ellwood by delivering a pouch to the Sky Lord. I am afraid, in my desire for haste, I forgot to ask the proper procedure for entering the Sky Lord's residence."

Obi nodded. "Come. I will show you."

Valiant followed Obi through a garden labyrinth at the end of which there stood an ornate gazebo made from the materials that adorned the residence in the sky. As soon as Obi stepped on the stair, five Central Realm bowmen appeared. They looked at Valiant and back at Obi.

Obi said, "Valiant has a pouch for the Sky Lord."

"We were told to expect Ash," one of the guards said.

"I was dispatched by the Forest Lord in Ash's stead." Valiant bowed.

A way opened, and Noll, Advisor to the Central Realm, appeared. "Well met, Valiant. Ridge informed me that you were on your way. You made better time than he expected."

"Ridge has always underestimated me," Valiant muttered.

Obi's lips twitched, but no one else heard Valiant's comment, or, if they did, they hid their response well enough.

"When next you visit, open a way to this location. No need to walk in from the labyrinth again. Come." Noll turned and opened a way to the residence. They exited the way onto a platform.

Valiant appreciated the tip but wasn't sure why Noll had helped him without being obvious about it. His eyes roamed the platform, which was at the edge of a garden housed in huge containers. He glanced over the side, unencumbered by rails. There were no rails. If someone attempted to leave the platform without permission, the bowmen would push them back. The interloper had better be able to fly because it was a long way to the ground.

He heard rustling to the left and glanced that way. Three ladies of the Central Realm approached. Lady Lekan and two females he didn't know.

"Oh." Lady Lekan pouted prettily. "I was expecting Father and Cloud."

"Lady Lekan." Valiant bowed and kissed her hand. "How pleasant that I am the recipient of your welcome. Obi and Cloud are behind us."

Lekan blushed. "Valiant, may I present the ladies Sky and Shimmer." She pointed to each of her friends as she said their names.

Valiant kissed their hands and said all that was proper. Lady Sky was the daughter of Queen Ceridwin and Lady Shimmer was the daughter of Quest, Sky Lord of the Central Realm. Quite the introduction to the Central Realm court. He grinned, knowing this wasn't the reception his father had in mind.

"Excuse us, ladies. Valiant has business with Lord Quest." Noll ushered Valiant away from the ladies as Obi and Cloud walked through another way.

Thanks to his shifter hearing, Valiant heard Cloud ask, "Will I still be allowed to attend the feast? I bet Valiant plays the lire and sings one of his songs. It would be a shame to miss that."

Entering the labyrinth that is every realm residence, Valiant smiled. This evening was turning out well indeed. Once his task was completed, Lord Quest invited Valiant to enjoy the repast with the Central Realm. They walked into the feasting hall to find Lady Shimmer waiting for them. Valiant wondered how long she had waited.

"If Valiant is to join the evening repast, he should join Lady Sky's table." Shimmer smiled at her father. "It's not a scheduled visit from the Northern Realm and many of our younger siblings are in attendance."

"Valiant, you may choose. An evening at the head table talking politics, or an evening in the company of your peers."

"Lady Sky's table looks inviting."

"Lord Ellwood is blessed to have such a wise son."

Valiant laughed and walked with Lady Shimmer. He stopped to speak to Cloud. Apparently, the younger members of the court were allowed their own table. No wonder Cloud had been disappointed when he thought he wouldn't be allowed to attend. Valiant would have enjoyed such a diversion when he was younger. Valiant had sometimes been allowed to join his cousin, Ciam, but only as adults were the Forest Lord's young allowed their own table. Lady Sky's table was nearly as rowdy as the kids' table and Valiant did indeed have a good time. He even agreed to sing a few songs.

"Cloud will be pleased with himself," Lady Lekan said. She leaned toward Valiant and added, "He loves your songs and wishes he was a bard, but alas, Kojo received that gift."

"I'm not a bard. I do enjoy playing the lire and singing, but that is not my destiny."

"Tis a shame. You are very skilled," Lady Sky said.

"Valiant has many skills, if the stories are true."

Looking over at Tero, Valiant laughed. Tero always wore his flying uniform. Not that Valiant blamed him. Tero was the newest member of the Central Realm's elite flying squad. The two enjoyed a friendly rivalry, normally over gaining a lady's attention for the evening. "The same can be said of you."

Tero smiled.

Many hours later, Valiant returned home to find Ridge waiting near his treehouse.

"It will be better for all if Lord Ellwood remains ignorant of the lateness of the hour when you returned."

"I'm not such a fool." Valiant would have pushed past Ridge but stopped and asked, "Why did you tell Noll I was coming in Ash's stead?"

"While the lords make decrees, we advisors work to keep the peace. No one wants an overzealous bowman to kill an unexpected visitor from another realm. That is how wars are started. Besides, I heard you had already secured the patronage of Obi. I'm almost impressed."

Valiant smiled. From Ridge, that was high praise indeed. Valiant nodded and entered his treehouse.

Chapter 9 – 4975 BCE

"I'm looking forward to the Seen. Kavi has promised me a few days of her time." Tempest grabbed her traveling bag.

"You spend more time with her than anyone else in the Seen. Why?" Valiant asked.

"Why not? You spend more time with Carwen than anyone else," Tempest retorted.

"Hush." Valiant looked over his shoulder, but no one else was around. The last thing he needed was for Father to learn of his interest in a shifter female. While Ellwood thought his interest in ladies of the court, any court, was acceptable – as long as he behaved properly – Valiant was sure the thought of a shifter female would be met with, at the very least, annoyance. Whatever plans Father had for Valiant, he was confident that it did not include a shifter wife.

Tempest huffed. "I tire of hearing of your escapades while I sit demurely with the elders."

"You have never sat demurely with the elders, or anywhere else for that matter," Valiant said. "You are the most sought-after lady in the five realms, and you delight in encouraging many males to make fools of themselves. You have plenty of admirers in the Seen as well."

"They don't interest me."

"Of course not. They're interchangeable." Valiant grabbed his traveling bag and led his sisters into the way. The first thing he saw in the Seen was Carwen and Taren. When Taren grabbed her arm, Valiant's eyes darkened. He dropped his bag and moved toward the duo. He pulled up short when Carwen twisted Taren's arm and threw him over her shoulder into the creek.

118

Tempest laughed. "Beautiful. Where did you learn such a move?"

"A visiting shifter from the east. He studied with a people further east on the other side of some high mountains."

"He's a crazy fool." Taren sloshed out of the water and onto dry land.

"Maybe, but his style of fighting worked well enough on you." Valiant placed himself between Carwen and Taren. "Why did you grab her arm?"

"None of your business, fae."

Valiant's hands balled into fists without his thinking about it.

Carwen laid a calming hand on his arm. "Doesn't matter. Come, Valiant, I would be pleased if you helped me search for herbs this day."

Valiant's grin was a dare that Taren didn't accept. Valiant turned his back on the others and left with Carwen.

Taren glared after the couple but didn't follow.

"Are you too befuddled from your unplanned swim to offer us assistance?" Temperance asked.

"What? Tempest injures anyone who tries to help her." Taren didn't take his eyes off the path, but Carwen and Valiant were out of sight.

"I don't." Temperance looked pointedly at her bag.

Taren reached down and grabbed the bag, tossing it over his shoulder. He glanced at Tempest. "I could carry yours as well."

Ignoring his offer, Tempest tossed her own bag over her shoulder and asked, "What do you know about this visitor?"

"Not much. His way of fighting uses the weight of your opponent against them. As you saw, it works well if you are fighting a larger foe." Taren cut his eyes to the girls. "You aren't gonna tell anyone, are you? Neither of you runs to tell your family anything."

"Course not." Tempest shook her head. "The fae believe that we should learn to protect ourselves. Not go running to someone to protect us. Besides, there's nothing to tell. Carwen didn't need our help."

"How about Valiant?"

"You do seem to go out of your way to anger him," Temperance said. "If he says anything, it will be in private, to you."

"Well, that's okay. I don't like Valiant, but your brother is fair in a fight."

Prized

"Come on." Tempest lengthened her stride. "I want to meet this visitor."

"His name is Esen. I'm sure you'll meet him. He's a friend of your uncle."

The next morning, Tempest dragged Valiant with her out to the field where Esen seemed to be dancing by himself. She approached and watched but didn't speak. After observing for a while, Tempest and Valiant began to copy his movements. The dance was similar to the forms they studied for hand-to-hand in the Farseen.

Eventually, Esen completed a form and walked over to them. "You move well. Who is your master?"

Tempest frowned. "I have no master."

"Nor do I," Valiant said.

Esen bowed. "I may have used the wrong word. In my language master is the one who trains others to fight."

"Like our Master-At-Arms. He trains the warriors." Tempest pursed her lips. "My father's people use similar movements to warm up before fighting."

"Aha. You, like young Taren, believe in brute force."

"No." When Valiant laughed, Tempest blushed and admitted, "Well, not always."

Esen grinned. "Shall we spar?"

Tempest smiled in return. It was what she had hoped for. Dropping into a fighting stance, she expected to grapple with him. Esen was a small man. Tempest was larger, both in height and weight, and expected to be victorious. While the move Carwen used would work well enough on someone with Taren's ego, she would never fall for such an obvious tactic.

For a few seconds, they alternated attacks. Neither gained the upper hand. Tempest moved in to grab Esen. With practiced moves, he blocked her attack, grabbed her arm, and tossed her over his shoulder.

She squeaked. Not in pain, but in surprise. He tossed her like she was a cloth doll.

"Are you okay?" Kyan leaned over and offered her his arm.

Tempest hadn't realized Kyan had been watching. She ignored the arm and jumped to her feet. "That was great. How did you do that? Can you teach me?"

Kyan laughed. "I told you she would want to be trained."

"And me as well." Valiant performed the same bow Esen had done early. "If it would not offend, I would be pleased to study with you."

"And me." Temperance had watched with Kyan.

Esen nodded. "I believe you will be worthy students."

As the group walked back to camp, Valiant noticed Kyan's arm. What is that on your finger?"

Kyan looked at his left hand. It indicates I am the sovereign's enforcer."

"True enough, though many call it the assassin's ring." Adair stopped beside his friend. "It's his own design as well."

"Impressive. Your skill with stones has grown," Tempest said. "And you still haven't told me how you are able to spell the objects."

"Perhaps we will talk later."

*****

"How goes the training with Esen?" Taren asked.

Valiant looked up from preparing the sling that they would use to transport the two stags back to the Alpha Clan. The sovereign had sent them out to hunt together. Both young men were aware that a few bets were placed on which would be the bloodiest when they returned, and not from the hunt.

"Why are you so opposed to his training?"

"I'm not. I just always resort to brute force. Can't seem to help myself."

Valiant laughed. "Your temper needs taming."

"You insult me." Taren's hands balled into fists immediately.

"No. I'm saying the same thing to you that everyone said to me before I stopped letting my temper..." Valiant stopped talking, not sure he wanted to share. After all, they weren't friends.

"What changed for you?" Taren held out his hands in a placating manner. "We aren't friends, but you fight fair, and I do, too. If you have a way to beat the anger, I would like to know."

"In fae circles, that would mean you owe me a boon."

"A what?"

"Boon. A debt to be paid later. The debt would have to be equal to what I do for you." Valiant grinned. No way would Taren agree to a boon.

"Not sure I want to do that."

Valiant's grin widened.

Prized

"How about this? You teach me to control my anger, and I'll quit pursuing Carwen. She only wants you anyway."

Valiant jumped to his feet with a snarl on his face. "Do you chase after her?"

"She's the smartest, prettiest girl in the camp. I had hoped to win her, but you're the only one that lights up her eyes."

Valiant's mind spun. Was Taren telling the truth?

"I teach you what I was taught, and you stay away from Carwen?"

"I'll not pursue her anymore. If she approaches me, that's different. I'll even warn others away from her."

"Others?"

"As I said, she's smart, pretty, and her father is wealthy." Taren shrugged. "You should stake a claim."

"I can't. It wouldn't be fair."

"I heard your father had plans for you. Is she a beauty, this fae your father picked for you?"

"I don't know."

"Tell him you already found the one you want."

Valiant barked a laugh. "The fae most definitely do not do that. The Lord of the Realm must be obeyed, especially in matters of mating."

"The sovereign is a dictator, but she allows everyone, even her offspring, to select their own mate. For once, I don't envy you." Taren picked up one end of the sling. "Do we have an accord?"

Valiant thought about it. He didn't spend nearly enough time in the Seen to adequately protect Carwen. "We have an accord."

"We still aren't friends. I loathe your privileged hide."

Valiant laughed. While he had money and plenty to eat, Valiant lacked the privilege of having a father who liked him. If Taren knew what his life was really like, he wouldn't call him privileged.

They walked for a while, carrying their load. Eventually, Taren said, "What's first?"

"First, you ask Esen if you can join the training." Valiant grinned, knowing that wasn't what Taren expected.

"What?"

"His forms are similar to forms the fae use for focus. Those forms will be the basis for you clearing your mind and taming your temper."

"Those forms are just dancing. It's silly."

"It works."

*****

As the summer season came to a close, Esen's most promising students stood before him. Everyone in the village who discovered a plausible reason to be in the fields had watched the competition. Tempest had won, but she was strangely subdued. Valiant rubbed a shoulder where she had tossed him into a tree. He had come in second. Again.

Today they would learn which two would be granted the privilege of training others. The chosen would regularly travel, via a way, to Esen's home, far to the east, for additional training. Looking at the others, Valiant hoped Carwen would be chosen to attend training with Tempest. It was a given his eldest sister had made the cut.

"You have all done well." Esen bowed to each student, commenting on their personal improvement. When he finished, Esen raised his voice. "Temperance and Taren will continue training with me."

Valiant's eyes widened. Tempest said nothing, but her accepting smile indicated to Valiant that she had at least suspected this as a possible outcome. Carwen was disappointed. Both Temperance and Taren were as shocked as Valiant.

One of the young asked, "Why not Tempest and Valiant? They were the two top competitors."

"Yes, they were. Both are fierce warriors, but my style of fighting is defensive, not offensive. As I have said many times, walk away if you can. If you must fight, use your opponent's strength to conserve your own. Temperance is not aggressive, and Taren has shown great promise in controlling his anger."

"Congratulations." Valiant hugged his younger sister and shook Taren's hand.

"Your assistance will not be forgotten," Taren said.

Carwen grinned. "Someone has been practicing not thanking a fae."

Taren smiled.

"I expect both of you to teach me everything you learn," Tempest said.

*****

Valiant left the forest and walked through the open pasture in no rush to return to the residence. His sisters, since reaching adulthood, were acting strange, and he tired of beating fools who thought his sisters were prizes in some type of contest. Valiant rounded the barn and saw Tempest and one of the farmhands kissing.

Face contorted in anger, Valiant marched over and pulled them apart. "Go home, Bryn. Speak of this to no one, and Lord Ellwood will never find out."

Bryn nodded and moved quickly down the path Valiant had just left.

"What were you doing?" Valiant knew without a doubt that Tempest had initiated that kiss. Bryn was not such a fool.

Tempest glared at her brother. "How dare you?"

"No, how dare you? If Father had found you thus, you would have been restricted to the residence. Irritating, but not life-altering. Did you think about Bryn? The punishment for kissing a daughter of the court without the Forest Lord's permission is death."

"As if you haven't kissed any daughters of the court." Tempest folded her hands in front of her chest.

"Name one daughter of the court you have seen me kiss. You can't because I haven't. Not in public, where anyone could see." Valiant waved his arms around.

Tempest noticed all the people who were suddenly within sight, and while she understood Valiant's meaning, she didn't appreciate his tone. "Think you that I fear any of them?"

"I know you don't but have a little compassion for Bryn's situation."

Tempest chewed her bottom lip, and admitted, "I just wanted to know what a kiss was like, but you're right. I shouldn't have done that."

Valiant shook his head and moved down the path through the Home Woods and the family treehouses. Tempest followed, lost in thought.

*****

Temperance entered Tempest's treehouse without knocking. "Why does Findarn follow me around?"

"Because he likes you." Tempest grinned.

"No, he doesn't. He likes the idea of exchanging vows with one of Ellwood's daughters, and he's afraid of you."

"If you don't like him, send him on his way."

Temperance chewed her bottom lip.

A sigh escaped Tempest's lips. "You could tell Lady Lindera that he's bothering you. She'll deal with her brother."

"No. I need to handle this myself." Temperance wrapped a blanket around herself and watched Tempest head for the door. "Where are you going?"

"For a walk."

When the door shut, Temperance muttered, "Fine. Leave me here in my misery." She pouted for a few minutes, fell asleep, and dreamed of a time when she would feel as confident and powerful as Tempest obviously did.

Tempest returned to her treehouse and snuck past Temperance, still asleep on the pillows. Once presentable, she shook Temperance. "Sister mine, have you been asleep all this time? It's almost time for the evening repast."

"Oh." Temperance opened sleepy eyes and saw that Tempest was already dressed for the evening. "Why didn't you wake me?"

As Tempest hoped, Temperance ran from her treehouse and didn't notice anything was amiss.

*****

Valiant waited for his sisters in the hall between their treehouses, as had become his custom. He was anxious because he had plans to meet Lady Talmai in the Hall of Battles, and his sisters were late. Lady Talmai was no Carwen, but she was a good friend, and spending time with her kept his father happy. It was no longer a secret that they were friends, and his father appeared to be pleased, which worried Valiant. When Temperance walked into the hallway, his question came out as a complaint. "What's taking so long?"

"Hush. If you plan to meet someone tonight, you can be a little late." Temperance adjusted her shawl.

"Or you could go without us. We can walk ourselves to the repast." Tempest joined them.

"Why? Still looking for someone to kiss?"

"Lower your voice," Tempest hissed.

Valiant turned to Temperance. "Have you noticed she's only quiet when it serves her?"

"If you two are going to snip at each other all night, stay away from me." Temperance marched down the hall. Valiant and Tempest hurried to catch up.

When they approached the Hall of Battles, ladies of the court were gathered around Lady Lindera.

"What happened?" Lady Talmai asked, her voice full of concern.

"Findarn won't speak of it. Not that he can. The healer said he can't use his jaw for at least a week. Father said it was probably..." Lindera saw the triplets and took a deep breath before continuing, "the brother of a lady Findarn is interested in."

"That doesn't reduce the suspects. Findarn has been interested in all ladies of the court who are not being formally courted. In fairness to the brothers of this realm, they have the right." Lady Talmai shrugged apologetically.

"I know. It's so embarrassing." Lady Lindera hung her head in shame.

"Maybe for him. Not for you." Lady Tempest said firmly. "It sounds like the issue has resolved itself. Come, Lady Lindera, I understand you devised a casting for the dress you wear tonight, and it changes color in the moonlight. I'm eager to see the effect."

Valiant watched the ladies, including Lady Talmai, walk out on the pavilion where the floating stairs stood, and the moon light beamed down. What happened to his plans?

"Did you beat up Findarn because of his interest in Lady Temperance?" Ridge whispered in his ear.

"Huh?" Startled, Valiant backed into one of the pillars. "Is Findarn interested in her? Is he bothering her?"

Shaking his head, Ridge pressed the bridge of his nose with his thumb and middle finger. "I was sure it was you."

"If he's bothering Lady Temperance, it will be me. At least once he heals."

"No, you won't. I thought it was you, but you have never gone so far before."

"Who else would beat..." Valiant looked over at Tempest. She looked up and smiled at him. "You don't think she –"

Ridge cut him off. "Yes, I do. It will be better for all concerned if you say nothing and allow the current rumor to stand."

"I suppose I'm being blamed for being overzealous. How is that better for me?"

"Everyone already thinks you did it. No harm done. There will be lots of harm if it is discovered someone else was involved."

Valiant pushed past Ridge and noticed how the court jumped out of his way. Realizing that those assembled assumed Ridge had just reprimanded him for beating Findarn, Valiant found a secluded spot to open a way and went to the cave. The same cave the triplets had used as a lair when they were young. Not only was he not spending time with Lady Talmai, but Valiant was also to take the blame for Tempest's temper. Again. No wonder everyone thought he had anger issues.

*****

It was over. No more clanging of metal, screaming, or elements thrown in every direction. The battle had been intense. Valiant looked around. The attackers were unaligned fae and not as well trained in the use of their powers as he would have expected, but they fought well enough. At least seven of his warriors were dead. And he did think of them as his warriors. Those who always volunteered to fight when the triplets were sent into battle.

Thanks to their shared bond, Valiant knew Tempest was fine, but he couldn't feel or see Temperance. His eyes darted over the battlefield. Valiant had grown accustomed to battle over the last two years and was able to look at the carnage without any show of sorrow or regret. Lord Ellwood had beaten that out of him. He heard a cry in his head. Tempest.

Valiant followed the bond they shared and found Tempest tending Temperance. He dropped beside her and asked, "What happened?"

"Short sword in the side." Tempest finished prepping the wound for travel. "She'll be fine, but I wish we weren't so far from the residence."

Valiant looked around and commandeered a cart. "We can fit seven additional injured on this cart with Lady Temperance. Who else is severely injured?" Once the cart was loaded, Valiant took the reins, opened a large way, and entered it. He exited at the residence and spoke to the first guard he saw. "Summon a healer."

Once the injured were attended and he had verification that Temperance would recover, Valiant returned to his rooms to clean up. He and Tempest had done amazingly well. Together, they were unstoppable, at least according to the songs the bards sang. He wasn't foolish enough to believe that. It helped that Lord Ellwood was not in attendance. Father always saw any misstep Valiant made and commented on it, usually in front of the warriors and bards. Especially the bards. He left his treehouse and raised his hand to knock on Temperance's door just as the door opened.

Tempest stepped back. "Temperance is sleeping, but you may check on her if you wish. I did."

Prized

Standing beside the bed, Valiant nodded. Temperance looked peaceful, but Valiant wasn't fooled. Once the herbs wore off, she would feel pain even after the healer had done her best. He and Tempest tried to protect Temperance on the battlefield, for she was a gentle soul, but it was hard as she wasn't as connected to them as they were to each other. He felt sorry for Temperance. It had been two years, and she hadn't shifted. In fact, the only shifter trait she had was a stronger sense of smell, which was sad. Shifting was amazing, and Valiant was so glad he had the ability. He placed a kiss on Temperance's forehead and left her to her rest.

Chapter 10 – 4973 BCE

"Lady Tempest, will you hold still? You act like you've never attended the feasting hall before. The men from the Southern Realm will like you just fine." The seamstress wiped her finger, where blood pooled from the pinprick and smiled. "Is there perhaps a male from the south who has caught your attention?"

Tempest turned up her nose. Ever since she became an adult, four years ago, the fae and the shifters had thrown men at her. As if she would accept any of the fools. What Tempest wanted was a male who wasn't afraid of her, or her father, or either of her grandmothers for that matter. A male who excelled in combat but was gentle. A male who lived by his own rules. A male like... Ridge. Her frown turned into a sly smile.

The seamstress saw the smile and sported a matching one. "Which one? Lugos, Lord Elros's younger brother, would be a fine choice."

Tempest laughed. "I'm sure Lugos is a fine male, but Lady Morgen might object." It was an open secret throughout the realms that Morgen and Lugos desired each other, but Lord Elros would not approve their courting. Tempest knew Elros, like most realm lords, waited to see if she would select someone from their realm for mating. Sometimes her ability to hear flashes of private thoughts from another was not welcome.

"As if anyone could object to you. Your shifter and fae powers far eclipse most. Strong, but fair on the battlefield, there isn't a male in the five realms that wouldn't consider you an acceptable match." The seamstress added a final pin. "Finished. Step out of the gown, and I'll have it ready for this evening's repast."

Prized

Tempest struggled out of the skintight cloth and donned her fighting leathers. "Your efforts to make me ladylike have not gone unnoticed. This is exactly the look I want tonight."

"The object of your interest must be special indeed."

"He is," Tempest murmured and left the fitting room. In the hallway, she whispered, "But he's not from the Southern Realm."

"Who's not from the Southern Realm?" Valiant stepped out of the shadows.

"No one." Tempest picked up her pace down the hall.

Valiant fell into step beside her. "Your deception would work better if I didn't know your mind, sister mine. Ridge is too old for you."

"You know nothing."

Valiant pulled her to a stop outside his rooms. "You've observed Ridge's every move as long as I can remember. You haven't seen twenty years, and he has seen more than seven hundred. He's too old." Valiant released her and opened his door. "Besides, he has completed his private residence, and everyone is sure he will move his chosen mate there."

"He has no mate... yet." Tempest added the last word after he closed his door.

*****

"What are you wearing?" Valiant looked Tempest over. The dress, if it could be called that, looked like spider webs, and barely covered anything. No sister, or any female relative really, should be in such an outfit. He rushed to stay with Tempest, who charged down the hallway.

"It's beautiful," Temperance said as she, too, rushed to catch up.

Valiant shook his head. Temperance never tried to compete with Tempest for attention, which was good. Tempest's dress would be the talk of the evening, and probably the season. "Um, does Mother, or Father, know about your new attire?" He spoke cautiously, knowing that Tempest planned such an outfit for the shock value alone. Hopefully, the seamstress wouldn't lose her livelihood over it.

"Father has repeatedly said he has no interest in what I wear," Tempest said, crossing into the Hall of Battles.

"No, but he'll care about what you don't wear," Valiant muttered. The sisters ignored Valiant, something they did when he interfered in their lives.

"And Mother?" Temperance asked.

Tempest flashed a wicked smile. "It's a surprise."

"If you are referring to that dress, it is most definitely a surprise, but yet it leaves little to the imagination." Ridge fell in step with the triplets. "Can I correctly assume that no one, not even your siblings, knew of this creation?"

Valiant raised an eyebrow. "You think we're that foolish?"

"You never know," Ridge murmured as they entered the Hall of Battles.

"Lady Tempest, you will outshine all tonight." Lady Morgen bowed.

Lugos turned and stared. He wasn't the only one.

Lady Morgen winked at Tempest before she leaned in and said, "Yes, Lugos, she is stunning, but if you continue to stare, I will remove your eyes and feed them to you."

Tempest returned the bow, pleased that the dress had the desired effect. Since Ridge had seen her, he had not left her side.

"Lady Tempest, you look ravishing tonight." Ahearn bowed and stood to offer his arm to Tempest. Ridge blocked his path.

"Lady Tempest has no need of your arm, Ahearn. I am here." Ridge's voice carried. As a result, the room turned and got their first look at Lady Tempest and her attire.

Tempest smiled as she took in the mood. The older members of the court smiled to themselves, thankful that their daughters had not thought to create such a display. The younger ladies of the court were jealous that they hadn't thought of it first, while the younger males of the court were in awe and fully aware that they would not be allowed near her this evening. Ridge made eye contact with every unmated male in the court, leaving them in no doubt that Ridge would remain by her side for the entire evening. Tempest couldn't help but preen a little, even though most assumed, incorrectly, that he was there on Lord Ellwood's orders.

Lord Ellwood and Lady Rayna entered the room just as Ridge helped Tempest to her chair. Ellwood barely glanced at his daughter and said, "I see you are sporting a new ensemble this evening, Lady Tempest. Charming."

Disappointed in her father's response, Tempest turned back to Ridge. At least he had the proper response to her outfit.

Ridge leaned in and whispered, "Did you think Lord Ellwood would pitch a fit in the feasting hall? If that was your goal, I doubt you've grown up very much at all."

Prized

"It wasn't Father's attention I wanted," Tempest hissed, loud enough that everyone at the table heard.

Lady Morgen laughed. "Lady Tempest, I'm sad to say that most males must have such things spelled out for them."

Ridge looked from Lady Morgen to Lugos with a confused expression.

Lugos shrugged, equally confused.

"I see what you mean. I thought at least some males were intelligent." Tempest replied.

"They are intelligent about many things. Other things remain outside their grasp. You must be patient." Lady Morgen patted Lugos on the knee.

Temperance watched the entire exchange, not understanding how anyone, regardless of gender, could miss the fact that Tempest was interested in Ridge.

The meal went exactly as Tempest had hoped. Ridge remained by her side throughout. When it was time to dance, Lord Ellwood led his eldest daughter onto the dance floor, following fae custom. Lord Elros had no daughters yet, so he led his wife onto the dance floor.

As the first song completed, Ellwood twirled Tempest into Ridge's arms. "Advisor, attend my daughter."

"Of course, Lord Ellwood." Ridge bowed and smoothly moved Tempest around the room. "Tell me, Lady Tempest, are you pleased with your new dress?"

"Indeed." Tempest smiled up at Ridge. "Does it please you?"

"I believe women should dress to please themselves." Ridge hid his smile when Tempest frowned.

They danced the first three sets without a break. Just when Tempest thought she would have to beg for a break, Ridge asked, "Do you care for some air?"

"I thought you would never ask."

Ridge placed his arm around Tempest and walked toward one of the balconies.

Tempest watched the court move out of their way. She knew it was Ridge's presence, not hers, that motivated others to move. One day she would instill such respect. For now, Tempest enjoyed the feel of Ridge's arm around her waist and the glares from ladies of the court who had never had the privilege of Ridge's attention. Never had she felt so alive.

132

At the end of the evening, Ridge walked Tempest to the entrance of the family treehouses. She lifted her face to his, expecting a kiss. She got one. Ridge lifted her hand to his lips and placed a gentle kiss on her knuckles. A perfectly acceptable way to say good evening if the male didn't have permission to court the lady.

Tempest watched in fury as Ridge walked away.

"What's the matter?" Valiant asked, his eyes twinkling.

"Hush." She turned and stormed into her treehouse.

Almost a complete moon cycle after the first bard sang *Dress of Webs*, the dress was commonplace at formal court functions. Many ladies in all five courts sported similar outfits, much to the despair of their fathers.

*****

Valiant, still in his court attire, blocked Tempest's path to her treehouse. "What did you do?" The question was rhetorical. He had watched Ridge kiss her in front of the entire court.

"Nothing." Tempest smiled slyly.

Temperance joined her siblings. "I think she used siren call on Ridge. I heard Mother say as much to Cwenhild before she left."

"Is it so hard to believe that Ridge prefers my company?" Tempest turned on her siblings as her eyes grew black, indicating she was pulling magic.

"Stop it," Temperance hissed.

"Unless, of course, you want to fight both of us." Valiant moved beside Temperance, his eyes darkening as well. "While Ridge, for some strange reason, enjoys your company, I doubt he would have kissed you where everyone could see without being under a spell. He doesn't have Father's permission to court you, and while Ridge is many things, stupid is not one of them."

"You know nothing," Tempest growled and pushed past Valiant. Before she had gone more than five steps, her path was blocked.

"Lady Tempest, Lord Ellwood demands your presence in his receiving room." Ash made no move to restrain her, but he didn't move from her path.

Tempest glared. "I'll go when –"

"Tempest Aerona Gundis Clotilda Astrid, you will go now. I shall accompany you." Lady Rayna moved calmly down the hallway. Without looking at her other children, she said, "You two are expected on the training fields."

Prized

Valiant and Temperance moved quickly to fulfill their mother's order, although what they would do on the training fields at night was anyone's guess. Rayna rarely displayed her temper, but her children knew well that when she appeared this calm, the time to argue with her had passed.

Rayna didn't speak again as she accompanied Tempest to Lord Ellwood's receiving room. Ash walked behind them. Tempest's temper was already the subject of songs sung by the bards, but Rayna was the one he watched. Lady Rayna had a fiery temper that most of the court had never seen, and those who had frequently died before being able to spread the word.

*****

Ellwood sat upon his throne, alone in his receiving room, waiting for his wife and firstborn. He was still angry, but time had cooled his temper. Time and two conversations. The first, with Ridge, had only required a few seconds for Ellwood to realize Tempest had enchanted the advisor. For that alone, she should be banished. Claiming someone without the Forest Lord's express permission was not allowed.

The second was more informative. Rayna had explained that females of the sovereign's line, once they reached adulthood, were able to use a power called siren call on males to control them. In the Seen, until the female had control of this power, she wasn't allowed to interact much with others.

Ellwood thought the power was more like enchantment, a fae gift, but he didn't tell Rayna of his suspicions. Some things his mate didn't need to know. He looked up from his musings when Rayna and Tempest walked in. Ellwood watched Tempest search for Ridge and hid his amusement. It was rare that Tempest lowered her guard enough to show how young she was.

When both women stopped in front of him, he said, "Mistress Tempest, you sirened my advisor. Why?"

Tempest raised her chin and glared at her father for the insult. He responded with a bored glance. "If you want the title Lady, you should act like one."

Before Tempest could respond, Rayna tapped her daughter on the shoulder and replied for her, "Lady Tempest has not yet learned to control this power. She will release her hold, but she must calm down to do so. Calm cannot be ordered. It comes from within."

"Would she benefit from some time with the Shifter Sovereign?" Ellwood asked the question he knew his mate wanted to hear. Rayna hadn't requested in so many words, but Ellwood understood his wife and her motivations. She wanted Tempest away from the court before their daughter ruined herself in the eyes of the fae.

"My love, that is an excellent idea." Rayna smiled.

*****

Dropping his traveling bag to the floor, Valiant asked, "Why are we going to the Seen?"

"We always travel to the Seen together. It would appear strange to the court if only Tempest went." Temperance nodded to the pixies who had packed her traveling bag, and they left her treehouse.

Valiant barked a laugh and claimed a chair by the fire. "No, it wouldn't. Everyone thinks we journey to the Seen as a punishment for Tempest. When Ridge arrives for the evening repast right after Tempest is gone, they will know for sure."

"Shh, don't let Tempest hear you."

"Don't let me hear what?" Tempest placed her traveling pack beside Valiant's and glowered at her siblings.

Valiant glared back. "Because of your actions, my plans for the evening are ruined."

"Your plans? Which lady of the court was to hold your attention tonight, brother mine? And why are you allowed to have dalliances with half the court while I can't kiss one male?"

"Have you ever seen me do more than dance or talk to a lady of the court? No. Discretion is something you lack, sister mine. I have observed you kissing, not one, but two separate males. How many have you kissed?"

Something in Temperance snapped. "Both of you stop. I tire of cleaning up your messes and soothing all around us. Valiant, no longer will I conceal your whereabouts from a suspecting father, brother, or uncle looking for a female member of his household. And everyone knows Tempest will do anything to protect you, so none will believe her if I stand against you. And you, sister mine, can fight this battle on your own. You were warned, repeatedly, not to chase after Ridge, and you ignored all recommendations of caution. For the first time in your life, you didn't get what you wanted immediately. When Ridge didn't respond to your advances, as was his duty, and the proper thing to do, you spelled him. When you release him from this spell the shifters call

135

siren call, he will not be happy with you." Temperance picked up her pack and said over her shoulder, "Come. I will open the way as I don't trust either of you to attend to such a task properly at this moment."

Valiant looked over at Tempest. "I didn't even know she could get mad. Did she mean what she said?" He depended on Temperance to run interference for him for many things, not just his nocturnal activities.

"Come." Temperance's sharp order came from the hallway. From the sound of her voice, she was moving down the living bridge at a fast rate.

"Yes, brother mine. She meant it." Tempest grabbed her pack and followed Temperance. For the first time in her life, Tempest was ashamed of herself.

*****

Valiant entered the way first. Any other time he would do so to make sure it was safe for his sisters, but today he rushed through to get away from his family. Father didn't show up to say goodbye, but that was a good thing. Although Valiant was irritated that his plans were changed without his approval, the rest of the family was mad. Who knew three unhappy females could wrench all the joy out of a room?

He checked the clearing Temperance had sent them to and smiled. Carwen stood at the edge of the clearing, picking berries. She was a lovely shifter.

Carwen smiled when she saw Valiant and said, "I did not realize you were returning so soon. 'Twill be pleasant to have you in camp for a while. Have you written more songs to sing?"

Valiant blushed. Only here in the Seen was he able to write and sing as a bard. Lord Ellwood did not want his son to follow such pursuits. Valiant had recently begun to realize that he was more at home in the Seen than in his father's court. "Perhaps a few."

Temperance pushed past him and whispered, "I won't cover for you here, either. Uncle Kyan will not be happy if you upset his friend's daughter."

Valiant glared at her back. He would never harm Carwen, daughter of Adair. Fact was, he liked her, probably a little too much. He knew he was expected to marry to further his father's plans, but until then, he could enjoy Carwen's company, even if all they did was talk.

"Well met, Carwen." Temperance walked past with her pack.

"Will you stay long?" Carwen asked.

"I'm not sure. Cwenhild sent for us." Tempest followed Temperance, leaving Valiant and Carwen alone in the clearing.

"Pray tell what happened?" Carwen asked. "Cwenhild returned from her visit to the Farseen in a rare mood."

"I'll bet she did. The story is Tempest's to tell, or not, as she sees fit. May I carry your basket?"

"That's very kind of you, but no. You have your pack to carry. I would enjoy your escort back to the village." Carwen smiled, showing off two dimples.

Valiant grinned. He did like dimples.

As they strolled down the path, Carwen asked, "Does Tempest's story have anything to do with our other visitor from the Farseen? I believe he's from the Northern Realm as well."

"What visitor?" Valiant stopped moving. Surely Ellwood wouldn't allow this to happen.

Sensing Valiant's mood swing, Carwen lost her smile. "Kyan introduced him to father as Ridge. Is he the same Ridge Tempest has spoken of so often? He is certainly handsome enough to be the same man."

"If he is, someone has some explaining to do." Valiant ground his teeth, a bad habit he developed as soon as his sisters showed interest in males.

"There you are. Carwen, your father desires your presence. Valiant is going hunting with me." Kyan's tone allowed no room for discussion, so Carwen left tossing Valiant an apologetic look.

Valiant turned on his uncle. "Is it true?"

"If you refer to Ridge's presence, yes. Cwenhild thought it would be better for Tempest to release the siren call away from court as Ridge will be entitled to the anger he will no doubt feel when this mess is over."

"Someone needs to order Tempest to release the siren call now."

"Unfortunately, it's not that easy. Since, according to Rayna and Cwenhild, Tempest does have feelings for Ridge, it's harder for her to stop what she started."

"Are you serious?"

"Yes, and we must start hunting now."

"Why?" Valiant raised an eyebrow in a fair imitation of Tempest.

Prized

"We're hunting Ridge. He took off, and we're not sure just how well he knows his way around our island."

"Tempest causes a mess, and I have to clean it up?"

"Essentially, yes." Kyan patted Valiant on the back. "At least you are spared the mood Tempest will be in after Cwenhild finishes talking to her."

Valiant silently agreed with the wisdom of that statement and adjusted his pack. "Where was he last seen?"

"Heading south, toward the strongest witch settlement on the island." Kyan shifted to his wolf and ran.

Valiant shifted to his wolf and matched Kyan's fast pace. Valiant picked up Ridge's scent before he picked up the scent of witches. Following Kyan's lead, he shifted back to human and settled into a traveler's walk. "How do we approach a coven of witches?"

"We walk into the witch settlement and ask nicely worded questions. They will know we are shifters as soon as they see us."

"Thought so. Just like witches in the Farseen, right?"

"Not sure. Witches from the Farseen are stronger, but I think it's only a matter of training."

"Why would Ridge come here?"

"Don't know. Not sure if he was searching for witches or picked this direction at random."

"Ridge was searching for me." A young woman stepped out of the thicket. "I am Delwen. Ridge is a relative of mine on my father's side. He does not wish to see any shifter."

"We're trying to help him," Valiant said.

"And how will you help him? Can you break the spell your sister placed on him?"

"No," Valiant ground out the words, "But she can."

"And will she? I have observed Tempest. She has a stubborn streak." When neither male spoke, Delwen added, "You cannot help."

Valiant stared at the witch. "You've been watching us."

Delwen smiled but didn't respond.

Movement in the thicket had Valiant and Kyan drawing weapons. Ridge walked out with his trademark smirk. "Since I'm the one who's been wronged, I have more right to draw weapons than either of you."

Valiant moved to put his weapon away.

"Fool. You have no idea if I'm friend or foe at this time. Why would you lower your defenses?"

Valiant grinned, knowing the answer for once. "To make it easier to shift into a wolf. In my shifter form, I always fair better in a fight with you."

"Some days, I think you can be taught, young one." Ridge's smirk almost returned, but he set his jaw in a hard line. "I will not return to Cwenhild's settlement. Not while Tempest is there, and I'm under this spell."

Kyan nodded. "She was sent here to break the spell. She must be calm to release it, and Rayna thought Tempest would calm quicker if she were away from Lord Ellwood."

"And why did Cwenhild want me here?"

"To protect you," Kyan said.

"You don't know that, and I don't believe it. Lady Rayna wants me here with Lady Tempest so that we can return to court together, leaving the court to wonder exactly what happened. If we are friendly with each other, many will assume the story was fabricated."

Valiant snorted. "I hate to be the one to say it, but the entire court saw you kiss my sister in the feasting hall. No one will believe it was a story concocted to cause trouble or amusement."

"Learn to play the long game, boy." Ridge set his face in a hard line. "If Lord Ellwood says I had his permission to court Lady Tempest, most will believe we kissed for the shock value before Ellwood made the formal announcement."

"You would never do that," Valiant retorted.

"But Lady Tempest would, and everyone knows it. I will become the fool who couldn't say no to her."

"No one who knows you would believe that. You, better than Father, can call my volatile sister to heel."

"Not always." Regret hung in the air.

Valiant rolled his eyes. "I don't like you. That's no secret, and even I blame Tempest for this mess, not you. You would never willingly harm her reputation by such a juvenile act."

"That changes nothing. I will not return to Cwenhild's settlement." Ridge turned and walked into the woods.

"My dwelling is the closest to these woods. You may check-in with me daily." Delwen winked at Valiant, tossed an apologetic shrug Kyan's way, and followed Ridge.

Prized

Kyan turned to start the long walk back to his home. "Boy, I don't want to hear about you spending time with Delwen. Let's not make this situation worse."

Valiant scowled at the back of Kyan's head and, for once, kept his mouth shut. To be honest, he never thought of other females when Carwen was nearby.

*****

Tempest shot out of Cwenhild's dwelling and shifted to her wolf. Temperance moved to stand in her way, and Tempest snapped at her.

"I bite back." Temperance's declaration would have meant more if she hadn't dived out of the way. Temperance had accepted that she would never shift and had declared to her mother she would no longer visit the shifters in the Seen. Rayna had begged her to return just this once, to help Tempest, and Temperance had relented, but she doubted she would be of any help.

"No. Leave her." Cwenhild's order stopped everyone in the camp who moved to follow Tempest, except Temperance.

Temperance snarled at her grandmother and ran after her sister. The only good thing about having so little shifter talent was she wasn't tied to orders from the shifter sovereign. She could not shift, but Temperance was swift of feet as were all fae. As she ran, she considered all the arguments she could use to convince Tempest to return to camp and behave. She knew none of them would work.

Thirty minutes into the run, Temperance realized where Tempest was going. Her headstrong sister couldn't be that devoid of intelligence. If Tempest didn't turn soon, she would run right into Cimil's colony of blood-sucking demons. The bloodsuckers were humans, male and female, infected with an aggressive sickness that somehow changed the human body so that only blood would sustain them. The type of blood didn't matter, but most preferred prey that feared them. The fae witches thought the bloodsuckers also fed on the fear, but no one knew for sure. The bloodsuckers were sensitive to the light of the sun. While the Farseen sun turned unshielded demons to dust, the sun of the Seen simply slowed them down.

"Tempest. Come back. You know Cimil is stronger than you." Temperance groaned when she realized her words were the worst thing she could have said. She slowed and watched Tempest disappear into the forest. She could feel the bloodsuckers nearby and knew she could go no further.

140

"I hope you know what you're about, sister mine." Temperance turned and, moving quickly, retraced her steps to the relative safety of the sovereign's land.

*****

When she heard Temperance call for her, Tempest sped up. For the first time in her life, Tempest had not been able to intimidate the family into submitting to her wishes. And for the first time, Ridge was angry with her. He usually found her antics mildly diverting or at least droll. She shouldn't have sirened him. She knew that. She didn't need her mother and grandmother yelling at her. Tempest growled, and her left lip turned up in a snarl. Normally, when she broke the rules, Ridge guided her and helped her find a solution. He wouldn't this time. She was young but understood that. Cimil was her only hope. His mind was powerful, and he would know what needed to be done. As for herself, Tempest had studied with Kavi for years and felt confident Cimil could no longer enter her mind.

"Hello, child. My how you've grown. What brings you into my woods?"

Tempest, with her mind closed tight, scratched her nose with her paw to make sure she didn't look into Cimil's eyes as she shifted to human.

Cimil frowned, but quickly placed a smile on his face. "Your mind grows strong. What can I do for you, Lady Tempest of the Northern Realm?"

Tempest almost looked up when he addressed her true, but she stopped herself in time. "I want to learn how to release a thrall."

"Now, why would I tell you that?" Cimil rubbed his smooth chin.

"I believe it is similar to a spell the shifters call siren call."

"I know of this siren call. They are not that similar. Who did you enchant, my dear?"

"No one. I just want the knowledge."

Cimil laughed. "For a fae, you do not lie well with the truth."

"If you can't help me, I'll leave."

"No, I don't think so." Cimil stood to his full height and said, "Look at me."

Tempest shifted and turned to run away. Two of Cimil's bloodsuckers grabbed her. Biting one in the jugular with her wolf canines piercing deep, Tempest turned to snap at the other. When she did, her eyes locked with Cimil's. She hadn't noticed that he had moved to stand behind his minion. Tempest closed her eyes tight, but it was too late.

"Look at me, Tempest."

She tried to ignore his command but failed. When Tempest complied, Cimil added, "Shift back to human. We're going on a trip."

Tempest shifted and walked beside Cimil. When one of the bloodsuckers got too close, Cimil said, "No. She is mine alone. None shall touch her blood save me."

Even enthralled as she was, Tempest shivered. For the first time in her life, she was in real trouble, and she doubted she was strong enough to get out of it. The walk back to Cimil's camp was longer than she expected, and those traveling with them did not seem to like her. When they finally arrived, she was surprised at the size of the colony.

"Stay by my side. The colony is not safe for you without my protection. Kyan has killed many of my people, and they would be pleased to take their revenge through you."

"I demand her blood."

Tempest glanced out of the side of her eye, careful not to look at his face. She wasn't sure if she could be enthralled by more than one bloodsucker at a time, but she wouldn't take the chance. The male who spoke looked a lot like Cimil, but where Cimil was svelte and built for fast movement, the newcomer was built for combat. He had impressive muscles, reminding Tempest of Ridge.

"You demand nothing from me, brother." Cimil grinned. It wasn't a happy expression. When no one else spoke, Cimil said, "We will return home. The shifters will come for this one, and I prefer to take my time. And Ahau, if you touch my prize, I will drain you."

Ahau's lip curled, but he didn't respond.

In no time at all, the colony had packed their tents.

"Tempest."

She could not ignore Cimil's call. "Yes?"

"Open a way to your new home."

"I cannot open a way to a place I do not know." Tempest frowned. Surely, he knew that. Besides, she understood Cimil could open ways.

"Yes, you can. I gift you the knowledge."

Tempest's eyes opened wide as she suddenly knew where Cimil's home was and exactly where the way should open. Knowing this was a show of power, of his control over her, Tempest opened the way as a single tear fell down her face. Her family would never find her. She walked through, followed by the entire demon colony.

Although she had seen into Cimil's mind and knew the water was clear, the sky was blue, and the air was warm as the Southern Realm, she had not truly believed. To see it in person was altogether different. This land was nothing like the island the shifter sovereign lived on. The air was warm and damp, even though it was sunny. Only in the rain forests of the Farseen had she experienced such weather. The breeze from the water reminded her of the Southern Realm. It was a welcome respite, cooling the perspiration that beaded on her forehead.

Tempest stood on a thin piece of land between the open water and a lake. A jungle butted up to the lake with trees and bushes that reminded her of the Southern Realm. A peninsula of land jutted out from the other side of the lake. On the peninsula sat a structure that resembled the Central Realm residence in that it was open and airy. If she wasn't surrounded by blood-sucking demons, she would have loved to explore.

"You may not open another way until I grant permission. Come, Tempest. I have much to show you." Cimil patted her shoulder and walked down a small path through the brush that quickly became a jungle canopy.

Tempest trailed behind her master, unable to control herself, but she was able to watch the world around her. Small bipedal creatures with long tails chattered and swung through the trees. Some type of reptile, longer and larger than an adult fae with four stubby legs and a long snout moved lazily through the river. Even with its mouth closed, the teeth were visible. When the creature opened its mouth, Tempest walked closer to the riverbank, hoping to get a good look at the teeth. There were a lot of teeth.

The creature moved faster than Tempest expected. She tripped as she jumped back. Cimil flew over her and grabbed the reptile, taking it into the river that churned from the fight.

Tempest watched the water but knew Cimil was alive. She still waited for his orders. Surely, if he was dead, she would not remain enthralled.

Ahau moved to her side while Cimil fought the creature. "You will be mine. I shall enjoy telling Kyan how you suffered."

She didn't stop her eyes from rolling. Ahau's threat had no weight. He had not enthralled her, and she had already planned how she would kill Ahau if Cimil didn't return, but she didn't think Cimil would die in the jaws of the beast.

Tempest's eyes returned to the water as it calmed.

*****

"Where is she?" Valiant stood in the center of the shifter camp and stared at his grandmother. "Why didn't you stop her?"

"She needed to burn off energy." Cwenhild stared back, surprised when Valiant didn't lower his eyes.

The shifters that hadn't left when Temperance announced that Tempest was with the bloodsuckers stepped back as a group. No one held the sovereign's gaze. Ever. Kyan eliminated the problem by stepping between them and pushing Valiant back. "Now is not the time for tempers."

"Oh, really? Well, Uncle," Valiant drew out the word, "Tempest is not on this land anymore. She's so far away that I can't feel her presence. For all I know, she's dead." Valiant crossed his arms over his chest, refusing to give the fear he felt more power.

Temperance sucked in air. "He can sense her anywhere in the Farseen. How much larger is this dimension than ours?"

"Never checked. I know the Seen is larger. That is all." Kyan remained a presence between Valiant and Cwenhild.

Valiant knew Tempest had not explored more of this world than he had. "How could she –"

"How doesn't matter. Kyan, trail her. Find her." Cwenhild's tone did not leave room for discussion.

"I'm going with him," Valiant said.

"No."

"Sovereign, you need to talk to your daughter. The one who gave birth to me." Valiant shifted and ran into the forest.

"Follow him. When you return I expect answers," the sovereign said.

Kyan nodded to his mother and followed Valiant.

Temperance walked toward the northern trail. "I'm going to see Kavi."

"Wait."

"Grandmother, we both know I don't have enough shifter blood to shift or be considered a shifter. While I feel your order as a weight in my head, I have no compulsion to follow it. Kavi might be able to see where Tempest is, and then I can open a way to her."

"If you find anything, you will return here to take a force of shifters with you," Cwenhild ordered.

"Perhaps." Temperance tossed the word over her shoulder as she continued to walk north.

Because she had entered the woods, Temperance didn't notice the clan backing away as the sovereign's eyes turned black as night.

Temperance ran through the woods, slowing to a walk only when she crossed the river near Kavi's home. Once Temperance was on dry land, Kavi stepped out of her cave. "I am pleased you finally arrived. There is little time, and you must open a way immediately. I will show you where we are going."

"Won't we need help?" Temperance had responded to her grandmother out of anger but knew she wasn't strong enough to fight the bloodsuckers alone.

"We have help." Kavi touched Temperance's shoulder.

Temperance sucked in air as she felt a sharp pain and saw Tempest on a sandy beach next to a jungle, surrounded by bloodsuckers. "What is this?"

"That is where we are going. Focus on that spot. The demons have already moved into the jungle."

Not sure what was happening, but feeling an overwhelming need to get to Tempest, Temperance opened a way.

*****

The demon camp was bare. Completely empty. Valiant yelled, and the sound echoed across the hills.

"Quiet, fool. Do not give away your location. Where's Tempest?" Ridge walked out of the forest. "I see you tracked her to this clearing as well."

Valiant looked over in disgust. "If I knew, would I be here?"

"Perhaps," Ridge retorted. "I felt she was in distress. What happened?"

"Not your concern." Valiant moved to push Ridge aside. The advisor didn't budge.

Kyan grabbed Valiant's arm. "We don't have time for this. We will need Ridge's help. Cimil has taken Tempest to his stronghold across the ocean. We must go there."

"Now, you know where she is?" Valiant raised an incredulous eye.

"Kavi just told me." Kyan rubbed the base of his neck.

"How, you're mind-blind."

Prized

"Kavi can push information into anyone's head."

"Bet that feels good," Valiant said.

"You're about to find out. She'll send everyone the location."

"Ow."

"Stop complaining. I'll open the way." Ridge opened a way and walked through.

"Guess Kavi told him as well." Valiant rubbed his head. He and Kyan followed Ridge. Nodding to Temperance and Kavi on the sandy beach, the men turned to watch other shifters join from another way. When it closed, Valiant asked, "Where's Cwenhild?"

Pointing to the shifter force that arrived, Kyan said, "The sovereign sent those fighters. She will prepare to fight Cimil in another realm."

Ridge turned to Kavi and held out his hand. She accepted it gratefully. "Lady Kavi, do you know where Tempest is now?"

"She is watching Cimil fight a legged serpent that attacked her."

"A what?" Valiant asked.

"Keep moving. Kavi can point one out on the way to Cimil's lair if she is so inclined." Ridge led the way down the single file path.

*****

When Cimil rose from the water, he tossed the creature aside. "Come, Tempest. I suspect your family will arrive soon."

Tempest winced as the other serpents fed on their dead companion. She fell in line beside Cimil.

She felt something watching her and looked up to see a large cat on the limb above her. Double her size, its coat was light brown, almost yellow, with black dots. The eyes were yellow. Tempest didn't want the animal hurt, so she dragged her eyes away.

Tempest felt three ways open, and she recognized all three signatures: Temperance, Ridge, and Cwenhild. Hopefully, they brought help. A lot of help. She glanced back at Cimil's vast following.

It wasn't long before they entered a clearing under the jungle canopy. An impressive stone structure, a residence of some type, rose toward the sky.

Cimil smiled and spread out his hands. "Welcome to my home, Lady Tempest."

Tempest didn't speak. She looked on in horror as she realized the bloodsucking demons didn't use all creatures for food, killing them quickly. Some were enthralled beasts of burden. Was that her fate? She could feel other shifters in the area and identified them as they walked around, unchained without guards, performing their tasks. Once enthralled, it appeared that the vampires didn't have to worry about their slaves.

She watched two shifters pull a cart into a central area. Once they secured the cart, anyone who wasn't a vampire ran for the food. They grabbed food, stuffing it into their mouths, pushing each other out of the way, and eating like animals. Tempest flinched at the sight. Was this her life now?

Cimil placed a hand on Tempest's shoulder. "Don't worry, my dear. As my personal property, food will be brought to you. You will eat in my private quarters."

Tempest shuttered again. That didn't sound better. It sounded like Cimil liked his food clean. She followed Cimil into the stone structure. She expected it to be musty inside because of the dampness outside. Instead, the smell of flowers was almost overwhelming. It was soon apparent why. Plants were everywhere. They crossed a vast room that resembled a dancing hall in the Farseen and took a set of stairs on the right. Up the steps, they climbed to the top tower. Cimil opened the door and ushered her in. The room was as ornate as her parents' treehouse. Tempest's lip curled up. The blood-sucking demon had the same love of creature comforts as the Forest Lord.

"You will remain here for as long as you please me." Cimil lifted the covers to reveal a feast on the table. "Eat. I shall return shortly. I suggest you not leave these rooms. It is not safe for you outside."

As soon as Cimil left, Tempest opened a way. At least she tried to. Nothing happened. Then she remembered. Cimil ordered her not to open a way until he gave permission. Could he do that? She tried again. Nothing.

Angry, Tempest sat down. Assuming he wouldn't poison his food, she tried some of the odd-looking fruit and found it tasty. The fermented drink was also good, but she only had a little of that. She needed her wits and strength. She ate her fill before searching the rooms. Tempest found nothing useful until she looked out the windows. Overlooking the forest, there were no guards or thralls on the backside of the fortress. She stuck her head out the window and looked east. There was the ocean she could smell. Looking down the walls, she saw that the building material would serve as handholds all the way down the outside wall. She could escape.

Prized

Her grin faded when she realized she wouldn't get far. Tempest already knew that Cimil could call her back to him whenever he wanted. Or could he? If she ran far enough away, perhaps he wouldn't be able to control her. Action was always better than inaction. Mind made up, Tempest crawled out the window and started the long descent to the ground.

*****

When he passed creatures eating one of their own, Adair asked, "Is that a legged serpent?"

"Yes." Kavi's voice grew weaker. "They are faster than they look on land and faster still in the water."

Adair watched Kavi wishing he could do something, anything to be of aid to her. When Kavi tripped, Ridge reached out and steadied her.

"Don't touch her," Adair snapped. Surely a fae as old and knowledgeable as Ridge knew Kavi could not stand the touch of another. Adair turned when Kyan placed a hand on his shoulder.

"Ridge can block his mind successfully. He will cause her no pain."

Adair nodded but wasn't appeased. If anything, it was more of a reason to dislike Ridge. Kavi had lived with the fae for some time many years ago. Many fae shared Ridge's ability to block others from their mind, and Kavi found it soothing. Another reason to dislike the fae.

Adair and Kavi had been friends as children. As one of Kavi's few friends, he had learned to never offer her assistance for fear of causing her pain as touch increased her mental link to others. They remained friends now, but he had wished for more. If Adair could block his mind from her thoughts, perhaps they could have had more. He looked on angrily as Ridge continued to steady Kavi on their journey.

Falling in step with Kavi and Ridge, Adair asked, "Is the press of minds too much? Temperance can send you home."

Kavi smiled at her friend and wiped the perspiration from her forehead. "No, I must remain. Ridge serves as a block to keep out the thoughts of others."

Adair stopped walking and glared at Ridge. Was there nothing this fae could not do?

*****

After scrambling down the side of the castle, Tempest ran into the forest. She considered shifting but wasn't sure it would be helpful. She

148

didn't think her wolf would be better at survival in this jungle than her human form.

She saw a golden-colored snake on a branch but had no idea as to its nature. Tempest gave it a wide birth. The chattering bipedal creatures moved around in the trees, and Tempest suspected the demons could track her by their noise. The swinging bipeds had been following her for a while, and Tempest had become used to their racket. Enough so that when they became silent, she looked up. Another one of the large cats with a black dotted, light brown coat lounged in the trees with a fresh kill. The cat looked on her with interest but didn't move. The cat yawned, showing great big teeth. Tempest moved past, keeping her eyes on the creature to make sure it didn't attack.

Tempest veered away from the river with its legged serpents. She saw more snakes in many colors, brightly colored frogs, and spiders, and realized she didn't know what was poisonous and what wasn't. Tempest was well versed in the dangers in all realms of the Farseen, including the creatures of the wastelands. In the Seen, she only knew the creatures of the large island where the shifter sovereign lived. She had traveled in the great landmass east of the shifter's island, but the animals here were nothing like the animals in the colder climates.

Tempest continued to move under the canopy of trees until she found a cave of sorts. Large boulders had fallen against each other and created a shelter. At least here she could watch in front of her and know that her back was protected. She sat down to rest, and for the first time, heard Cimil call to her, but he was far away, and she thought she could resist. As the call became more urgent, Tempest realized her plan would fail.

She lay back on the ground and immediately felt a sting, and then another and another. Jumping up, she saw ants crawling all over her body. She tried to brush them off, but they continued to sting her back, Tempest knew true pain for the first time in her life. Pain received on a battlefield was nothing to what she experienced now. Her entire body exploded in agony, and her heart pounded in her chest. Shaking and sweating, she moved away from the cave with no understanding of what had happened. She had only taken a few steps when she fell down unconscious.

*****

Prized

Cimil entered his quarters, ready for a taste of his newest prize. He had put off feeding to prolong the pleasure of anticipation. Tempest was powerful and her blood would be equally powerful, enhancing his magical strength as well as curing his hunger for a while.

He looked around. "Tempest? I did not expect you to hide from me. You know there is no place to go. I can follow your mind anywhere."

The spike of anger he felt was replaced with eagerness for the hunt. She was a rare find and he would enjoy breaking the shifter. Cimil opened his mind. The curse that left his lips was heartfelt. How did she get into the jungle without the guards noticing? He peered out the window and saw no guards.

"Ahau, you are a fool," Cimil muttered. Ahau had removed the guards from the back of the castle to guard the front in anticipation of the shifters arriving to reclaim their daughter, exactly as Cimil had told him not to do.

Cimil moved silently out of his rooms and down the hallway. Ahau had just caused his final warrant. Cimil would kill Ahau himself. Why let all that power go to waste? Of course, that would delay the tracking of Tempest, but such was life. Duty before pleasure.

Rather than track her, Cimil called her back to him. It wouldn't be as much fun, but it would save time. He continued to the center courtyard where he found Ahau feeding on his favorite pet. If he didn't drain her soon, she would become one of them, but that wouldn't be a problem soon.

Cimil grabbed the pet and threw her across the room. The action ripped open her throat as Ahau's teeth were attached to the vein of her neck at the time.

Ahau jumped to his feet and pulled his sword.

Cimil grinned. He would enjoy this kill.

The fight was quick, and the outcome inevitable. Once Cimil drained Ahau he stood and faced his people. He looked each of them in the eye, enjoying the lowered eyes and nervous stances. Fear was an excellent motivator.

His thoughts returned to Tempest. Where was she? Cimil couldn't hear her mind at all, which meant he couldn't track her. How did she break his control over her?

*****

"How many demons will we find?" Ridge asked.

"No more than twenty-five," Kavi said weakly.

Adair gritted his teeth, but said, "Ridge, you must take her to safety."

"No, he must take me to Tempest."

"Surely, you are not needed for the battle."

Kavi shook her head. "Tempest is no longer enthralled to Cimil."

"How?" Ridge asked.

"I don't know, but she is in great pain, and Cimil cannot find her."

Ridge and Kyan exchanged a look.

"Go," Kyan said. "If you find Tempest, we will leave without fighting the demons. While we wait, I'll make plans for battle."

Ridge nodded. He and Kavi moved away from the shifters and traveled north. As they put more distance between them and everyone else, Kavi grew stronger.

Ridge asked, "Did you really need to come?"

"Yes," Kavi stared at a golden snake, and it slithered away.

"You should have married Lord Elros. He now rules the Southern Realm."

Kavi laughed. "He didn't love me. He loved the idea of saving me. There is a difference."

"Indeed. What about Adair? He loves you for you."

"Yes, but he can't shield his mind."

"That's unfortunate."

"I certainly think so." Kavi stepped over another log wishing they were on a path, and at the same time wondering if there were any paths in this jungle. "What will you do about Tempest?"

"She enthralled me for lack of a better word."

"She loves you."

"Does she? I'm not so sure. Perhaps she is in love with the idea of loving me."

Knowing Ridge turned her words back on her, Kavi shook her head. "She's close. This way."

When they topped a hill, they saw Tempest lying on the ground. Ridge ran to her. When he touched her, she whimpered, and tears streamed down her face.

Tempest opened her eyes and cried, "I hurt you. It's my fault. I caused everything."

Ridge blinked at the words he never expected her to say. "Hush. Rest. I'm here now. Everything will be fine."

Prized

"Don't be mad." Tempest sighed. Still shaking and sweating, she snuggled into Ridge. He held her until she fell back asleep.

When she was resting quietly, Ridge turned his attention to Kavi. "What happened here?"

"I don't know." Kavi moved around slowly and finally walked up on the rise in front of the boulders. "Aha."

"Aha, what?" Ridge's voice was sharp.

"She must have been up here."

"And?"

"There's an ant nest underneath the canopy of the trees."

"Ants?"

"These ants are unique. Their sting can cause a full day of pain and apparently can break a demon's mind control."

"Ants did this?" Ridge looked down at Tempest. She was still writing in pain. Luckily, she was unconscious again.

*****

Valiant peered through the dense undergrowth at the residence. It was open and airy but not very well defended. The guards had moved to watch something in the center court. It sounded like a fight. "Shall we attack?"

"The demons are dangerous."

When Kyan said nothing more, Valiant frowned. "Are those shifters?"

"Yes." Adair moved silently to Valiant's left. "Not all thralls are used for food. Some are workers."

"Why don't they leave? Why don't you rescue them?" Valiant gaped at Adair. Not even Lord Ellwood would leave his subjects in such a state.

"They are thralls. They have no will of their own. We used to rescue them, but they always run away and return to their master."

"But —"

Kyan cut Valiant off. "There is nothing we can do for them. If we attack the demons, the enthralled will attack us."

"Would it not be kinder to kill them?" Valiant asked.

"For them, yes. We tried that, too. The demons simply took more as thralls for labor. Know this, if Tempest is already a thrall, and we fail to kill Cimil, we will be forced to kill her. She's too powerful to leave her with the demons and she will always be a thrall."

Valiant glared at his uncle who had to know that Valiant would never leave Tempest in such a state or allow her to be killed. Before he could respond, Valiant grabbed his head in pain. Kavi had sent another mind message.

*****

For the next few hours, Tempest moved in and out of consciousness. When she was aware, Tempest thought of nothing other than the pain, although once or twice she thought she heard Ridge speaking gently to her. His voice comforted her.

When she finally woke without pain, Tempest sat up. She felt fantastic, ready to take on the world.

"Finally."

Tempest swerved her head around. Ridge sat behind her, reclining on a tree trunk. A tentative smile played on her lips. "I thought I dreamed you."

"You did not."

"I meant what I said."

Ridge raised an eyebrow, imitating the expression she was already well known for.

Tempest grinned for real. "I am sorry. I should not have used siren call on you."

"You are now in my debt." Ridge spoke the words they both knew to be true.

"I've always been in your debt. Do you think I don't know how you protect me from Father's anger?"

Ridge shrugged.

"I'm calm enough now." Tempest closed her eyes, inhaled deeply, and released it. The breath wasn't all she released.

Ridge felt a calm settle around him as a cool breeze hit his face. Released from her spell, Ridge did something because he wanted to. He pulled Tempest into his arms and kissed her.

"I knew it!" Valiant pushed through the jungle and placed his hands on his hips. "Tempest, release Ridge."

Kavi moved to stand in front of Valiant. "She did. This time Ridge is kissing her of his own free will."

"Then, he dies."

Adair grabbed Valiant's sword arm. "Whatever rules govern actions in the Farseen, in the Seen, if the female has attained her majority and is willing, the male may kiss her. Tempest does not appear

Prized

to mind, and I do think he's earned the right." Besides, Ridge wasn't kissing Kavi.

Ridge stopped kissing Tempest and said, "I like the way Adair thinks." Then he returned his attention to more important matters.

Valiant frowned. He didn't like this at all.

Chapter 11 – 4972 BCE

For the first time in his life, the Dark Woods offered Valiant no relief. On the contrary, he was angrier than before he entered the forest. Tempest had finally gotten what she wanted. Even though she tricked Ridge, Lord Ellwood had given his permission for Ridge to court her, and she had accepted him as her consort. They were now inseparable. Temperance was sure they were truly in love. Ridiculous. Tempest simply wanted Ridge because he was the best, and she would not accept anything less. As for Ellwood, Valiant understood his motivations. Ridge, better than anyone, could rein in Tempest and her wild tendencies.

As was his custom, Valiant moved silently through the woods. So ingrained was his training, that Valiant, regardless of form, was unaware of his stealth. When he heard taunting voices, he slowed. Peeking through the underbrush, Valiant saw four water dragons, three large, one small. When he focused on the smaller whelp, Valiant realized the dragon was some type of half-breed. It had the horns, claws, and wings of a regular dragon, but its body was longer and leaner. The whelp wasn't just one color, but a mix of colors more suited to a river dragon.

"You are an abomination." The largest of the river dragons, claws extended, stood over the whelp.

"We should kill him." The second river dragon suggested.

At those words, Valiant's anger exploded. His entire life, he had been put down for being a half-breed. Valiant stepped out from the underbrush and called water, turning it to ice and throwing the large shard at the largest river dragon. The shard did not hurt the enormous dragon, but it did surprise him. Valiant moved to stand between the whelp and the river dragons, and said, "Mind your manners. This land belongs to the Forest Lord of the Northern Realm, and you will not harm our guest."

When the adult dragons looked at Valiant, he blushed. He didn't really know the story, but he would no longer sit by while someone who was different was made to feel less. Within the Farseen, different was considered weak or bad. The children of the Forest Lord were the exceptions, as their powers had come in stronger than most, but until their full powers had manifested, they had been the subject of ridicule. Valiant had been more susceptible to the harassment than his sisters. It didn't hurt that more ruling fae feared angering Tempest than Lord Ellwood.

When one of the river dragons threw fire at Valiant, he gathered it up, and turned it back on the dragons, adding more heat to the flames. The dragons dove for the river to escape the fire. River dragon scales were not as resistant to fire as those of regular dragons.

The three river dragons rose from the water and advanced. Valiant set his stance and sirened the dragons, freezing them in their tracks. None were more shocked when it worked than Valiant. He had expected the dragons to pause to laugh at his feeble attempts to stop them.

Knowing it wouldn't last long, Valiant turned to the whelp. "Are you injured?"

"I'm fine. Leave me alone." The whelp tried to spread his wings, but the left one hung wrong.

"Let me help."

"I need no help," the whelp replied.

"Yeah, I know that tone." Valiant's tone softened. "It's the one I use when I'm scared.

"What do you have to be scared of? You're ruling fae."

Valiant laughed. "My father is ruling fae, and my mother is a shape shifter from the Seen. I'm not sure what I am."

The whelp eyed the fae. "You are Valiant, the son of Lord Ellwood, Forest Lord of the Northern Realm, and Lady Rayna of the Alpha Clan of shifters."

Valiant never understood why the lesser fae used full titles when determining whom a ruling fae was, but they always did. Performing a bow, Valiant said, "Valiant, at your service."

"Greetings, Valiant. I am Kulvir, son of Tulvir, Matriarch of the Greens. I have not met my father." Careful of his injured wing, the whelp returned the bow.

Valiant nodded his understanding. "So, you were checking to see if the river dragons in the Northern Realm would claim you."

"Yes. Obviously, a flaw in my thinking."

Valiant noticed that the claws of the largest dragon moved. His spell would dissipate soon. "Come. When we were young, my sisters and I hid nearby from our duties. It will be a safe place for you to recover."

"Why would you help me?"

"We half-breeds have to stick together." Valiant took off down a seldom-used trail. He wasn't surprised when Kulvir followed.

Helping Kulvir took longer than Valiant had planned. Returning to the residence three days later, he was greeted by two angry sisters and an irate mother. All three, plus Ridge, had gone to great pains to keep the Forest Lord from discovering his son's absence. Valiant adjusted his court attire and hid another blade in his left boot. Thanks to his father's not so gentle training, Valiant was always prepared for battle. When he opened the door to the hallway, Valiant was not surprised someone was waiting to lecture him again. But he was surprised by who was waiting.

"Skip out of court as much as you wish. I don't begrudge you that, but you will make sure Lady Tempest knows you will be gone. She was worried, and when she's worried, I want to kill something. Don't give me a reason for that something to be you." Having said his peace, Ridge turned and walked away.

"Doubt you would have the guts to kill without Tempest's permission," Valiant whispered toward the retreating form.

"You know that's not true." Temperance stopped by his side. "And Ridge has to put up with Tempest's foul mood. She is almost as bad as Father when she's upset. I believe you are old enough to know your own mind, and as a male, you can leave anytime you wish, just make sure Tempest knows what's going on."

"I don't answer to her."

"No, but as a kindness to the rest of us who have to live with her mood, tell Tempest something so she won't bring the elements down upon us.

*****

Prized

This meal must end sometime, and I will not dance with any female in the hall.

Valiant repeated the sentence as a mantra in his head. He was bored with the Northern Realm. Perhaps it was time to visit the Seen for an extended period. Now that Ridge and Tempest had the approval of Lord Ellwood to court, there was no one to fight. Before, when any male came near his sisters, Valiant enjoyed tracking down the fools and beating the offenders for even looking at Tempest or Temperance. Not that Tempest needed his protection, but the only benefit as a brother was bloodying any male who thought his sisters were available. Now, no one wanted to take on Ridge, so the court had calmed down. On some level, Valiant thought that might have played into Lord Ellwood's decision when he granted permission for Tempest and Ridge to be together.

Valiant glanced at Temperance. She needed to be protected. Not from her own bad decisions, as Tempest did. No. Temperance was gentle and too trusting by far. She never caused a scene and would never do anything to displease Father. Valiant had often wondered how Rayna had named the girls so accurately. Someday he would have to ask. But for now, until Temperance was settled, Valiant knew he wouldn't leave her unprotected.

The entire court looked over as a bowman approached the Forest Lord's table. The message would have to be urgent to force an interruption of the evening repast.

"Lord Ellwood, Tulvir, Supreme Matriarch of the Greens, has requested an audience with Valiant the Bold. She awaits him at the floating stairs."

Every eye turned to look at Valiant. Dragon Supreme Matriarchs didn't ask for an audience. They demanded others to appear before them in their lairs. Valiant shrugged. "She can't mean me."

"No one else has the name Valiant." Tempest stood from her table. "Come, brother, let us see what Tulvir wants."

Valiant joined her only to have the entire court, including Lord Ellwood, follow them to the main entrance of the Northern Realm residence and the floating stairs. What happened next became the first song ever written about Valiant that didn't include Tempest. "Valiant the Bold" became a staple in the repertoire of the bards.

The feasting hall grew still and silent
The green supreme matriarch waited.
She demanded to meet a fae of the realm
Valiant the Bold, she indicated.

Valiant shrugged his shoulders and left the hall,
To meet the dragon matriarch.
Those in the feasting hall followed suit,
Even the Northern Realm's patriarch.

Silently waiting, the crowd looked on,
Valiant spoke for all to behold,
"Valiant is my name, 'tis true,
But none have called me bold."

The dragon smiled with sword in hand,
"Valiant the Bold, I call you thus.
Three river dragons you fought alone
And defeated them with no fuss.

River dragons for my son you fought
They singled him out, you knew not why.
You rushed to his aid against great odds.
My son is dual born, I cannot deny.

You stood as his patron, no fear for yourself.
This sword I present you, forged by my fire.
Keep yourself worthy and pure of motive
And it will defend you, when times are dire.

The Patron's Sword I have crafted
For one with others to protect
It will fight for you, my friend
Unless you offend it with willful neglect.

Regardless of who wields this sword,
It holds its faith to you.
Be a patron for the underdog,
And it will ever be true."

Valiant the Bold accepted the sword,
And bowed to the dragon with flourish.
He wielded the sword with bravery and honor,
And never lost a skirmish.

*****

The next day, Valiant fought with a precision he had never felt before. Almost as if the sword knew what his opponent was going to do next. Valiant disarmed Ciam and leaned down to offer him a hand up.

Ciam waved away the assist and jumped to his feet. "Impressive. How does the sword feel?"

"Like an extension of my arm. It's marvelous." Valiant made a figure eight with the sword before sheathing it.

"I've never seen you move so well. The Patron's Sword is a great gift." Tempest eyed the sword. "Might I give it a try?"

Valiant almost refused, but that would be petty. He turned the handle end toward Tempest and bowed. "Shall we spar?"

Ciam handed Valiant his sword and stepped back. At first, the siblings fought without much of an audience. Tempest and Valiant sparred frequently, and Tempest always won. When Valiant landed the first hit, knocking Tempest off balance, those in the training area took notice.

Tempest looked at the sword in her hand and snarled. The sparring session turned into a fight. A fight Tempest eventually lost, when Valiant knocked the sword out of her hand and sent her tumbling. She lay on the ground breathing hard. Valiant appeared rested and relaxed.

Ridge walked out and extended his hand to Tempest, asking softly, "Did you forget what the sword does, my lady?"

"What?" Tempest was distracted as she picked up the sword and glared at it.

"Tulvir spoke plainly enough. The Patron's Sword holds its faith to Valiant. Even if someone else is wielding it, the sword works for him."

Tempest scowled and handed the sword back to him, who accepted the sword with a grin. For the first time, Valiant defeated Tempest in a sword fight.

A few hours later, Valiant leaned on the hall of the living bridge. Still smiling over his success on the training field today, he anticipated a fun evening. He had been warned that his defeat of Tempest was well-known now. He expected a few taunts about needing a magic sword to defeat his eldest sister. But since she had not lost to anyone, except Ridge, since attaining adulthood, the mocking would trivial.

Temperance opened the door and sighed. "You don't have to wait for me every evening. We both know you and Lady Talmai will meet up later. Go ahead and join her."

"What do you mean? I've been careful." The last thing he needed was for the courts to decide he had selected Lady Talmai as his mate. She was fun, but in his heart, Valiant knew that no other female would ever compare to Carwen.

"Yes, you have." Temperance patted his arm. "Fear not. Father has not observed anything to cause a display of anger. I know you better than most."

Valiant grinned in relief. As they approached the Hall of Battles, he asked, "Is there a male you favor? I could help you meet him, assuming I approve of your choice, of course."

Temperance laughed. Before she answered, she looked around to be sure no one, not even pixies, was around. "No. I would prefer someone who would move me from the Northern Realm."

Valiant nodded. He fully understood her desire. He wanted to leave the Northern Realm as well. They arrived in the feasting hall to find the Forest Lord talking with Algar, Ellwood's oldest assassin. Turning to face his son, Lord Ellwood smiled. "I hear you defeated Tempest this day. I am pleased you finally succeeded after so many failures."

"Thank you, Father." Valiant returned his smile. "I find a dragon-made sword to be a powerful ally."

Lord Ellwood looked confused, but a smile graced Algar's lips, and he nodded his approval. The smile was so rare that Valiant grinned as he walked Temperance past.

"Excellent response," Temperance whispered so that only a shifter would hear her. While she lacked their superior hearing, she did know how soft she could talk and still be heard.

*****

Valiant threw open the door to Tempest's treehouse. "Come."

"Really, brother mine? An order so early in the day? Carwen will be in camp when we arrive. She always is." Tempest closed her travel bag, and they walked down the hall to take their leave of Lord Ellwood.

Valiant didn't contradict Tempest, but he knew better than to assume Carwen would always wait for him. After taking their leave of court, Valiant opened a way, and they entered an open field near the sovereign's camp. It was Carwen's favorite place to gather herbs this time of year. He turned and looked in every direction. His face fell when he didn't see her.

Tempest patted him on the shoulder. "She can't sit around all day waiting for your arrival. I'm sure you'll find her in camp."

They arrived in camp to find Temperance and Taren demonstrating what they had learned with Esen. Two of the camp warriors attacked Temperance. True to form, she used the weight of one to toss him into the other. Both men landed in a heap.

"Nice." Tempest nodded.

Taren grinned. "Would you help with the next demonstration? Attack, no elements, but any weapon you choose."

Valiant shook his head, but Tempest dropped her bag and settled into a fighting stance.

"In your own time." Taren looked unconcerned. After nearly a minute, when Tempest didn't move at all, he added, "Whenever you're ready."

A few more seconds passed, then Tempest disappeared. Taren moved in a slow circle, trying to find her. "I should have said no spells, either."

The children laughed. Cadel pointed to the largest oak tree at the edge of the forest. The one the kids climbed.

Fully visible, Tempest sat on a large limb, feet swaying. She waved to the group and dropped out of the tree. As soon as her feet touched the ground, she ran full out. No weapons were drawn. She was going for speed and brute strength. When she jumped, Taren swooped down, kicking her off balance as he dove out of the way.

Tempest went tumbling across the ground. When she sat up, Taren offered her a hand, which she accepted. Taren said something softly to Tempest, and she laughed.

Valiant frowned. He never monitored either sister in the Seen as both seemed to favor the men of the Farseen. Was he wrong? Did Tempest think to have a fae in the Farseen and a shifter in the Seen? That would make a song worthy of the anger it would invoke.

Temperance and Taren explained what they had done and why. After the training, Tempest and Valiant walked Temperance to the field, where she opened a way and left. As they returned to the Alpha Clan's camp, Valiant asked, "Do you favor Taren?"

Genuine surprise covered Tempest's face. "No. I could see the attack he hoped for in his mind and provided it. He realized what I had done and told me so."

"Why help Taren?"

"Why not? You aren't the only one to notice he's changed. Like the rest of us, he grew up. Besides, he's always been kind to Temperance. While he made fun of you, and even me, he never did so to her. I always appreciated that about him."

"Do you think he and Temperance…"

Tempest slapped him on the shoulder. "No. He's kind to her. He's kind to anyone weaker than himself. You just never noticed because the two of you were too busy fighting over Carwen."

"Did you know he was interested in her?"

"Everyone knew he was, even Carwen."

*****

"Where are we going?" Valiant ran to catch up with Kyan and Tempest.

"You don't remember the way to Kavi's?" Tempest asked with a whole lot of duh.

"Of course. We're going to Kavi's. Where are we going from there?"

"We're going to explore the landmass to the west."

Valiant's mouth dropped open. "Cimil's land?"

"No." Kyan shook his head. "The land north of there. It has the same type of weather as we do. It's huge and much less populated than here, and Kavi enjoys getting away. We will travel mostly in our wolf forms."

"Why?" Tempest asked.

Kavi stepped out of the clearing. "The people of that area have skin that is reddish and darker than our own. They all have black hair and brown eyes."

"All of them? Are they shorter, like Esen's people?"

"Yes, all of the peoples in the west share straight black hair and brown eyes. And no, they range in height much as we do."

Kavi opened a way and walked through. Tempest and Valiant followed while Kyan brought up the rear. The thunderous sound of water rushing over the falls drowned out talk. Valiant grinned. Kavi brought them to waterfalls that would give even the Water Lord of the Western Realm pause. The most striking waterfall boasted a half-moon shape. The second, small by comparison, resembled any fast-moving water that plunged down a cliff. The third fell the same height as the first, but the width was a third the size. The waterfalls, caused by a drop from one enormous lake to another, provided a most impressive sight. Valiant couldn't take his eyes off the falling water. Eventually, Kavi tapped his shoulder and led them to a path. Valiant followed, but his eyes returned to the falls again and again. Following Kavi's example, they shifted and roamed the area as wolves. Only at night did they take human form to talk, and only if they found the shelter of a cave for privacy.

"This land is as green as the Northern Realm." Valiant popped a berry in his mouth. They ate meat in wolf form because they didn't want to make a fire that might draw attention their way. The hunters they had passed did not seem interested in killing wolves when more edible creatures were around, but Valiant suspected that they would kill for the warm fur. And he was certain they would kill other humans, especially ones that looked nothing like the inhabitants of this area. Regardless of dimension, anyone different was suspect. It had always been so.

"Wait till tomorrow." Kyan reclined on the cave entrance and watched the land below them as the sun dipped behind the mountains.

"What's tomorrow?"

"Enough talk. We sleep as wolves." Kavi shifted and got comfortable.

The next morning, the four wolves continued west. They passed the last of a series of enormous lakes and entered open plains. The grasslands were flat with rivers and streams that provided plenty of water. The wolves made good time for prey was plentiful, and the vast land allowed the wolves to stay away from the local humans.

They trotted through the fields. Tempest slowed and growled at a stand of trees. Valiant would have joined her, but Kavi yelled in his head to stop. He did, mostly because the scream hurt his head.

Kyan leaped ahead and stood between Tempest and the wolf that came out of the forest. He snarled before turning his back on her and facing the wolf.

Valiant finally smelled what Tempest had. The new wolf was a shifter. The new wolf stopped a few feet in front of Kyan, both wolves bowed and moved into the forest together.

Guess they know each other. Tempest spoke to Valiant mind-to-mind.

Valiant nodded. It appears so. They could have warned us.

We weren't sure we would see him on this trip. We never are. Kavi passed Valiant and Tempest following Kyan, who shrugged their wolf shoulders and followed.

When they neared a cave, the unknown wolf shifted. "Who are the young pups?"

Tempest shifted as well. "Tempest. This is my brother, Valiant. Who are you?"

"I'm Ilar. You must be Rayna's young? That makes you my grandchildren."

"Your Cwenhild's mate?" Tempest raised a disbelieving eye on a male she had never heard of.

Ilar laughed. "I was for many years. In time I found life as the mate of the sovereign was not for me. I convinced Rayna to open a way to this area and settled here."

"Are there no other shifters living with you?" Valiant asked. He had assumed Ilar had his own clan, but he sensed no other shifters.

"No. I prefer it that way, as Kavi and Kyan well know."

"Brother, you always enjoy our visits." Kavi shifted and ignored his growl. "Don't growl at me. I know you are happy to see us. My sister may not appreciate you, but I do."

"I enjoy your visit. Kyan's, not so much." When Kyan growled, Ilar said, "I don't begrudge you your anger, son, but you are better suited to the job than I ever was."

"Will you not shift, uncle?" Valiant asked Kyan.

"It's better if he doesn't. He and Ilar fight if they are both in human form," Kavi explained.

Valiant raised an amused eyebrow. "You have father issues. The man who lectured me about respecting my father, at least to his face."

Kyan shifted and focused on Valiant. "Your father, for all his faults, didn't leave the day you attained your majority saying, "You're an adult now. You can serve as the sovereign's assassin.""

"In truth?" Valiant turned a disbelieving eye to Ilar. "That was not very well done, Ilar."

"Why have we never heard of you?" Tempest asked.

Prized

"I suspect Cwenhild still has a mandate that no one shall speak my name in her camp." Ilar reached for a waterskin, took a swig, and passed it to Kyan.

Kyan growled but took a sip and passed it to Tempest. "This is Ilan's best skill. His ale will warm any heart."

Tempest took a swig, nodded, and passed it to Valiant, who took a long draw and smacked his lips together. "No one in the five realms makes an ale this smooth."

"Will you not share, nephew?"

Valiant blushed and handed over the skin. "Didn't think you would want any. You don't normally partake of strong liquids."

"You and Father do not bleed your emotions and thoughts. Kyan is mind-blind, and Tempest locks her mind from all. There are only animals nearby, meaning I can have a sip or two. If the libation lowers my blocks, it will not be too painful."

Valiant settled in and watched Kyan with Ilar for a while. Kyan didn't really seem as angry as Kavi indicated, but he wasn't overly friendly either. After consuming more of the ale, Valiant walked outside to clear his head. He ended up sitting on a rock, watching flashes of fire cross the sky. The fae sky watchers said they were bits of rock flying through space. He had never seen so many at one time. Valiant was surprised when Ilar joined him.

"How is Rayna?"

"When did you last see her?"

"The day I left. She has never come to visit, and I cannot open a way to the Farseen. Even if I could, I have never been to the Farseen. And I dare not return to the sovereign's lands."

"Rayna is well. She is powerful and well able to protect herself."

"You have the ability to take more than one form. You should, but be sure to keep a couple hidden. You never know when the fae might start another war."

"What do you know?" Tempest asked as she and Kyan joined them.

"I sometimes see flashes of the future, but it could change. You should both be prepared." Ilar walked back into his cave.

"Interesting. Do you think he's helping us or making us worry about the future for no reason?" Valiant asked.

"Perhaps both," Kyan retorted. "He is always cryptic with his visions, but it normally pays to listen to his words."

They stayed with Ilar a couple of days before they continued their journey west, but he wouldn't speak of his vision again. They traveled until they saw a mountain range. The high mountains extended beyond where trees could grow, running north to south as far as the eye could see.

"How large is this landmass?" Valiant asked when they stopped traveling one evening. They had moved closer to the mountains but were still a solid day and a half from the mountain base.

"We are a little over halfway to the other large body of water. This landmass alone is twice as large as the entire Farseen dimension."

Tempest asked, "Why does the sovereign not claim this land? Diverse wildlife and fertile land. There is nothing to want here."

"We cannot blend in with the population here. At least not most of us. Ilar remains in wolf form most of the time. There aren't many shifters who can do so without losing themselves to the animal. I believe we've traveled enough. Time to return home." Kyan opened a way and returned them to Kavi's land.

"Why did we take that trip? I enjoyed myself, but why?" Tempest asked.

"Because that was the only way you would ever meet your shifter grandfather. You may tell Rayna you met him or not. That decision is yours. You must never speak his name in Cwenhild's presence or anywhere within her camp." Kyan bowed to his aunt. Farewell, Kavi."

As they returned to the sovereign's camp, Valiant asked, "Should we mention him to Temperance?"

"To what end? She no longer visits the Seen and has expressed she has no interest in shifter matters," Tempest said.

Valiant shrugged. He always thought Temperance made that statement to save her the hurt of knowing she would never shift, but he knew he would follow Tempest's lead as he did in most things. It made life easier.

A few weeks after they returned to the Farseen, Valiant approached Tempest as she meditated. "Did you choose a new form?"

"Yes, the large falcon we saw on our visit west of the waterfalls. Did you?" Although they had seen many waterfalls on that trip, Tempest didn't clarify which waterfall. No need. The cascades in the west were impressive, but none compared with the three waterfalls where Kavi had opened a way on their first visit.

"Eagle. The one with the brown feathers, not the white head."

Prized

"Good. The white-headed eagle is too distinctive."

Valiant smiled tightly when Tempest approved of his chosen form. Though he had picked his flying form for the reason she had stated, it irritated him that she gave her approval. "Exactly. I'm ready to return to the large landmass anytime. Our new forms will blend in and allow us to travel easier."

At the next full moon, Valiant and Tempest shifted into their wolf forms and left the residence heading for the cave they frequented in their childhood. To protect their new forms, Tempest layered a privacy spell over the entire cave. Within the safety of the cave, they shifted to their new bird forms and practiced flying.

Birthing Explosion

4905 BCE – 4897 BCE

Chapter 12 – 4905 BCE

"What's taking so long? Can nothing be done?" Valiant prowled the living bridge between his treehouse and the one assigned to Tempest. Tempest and Ridge still used those rooms when they visited the Northern Realm residence, which was frequent. It was something Valiant didn't understand. If he had another place to live, he would never be here.

"In my experience, no. Females give birth on varied timetables. The process cannot be hurried." Ridge didn't pace, but he fidgeted with a puzzle box, a sure sign he was restless.

"Is she in labor?" Kyan asked. When the other men glared at him, he shrugged. "In my experience, a woman in labor yells."

"You thought Lady Tempest would yell?" Valiant asked, incredulously.

"Your point is valid," Kyan agreed.

"Oh, my," Lady Rayna's soft voice echoed through the bridge. She had been pacing.

Kyan rushed to her side. "What is it, sister mine?"

"My water broke."

"Come, I'll walk you to your treehouse." Kyan took Rayna's arm and moved her down the hallway of the living bridge.

Valiant watched them go. "Will everyone give birth today?"

Ridge didn't look up from his puzzle box. The servants and guards stood silently. As the sun dipped behind the mountains, Kyan returned.

"What news?" Ridge asked.

"Rayna has given birth to triplets," Kyan said. When Ridge stood, Kyan added, "Lord Ellwood has instructed Ash to attend to the notifications. You have leave to remain here."

Prized

Ridge leaned back on the wall and returned to his puzzle box.

Valiant was glad that his mother had delivered healthy children, but still, he glared at Kyan. "How is it that Lady Rayna delivered first when Lady Tempest has been in labor longer?"

"There are no rules to the birthing process," Kyan explained.

"I don't like it." Valiant resumed pacing, and asked, "Have these triplets been named?"

"Saffron, Clarity, and Fauna in order of birth."

Valiant frowned. Three additional sisters. He had hoped for at least one brother. Perhaps a brother would have given Ellwood the son he wanted, and Valiant would be free.

Temperance approached the men. She had been in the Seen for the past few weeks training with Esen. "Cwenhild gave birth to Loane, Jocosa, and Katell this morning. I returned to announce the news and find that Mother has given birth, and Tempest soon shall."

"Three girls?" Kyan asked.

Temperance nodded.

Kyan sighed. His life was overrun with females.

*****

Lord Ellwood looked at his three daughters asleep in their bassinets. Daughters? He had expected at least one boy who would become the power of this set of triplets. Valiant was a disappointment, always following Tempest's lead, and neither child obeyed him without question.

Looking between the bassinets, Ellwood saw no difference between the girls. Similar in looks, they weren't identical, but he hadn't expected them to be. Fae rarely were, though Tempest and Temperance were except for their hair color and temperament. He saw no hint as to which child would be the power.

Lord Ellwood turned to the door when he heard a noise out in the hallway. When he heard a faint knock, he said, "Enter."

"My Lord, Lady Tempest is in distress."

Ellwood didn't notice the nannies move in as he rushed past them to check on his eldest. She was still in labor twelve hours after Rayna gave birth.

Ellwood stopped by Valiant. "What happened?"

"The midwife said the baby is still turned wrong." Valiant didn't take his eyes off the door.

Ellwood scoffed. "That's easy enough to fix with animals. Surely, it's not a problem for our females." Looking around for his advisor, Ellwood asked, "Where's Ridge?"

Valiant shrugged. "He joined Tempest in her chambers."

Ellwood and Kyan exchanged looks. The father was never invited into chambers until after the birth unless it was to say goodbye to the mother.

A few minutes later, a relieved Ridge opened the door. "Lady Tempest has gifted me a son. His name is Layton. Both are doing well."

Valiant twirled Temperance around as they laughed.

Ellwood placed a smile of approval on his face, but the smile didn't reach his eyes. Ridge had the one thing Ellwood wanted, a son to mold in his image. With Tempest and Ridge as parents, Layton should be a power in his own right.

*****

Valiant opened a way to the Seen. When Kyan attended the younger triplets and Layton's first day in court, he had told Valiant that a visit to Ilar was necessary. That's all. Kyan refused to say anything else. Now that Tempest and Rayna were busy with their new babies, it seemed like a good time to take a trip. Besides, the triplets could be loud when they weren't happy, and Rayna wanted them with her instead of in the nursery.

Valiant flew through in bird form near the valley where Ilar lived. He watched Ilar for a while, wondering what was so important.

Ilar, in human form, stoked his fire. "Grandson, I know you're there. Shift and join me."

Dropping down from his perch, Valiant shifted as he touched the ground. "Kyan said you wanted to see me."

"Yes, Kavi said you have my gift. It's time you were trained."

"I am trained."

"No, you wield power you don't yet control." Ilar handed Valiant some dried meat. "Have you noticed that elemental powers arc away from you?"

Valiant shrugged. There was something strange about how elements behaved around him, even with Kyan's training. Valiant thought he was lucky.

"It's not luck, boy. You have a personal shield that repels elemental powers. It also repels elementals. Makes 'em sick, according to my mother. To be clear, a strong elemental can fight through the repulsion and kill you."

So that's why elementals never bother him. He fingered the carnelian dagger Kyan had given him.

Ilar grinned. "You should continue to wear that blade, but it isn't necessary for your protection."

"How does this protection work?"

"I don't know how it works. I can tell you how to make use of it."

Narrowing his eyes on Ilar, Valiant asked, "Can you read my mind? Really read it?"

"I can hear what you think if I want. It's one of the reasons I like being alone."

Valiant would have growled at the invasion of privacy, but he was more interested in the protection power. Finally! Valiant had a skill, a useful one, that Tempest lacked. "Let's get to it."

Days later, when Valiant returned to the Farseen, Ilar had taught him many other things besides how to control his rare gift. As Valiant opened a way, he knew two things. He was a lot more powerful than he thought, and he wouldn't tell Tempest. It was nice to know something about himself that no one, except Ilar, knew.

*****

"Don't we have a nanny for this?" Ridge looked over at Tempest. She laughed at him. Laughed. At. Him. He was one of the scariest beings in the Farseen, and she didn't even try to hide her mirth. No one else would dare, at least not to his face. In disgust, he turned back to his task, wrapping the triangle of cloth around his son. Mission complete, he held Layton up and watched the material fall away from the child. Layton took this moment to relieve himself.

Tempest's laughter filled his residence. Her laughter always warmed his heart, but he didn't like the reason she was laughing.

"Seriously, where is Nanny?"

"I gave her leave to visit her mother, who just delivered a baby." Tempest walked over, took the boy, and quickly placed the cloth properly and securely.

Perhaps all women knew how to do these things. Ridge smiled and kissed her on the forehead. "Enjoy this time with our son. I have a task to complete for Lord Ellwood."

"You do not." Tempest glared at him.

"Yes, I do." Ridge left the nursery. As far as he was concerned, Nanny had better enjoy her free day. She would not be allowed another until Layton was old enough to relieve himself without assistance of any kind.

Cleaned up, Ridge took the path by the Kaveri River, passing Psyche Falls before turning left. He skirted the southern edge of the wastelands until he was near Father Aldous's northern residence. Father Aldous was the oldest and scariest fae Ridge knew. Why he was called father by everyone was a question no one could or would answer. Even the fae queens called him thus. Ridge knew of no one who willingly argued with Father Aldous and every realm provided land – chosen by Aldous himself – where the powerful fae built a home. Aldous was the original unaligned fae, not because he was expelled from the courts, as were most unaligned fae, but because he was that strong.

Ridge topped a hill and saw Father Aldous's treehouse surrounded by the red dragons who were loyal to Aldous and not the red supreme matriarch. At least, that's what everyone said, though no one knew who said it first. The dragons looked at him but made no move to block his path. Having made this trek before, Ridge took that as permission and crossed the creek to climb the steps and knock on the door.

A smile spread across Ridge's face. He had been assigned this task a couple of days ago. It was a minor task that did not need to be performed this day, but it was a task he was assigned by Lord Ellwood. Scary or not, Father Aldous just got him out of diaper duty.

Chapter 13 – 4901 BCE

"You're back early." Tempest remained on the ground while Layton ran around in circles, throwing drops of water on the flowers and anyone walking by. It was a pleasant warm afternoon, and most were amused by the antics of the child Lord Ellwood doted on. When Layton threw water at Valiant, Valiant grinned and pushed the water into the river, causing Layton to laugh and chase the water.

"Yes, the Southern Realm was boring," Temperance said. She watched the merfolk in the Kaveri River toss water back and forth with Layton.

Valiant tossed his pack to a waiting pixie and bowed to his sisters. "Come, Layton, I'll show you how to hold a bow."

"Can I shoot an arrow?" Layton ran and jumped into his uncle's arms.

Valiant caught Layton, amazed at the boy's ability to trust, and said, "I don't see why not."

"Be careful," Tempest said absently. She wasn't worried. Valiant and Tempest worked hard to prevent Lord Ellwood from doing to Layton what was done to Valiant. Once they were out of sight, Tempest asked, "What happened?"

"I tire of fools who want to claim me as if I'm a prize."

Tempest laughed. "You are a prize, sister mine." She looked over as her youngest siblings ran into the garden with their mother trailing behind. Saffron ran to the river merfolk to play, while Fauna talked to the plants. Tempest didn't look closely enough to see if the plants were talking back or not. Perhaps Fauna was talking to pixies or woodland fae. Clarity stood with Rayna, plotting who knew what.

"Did the Western Realm offer no amusements?" Rayna asked.

Temperance dropped to the ground beside Tempest. "Lord River is a fool."

"Then why is he the lord of the realm?" Clarity asked.

"The queen's pleasure, and fighting skills, not intelligence, determine who is lord of a realm," Tempest explained.

"Question you my intelligence?" Lord Ellwood asked.

Tempest knew he had been listening for a while and knew which realm lord was being discussed. Before Tempest could respond, Clarity said, "Not you, Father. Lord River. Lady Temperance said he is a fool."

"And so, he is." Ellwood laughed. Turning to Temperance, he added, "But surely that's not the only reason you rejected him."

"No, Lord Ellwood. While at court, it became obvious to me that Lady Aerten holds Lord River's favor. I will not exchange vows with a male who loves another, regardless of the benefit it would bring both realms." Temperance took a deep breath. It was the first time she had ever spoken thus to her father, and she doubted he appreciated her point of view.

Before Ellwood could respond, Rayna nodded her head. "Quite right. Vows are hard enough without fighting a cast-off consort, especially one the entire court dotes on. Did anyone in the Western Realm catch your interest?"

"No. But since someone is sure to mention it, Father Aldous and I spent a significant amount of time together."

Lord Ellwood smiled. That would be a worthy union. Much better than a blending with the Western Realm.

Temperance stood, dusted off her traveling clothes, and turned her gaze on Tempest. "He asked a lot of questions about you, sister mine. None at all of me. If you ever decide to drop Ridge as your consort, I believe Father Aldous will be standing by to heal your wounded heart." Temperance walked away.

Tempest gaped after her sister. Why would she ever turn Ridge away?

"Can you have more than one love at a time?" Clarity asked.

Lord Ellwood laughed, kissed his wife on the cheek, and returned to his duties.

*****

Valiant opened a way and led Tempest into the Seen. Not to the shifter sovereign's home or to the large landmass to the east where they had made a few friends, both human and shifter, but to the northern portion of the immense landmass west of the sovereign's territory. Their first trip had been with Kavi and Kyan to a spectacular waterfall before going to visit Ilar.

This time they came alone. Tempest and Valiant flew out of the way west of Ilar's home at the base of the high, rocky tipped mountains in their bird forms that no one but them knew about. They didn't stop to visit with their grandfather but flew past the vast plains blessed with vegetation and game into the arid mountains. The peoples of this area had black hair and a skin color similar to Cimil, the blood-sucking demon Tempest still feared. Cimil's home on this land was far south of their current location. Going further west, they flew over the high mountain range. Together they found a good site for a way far from humans high in the mountains. This location would become their point of arrival for future trips.

The next day they flew west from their mountain retreat, traveling further than they ever had before. Enormous canyons with striking stone monoliths and impressive arches were common. Humans were not so common, but a few made their homes near the large river that cut through the area. They followed the river and discovered that canyons were common in this part of the Seen. They continued for a while until Valiant dove for the ground.

Valiant had been unable to stop himself from landing and taking human form. Something he probably shouldn't do here as it was doubtful these humans had ever seen blonde hair and pale skin.

Tempest joined him and shifted to human form. "Amazing."

They stood on the rim of the largest canyon they had yet to see. Horizontal stripes of color gave the gorge a stunning look.

"For a desert, there is much life here." Valiant pointed to sheep with large horns, deer, and many types of birds. "This river must be enough to sustain them."

Sound alerted them to visitors. Both shifted back to their bird forms and flew across the gorge to hide within the safety of tree branches.

A group of humans stopped on the rim and performed a death ceremony. Once the body was ashes, and the fire died out, the humans left, leaving behind mementos of the life lost.

The duo flew back across the canyon. Valiant picked up a weapon he had seen before, but only from a distance. "Do you think they will miss this? I want to make my own atlatl, and this could be my guide."

"We don't know their customs. Perhaps they will come back for it."

Valiant nodded and returned it where he found it. They flew again, continuing to follow the river. Waterfalls were a surprise in this desert area, and they stopped by a large one, shifted back to human, and swam for a while. Careful to not be seen by the humans, they stayed for a few days, exploring.

"We should return to our camp. I'll open a way."

"No, I want to fly over the river again." Valiant shifted and flew.

Tempest shrugged but followed her brother. When he flew to the location of the ceremony they had witnessed, Valiant shifted and picked up the atlatl.

"You still want to take that," Tempest said. It wasn't a question.

"Yes, but I don't want to show disrespect to their dead."

"Leave something in fair exchange."

Valiant pulled out his slingshot, but the Seen did not have the necessary materials to create such a weapon, yet. He placed it back in his sack and pulled out a boomerang. Unlike the basic boomerangs found in the Seen, his was layered with different types of wood to create a design. It had been a gift from Lady Talmai. He was fond of the weapon, but for the fae, the exchange must be a match for what was taken. He desired both the atlatl and the boomerang. He laid the boomerang down and placed the atlatl in his bag.

The siblings shifted and flew away.

A young boy who was almost a man watched the bird people fly away. Crawling out of the rocks where he had hidden when he saw the people who were fair of skin and hair, he approached his father's things. Today he was tasked with retrieving the items. As the oldest son, they were now his to use. His father's atlatl was of good design but common. The thing the birdman left was unique. A gift to be treasured and a tool to learn to wield.

He returned to his tribe, wondering if anyone would believe him when he told the story of what he had seen. Perhaps one of the elders would know how to use the gift from the birdman.

*****

Prized

"Lady Tempest." Sorbus stopped in front of her and bowed low, ignoring Ridge and Valiant. Saffron and Clarity shuffled behind him. Both appeared to have been in a fight.

"Yes?"

Her icy question did not bode well, but it didn't stop Sorbus, who forged ahead. "Mistress Clarity and Mistress Saffron had a small disagreement that spilled over to the practice field, disturbing the warriors' training. Pinus brought them to the Forest Lord's receiving rooms. Ash suggested that you might wish to deal with them. Less disturbance to the court schedule."

Valiant watched both girls lift pleading eyes to their eldest sister. They had obviously been fighting. A fact that would heap a lot of trouble on their young heads if Father was apprised of the event. Lately, Tempest had been called upon to deal with her younger sisters as if she were their mother for just that reason. More of the guards feared Lady Rayna's temper than they did Lord Ellwood's.

Ridge walked away with Layton in tow. Tempest rolled her eyes as he retreated and turned to Sorbus. "You may entrust them to me."

Sorbus bowed and followed Ridge.

Tempest turned back to her sisters. "Explain."

The girls tried to speak over each other. Each wished to be the first to tell their side of the story.

Valiant winked at Tempest and whistled loudly. "One at a time."

"Ow, that hurt." Clarity placed her hands over her ears.

Saffron huffed, but said, "You go first."

Clarity shot her sister a superior look. "Saffron was showing off. Using wind just to irritate me."

Tempest raised a single eyebrow.

"Well, she did. She does it all the time. Calling elements whenever I'm nearby, just because she can call all four, and I can't."

Saffron shook her head. "I was practicing calling a little wind at a time, as Temperance instructed me to do. No one was around when I started. When Clarity showed up in the garden, I realized I had called wind too long and had to release it slowly. If I had just dropped it, I would have flattened cook's garden."

"I think Saffron was right to slowly release her wind, don't you, Tempest?" Valiant chuckled.

"Why?" Clarity looked between the two.

"Tempest knows all about upsetting cook. It's not something you girls want to do." Valiant bowed and left them.

Later that evening, Lord Ellwood approached Valiant. "Why did you and Lady Tempest discipline your younger siblings? They should have been brought to me or at least Lady Rayna."

Valiant hid his irritation. Valiant hadn't done anything.

"Lord Ellwood, Mistress Saffron and Mistress Clarity were brought to me, not Valiant. They had a silly spat. They should have been turned over to Mother, but I saw no reason for their escort to spend the day looking for her with two tired and unhappy children in tow." Tempest stood by Valiant, facing their father. "Both were punished for disturbing the warriors in their training."

"And the fight?" Ellwood asked.

"I told them what you told us when we fought as children." Tempest grinned. "I told them to do so away from prying eyes."

Lord Ellwood laughed and walked away.

Valiant's eyes narrowed on his father's retreating form. Had he said those words, anger, not laughter, would have greeted them.

*****

"I very much want to." Layton peered out the window.

Back from his trip to the Seen, Valiant slowed his movement at Layton's words and angled toward his nephew. The hallway was empty except for the two of them. Valiant peered out the window but didn't see any Farseen creatures hovering. Was someone trying to use Layton for some scheme? It didn't seem likely. Most feared the ire of the boy's parents. "Who are you talking to?"

"N... No one." Layton stepped back.

Valiant raised an eyebrow in a fair imitation of Tempest's trademark expression.

"I want to see a gargoyle move." Layton hung his head.

Valiant laughed. "As do I, but they only move if someone in the house does something to lose the gargoyle's protection, or if they are defending the residence."

"You've never seen one move?" Layton asked.

"No one has attacked our residence since I was born, so no. If you ever observe one, let me know. I would like to see that as well. I'm going to the practice fields if you wish to attend me."

Layton grinned and fell in step with his uncle. Too young to wield actual weapons, when they entered the field, the nymphs brought

Layton his bow with seven soft-tipped arrows in the quiver. They handed Valiant his bow and a quiver of silver-tipped arrows.

"Do you remember what we discussed last time?" Valiant fired three arrows in rapid succession. All three hit the center of the target. No one commented, but he didn't expect them to. His entire life, the only comments he received on the practice field were taunts.

"Steady hands, calm breathing, and focus," Layton said.

"Very good. Show me."

Layton looked at the target which had been moved in for him and snarled.

Valiant grinned. "The target will move back as you grow. Your arms cannot pull a bow with the same power as mine. At least not yet." Valiant had insisted that Layton be allowed to grow into his future role. Valiant's most miserable memories centered around attempting to hit a target that no young child could have hit. He would not allow Ellwood to do to Layton what was done to him. "Forget your anger. The only thing that is important right now is the target."

Layton took a deep breath, held it, and let loose his arrow. The arrow hit the center of the target but fell to the ground because of the soft tips.

"Perfect."

"Nice shot."

Layton beamed at the praise. Valiant smiled, still surprised that the warriors were so kind to Layton when they had been so cruel to him. Of course, Ellwood doted on his grandson as he never had his son.

Chapter 14 – 4899 BC

"Are you sure we're allowed?" Fauna asked. She peered inside the cave. Although some attention to comfort had been made, and there were supplies within, it was apparent the cave no longer saw regular use.

Saffron and Layton exchanged shrugs. Fauna was the timid one, never knowingly disobeying her elders. Saffron said, "We weren't told we couldn't."

"Because we didn't ask," Layton muttered under his breath, knowing only Saffron heard him. Layton had learned long ago that Saffron was the only one of the triplets whose hearing matched his. When Saffron grinned, he raised his voice and added, "If Mother, Temperance, and Valiant played here, why can't we?" Layton asked.

"Of course, we can." Clarity pushed past the others and walked in.

Layton had expected that. Clarity would do anything Tempest had done if only to prove herself Tempest's equal.

"It is nicely organized." Fauna tapped a pillow, and dust filled the room. "But it could do with a good cleaning."

Layton looked around the cave. "We should thank Temperance."

"Why?" Clarity's eyebrows popped up.

"Do you think Tempest or Valiant would bother to organize the cave into functions?"

"Excellent point." Saffron watched a cadre of pixies fly into the cave.

A pixie hovered in front of Saffron. "I am Duni, leader of our coterie. Are you returning to play? We used to keep the place clean for

Valiant and the ladies Tempest and Temperance. We would be pleased to do so for you."

"Great. That's settled." Clarity's eyes lit up, and she twirled around in the cave. "Come, Fauna, let's check out that nook."

As Clarity and Fauna moved further into the cave, Saffron moved closer to the pixies and whispered, "Whom do you report to?"

Duni looked nervous, and her brethren moved closer to the entrance.

Layton raised his eyebrows, "Who?"

"Your father has always been kind to us." Duni kept her voice soft.

"Are you saying Father protected the others and now us?" Layton also whispered.

"I would prefer not to say that," Duni said.

"Did Tempest know?" Saffron asked.

"She knew we cleaned," Duni replied.

Layton narrowed his eyes on the pixie. "What didn't she know?"

"How would I know such information?"

Saffron grinned. "There must be another group, perhaps nymphs who watch this place, probably for Ridge."

"And Mother didn't know?" Layton shook his head. "I, for one, will not mention it to her."

"Agreed," Saffron said. She bowed to Duni. "Having pixies keep the place clean will be nice."

*****

Ellwood approached his youngest triplets and his grandson identifying plants in the garden. "How are you this fine day?"

"Lord Ellwood." The greeting came in unison from his daughters, who curtsied and his grandson who bowed.

Lady Adaryn, their teacher, turned and bowed. "They have mastered their studies for today and have the afternoon free."

"Excellent. Layton, attend me." Ellwood walked away with the assurance of someone accustomed to having their orders followed.

Layton ran to catch up. He had seen the fire in Clarity's eyes and knew she would corner him later. She didn't understand that being the focus of Lord Ellwood's attention was not always a good thing. He fell into step beside his grandfather but didn't speak. It was all he could do to keep up with Ellwood's stride. Layton wasn't surprised when Ellwood turned toward the training fields.

Sorbus, one of Ellwood's private guards, waited with an assortment of weapons for the Forest Lord.

Layton swallowed. He had heard the stories and knew Ellwood had mocked Valiant often. Layton had never been so treated. Was now his turn?

Ellwood handed Layton an atlatl. "Have you seen this weapon before?"

"Yes. Valiant has one from his travels in the Seen. He's very accurate with it."

"So I hear," Ellwood murmured. "Has he instructed you in its use?"

Layton squirmed. "I have watched him use it and tried it once."

"Show me." Ellwood handed him the atlatl.

Taking his time, making sure to calm his breathing, Layton took aim and let the dart fly. He watched the dart fall short of the mark, but his aim had been true. He glanced up to see his grandfather's reaction and was surprised to see a smile.

"Acceptable. With some practice, you will become proficient."

"I am pleased you find my attempt agreeable."

"If you were older, I would expect you to hit the target, but at your age, I am content."

After Ellwood's words, other warriors on the field offered words of encouragement as well.

Ellwood turned and saw Valiant watching. Raising a beckoning hand, he said, "Come Valiant. Your student awaits." Only after Ellwood walked away did he allow the smile to touch his lips. Ellwood had always been able to read his children better than they thought. Valiant had been relieved that Layton was being treated fairly, and then he had been angry that he had never received encouragement from his father. Just as Ellwood had planned.

Chapter 15 – 4897 BCE

Layton calmed his breathing and marched nervously onto the practice field alone. Always before, someone walked with him. He doubted he would receive the same deference from the warriors without an escort.

"Young Master Layton. What weapon are you training with today?" Pinus asked.

Layton glanced at his bow and quiver of arrows. Before he could stop himself, he asked, "Is your eyesight failing you? Is there nothing the healers can do?"

The laughter from the warriors told Layton they disliked Pinus more than him. That was good news.

Cypress clapped Sorbus on the shoulder. "I believe Layton will be a nice addition to the guard."

"Indeed." Sorbus walked over and stopped beside the post where Layton placed his quiver. "Were you given a specific area to work on this day?"

"No. Father said to practice, and he would join me later. I thought to work on various stances."

"A worthy goal to be sure, but Ridge will provide the best instruction on that. Might I suggest you simply use this time for target practice."

Valiant joined them, no longer jealous but pleased his nephew wasn't taunted as he had been. "Sorbus is right. Let us take aim at the target."

Layton watched the warriors move away. Valiant wasn't a favorite with the guard, but he didn't know why.

186

*****

Valiant escorted Temperance to the feasting hall. He wished his sister would pick a fool and exchange vows, or at least pick a consort as Tempest had. For nearly one hundred years, Valiant had stood as opposition to any male who thought to garner his sister's favor. He didn't like Ridge, but at least he didn't have to worry about Tempest. Not that he ever had. He frequently beat a beau before Tempest could, knowing that the guy would survive the humiliation of being beaten by a brother better than taking a beating from the lady he pursued.

He felt Temperance stiffen and turned as Pinus stepped out from behind one of the pillars. Valiant said, "Admiring the Forest Lord's fighting prowess?"

"Huh?"

Valiant rolled his eyes. Pinus had zero social skills. Pointing to the pillar, Valiant said, "The Battle of the Home Wood. It's one of my favorites." Mostly because it was a battle fought by the previous Forest Lord and not his father.

"Oh yes, good fight." Pinus moved closer to Temperance and held out his arm. "May I escort you to your table?"

"She's on her brother's arm, you oaf." Elm turned to Valiant. "Lady Talmai is looking for you, Valiant. I can escort Lady Temperance to her table if she does not object."

Lady Temperance took Elm's arm. "Go. See what Lady Talmai wants."

Valiant bowed and left. Elm was his friend, and Temperance had mentioned that she always felt safe with him. He turned back. He didn't want his best friend and his sister involved with each other.

"There you are," Lady Talmai said from across the room.

Valiant forgot all about Temperance. Lady Talmai was in a lovely green gown cut in the most fascinating way. The back was cut low to the small of her back. Somehow, the front was lower. The skirt was cut from the floor straight up the thigh on her right side. She walked toward him, and he found it hard to take his eyes off the sway of the skirt that offered promise but revealed nothing. Valiant forced his eyes to look up at her face. 'Twas a lovely face. "I came in search of you as soon as I heard you were looking for me."

"How kind you are."

Prized

"Allow me to escort you into the feasting hall." Valiant held out his arm and bowed. She slid her arm through his, and they strolled into the hall. Neither noticed the pillars of great battles fought.

After the meal, and dancing, Valiant took Lady Talmai out on the balcony for some air. They were in a secluded area, completely hidden from view by the many strategically placed plants. He knew they were safe from prying eyes because Valiant had seen to their placement just this afternoon. She leaned in, and Valiant closed the distance. The kiss was gentle and full of promise.

"How dare you." Temperance's voice was a furious whisper.

Valiant jumped back. When he didn't see Temperance, he looked through the plants and saw Temperance in Pinus's arms. Valiant pushed through the plants, knocking over pots. "Lady Talmai, please escort my sister back to the main hall. Take her to Lady Tempest."

Talmai sighed but did as instructed.

Valiant closed in on Pinus. Pinus was a fool and had destroyed what had promised to be an enjoyable evening. The fight, if it could be called that, was quick and decisive. Valiant was accomplished in hand-to-hand, and Pinus possessed no offensive or defensive skills. When it was over, Valiant was not surprised to see many of the males in court watching. He was concerned that a couple of bards had observed the exchange. There was naught to be done about it now.

The next morning Valiant chose to have first repast in his rooms. He left immediately after to meet with the Eastern Realm on Lord Ellwood's order. As a result, he barely returned in time to change and rush to the feasting hall for the evening repast.

"Father knows about the bard's new song," Temperance said as he sat down.

"What new song?" And why did he care? The bards were always writing new songs.

"The Unlucky Suitor." Elm grinned. "Next time you assault someone for addressing your sister, you should make sure there are no bards around."

Valiant winced. Another song his father would use to taunt him.

*****

Saffron heard Tempest approach before she saw her. Excellent hearing was a gift Saffron had had from birth. She watched Tempest, wearing a flowing skirt instead of the fighting leathers she wore most days, drop to the sand beside her.

188

"Mistress Saffron, why aren't you in court as Father requested?"

"Are you here to make me go back? It's boring." Saffron couldn't keep the whine out of her voice.

"No, sister mine, but others might, if only to preen before Father. You should go deeper in the woods to stay hidden if that is your goal, but you must have someone with you."

"You never took a guard," Saffron replied indignantly.

"And for that reason, I had to kill a werewolf when I was your age. Always enter the woods with a friend, if not a guard."

Saffron used a stick to draw in the sand and admitted, "All of my friends are too afraid of Father to do anything without approval. Even Clarity and Fauna run to him for everything. Fauna for permission. Clarity for approval."

"It sounds to me like you need to make new friends." Tempest stood and brushed sand from her skirt while peering into the reeds. "You are not to go exploring without a friend, but remember, new friends can become best friends. Trust your heart, for yours is pure and will not lead you astray." Tempest left.

Saffron sighed. Tempest spoke in riddles whenever she wanted to teach. It was irritating and hard to understand what her eldest sister was really saying.

Something large splashed in the river. "Who's there?" Saffron's demand lost its punch since her voice wavered.

Tehuti used his wings to hover above the reeds. "Only me, Tehuti, and Kailani, my sister. She is sleeping. We didn't mean to scare you."

Saffron looked Tehuti over. He had nymph wings and merfolk tail fins. "I wasn't afraid. Well, not much," she conceded before walking past the reeds to the edge of the river, "You are new to my father's land."

Tehuti nodded, "Indeed, we are."

"Where were you before? Why did you leave? Where's your family?" The questions came rapid-fire as Saffron eyed the newcomers.

"So many questions, but you didn't ask what we are," Tehuti smiled just a little. She was the first person he had met who didn't immediately demand verification that they were not fully one thing or the other.

Saffron pointed at their tail fins and wings. "You can only be the Water Sky twins. Tempest sang your song the other day. Your mother is a mermaid and your father a forest nymph, which means you are at home in the sky and the sea. It must be marvelous to be you. I'm sure no one tells you what you can and can't do."

Tehuti nodded. "'Tis true, no one tells us what to do, because no one cares. I'm sure the rules that are imposed on you are to keep you safe."

"That only proves you haven't met Father," she pouted. She looked over as Kailani woke up and smiled, "I bet you're the new friends my sister told me to find."

Kailani scurried to hide behind her brother.

Saffron frowned, "Why do you hide?"

"Forgive Kailani, we were hiding from those who harmed her. She just awoke and didn't know your intentions."

"Who in Father's realm harmed you?"

"No one. We came here from the Eastern Realm." Kailani peeked out from behind her brother to better see the child.

Saffron stood to her full height, "Oh, then you should stay here. None will harm you here."

Tehuti sighed, "I wish that were so, but we are half breeds, as you pointed out earlier. Without the sponsorship of a ruling fae, we will always be in danger."

"Then I shall be your... patron. That's what Valiant and Lady Tempest would say. I shall be your patron, and none shall harm thee," Saffron smiled, pleased with herself.

"I would welcome your patronage, but I think perhaps you should check with Lady Tempest. I don't want to be accused of tricking you," Tehuti smiled. He couldn't have asked for a better introduction to Lady Tempest, the ruling fae he had been trying to meet for days.

"Don't be silly. She knew you were here, and she approves, or Lady Tempest wouldn't have left me alone with you. Since we're to be friends, we can walk in the woods. She said I could walk in the woods with friends." Saffron smiled in anticipation.

"I think it's a lovely day for a walk," Tehuti responded.

*****

Layton grabbed his traveling pack and joined his father. "Why do I have to go? I'm only one-fourth shifter. No one believes I will shift."

"No one knows if you will or not. You will join your aunts for a season of shifter training. It wouldn't hurt you to make some friends in the Seen," Ridge said.

"You want me to go to watch out for Saffron, Clarity, and Fauna."

190

Ridge clapped his son on the back. "Always. Your aunts need your protection, whether they know it or not."

Layton bit his lower lip and immediately stopped. It was his mother's habit, and he didn't want to become known for it. "Father, will the shifters trust me at all?"

"Depends. Most will wait to see how you act. Trust Kyan. He'll protect you if for no other reason than you are family."

"I've never met Kyan. Why would he help me?"

"Shifters are big on family ties, and he's fond of your mother. Now, remember what you've been taught about the Seen. And no matter what, stay away from the blood-sucking demons. Your mother has done more than enough to anger them." Ridge patted Layton on the back. "Go. Join your aunts."

Layton sighed. He had been unable to get anyone to tell him what his mother had done to anger the blood-sucking demons. There weren't even any bard songs to provide a hint. Maybe a shifter would tell him. He joined his aunts, who, like him, were dressed in the unadorned leathers the humans wore for everyday travel. The clothes were comfortable enough, so he didn't care, but the girls did not look happy.

"Must we wear these leathers?" Saffron asked.

"Yes, if only to fit in," Ridge said.

"Who will open the way for us?" Charity asked.

"I shall." Valiant, carrying a small traveling pack, entered the hall.

"Are you going?" Layton asked. Although he expected Uncle Kyan to be his guide, it would be nice to have Valiant along for this first trip to the Seen. Layton had only met Kyan once.

"Yes." Valiant opened a way and looked over the heads of the kids to Ridge. "I'll keep them out of trouble." Valiant turned and walked into the way.

Smiling, the triplets followed with Layton bringing up the rear.

As the way closed, Ridge murmured, "I wonder who will keep Valiant out of trouble."

*****

Layton stepped onto the soil of the Seen for the first time. As he looked around, he was unhappy to discover the land looked much like the Farseen. Trees, flowers, and bushes — at least the ones nearby — looked very much like home.

191

"Disappointing. I wanted to see plants like the ones Lady Tempest collects," Clarity said.

"She collects plants from a climate warmer than the Southern Realm as part of her travels in the Seen. You will have to ask her where she finds the more exotic ones," Valiant said. They walked for a while with Valiant pointing out various landmarks.

Topping a hill, Fauna squealed, "Horses. They are bulkier than unicorns, and they don't have a horn, but otherwise are lovely."

Layton watched the herd run. "Can they be ridden?"

Valiant herded the triplets down the path. "I know of no one who has tried. Horses are wild but live throughout the Seen. There's a group of nomads far to the east that I've been watching. They want to use the horses to carry loads, maybe pull a cart, for them. It might work. Horses have no magic and can probably be domesticated like dogs and cats."

"Forget loads. I want to ride one." Layton continued to watch the herd run. It was a graceful, swift-moving dance. Unicorns were too skittish and used their magic to attack anyone in the Farseen who attempted to get near them. Riding a horse would be grand.

"A worthy goal to be sure, but for today we need to get to the Alpha Clan's camp." Valiant ushered the kids down the path, watching the four-went-way. It looked like they would reach the crossroads at the same time as a small group of humans. "Watch your words. You're about to meet humans. Call me Uncle, like we talked about."

Layton nodded but kept his eyes on his first humans.

"They look normal," Clarity said. Her tone did not imply that normal was good.

"What did you expect, sister mine?" Saffron asked.

Layton grinned but didn't comment. Clarity had a mean streak, but Saffron could be counted on to contain her more wild outbursts.

"Good day to you, Valiant." A human male walking alone extended his hands, both palms up. "How is it that you remain young as I have aged?"

"You would fare better if you laid off the ale, friend." Valiant extended his hands in the same manner and grinned when the man laughed. "Mungo, meet my sister's children."

Mungo eyed the children. "A fine healthy lot. Where are you headed to this time, my wandering friend?"

"North. They will hunt with me." Valiant pointed to the kids.

"There are much better places to hunt. The creatures there do not behave as they should. 'Tis a dangerous place to take the young."

"Fear not. I am meeting other hunters. My sister's young are safe."

"Of that, I have no doubt. They are with you." Mungo called over his shoulder as he walked away, "Try to look a little older when next I see you."

They passed a few other humans. Some traveling alone, some in groups. While they didn't all speak, all adults made the same hand movements Valiant and Mungo had.

"What type of greeting is that?" Saffron asked.

"Holding out the hands, palms up, show that weapons are not being drawn," Valiant explained.

"But you can call the elements. What does it matter if you don't have a physical weapon in your hand?" Clarity protested.

Saffron sighed. "Humans can't call the elements and must draw a weapon to attack."

Valiant nodded. "Normally, the humans would be more afraid of me because of my size, but with four children with me, they appear to see me as less of a threat."

Clarity frowned. "If humans are so weak, we should rule over them, like we do the lesser fae."

"We don't rule the lesser fae. We coexist with them. Some of the so-called lesser fae are far more powerful than we are." Saffron said.

Clarity harrumphed but didn't argue.

Valiant turned right onto a lesser used path. "We're nearly there. Remember your instructions."

Layton watched the tree line where he could sense other shifters. He didn't know he could do that. "Who waits for us in the woods?"

"Some from the Alpha Clan camp." Valiant raised his voice and said, "I was not expecting to be greeted thus."

"We had to move. One of our new adults was out late on the afternoon of his second full moon as a shifter and shifted in front of a human. We knocked the human out and managed to convince him that he imagined it, but it's not safe here now."

"How long have you been waiting?"

"We returned today to await your arrival and collect the last of the camp supplies," Taren said.

Although Taren and Valiant fought as youths, they had grown to be friends. Valiant asked, "What can we carry?"

Prized

Taren handed out appropriately sized bags to the kids. Then he grabbed one end of a pole with many bundles on it. Valiant grabbed the other end. The remaining shifters picked up their burdens and entered the way Kyan opened.

*****

Layton was the first of the kids to exit the way. It was his custom to precede his aunts, looking for danger.

Clarity stopped beside him and took in the scene with her trademark sneer. "Huts with thatched roofs and what I'm sure are dirt floors. Are we expected to live here for the warm season?"

"Hush," Saffron said. "Don't be so negative."

"Negative? How is the truth negative?"

Fauna tapped Clarity on the shoulder. "'Tis a lovely village and the first we've seen here. Since the shifters move every few years, it doesn't make sense to build permanent structures."

Clarity turned up her nose. She would never leave the comfort of the Farseen for this.

Layton and Saffron exchanged a shrug. When a female shifter approached Valiant and placed a kiss on his cheek, Layton grinned. This must be Carwen. Although no one ever spoke of Carwen within Lord Ellwood's hearing, she was the subject of an ongoing argument between Tempest and Valiant. Tempest thought Valiant should mate Carwen and bring her to the Farseen. Valiant was reluctant to do so for some reason Layton didn't understand.

"Carwen, meet my younger siblings: Saffron, Clarity, and Fauna. And this is Layton, Tempest's son."

The girls smiled, and Layton bowed after Saffron poked him in the ribs.

Carwen's eyes danced with laughter, but she bowed in return. "Welcome. I hope you enjoy your first trip to the Seen. Come Valiant. You may help me gather herbs."

"You gather herbs?" Clarity's eyes shot up.

"Only with Carwen." Valiant took Carwen's hand, and they walked into the forest.

"What is he doing?"

"Hush. Valiant has friends here in the Seen. It is not unexpected."

"I wonder if Father knows." Clarity's face took on a calculating look.

"What Father knows is irrelevant. He shouldn't hear it from us." Saffron spoke with a finality that made Clarity's eyes narrow on the sister who was three minutes her elder.

Kyan motioned for the kids to follow him. "Come. Settle into your home for the season."

Fauna and Saffron fell in step beside Kyan. Layton rushed to catch up. Clarity trudged behind.

*****

"They expect us to cook and clean. When we aren't doing that, they expect us to study. At least back home we can use what we are taught. When will we ever cook?" Clarity laid on the bedding she had claimed, furthest from the door. That way, if they were attacked, she would have time to gather her weapons.

"There are no pixies in the Seen. Someone has to cook and clean," Fauna said.

"Well, it shouldn't be me. I'll bet the shifters never asked Tempest to cook or clean." Clarity jumped when the flap opened.

Valiant walked in. "Actually, they did. Her response was the same as yours, at first. Then she found she enjoyed prepping food, although I don't think she ever got the hang of cleaning." Valiant eyed the room and nodded to Saffron. "I thought you would take the same spot as Tempest had. Closest to the door, ready to fight at a moment's notice."

Saffron blushed at the praise. When she saw the flash of anger in Clarity's eyes, she said, "I wanted to be close to the door. I like to walk at night."

Valiant tapped on the curtain between Layton's bedroll and the girls. "I think this is the same curtain from our visits." He looked over the cloth and smiled. "It is. See that burn mark. It was the summer Tempest finally got control of fire. She left scorch marks on everything."

"Is that cloth the reason the room smells musty?" Clarity asked.

Valiant ignored Charity's question. "Come. We're going north today. There's someone I want you to meet."

"Are we going to meet Kavi, one of Mother's elder sisters?" Saffron was the only one who seemed interested.

"What do you know of Kavi?" Valiant asked.

"Not much, just a couple of things Temperance said. Kavi is a powerful mind walker, but she can't block people. Sounds lonely."

"I suppose it can be, but she seems happy enough."

*****

"Why just the two of you?" Clarity stared at Saffron and Layton. "Why are Fauna and I to remain here?"

"How should I know? Ask Kyan." Layton stuffed supplies in his pack and waited for Saffron at the door of the hut.

Saffron shrugged. "We weren't told the whys, and we weren't asked if we wanted to go. I assume this is something Cwenhild decreed. She used to do the same with Tempest, Valiant, and Temperance." Saffron shrugged on her pack and left with Valiant.

"Come, we're meeting Kavi." Kyan took off in long strides.

"Kavi. I didn't think she traveled where people were." Saffron struggled to keep up.

"She has wanted to visit Esen's settlement for some time. Since I'm going on business, it's the perfect time to take you two and Kavi."

"Clarity wasn't happy." Layton pushed the sweat out of his eyes. He also struggled to keep up with Kyan. "Is there a reason we're hurrying?"

"We're making a side trip. I was just informed that the run started."

"What run?" Saffron asked.

They entered a clearing where Kavi waited. "Took you long enough."

Kyan nodded and opened a way.

"Where are we?" Layton asked.

"Far to the west on the fertile landmass across the massive water.

Layton and Saffron exchanged a grin and followed Kavi into the way. If even half of the songs Valiant wrote about this land were genuine, they were in for a treat. They exited onto a ledge next to a river. Layton and Saffron watched the river with open mouths. Large red fish swam upstream. Huge brown bears, much larger than any they had seen before, stood in the river catching their dinner.

"What is this?" Saffron asked.

Kyan grinned. "The fish swim upstream every year at this time. We wanted you to see this amazing bit of nature before we go on to visit Esen."

"Esen's land is further away?"

"Yes. Esen is further west from here, across another large body of water," Kyan said.

"Another large body of water? How large is this dimension?" Layton didn't look up from watching the enormous bears.

"At least three times as large as the Farseen."

The bears were much closer together than Layton would have thought predators would be. They used massive paws, or powerful jaws, to snag fish. "Do these bears hunt in a pack, like wolves?"

Kyan grinned. "No. They're loners. This is about the only time you will see them in groups. Come. We have other places to see."

When Kyan opened the way, Kavi and Saffron entered immediately. Kyan prodded Layton, who looked back at the bears as he walked into the way. On the other side, Layton stopped by Saffron. She stood at an overlook on the trail. Layton could see a village that he assumed they would hike down to, but what caught his attention was the land.

This land was mountainous in the same way as the Northern Realm, a few mountain peaks above the tree line, clear water, and, of course, lush, green valleys.

Saffron grinned. "It feels like home."

Layton nodded.

"Be aware of your surroundings. Go nowhere alone. Esen's clan will not be surprised by fair skin and hair, but others in the area may be," Kyan said.

Layton looked at Saffron and Kavi, both had light blonde hair. Thankful his own hair was dark, like his father's, Layton vowed to himself to keep an eye on the females.

"Look." Saffron pointed down into the valley at a huge striped cat with three cubs trailing behind her. The cats approached the river to drink. "It's beautiful."

"And deadly. Stay away from her. Tigers will kill," Kyan said.

"As will most females with young." Kavi walked down the mountain trail toward the camp.

As they entered the camp, Layton noticed the clan pointing and grinning. They weren't focused on the fair-skinned blondes. No, the shifters were making fun of him. Thanks to his fae heritage, within a couple of hours, he understood their words and knew he had been right about their comments. Tiring of the observations about his parentage, Layton said, in their language, "You're right, I may never shift, but I already control fire and water." He proved his words by creating a fire in the pit that was used for roasting large animals. "Shall I leave the fire or put it out?"

Prized

"Put it out. Now." Kyan's order left no room for discussion, but Layton was slow to smother the flame. The clan members silently returned to their work.

Knowing Kyan expected it, Layton followed his uncle into their hut.

"Why?"

"Did you not hear them? They were making fun of me, because of who my parents are. I thought they should know I wasn't weak." Having never been picked on, Layton found he didn't like it and thought a warning was called for.

Kyan shook his head. "You're more like your mother than I thought."

Layton grinned.

"That wasn't a compliment." Kyan rubbed the bridge of his nose.

*****

"Saffron. Today we leave the men behind."

"I thought we were to stay together." Saffron looked up from her task.

"Esen will guide us to a secluded place where we won't see anyone. I can always open a way if we need to escape quickly. I need a few days away from the minds in the camp."

Saffron nodded and gathered her pack. The trio walked for nearly half a day until Esen showed Kavi a cave that looked like it had once been someone's home.

"This is where my aunt lived. No others will come here, for she was powerful and killed any who approached except for a couple of her family members." Esen ushered them into the cave. "She died a few months ago, but it will be a while before others realize it. I am the only one still living that she allowed to visit, and I have told no one."

"This is perfect." Kavi looked around and placed her pack on the ground. "We will be fine."

Once Esen left, Saffron turned to Kavi. "Why are we here? And don't say it's to give your mind a rest. I've been watching you. I think you have better control than you let on."

"I do when awake, but not when I sleep. I want a few nights of real sleep."

Saffron raised a single eyebrow as Tempest did.

Kavi grinned. "I do want a couple of restful nights, but you need proper training."

"What do you mean?" Saffron forced herself to not react. She didn't think anyone knew, not even Tempest.

Rather than answer her niece's question, Kavi asked, "What is the bird form you take? It's mostly red with gold feathers on the tips of the wings and a gold leaf design on the chest."

Saffron's mouth dropped open.

"My dear, I told you I can't block anyone's mind when I sleep. No one else knows." Kavi's expression was kind, and her words soft.

"What else do you know?" Saffron balled her hands into fists.

"More than you would like. Take comfort in the fact that I am blessed with the ability to keep my mouth closed."

"I'm an aberration. No one shifts this early."

"Child, your father is a powerful fae. Fae come into their powers early. It is not surprising that a union between your father and mother would create a few oddities."

"Who else?"

It was Kavi's turn to raise an eyebrow. "You wish me to share your siblings' secrets with you? Then you will not mind if I share your secrets with them."

Saffron shook her head. "Never mind."

"Good. Then we shall begin."

Hours of training both mind and body left Saffron tired. She watched another female tiger and her cubs eat a boar. She didn't even look up when Kavi placed a large amount of food in front of her, but Saffron picked up the dried meat and chewed.

"Still watching the tigers?" Kavi sat beside her, eating a smaller portion of food.

"They are powerful and beautiful." Saffron didn't take her eyes off the mother and cubs.

"Just like you, my dear."

Saffron grinned. "Did you bring me here because tonight the moon will be full?"

"Yes. You may shift into your other form without worry."

"I normally sneak out of the residence and thought I could escape the clan as easily."

"Doubtful. Your living quarters in the Farseen are removed from the formal court. In the Seen, you would have to sneak by the clan guards, and they have a better sense of smell than the fae."

Prized

"I hadn't thought of that." Saffron watched the sunset. Her vantage point gave her a perfect view of the cat family. When she felt the call of the moon, she embraced it, spreading her wings so she could fly.

Nothing happened. She had no wings. Saffron looked down and saw paws. Furry paws. She was a tiger, younger than the mother, but older than her cubs.

"I'll not take my wolf form. No reason to rile the predator within each of us." Kavi shifted into a falcon and flew next to Saffron as she ran. *How do you feel?*

Saffron heard Kavi's voice in her head. Good. I like this form. I didn't realize it was so easy to pick another form.

For most shifters, it isn't. We must run away from the mother and her cubs. You don't want to fight her.

Saffron nodded and cut right, toward the mountains. There she found a herd of deer and was surprised how instinctual the hunt was. She bit into the doe with relish and looked at Kavi. *You could shift and join me. There's plenty, and I hate to waste.*

Kavi nodded and took her wolf form.

In the tall brush, under a full moon, a wolf and a tiger shared a meal.

*****

Layton watched the shifters run and play in their other forms. He, and other children too young to shift, were restricted to the camp, guarded by a menagerie of adults in their shifter forms. Without Saffron to talk to, Layton kept to himself. He didn't need mind powers to know that most of the clan didn't like him. They made that clear enough before the adults realized he understood them. Now they didn't even look at him, much less speak to him. The young took great pleasure in telling Layton that he, with only one-fourth shifter blood, would never know the joy of shifting. The thing that angered Layton most was that he agreed with them.

So, he sat alone, watching a herd of horses running across the plains while the full moon shone overhead. The horses were beautiful. Heavier built than the unicorns of the Farseen, the horses didn't shoot lightning out of a horn when angry or scared. Wondering if humans would ever ride horses, he kept his eyes on the herd and his focus on the person approaching from the path to the camp.

Solongo, Esen's daughter, who was near Layton's age, joined him on a rock. She sat down but didn't speak.

"You don't have to," Layton said.

Solongo tilted her head. "What?"

"Esen sent you over so I wouldn't be alone. Don't bother. Go back and tell him I sent you away. Then you can go play with your friends. It looks like they have a good game of chase going."

"What?"

"You heard me."

Solongo stood and crossed her arms in front of her chest. "Yes, I did. I'm not here because of Father. I was interested in hearing about the Farseen, the interesting creatures, and the realm courts. I thought maybe you would like to talk. I didn't realize you didn't like any of us."

"Wait." Layton scrambled to his feet and blocked her path. "It's your clan who dislikes me. I heard them. They don't want me here."

"Some of them don't. Some of the shifters don't want me here either. My mother was human. What difference does their opinion make?" She stopped trying to move past Layton and said, "You embarrassed those who spoke ill of you. That's why they ignore you."

"They started it."

"Yes, but you have the power. You were the injured party. Until you forgive them, they will not speak to you."

"I don't understand."

"Those who made jokes when you could understand them have embarrassed the clan. They cannot, by our laws, speak to you until you make the first move, meaning you excuse their bad behavior."

"I have to forgive them?"

"Not exactly. You have to be the first to speak to those who were rude. It means you are willing to overlook their conduct, but you expect it to not happen again. Had you not understood the comments, it would still have been bad manners, but it wouldn't have been an embarrassment to the entire clan. Don't the fae have rules of conduct?"

"Yes, but mostly if a fae is injured by another, they meet on the killing fields, a place in each realm where differences are settled."

"Would the fae kill over such a minor offense?"

"Depends on the fae, some would."

Prized

"How odd. Come back to camp with me and speak to some of those who laughed at your expense. You will find most will be happy to be released from their shame."

"Shame. Making fun of someone brings on shame?" Layton shrugged but followed her down into the camp. He did not understand the people of the Seen.

*****

Back at the sovereign's camp, Clarity ignored her brother's glare, climbed the rock formation, and sat between Valiant and Carwen. "When will we go to the large landmass? The one with the huge waterfalls, open plains, towering rock formations, and deep gorges."

Carwen chuckled.

"When you're older," Valiant growled the words, irritated by Clarity's lack of tact and Carwen's unbecoming humor. It wasn't often he was able to be alone with Carwen. Charity's arrival put an end to his plans.

"Why can't we go now?"

"You won't go until Kyan or I decide to take you."

"I want to go now. I need to see this land for myself."

"You haven't seen much of the sovereign's land yet. Why the hurry?"

"I want to go." Clarity's face contorted into her characteristic snarl. "You and Tempest have seen it."

"Not until we were adults. The odds of you getting what you want would improve if you paid more attention to others." Valiant walked off.

"Whatever did he mean?" Clarity stared after her brother.

Carwen laid back on the rock and laughed.

Valiant shook his head. Even when he was angry, Carwen's laughter made him smile. He left the rocks in the meeting area and strolled up into the hills. The sun was bright in the sky and, even though he was irritated with Clarity, he was relaxed. He always was the day after a full moon. Valiant reached the top of a knoll and turned back to see the Alpha Clan Camp. It was peaceful or would have been if the sovereign wasn't such a tyrant. At least Lord Ellwood was easy to understand. The sovereign always smiled, but Valiant had observed that she was as quick to cut a throat as Lord Ellwood. She just didn't give a warning.

He heard a noise behind him and turned to see Fauna and Gilmer playing. Valiant watched as Gilmer taught Fauna the rules to a game of chase that the shifters loved. Valiant observed awhile and then eased away to allow them to play without supervision. In a couple of years, Fauna would not be allowed such freedom, but for now, he saw no harm in allowing the young to be young, and Gilmer was a good boy.

Prized

More Come of Age

4892 BCE – 3726 BCE

Chapter 16 – 4892 BCE

With the sunrise to his back, Layton threw three spears in rapid succession. All three connected near the center of the target, forming a triangle. He grinned, pleased with his performance.

"Excellent arm," Pinus said before he threw his own spears.

Layton didn't respond. He was almost an adult and knew the only reason Pinus spoke to him was that Pinus desired to move up in court. His chosen method was to exchange vows with one of Ellwood's daughters. What Layton couldn't understand was why Pinus, at least as old as his mother, would speak to him on the practice field. But he always did.

Layton waited until Pinus completed his throw. Only then did Layton approach his target and retrieve his spears. Pinus tended to throw wild.

Pinus ran to catch up. Grabbing his own spears, which had not found the bullseye, Pinus asked, "Will Lady Temperance be at the repast this evening?"

"I suppose. Where else would she be?" Layton walked away from the annoying man.

"True enough." Pinus grinned.

Layton reared back and considered throwing his spear into Pinus's chest. He took careful aim and threw the spear into the target. If he killed one of his grandfather's subjects on the practice field, without due cause, his evening would not be pleasant, although the other warriors would surely applaud his efforts. The other two spears also landed in the bullseye.

"Good arm," Valiant said.

Prized

Layton grinned. He knew Valiant had walked up behind him. Pinus had never been able to hide his fear of Valiant the Bold. Layton didn't know what the story was, but he wanted to. Maybe when he reached his majority on the morrow, he would find out the true history of the more curious stories about the family.

"Come. We should get ready for the morning repast."

Layton grabbed his weapons and followed Valiant off the field.

*****

Valiant moved out of the way as his youngest siblings darted through the Hall of Battles, heading for the morning repast.

"What's the hurry?" Valiant grinned.

Fauna grinned back.

"It's our birthday. We're adults. We'll shift soon and have a place of honor in the realm and in a shifter clan," Clarity said excitedly.

"Well, you might shift, but it could take a few months," Tempest joined them in the hall with Ridge and Layton by her side. She smiled at Fauna, "There's no shame in not shifting. It will simply mean your fae blood is stronger than your shifter blood."

"Oh, I must shift," Clarity wailed. "I want a place of honor in both the fae and shifter worlds."

"Well then, I wish that for you as well," Ridge smiled. "But Milady spoke the truth. It's okay if it doesn't happen."

"You're wrong. I shall shift." Clarity turned to Valiant, "Brother mine, would you escort us to the feasting hall?"

"It would be my great pleasure to accompany three such lovely ladies to the hall." Valiant bowed with great relish and extended an arm to Clarity and Saffron, walking his young sisters down the hall. "Come, Layton, you come of age on the morrow. You should accustom yourself to escorting females."

"Yuck," Layton muttered. When he saw his mother's eyebrow, raised in annoyance, he ran to catch up with Fauna and offered her his arm. He watched with interest as his aunts received leather-bound scrolls from their father for their coming of age gifts as part of the morning repast. In this, Layton agreed with Clarity. He wanted weapons, not books.

At the mid-day repast, the new adults ate quickly and ran to check out their treehouses. No longer would they share the nursery rooms. Layton went with them. The new accommodations nearly matched. Saffron's treehouse had walls the color of the tree bark in the dark woods with cloth hangings stitched in the form of various herbs. Clarity's treehouse matched Tempest's in terms of color but not in size. Fauna had pale green walls and flowers on all materials. Her treehouse suited her perfectly. Of the three, Clarity was the least satisfied with her rooms. No surprise. She was rarely pleased.

At the evening repast, the ladies received many gifts from all five realms. When Lord Ellwood entered the hall with presents, a hush descended in the hall as everyone gathered to see what their next gift would be. Layton looked on enviously as the girls received weapons and fighting leathers. He hoped to get his own when he came of age tomorrow. Layton picked up Saffron's short sword. He could tell by the balance they weren't made by the Forest Lord. Mother had been right. He was pulled from his thoughts by his mother arguing with his grandfather. It was a common enough occurrence, but it was always good to pay attention when they became angry. That way, he knew which topic to avoid for a day or two.

Tempest narrowed her eyes on her father, "Don't you mean me, Father mine?"

"Indeed, Lady Tempest or Valiant are both better choices for her training, Lord Ellwood," Temperance added earnestly.

"True, my daughter, but they don't need to spend more time on war skills. You do. I overheard Lady Clarity say this morning that she would prove herself worthy of weapons made by my hand. Her desire should overcome any impediment that training with you will bring her."

Layton winced when Tempest and Valiant both gritted their teeth to keep from speaking. Ellwood had just set Clarity up to fail and make Temperance look like a fool. He wished he understood why his grandfather did things to make life hard for his children, but he always did.

Rayna smiled sweetly at her children before turning to her husband. "When Lady Temperance and Lady Clarity prove you wrong, husband mine, I think you should provide each of them a boon."

"A competition," Ellwood grinned. "What terms?"

"In three months, Lady Clarity will spar with Sorbus. If she can surprise him in a category, to be determined by Ridge, you will concede that Lady Temperance is an excellent teacher of war skills and that Lady Clarity is an excellent student, worthy of the weapons you shall gift her."

Prized

"And if Lady Clarity fails against Sorbus?"

Rayna's smile widened, even as her eyes narrowed. "If she fails, Lady Clarity will forfeit the right to have weapons made by your hand."

Layton hid his surprise. He knew Clarity desperately wanted weapons made by the Forest Lord. Clarity wanted everything Tempest had. He had never met anyone more jealous of another person than Clarity was of Tempest. He didn't truly understand why. Tempest and Ellwood fought frequently. Layton's personal ambition was to never engage in conflict with Ellwood. He even considered moving from the Northern Realm, but that would require planning and a bit of luck. If he stayed, he would eventually be forced to participate in court life, and Layton wasn't interested in becoming Grandfather's puppet.

After the repast, Layton watched as his aunts danced with those the Forest Lord approved as suitable partners. He was surprised at the number of males — of all ages — who had solicited dances with Lord Ellwood's youngest daughters.

*****

The day after the triplets came of age, Layton escorted his aunts to the garden where they had played as children. Saffron, Clarity, and Fauna were so close in age to him that they were more like siblings, than aunts and nephew.

"Everyone says it means something. Your coming of age day and all three moons full on the same day. Many expect you to shift," Saffron said, dragging Layton away from the river's edge where Tehuti and Kailani slept.

"Don't be silly," Clarity scoffed. "Do you know how rare it is for a full-blooded shifter to shift on the day they become an adult? It doesn't happen. Layton is only one-fourth shifter. I doubt he'll shift at all."

Layton snarled and walked off. Of course, Clarity would say out loud his worst fear. What if he never shifted? He didn't think his parents or Rayna would care, but his Forest Lord grandfather and shape-shifter great-grandmother would care. They would care a lot. Layton still didn't know what he wanted.

"She didn't mean it," Fauna said. She stood just inside the woods. Fauna was the most unthreatening of the triplets. She didn't like conflict and frequently hid in the woods, saying they calmed her.

"Yes, she did. You know she did." Layton kept walking.

Fauna dropped into step beside him. "Maybe, but she, more than the rest of us, wants Father's approval. She believes shifting will garner his respect."

Layton held back a limb so that Fauna could walk unencumbered on the rarely used trail. "I wish her luck. He doesn't approve of anyone."

"True." Changing topics, she said, "Are you ready for your present?"

Layton grinned. As a grandchild of Lord Ellwood, he would receive one present from his grandfather today. It would be delivered at the mid-day repast and was the reason he had stayed in his mother's rooms at the Northern Realm residence for another day. "Yes, regardless of what books or weapons I receive, I will say all that is proper with a smile upon my face."

They arrived at the cave where Ellwood's children had always gone to escape the world. They plopped down on rocks and talked for a while. Layton felt the anger float away. Fauna was good at calming him down.

Eventually, Fauna asked, "What if you do shift this evening? I have noticed how much you've been eating lately, and normally you wouldn't get angry at Clarity for making one of her spiteful comments. You're showing the signs, so you might shift. Have you considered what form would be most useful to you?"

"Yes. I've considered it." Layton stood and offered her his hand. He had thought of nothing else for weeks, and neither his parents nor grandparents offered any detailed suggestions. They were strangely silent on the subject. "Come, we don't want to be late."

Fauna accepted the snub with a smile. "I look forward to when you share your chosen form."

"And remember your promise. Don't leave me alone with any female." Both his father and uncle had warned him that some females would want the position having him as a consort would bring, but not necessarily him. He didn't feel ready to deal with court plots yet. More importantly, although his father had discussed the matter with him, Layton still wasn't sure he would know what to do with a female if she offered companionship for the evening. The one thing he did know, he didn't want to become the subject of a joke or a song that would follow him forever.

Prized

They stopped by the garden to join the others, but Saffron and Clarity were gone. They arrived at the feasting hall, and Layton immediately discovered Ridge and Valiant were right. Some of the ladies trying to catch his eye were as old as his mother. One was ancient, at least as old as his father. He tightened his grip on Fauna's arm.

"Don't worry, nephew," Saffron whispered in his ear as she took his other arm. "We shall protect you from the scary females."

Clarity scoffed as she came to stand beside him.

"What a glorious day. Layton attains his majority at last." Lord Ellwood stood at the top of the stairs with Sorbus, who held something under a blanket. "Come grandson. I have a small gift for you."

Layton bowed to his aunts and walked up the steps to join his grandfather. He lifted the cover to find weapons and leathers, as expected. He picked up one of the blades. The balance was perfect. Layton looked at his grandfather and bowed. "You honor me."

"Nonsense. You must have proper weapons. One day you will take your place by Valiant's side, leading my troops into battle. You must be properly armed. Sorbus will attend to your training, not that you require additional training. Your feats on the training field are well documented, but extra practice will not hurt."

Layton was still looking at his weapons, when his aunts joined him. He now possessed arms made by the Forest Lord himself. Saffron and Fauna congratulated him. Clarity looked at the weapons and snarled. The others ignored her, accustomed to her mood swings.

Later that evening, Layton waited in the hall of the family treehouses. In the past, he hated escorting his aunts to the feasting hall, but today he was thankful for the task. Not only was he there to make sure no male approached them without permission, but he also needed them as a buffer from the ladies of the court.

"Afraid to enter the Hall of Battles alone?" Clarity asked.

"You would be too if you saw the horde of ladies lying in wait."

Clarity laughed. It was a real laugh, and her face was transformed. "Lady Abbie has always liked you. You just didn't notice before."

"She likes to spar with me because we're evenly matched."

"She likes to look at you. Sparring is a great way to look at someone without drawing attention to your motives," Fauna said. "She is kind. You should ask her father for permission to dance with her."

"What?"

"You're an adult now. As an unmated male, you are expected to dance after the repast," Clarity said. "Why do you think you've been practicing with us for the past year?"

"Because you needed a male to dance with." Layton stopped moving as an ugly truth presented itself. "I have to dance? In public? Tonight?"

"Of course, and you must ask someone other than us. Lady Abbie is a good choice. You could ask your aunt, Lady Sierra, as well. Lady Adaryn — as our teacher — is another good choice," Fauna said.

"And remember, it is always good form to ask your mother and grandmother to dance the first evening of your adulthood." Saffron placed her arm through Layton's and pulled him down the hallway.

"Dance?" Layton wasn't sure why he kept repeating that word, but he did. At least he didn't have to ask for permission to dance with relatives. That should fill up half the evening.

When they arrived in the feasting hall, Clarity gave him a little push. "Go on. Line up at least two dance partners for the evening."

Layton walked away to follow their suggestions, his feet keeping time to the laughter from his aunts.

When he sat down at his aunt's table, he had dance partners for six dances. Layton expected to fill the rest of the evening with various relatives whom his aunts had reminded him would expect his attention. Layton watched his aunts, still laughing. Females had it so easy. No fear of rejection. Just show up and watch males grovel for the chance to lead them out on the dance floor. No public humiliation if the father said no. He noticed Lady Arolla, Pinus's sister. She always sat with family, and Layton didn't remember her talking or dancing much, but he wasn't in court that often. Maybe she didn't like to dance, or perhaps she was shy. Layton excused himself from the table and returned as the first course was served.

"You were almost late," Clarity said.

Valiant nodded his agreement as he sat.

Once the repast was over, the dancing began. Layton could feel the eyes of most everyone watching to see who he would dance with first. He had planned to sit out the first dance because he didn't want to give the gossips tinder for their fire, but he had changed his mind.

Once the opening completed and everyone could join the dance, he walked over, bowed to Lady Arolla, and led her out on the dance floor. She danced beautifully. A good thing considering the stares.

Some in surprise, some in anger, and a few — including his mother and grandmother — in approval. Pinus had done much to lose face with the court, but his sister, only a couple of years older than Layton, had done nothing to earn such condemnation. He checked with a couple of friends, and they had stayed away from Lady Arolla because of her brother. Deciding his standing as the grandson of the Forest Lord, and the son of Ridge and Lady Tempest, should mean he was made of sterner stuff, he asked for a dance. Her father had looked downright grateful.

When the dance was over, Layton walked Arolla off the dance floor.

"I enjoyed the dance. You are very kind," Arolla said.

Before Layton could respond, Cypress joined them. "I believe the next dance is mine."

Arolla saw her father's nod and blushed. She walked away on Cypress's arm.

Layton walked across the floor to Lady Abbie to claim his dance. He took a moment to notice the sunset. It was beautiful. With all three moons reflecting the sun's light, it would not get very dark tonight. At that moment, he doubled over in pain.

"Do you feel the moon's call, my son?"

Layton had no clue when or how his mother arrived by his side, but he was grateful. He looked up at her and shifted.

"Come. We shall hunt." Lady Tempest shifted to her wolf, ran out on the balcony, and jumped to the ground. Layton followed. When he jumped, he flapped his wings and wobbled a bit. After scraping the ground with his underbelly, his wings took over, and he flew.

"It's a good thing he is young," Ash commented. "Otherwise, he would have brought down the residence."

"Indeed." Ridge watched Layton, a black dragon whelp, fly into the night.

*****

Three months later, Layton entered the killing field with his parents, though there would be no killing today. It was the only venue that would hold everyone in the five realms who wanted to see the competition Lady Rayna and Lord Ellwood had devised. As always, the crowd quieted when Lady Tempest entered the stands. Layton wondered if anyone else knew his mother was a source of more fear in the Northern Realm than Lord Ellwood. Although the reasons were different. The fae would probably like Lady Tempest better if they knew she was loyal to the fae and not to her shifter family. Even Layton was unsure where her true loyalties resided, perhaps because Lady Tempest wasn't sure herself. Layton and Ridge followed her to their seats and got comfortable.

At the appointed hour, Lady Clarity walked out in her leathers, walking stick in one hand, and wearing a sai over each shoulder. Her long hair was braided and wrapped around her head in the style Lady Tempest wore when in battle. As this was a sparring competition between a trainee and an experienced warrior, she could use whatever weapons she wished. Sorbus, as the experienced warrior, was allowed only his tapered walking stick.

Lady Clarity walked with purposeful steps to the center of the arena and bowed. Sorbus returned the bow and stood poised and ready. Clarity dropped her walking stick, pulled a sai into each hand, and charged. Aggressively, she attacked. Sorbus took a half step back and swung his stick in an arc, sending one sai flying. The other sai she grabbed with both hands and lunged for his left arm. Sorbus blocked the strike and smiled grimly.

Layton nodded to himself. He knew Sorbus had an old wound that made him a bit slower with his left arm. Not much, but it was a weakness. Good for Clarity. She had prepared well.

Clarity twirled with the sword, and Sorbus dropped to the ground, using his stick to bat the sai away and his legs to knock her to the ground. Clarity rolled and grabbed her stick, and they spent a few seconds striking at each other. With this weapon, Clarity showed advanced skill. Not surprising, since the walking stick was Lady Temperance's best weapon. Sorbus blocked her next strike with enough force to disarm. A second later, a small dagger flew through the air and embedded in his walking stick.

Layton clapped. Clarity's small dagger was a surprise. It should be enough to allow her to hold her head high. Layton knew she was too young to truly defeat the old warrior. Only Ridge consistently defeated Sorbus on the training field.

Sorbus waited for Clarity to stand. Instead, she shifted into a wolf and pounced. Tilting his walking stick, Sorbus sidestepped her attack. He had sparred with Lady Tempest and Valiant enough to know how to battle an intelligent wolf. Clarity rolled with the fall and turned to attack again.

Prized

Clapping wildly along with everyone else, Layton looked over at Saffron and Fauna. They hadn't known she could shift either. Layton was relieved. Clarity had been angry when he shifted first.

"Enough!" Lady Rayna called from the stands. "What say thee, my husband? Has our daughter proven herself worthy of the weapons you shall bestow upon her?"

At Rayna's command, Lady Clarity and Sorbus bowed and walked over to stand before Lord Ellwood.

"Indeed, her skill was most impressive." Ellwood looked over at Temperance, "When did you learn to wield a small dagger well enough to teach the art? I have never seen you use one in combat."

"Lord Ellwood, I believe the fault is mine," Ridge admitted.

"Yours?" That one word was said with enough venom to scare lesser men.

Ridge smirked. "Valiant gave each of the triplets a small dagger when they attained their majority. I decided to teach them to use it properly since both Milady and Valiant are a bit too wild in their throws."

Layton chuckled along with the warriors when Tempest and Valiant exchanged looks that said Ridge would pay for that remark.

"I believe you will find Lady Saffron and Lady Fauna wield the small daggers in their boots with equal ease." Ridge motioned toward the younger sisters of his mate.

"Daughters mine, is this true?"

In answer, both Saffron and Fauna pulled their daggers in practiced moves and threw them at the center of a practice box. Both landed near the center of the mark.

Those in the stands applauded. Clarity looked over in surprise. Layton could tell she was disappointed that she wasn't the only one to receive focused training from the Realm Advisor.

"Sorbus, was my daughter's fighting acceptable?"

"Indeed, Lord Ellwood, Lady Clarity twice surprised me with a move I would not have thought her capable of at this point in her training." He turned to Clarity, "Your skill will only improve as your strength grows. Congratulations on your shift."

Ellwood looked down at his daughter, "And who assisted you with your shift?"

"Mother. I hoped to surprise you with my chosen form," Clarity bowed.

216

Ellwood laughed, "You did indeed. Lady Saffron, Lady Fauna, have either of you another form to show me?"

"No, Father," Fauna replied.

Saffron shrugged.

"Ah, well, maybe when next the moons are full. Come, Lady Clarity, walk with me."

Layton winked when Clarity walked by, but she didn't notice. She was focused on her father. He was happy for his aunt. This result was all she had hoped for.

Chapter 17 – 4889 BCE

Valiant walked the path around the island, thinking. Every morning, he made sure Temperance was comfortable and prepared for a day of study. Then he had nearly six hours to himself. He always found himself here, on this cliff, where he practiced his warrior skills. He liked the view and the silence. Few wanted to walk so far away from the library.

One of the larger human settlements was visible from this point. The island, home of the greatest preternatural library in either dimension, was veiled. The humans didn't know Atlantis was here. There were rumors and stories of a great city of knowledge, but most humans thought it was a bard's tale. It was. He wrote the original himself at his great-grandmother's request. The fae queens wanted a story to hide behind to explain the rumors.

Valiant finished his workout and headed back to the city center. Temperance rushed up to him, carrying both of their travel bags. She tossed Valiant his pack. "We have to return to the Farseen. Now."

"What happened? I thought you loved it here. I expected to drag you home next week." Valiant looked his sister over. No injuries, but she did look concerned.

"It is more wonderful than any place I've ever been," Temperance said. "The free exchange of knowledge is inspiring."

"Then what's the problem?" Valiant shrugged on his pack.

"Queen Niamh told me to find you and leave immediately. I didn't do anything to upset her." When Valiant raised an eyebrow, Temperance stomped her foot. "I didn't, but Grandmother is furious."

The ground shook, and Valiant could see cracks forming in the buildings.

"Time to go." Valiant grabbed Temperance by the arm and opened a way. They walked through accompanied by dust and debris into the family gardens in the Farseen.

"What was that?" Valiant asked.

Temperance looked around, wide-eyed.

"You're back early," Saffron said.

"Yes, we are," Temperance said. She watched the merfolk in the Kaveri River toss water back and forth with Saffron and with the merfolk-nymph twins. "Grandmother was angry."

Tempest leaned forward. "Someone angered Queen Niamh? On purpose?"

Valiant tossed his pack to a waiting pixie and bowed to his sisters. "Come, Layton, tell me what has transpired in court while I was away."

Once they were out of sight, Tempest asked, "What happened?"

"The queens learned that some have been hiding knowledge. A direct violation of the agreement with the Tetrad."

"Starless night."

"Temperance, I'm pleased to see you safely home." Rayna joined them.

"Do you know what happened?" Tempest asked.

"Yes, Queen Niamh dropped Atlantis into the ocean. She warned only a handful of people to leave before she destroyed it. No one remaining survived."

"I'm sure that made the Tetrad happy," Tempest said.

"I'm sure it did not," Rayna replied tartly.

Tempest excused herself and went to join Saffron. "Sister mine, you should be more careful."

"Why?" Saffron's stance and facial expression were very similar to Tempest's when caught doing something she shouldn't.

"Because I know you are here with your friends. I don't mind, but care must be taken. There are those in the court who would use this knowledge against you."

"How? We are all patrons. I might be young, but I'm an adult now, and my patronage counts for something." Saffron stomped her foot.

"I do not fault you. I do think you should consider your friend's safety instead of your own ego." Tempest bowed toward the water. "Well met, Tehuti and Kailani."

Prized

"Well met, Lady Tempest," the twins replied.

They were the offspring of a mermaid mother and a nymph father. Without the patronage of a ruling fae, the twins would have died a few years ago. Saffron was right about that. Her patronage did count, but she was barely an adult and did not yet understand that such kindness could be used as a weapon.

Saffron blushed at Tempest's reprimand. She didn't mean to put her friends in danger. "How can I keep them safe?"

Tempest smiled, pleased with Saffron's question. "Go to Father's receiving hall and request that Kailani be given a position within the court, perhaps in your schooling. Something where she would spend time with you. Tehuti is strong and could monitor the river access to the family treehouses."

Saffron pursed her lips. "I've never made a formal request before."

"Ask Temperance to help you with the wording." Tempest walked off.

*****

Saffron walked into the Receiving Hall, dressed for court. It was the first time she had worn the flowing skirts and billowy shirts fae females considered essential for a day in court. Up to now, the triplets wore the Northern Realm colors in fighting clothes. Saffron smoothed the front of her skirt, loving the feel of the fabric and the way it made her look. She was an adult.

There was a press of people in the hall. Most wore the colors of the Northern Realm, but Saffron also spied representatives from the Central and Southern Realms. It is sobering to know that all would await her pleasure as family held the highest priority when they were scheduled to be in court.

"Master-At-Arms Ash, I have an appointment to see the Forest Lord." Saffron was careful to use his title and not the more mundane address of Father.

Ash bowed. "Indeed, Lady Saffron." Ash opened the door, and she walked in.

*****

Ellwood watched his daughter approach. "Morning, my child."

"Lord Ellwood." Saffron bowed. "I petition you, not as your daughter, but as a member of the court."

220

"Indeed." Ellwood leaned back into the throne and hid his smile. His spies had already told him that Temperance had helped Saffron prepare.

Now that Saffron was in the receiving room, she was surprised to find that she was nervous. There were a lot of people in the room. She had not expected that. "I am patron to Tehuti and Kailani, twins born of a mermaid mother and a nymph father."

"A fact of which I am aware."

Saffron sighed at her slip. Of course, he knew. "Both have offered their services to your realm."

"I see. Have you a task in mind?"

"Yes, Father. Tehuti is strong and well suited to guarding the waterways outside our treehouses. Kailani would be an excellent addition to our teaching staff."

Ellwood pretended to consider the issue, but he knew what his answer would be. It would be interesting to see how Saffron handled her first responsibility. It would also be interesting to see Fauna and Clarity's response, especially Clarity's.

*****

Fifteen minutes later, Saffron left Lord Ellwood's receiving room with everything she wanted. Kailani was to be her aide; hopefully, her elder sisters could help her define duties for an aide. Tehuti was charged with protecting the waterways around the family treehouses. Saffron understood that, regardless of what he said, Ellwood agreed to her plan for his own reasons. That didn't matter at this moment. Giddy with her success, Saffron ran to the study rooms and threw open the door. "I did it."

"Did what?" Clarity asked without looking up from her scrolls.

"I petitioned Father. He approved my request."

"Your what?" Clarity tossed her scrolls aside. She wanted the prestige of being the first to petition their father. How could Saffron do with ease what Clarity wished to do?

Saffron noticed Clarity's change in attitude but didn't have time to deal with her volatile sister. "I'm going to Ridge's residence. Tempest will want to know it worked." Saffron grabbed her cloak and ran from the room.

Clarity threw the chair she had been sitting in against the wall.

"Tell me that dispelled your anger? If you arrive at the evening repast in such a state, Lord Ellwood will make use of your mood."

Prized

Fauna didn't look up from her needlework, accustomed to Clarity's frequent displays of temper.

Clarity threw another chair, took a deep breath, and molded her face into a peaceful mask. "I'm better now."

"Good. Let me braid your hair. You like the style Temperance has worn of late, and I've mastered the technique."

Clarity allowed Fauna to pull her into a chair by the window. While Fauna braided hair, Clarity plotted.

Chapter 18 – 4880 BC

"What is this?" Ridge looked at the sword in Aatami's claw. Aatami stood beside the floating stairs of the Northern Realm residence. With him standing on the ground far below, the ancient red dragon was eye level with Ridge, Tempest, and Ellwood.

"Mine." Ellwood reached to grab the sword.

Aatami pulled it back. "Listen to the instructions before you touch."

Tempest placed a hand on her father's arm, inclined her head to Aatami, and asked, "Is this the sword you offered to make?"

"Offered? What an interesting way of saying I lost a bet." Aatami blew smoke out of his nostrils but grinned. "Yes, Lady Tempest, this is one of the Five Swords of Virtue. One sword going to each realm lord. The Northern Realm shall receive Veracity. With this sword, you can reform the universe to match your words."

Tempest gasped, and Ridge stepped forward. "None should have such a sword." Though the guards didn't hear the conversation, they looked at the sword with interest. Dragon made objects were far more powerful than objects made by any other in the Farseen.

"The realm lords wanted swords of great power. This is a sword of great power. Fear not. There are rules. Only the three of you shall be given the instructions to wield it. You may do with that knowledge whatever suits you." Aatami smiled and spoke into each of their minds. *Veracity is the Sword of Truth. Hold the sword thus* (Aatami raised the sword in the air) *while speaking the incantation, and Veracity will reform the universe to match the words you speak aloud.*

Prized

Ridge didn't so much hear the incantation as he suddenly knew it. He was sure Tempest and Ellwood received it as well. "I repeat, none should have this sword."

"What is that tune?" Tempest asked.

Ridge nodded. He had been wondering about that as well.

"It is the song of the sword. When the five swords are together, their melody is… intoxicating."

"Is the desire for the sword strong with us because we know how to use it?" Ellwood asked.

"No, the sword calls to any fae, but the call is strongest for those who are powerful or desire to be so." Aatami grinned

Ridge growled. That fool dragon might actually destroy the realm. The song of this one sword pulled at Ridge, demanding that he hold it, no, wield it. Without noticing he had done so, and in sync with Tempest and Ellwood, he stepped toward the sword. Realizing what they had done, the trio exhaled and backed up, still in sync.

"I have fulfilled my part of the wager, Forest Lord. My debt to you is paid," Aatami said.

Lord Ellwood stared at the sword but didn't speak until Tempest nudged him. Still eyeing the sword, Ellwood said, "The sword satisfies the terms of the wager. Nothing owed on either side."

Bowing, Aatami laid the sword on the short wall and flew away.

Full of desire, all three stepped toward the sword again, each reaching out a hand to grasp it. At the last second, Ridge turned and blocked Ellwood and Tempest. With the sword at his back, he said, "I think it is an exceedingly bad idea for us to touch this sword."

Ellwood drew his body up to his full height. "Probably, but the desire to touch it is tremendous."

"The song is lovely." Tempest moved to step around Ridge.

Ellwood narrowed his eyes on his eldest. "The sword is mine."

Ridge saw Lady Fauna sitting in an alcove with a scroll in front of her. She was the gentlest soul in Ellwood's family, probably in the realm. "Lady Fauna, I have a small task for you."

At Ridge's summons, Lady Fauna hurried over. Ridge pointed to the sword. "Take this sword from the wall and place it in a secure location. Let none touch it, save yourself, and tell no one – not even the three of us – where it is. Lord Ellwood will call you to his meeting hall later today, and there the three of us will meet with you on this topic. All three of us must be there before you discuss the sword."

Confusion spread across her face. The sword had no sheath. After a minute, Lady Fauna picked up the sword, hid it in the folds of her skirt and left, humming the song of the sword.

Even as Fauna walked away, Ridge wanted to call her back and claim the sword for himself. The further away she was, the less he felt the sword's call, but still, the desire to chase her down and retrieve the sword was tremendous.

"Fast thinking. If, as Aatami stated, the sword calls to the power-hungry, Fauna is the person least likely to try to wield it." Tempest still stared in the direction Fauna had left. "I would have fought the two of you for the sword."

"As would I." Ellwood grinned. "It would have been a glorious battle."

"But one that would serve no purpose." Ridge shook himself. "If the other four swords are as powerful as this one, the realms may once again go to war."

"Will, not may," Tempest corrected. "What shall we do with it?"

"We should ponder that thought until after the noon repast. Then we will reunite in the meeting hall and discuss before Fauna is called," Ridge said.

"Wise counsel from my advisor." Ellwood walked off.

"I promised Mother I would join her this day." Tempest smiled when Ridge leaned down and kissed her cheek.

"We'll meet at the noon repast, Milady." Ridge watched her go. She was still thinking of the sword, as was Ellwood. He should probably protect it from them for their own good. He was strong enough to resist the call. Ridge entered the building using the same entrance Fauna had. He had a good idea where she would go, and the sword should be protected.

Ridge stood outside the library, wondering what had happened. The call of the sword faded a short while ago. Did Fauna find a way to hide the sword so that the song could not be heard? How very surprising of her. He opened the door to discover he was the last to arrive.

Lady Fauna sat in the middle of the library at the large desk used by scholars with Lady Rayna on her right and Valiant to her left. Standing before them, Lord Ellwood and Lady Tempest did not look happy.

Rayna smiled at Ridge. "Come, join us. Fear not. Lady Fauna asked for our help but wisely did not tell us details."

"All we know is Aatami gave something to the Northern Realm, and you told Lady Fauna to hide it. She hid it before contacting us." Valiant didn't bother to hide his irritation that he didn't know what was going on.

"And she hid it well. I can't feel it anywhere," Tempest said.

"Did you search the entire residence?" Ridge asked.

"Hardly, I followed the song until it disappeared. The last place I heard it was in Lord Ellwood's receiving room. This library is where Lady Fauna is most comfortable, so it is where I started my search."

Ridge nodded. It was what he had done as well.

"Where is my sword?" Ellwood demanded.

Fauna looked nervous, but she said, "As I searched for a hiding place, I realized everyone I passed turned and followed me. The... object called to everyone. Even pixies followed me. I remembered that in Father's receiving room, there was a box where items of power could be placed and hidden from the senses."

"My sweet child. You placed it there. Very well done."

Ellwood was at the door when Fauna said, "It's not there anymore."

He turned and looked at her. "Then where is it?"

"I told Ash I had something to deliver to your room in private. He opened the door to let me in, but I had to close it to keep everyone else out. I was relieved that no one else was in the room at the time. Once I placed the sword inside, I took the box and hid it, as Ridge requested. I left from the private exit so as not to be observed. No one followed with the sword in the box. After hiding it, I returned to the receiving room and left out the main door. Apparently, once they couldn't hear the song, they forgot why they were following me."

"That only works if they don't see it and don't know how to use it," Tempest muttered.

"Lady Fauna, you must tell me where it is. I shall protect it." Lord Ellwood smiled at his daughter.

"You don't want to protect it. You want to wield it." Tempest relaxed her arms, ready to fight her father.

"As do you, sister mine." Valiant didn't move from his position beside Fauna.

Tempest looked like she was ready to fight Valiant, so Ridge said, "As do I. Seeing the object, knowing what it can do, makes the pull stronger. At least that's the way it appears to me." Ignoring the others, he spoke to Fauna. "I should not have put the object in your care. I thought it would cease to be an issue when out of sight, and I didn't think it would call to all fae."

"You put my child in danger." Ellwood, eyes shining in anticipation, advanced on Ridge.

Ridge settled and waited for the attack. Though they sparred regularly, Ellwood had never beaten Ridge in hand to hand. Today would not be that day.

"Ridge, back away. Lord Ellwood, stop." Tempest used wind to separate the men.

"Milady, do not interfere." Ridge regained his feet and ran at Ellwood, who charged him as well.

"Ellwood. Now is not the time." Rayna threw her hands in the air as the fight began.

"Oh, Mother, I think now is exactly the time." Valiant grinned. When he saw Tempest moving toward the men, he added, "Protect Fauna. I'll delay Tempest." Valiant pulled the Patron's Sword and advanced on his sister.

"I tire of you always leaning on that sword." Tempest didn't pull a weapon from her body. She called wind.

Valiant smiled grimly and called water. Tempest had learned long ago not to attack him with any type of sword or made weapon when he drew the Patron's Sword. He was no match for her with elements, but he didn't need to defeat her, just delay her. His water hit her wind, and, in a bazaar twist of magic, a small hurricane formed inside the library. The swirl splattered water around the room, soaking the scrolls. Valiant sighed. He would get blamed for that. Knowing that her command of the elements would be his undoing, Valiant opened his mouth to plead with his sister and saw that she wasn't looking at him.

Valiant followed her eyes, and his mouth dropped open. Ellwood stood within a circle of fire. Ridge stood within another. Wind held both men in place. Rayna had never displayed that type of power before. Not against the powers of someone as tough as those two.

Tempest took the moment of her brother's distraction to run at Fauna. Valiant threw caution to the wind and tackled her. They rolled away from each other and jumped up into fighting stances. Tempest tossed him into the hurricane. With Tempest focused on Fauna, Valiant was able to dissipate the wind. He pushed the water at Tempest. Too late, he realized he would drown Fauna as well, and she couldn't defend herself well from the elements. He tried to place a shield around her, but something blocked him.

The shield that circled her was a surprise. Fauna couldn't create a shield. Rayna was too busy and had never been able to shield anyone else. Neither could Tempest, but she beat on the shield and looked at Valiant. In her anger, she jumped from Fauna's side and pulled a sword as she landed in front of Valiant.

Valiant gripped the Patron's Sword and smiled. For the first time, Tempest was so mad, or drunk on the song the dragon made item sang, she forgot the details. Their swords met, and Valiant thought he might actually win the day if he could keep her focus on swordplay. He spared a glance to see that Fauna was still safely inside a shield. Unfortunately, while he was distracted, Tempest lunged. The cut to his side stung, but it was just a flesh wound.

Pushing all other thoughts from his mind, Valiant battled Tempest. Valiant had never listened to his sword so closely. He quit attacking Tempest and let the sword lead the dance. Never had he been so sure of his movements. One moment they were fighting, and the next, he took the hilt of the sword and knocked her out.

No time for rejoicing over his unexpected victory. Ridge had made it through the fire and, ignoring Rayna, talked to Fauna. Valiant knew from personal experience that Ridge could be brutal when he spoke softly. Rayna and Ellwood continued to battle, so Valiant ran at Ridge with the Patron's Sword. It was a suicide move, but he couldn't leave Fauna unprotected.

Valiant raised his sword. His only hope against the realm advisor was a death blow. At the last second, Ridge's sword shot out and blocked Valiant's attack.

"I'm surprised you were able to hold a steady shield around Fauna while you fought Tempest. Your skills have grown."

"You always sound surprised when you say that." Valiant gripped the sword tighter. Ridge used words to lull his adversary into a trap.

Ridge looked at Valiant's grip and twirled his sword in a relaxed move. "Are you sure you want to do this?"

"Give me a choice that doesn't forfeit Fauna's life." Valiant turned, keeping Ridge in his sights.

"Fauna is in no danger once she gives me the item."

"That's a problem for me."

Ridge tired of Valiant and said, "You don't even know what the sword is, what it does."

"Don't need to. If it makes you and Tempest act like vicious marauders, it's bad." Valiant grinned. "I am pleased to learn it's a sword."

Ridge growled.

Valiant caught movement in the stacks on the second level of the library and saw Saffron hiding in the shadows. Great. Another sister who couldn't defend herself well. Ignoring everything else, Valiant once again let the Patron's Sword lead the dance. Ridge, more realistic than Tempest, realized the sword would be his undoing. He charged Valiant and slipped on a puddle of water.

Realizing now was his chance, Valiant once again used the hilt of the sword to knock Ridge unconscious. He turned toward his parents in time to see Rayna knock out Ellwood by dropping a column on his head.

"Father will not be pleased when he awakens." Valiant walked over to Fauna.

"I suspect not," Rayna replied. "You may drop your shield now."

Before Valiant could explain it wasn't his shield, the shield dropped. He caught Saffron out of the corner of his eye and watched her disappear through a door. He pointed to the three unconscious warriors and asked, "What do we do now?"

"You will go find Aatami and determine what is to be done with the item from that ridiculous wager. I suspect he is with his daughter." Rayna gathered Fauna in her arms. "Are you alright child? I will never forgive Ridge for this."

"I'm pretty sure she is the only member of this court who did not want the item. I say he made a good choice."

Rayna turned her wrath on her son. "Do you? And why are you still here? Go. Find out what can be done with that stupid thing."

*****

"What did you do?" Ralliner, matriarch of the red dragons, glared at her father.

"I lost a bet. I paid my debt."

"You made swords of great power and gave one to each of the realm lords. They will destroy each other."

Prized

"Probably."

"Don't look so pleased with yourself. If the ruling fae destroy themselves, the dragons will have to rule. The matriarchs don't want to rule. It's too much work. We have long worked behind the scenes to keep the ruling fae ruling. Your actions could destroy all we have built."

"But it will be amusing." Smiling, Aatami dropped into the river and left his daughter to her anger.

Ralliner blew fire and prepared for the arrival of whoever the realms sent to address the issue.

*****

Angry at his mother's attitude, Valiant sheathed his sword and left the library, opening a way to the entrance to Ralliner's nest. The two dragon guards advanced on him. Ortinoth said, "Enter in peace. Congregate in peace. Leave in peace."

"Or make the blood price so high your enemies will desire peace," Valiant said.

"Just so, Valiant the Bold. Ralliner is not expecting you."

"Her father gave my father an item of power." Valiant left the explanation there.

Ortinoth laughed. "That's why she's so angry." He bowed and made room for Valiant to pass. "I believe you know the way."

"I do, indeed," Valiant retorted. He wasn't surprised that there were no whelps pointing the way. He had not been expected. Of course, it was possible this was a test to see if he would get lost. He didn't. He walked into Ralliner's lair to find her resting on a rock.

Ralliner opened her eyes. "You may as well get comfortable. I suspect the other realms will send representatives as soon as possible unless they destroy themselves first."

Valiant dropped to the cave floor and followed her advice. This was gonna take a while. He busied himself tending his wounds.

Eventually, Cloud from the Central Realm arrived. Valiant looked up and smiled. "Are you here because of an item crafted by Aatami?"

"Yes." Cloud grinned and admitted, "I wasn't given any additional details as to why those on my lord's balcony were fighting."

Valiant nodded. "Join me. We'll have to wait for the rest of the realms to send a rep."

Soon after, Lugos, of the Southern Realm, and March, of the Eastern Realm, joined the vigil. When Prosper, of the Western Realm, arrived, all the realms were represented, and they waited for Ralliner to appear. Dragons, especially dragon matriarchs, did things in their own time, in their own way.

March, the son of Lord Leaf, raised an eyebrow at Valiant. "Perhaps you know why we're here."

"Aatami lost a bet with the realm lords. He created for them items of power. The one in the Northern Realm caused havoc. I'm here to see what is to be done."

"I know only that Lord River, his Master-At-Arms, and his realm advisor fought. All three were seriously wounded before Father Aldous intervened," Prosper said.

"Count yourselves lucky," Lugos said. "My brother, Lord Elros, had a similar fight when Aatami presented him with an item on the training field. Many warriors heard the presentation as they were on the field, armed, and ready for battle. Wounds were still being tended, and seven were dead when I was sent here."

Ralliner rose from the depths of her underground pool. "You are here because the realm lords and Aatami made a bet. Aatami lost. I will give you details if you agree to surrender to me the item from each of your realms. I will guard them and keep them safe from any fool who desires to wield them."

"And if we refuse?" Prosper asked.

"Then, I will leave the item in your realm. Once your realm is destroyed, I will simply retrieve it." Ralliner's eyes turned gold, and her teeth shown in the light when she smiled.

"Once the item is removed, will those affected by it return to normal?" Valiant asked.

"Once I have secured the sword, the affected will be free. They will remember what has happened and will desire the sword, but they will not feel the pull to wield it as they do now."

"Good enough for me," Valiant said. He didn't think the Northern Realm would survive a true fight between Lord Ellwood, Tempest, and Ridge.

"I agree with Valiant," Cloud said.

"I wish to hear the details before I agree," Prosper said, and the others nodded.

"Then gather around and hear the tale." Ralliner motioned for the men to move closer to her. "Valiant the Bold, Bard of the Northern Realm, you shall sing this song for all bards to share."

Prized

Valiant didn't bother to contradict the dragon. They named a person true. If she said he was a bard, everyone — excepting his father, of course — would consider him a bard.

Once Ralliner explained about the swords and completed her song, she said, "You five will travel together to the Queen's Court and present to them, and your realm lords, what you have learned. Goodbye." The red matriarch dropped into the watery depths.

"Who can open a way to the Queen's Court?" Cloud asked.

"I have been instructed to do so. The queens and realm lords await your arrival."

As one, the five men turned to see Theron, Master of the Hunt, and his daughter, Mistress Kanda. They worked for the five queens and obeyed no realm lord.

"Come." Theron opened a way, and Kanda walked through. The men followed her with Theron bringing up the rear.

The queens sat on their thrones with each realm lord standing beside their queen.

"We have heard from each lord. Tell us what Ralliner has said," Queen Niamh of the Northern Realm said.

The others looked to Valiant as he was her grandson. He said, "I have a song to sing after each of us describe the sword given to our realm. The Sword of Veracity was given to the Northern Realm. It reforms the universe to turn the words spoken by the wielder into truth."

"How is this accomplished?" Queen Ceridwin of the Southern Realm asked.

Valiant grinned. "Only those who were with the Forest Lord when he received the sword know the answer to that question."

Queen Ceridwin nodded. "Next."

"The Sword of Tenacity, in the hand of its wielder, will enjoy the complete confidence of all in his purview. Even the wielder will assume he can do no wrong." Lugos of the Southern Realm licked his lips and added, "I was not with Lord Elros when the sword was presented."

Prosper stepped forward. "The Western Realm received the Sword of Invincibility. As long as that sword is in the hand of the wielder, he will be full of courage and receive no injury; however, those who follow him can be killed. Each time the sword saves the wielder from harm, someone close to him dies."

232

"The Sword of Diligence came to the East, giving the wielder complete focus. Once the wielder releases the sword, focus is lost completely, leaving the wielder in a daze until the next sunrise." March nodded to his father, Lord Leaf.

Cloud, the youngest of the group, stepped forward. "The Central Realm received the Sword of Alliance. It unites any creature within the presence of the wielder. The unifying effect goes away as soon as the sword is sheathed."

Queen Niamh shook her head. "Every realm lord should know better than to make a bet with a dragon. Win or lose, you will lose." She turned to Valiant. "Grandson, sing for us."

*****

As the evening repast completed and the assembled made ready to dance, Valiant walked to the center of the room and said, "I have a message from Ralliner, matriarch of the red dragons. She desired I sing this song for all bards to share. It is titled, *The Five Swords of Virtue*."

Lord Ellwood nodded his head, and a pixie delivered Valiant's lute to him.

The court moved closer to hear. It was rare Valiant sang in the Northern Realm court, and everyone had heard that something happened, but no one had details.

"The realm lords bet with Aatami.
A foolish thing to do.
The dragon lost the bet that day
And left in quite a stew.

Five swords of power he did carve
And gave each a virtue.
But dragon made means powerful
And fighting did ensue.

Veracity, the Sword of Truth,
Went to the Northern Realm.
The wielder holds the truth in hand
And none should take the helm.

Tenacity gives confidence,
The Southern Realm will stand.

233

Prized
With sword in hand, no doubt is felt
By any in the land.

Invincibility offers
Courage to the West.
No harm to he who wields the sword.
Just he will be so blessed.

Diligence, the Sword of Focus,
Did travel to the East.
Sharp focus to the wielder but
Recovery's a beast.

Alliance, Sword of Unity,
The Central Realm will find,
Unites all with the wielder true,
But leaves them in a bind.

Each realm lord and those in his view
Received the needed tools,
To wield the power of their sword
Within the given rules."

"What does that mean?" Ash asked.

"It means the realm lords gave the swords to Ralliner to protect." Ellwood looked around his court. "The only time the five swords of virtue are to be mentioned in my court is when someone asks for the song to be sung."

Valiant turned to leave, only to find Tempest blocking his path. When she didn't move, he said, "I have to go to the other realms this night. I am to sing this song in every court."

Tempest nodded and backed away. "We'll talk tomorrow, brother mine."

"Not if I can help it." Valiant opened a way and left.

He returned home before the sun came up. Valiant was tired from his travels and not in the mood to deal with anyone. He entered through the garden, hoping to bypass everyone and get some sleep. He turned the corner and saw Tempest sitting on the windowsill.

"Go to bed."

"I want to know what happened with the swords."

"Go ask Ralliner. I don't have a clue."

"You must have some idea."

Valiant pushed past his sister, entered his rooms, and closed the door in her face. He had no intention of sharing what little he knew with Tempest. She was too interested in the swords.

*****

Valiant found Saffron sitting at the water's edge with no other siblings in sight. Finally. It had taken a couple of weeks for him to find her thus. When he sat down on a rock nearby, Tehuti and Kailani rose up out of the water.

Saffron winced but said, "Leave us. I believe my brother has something he wishes to say to me alone. I'm quite safe with him."

When the twins left, Valiant asked, "Do they often guard you?"

"Yes, they feel it is their payment for my patronage. I can't seem to explain that it is unnecessary." Saffron blushed.

"I would say caring guards are always useful."

"I suppose." Saffron pressed her skirts to remove wrinkles that weren't there. It was a nervous habit. "Do you have something to say, brother mine?"

"Are you hiding your abilities from the family?"

"I believe you already know the answer."

"I know that you can set a strong shield. What else can you do?"

Instead of answering the question, Saffron said, "I've watched, you know. Father leaves Temperance alone because she is not as strong as you and Tempest. I prefer to be left alone."

"I can respect that, but if no one knows your powers, how can we help train you? Have you shifted?"

"Can you block Tempest from your mind?"

"Tempest isn't the problem."

"Not yet," Saffron agreed, "But she is more like Lord Ellwood than any of the rest of us. You see that, don't you?"

Valiant cocked his head to one side. "No, I don't."

"Then we have nothing more to discuss."

Valiant opened his mouth to argue but closed it without speaking. After a few moments, he said, "You might benefit from a visit to Kavi."

Saffron smiled. "I am staying with her next month. It will be my last trip to the Seen as I have not displayed shifter gifts."

Prized

Valiant nodded and left. He took the conversation and buried it deep in the place where he placed knowledge he didn't want to share with Tempest. It was the one part of his mind she couldn't enter. He added one other fact. He had seen an orange tiger from the Seen in the woods recently. It was a breed Valiant had observed in Esen's territory. He had thought Tempest had taken another form. Now he wasn't so sure, but he would never ask.

Chapter 19 – 4869 BC

"Why are you escorting me?" Clarity gave Layton a withering stare.

"Saffron and Fauna went to the Southern Realm. You didn't want to go, so you're stuck with me."

"I don't need a bodyguard."

"Lady Clarity, if you object to your nephew as an escort, perhaps I will be acceptable."

She turned and stared at Ash, as did Layton. The Master-At-Arms, though old, was a handsome man, and Layton knew the moment Clarity decided to use Ash to escape Layton's escort. Clarity smiled and dropped her nephew's arm for Ash's. Layton watched, unsure what he should do. He didn't object to Ash, but would the Forest Lord?

"Don't worry. Lord Ellwood knows of Ash's interest in Clarity, and while he hasn't given permission, he has been lenient." Ridge stopped beside his son.

"I would have thought Ash would want a more pleasant companion."

Ridge laughed. "Ash has always liked his women strong-willed."

"Then, he has chosen well." Layton didn't look his father in the eye when he asked, "Why do you allow Mother to flirt with Father Aldous?"

"Allow? Son, no one, not even Lord Ellwood, ever allowed Lady Tempest to do anything. She does as she sees fit."

"Just so, my consort." Tempest stopped between Ridge and their son. "Do you have a question, Layton?"

"No, Mother." Layton walked off to join his particular friends. He wasn't interested in getting involved in the storm brewing between his parents. When he entered the Hall of Battles, Slate was unhappy. "Why the frown?"

"Not angry, annoyed." Slate pointed toward their friend, Night. "I saw her first, and he swooped in and is giving her the tour of battles."

Layton followed the pointing finger and stopped breathing. She was beautiful. "Who is she?"

"Lady Nolween of the Central Realm. A cousin of Lady Lindera's, visiting for the season."

Layton patted Slate on the shoulder and walked away. Night always followed the same path when showing a female around the columns. And wasn't that nice. When Night brought Lady Nolween to the first battle Lord Ellwood fought after being named the Forest Lord, Layton edged around and bumped into her.

"Forgive me. I am Layton, a clumsy fool." Layton smiled as he kissed her hand.

Nolween smiled back.

"Do you enjoy tales of heroics on the battlefield?" Layton asked.

"Why? Do you have tales of brave deeds to tell?"

"As clumsy as I am? I fear not. Sorry to have interrupted your tour." Layton stepped back and bowed.

Night growled at Layton as he continued on with Lady Nolween.

"Clumsy? Not even close." Slate whispered in Layton's ear. "I thought you would sweep her out of Night's arms."

"No reason." Layton smiled as Lady Nolween turned and looked back at him.

After Night returned Lady Nolween to the table with her cousin, he joined his friends at the table Lord Ellwood's girls had claimed.

"Why so glum?" Slate asked.

"Lady Nolween had no dances left." Night looked at his friends. "Did either of you secure a dance while I was showing her around?"

"Of course," Slate laughed.

Once the repast completed, Slate was the first to lead Lady Nolween onto the floor. As the evening progressed, Night watched Layton with interest. When Layton escorted his aunt off the floor, Night asked, "Did you not secure a dance either?"

Clarity followed Night's eyes and smiled. "Layton learned from the best. I'm sure he secured the last dance with Lady Nolween."

Layton bowed to his aunt and walked over to Lady Nolween as the last set started.

"Why the last?" Night asked.

"He'll be able to leave a lasting impression," Clarity explained. It was the signature move Valiant was known for. No longer did parents watch who he danced the opening dance with. Everyone watched to see who he led onto the dance floor for the last dance of the evening.

*****

At the next triple full moon, Ridge stood on the balcony of his fortress, his untied shirt blowing in the night breeze. He watched Layton flying in his dragon form. Lady Nolween from the Central Realm sat in the harness Layton had made for her. Perhaps she was the one who would make him happy.

In her jaguar form, Tempest exited the Dark Woods. He knew the second she saw him. He waved. Between one breath and the next, Tempest shifted into a bird form. Ridge's eyes opened wide. He had not known she had taken a bird form, but he wasn't surprised. There were many secrets she kept from him now. She flew to the balcony and shifted to human as she landed.

"I love the feeling when all three moons are full."

"What did you do this evening?"

"Ran the Dark Woods. Father Aldous was searching for herbs under the light of the full moons. He ran with me for a while."

She didn't look at Ridge, but he knew she was focused on his response. "He flirts with you."

"I don't respond."

"Not with intent, no, but you enjoy the attention."

"To be admired is gratifying."

Ridge reached out and gently clasped her arm, effectively holding her in place. "Does my attention no longer gratify you?"

"You're being ridiculous." Tempest removed his hand and walked away.

Ridge turned back to the night sky, and muttered, "No, I'm not." He watched Lady Nolween put her arms around Layton. Her embrace didn't cover more than a few scales, and he was still young. If his dragon size aged as a true dragon, he would be one hundred years old before he was an adult-sized dragon. Lady Nolween giggled, and both looked happy. They had become inseparable as the season had progressed. Ridge could remember when he and Tempest were like that.

Prized

The next morning Ridge left early and marched toward his object. He wouldn't open a way to his destination. That was suicide. This was already a fool's errand, but things could not go on this way. He left the edge of the Kaveri River and cut through a pass. When he reached the valley, he could see Father Aldous's home at the base of a mountain range, his dragons were everywhere. Some flew, some slept, and some played, but every dragon stopped and stared in his direction when Ridge stepped foot in the valley.

"I've been expecting you." Father Aldous lay on a large rock, sunning himself.

"Have you?" Ridge spat the words.

"Yes. Your status as consort is wavering. You should do more to secure Lady Tempest as your wife."

Ridge raised an eyebrow. "Do you think you will have better luck in that regard?"

"I doubt anyone will have luck in that regard until she issues an invitation."

"On that, we can agree."

"Why have you come?" Aldous sat up and crossed his legs at the ankle but remained on the rock.

"Why have you been expecting me?" Ridge countered.

"Fighting me will not improve you in Lady Tempest's eyes."

"A fact I know."

"Yet, here you are."

"Perhaps a fight will improve me in my eyes."

"Good enough. Let us fight." Aldous whistled. As one, all the dragons in the sky and on the ground turned and looked at Aldous. He whistled again, and they all turned their backs on him. "They will not interfere."

Ridge nodded. He had heard Aldous could command the dragons thus. Until now, he had not truly believed that.

Both men bowed. Before they stood upright, Tempest appeared between them. "Fools. You dare to fight for the right to be my consort?"

"Actually, Ridge and I fight for his peace of mind. You don't have much to do with that." Father Aldous grinned.

Ridge rolled his eyes. "Leave us."

"No, if anyone is going to fight for me, it will be me."

"In truth, we are fighting because of you, not for you," Ridge said.

240

"What's the difference?" A wave of confusion crossed her face.

"Before you arrived, we acknowledged that you alone will determine who your consort is."

"Then why fight?"

Ridge sighed and said, "Because I need to do something."

Tempest glared at both men. "You shall not fight."

"You say that as if you can stop us." Aldous's eyes twinkled and a smile graced his face.

"If I must." Tempest raised both hands. With her right hand, she used wind to send Father Aldous across the valley. He landed in a heap in front of the eldest of his dragons. Father Aldous didn't move from the ground, but his laughter echoed throughout the valley. The wind in her left hand sent Ridge flying through the pass and dumped him in the Kaveri River.

Ridge sat up in the middle of the flow and spat out water. Water dragons watched from the bank. A water nymph swam over. "Have you need of assistance, Ridge, Advisor to Lord Ellwood?"

"No." Ridge stood and left the river. Wet though he was, he took a leisurely stroll back to his fortress. He suspected Tempest would be gone when he arrived.

He was not wrong.

*****

"What happened?" Valiant blocked Ridge's path

"You have what you have long wished for. Lady Tempest no longer desires me as her consort."

"What did you do?"

Ridge gritted his teeth and noticed no one else was around. Giving thanks for small favors, he said, "If you must know, Milady took exception to a fight Father Aldous and I were going to have."

Valiant grinned. "Who won?"

"Lady Tempest. She tossed both of us in opposite directions." Ridge narrowed his eyes on Valiant. "If I hear a song of this tale, I will blame you."

"Too late. Three songs have already been written, though none by my hand. I just wondered which was correct. Turns out, none of them are." Valiant turned and walked away, laughing as he went.

Ridge rubbed the bridge of his nose. This was going to be bad.

Ridge had been right. Three weeks later and he was still being ridiculed. He could deal with that. He had always known that when

Tempest sent him away, he would be the court joke for a while. But he had not counted on the fights that would break out as young fools tried to prove themselves to Tempest by beating each other up. What a waste.

If something didn't change soon, he would have to come up with a way to put a stop to it. None of the fools would ever earn Tempest's favor. She didn't like to be chased. She liked to chase.

*****

Tempest had had enough. She snuck out of the family treehouse part of the residence without Valiant or Temperance, and she walked into the feasting hall alone, tired of the stupidity. Since Ridge was no longer her consort, every unmated male in the five realms had attempted to console her. Even the shifters had invited her for an extended visit. As if everyone expected her to replace Ridge. Ridiculous.

Using her peripheral vision, she could identify at least three fools bearing down on her. She stopped moving and raised her voice so that it would carry throughout the hall. "Concern for my wellbeing is neither expected nor required. I do not need to be consoled, nor do my spirits need lifting. Any male who approaches me thus will be castrated by my hand. The same fate awaits any who approaches me saying they have been given permission to address me by my father. If I want your attention, I will tell you."

Lady Rayna raised an eyebrow at her daughter, but Lord Ellwood looked pleased. Ridge and Ash, also sitting at the Forest Lord's table, didn't bother to hide their smiles. Ridge went so far as to chuckle.

Valiant escorted Temperance into the feasting hall, looked around the room at the wide-eyed crowd staring at Tempest standing regally in the middle of the room, and asked, "What did we miss?"

"Fear not. The bards will surely write a song, or three, about it," Ash said.

Chapter 20 – 3726 BCE

Saffron crossed the Kaveri River and walked through the Dark Woods. When she was sure no one was around, she shifted and ran toward her destination. In tiger form, she swam across the river to an island. Her island. Exiting the water, she shook before she shifted. Her next shift would be wet, but she didn't care.

A forest covered her island, but there was an opening that would be perfect for a treehouse. No one knew why she had petitioned the Forest Lord for ownership of the island, although she suspected Valiant knew. He had watched her closely of late, and she was sure he knew more than she would like.

She had expected Tempest to approach her, but it appeared that Valiant could keep Tempest from knowing all he knew. Apparently, Kavi had been right. Everyone in the family had a secret or two. When she arrived at the clearing, Valiant, Kyan, and Ridge waited for her. The three of them together, not fighting, was as surprising as it was lovely.

"What is this?" She asked.

"If you intend to live on an island, you will need a place to rest," Kyan said. He had brought a chair and a small table from his home. She had frequently admired both. She liked things made of wood, and Kyan had carved both.

Saffron raised an eyebrow, using Tempest's signature move, but she didn't speak.

Valiant grinned. "Don't worry. We made no specific plans. We are waiting for you to decide what you want.

Prized

"I want a place to myself where I can grow herbs and do as I like. I tire of court life."

"Don't we all," Valiant muttered. Louder, he said, "What should we build first?"

"Shouldn't you ask me?" Rhus, the most sought-after builder in the Northern Realm, joined the group. "Since I had to wade across the shallows to get here, might I suggest we start with a bridge?"

"Who sent you?" Ridge asked.

"I solicited Rhus to build my new home." When the others stared at Saffron, she smiled. "Did you think I would build my own home? Or better yet, did you think I would not even think about the necessity of having a residence?"

While the others looked sheepishly at each other, Rhus laughed. "Come. You three may build the bridge while I show Lady Saffron my design."

Weeks later, Valiant returned to Saffron's island to check the progress. Crossing the bridge, he was pleased that he had at least helped that much, even though it had been an easy task. Rhus had already cut and prepared most of the wood for the bridge, requiring little effort from Kyan, Ridge, and Valiant – working together – to complete the crossing.

The castle in the trees, as it was already called, was a statement piece. Mostly it said, stay out. Another bridge was being built high in the sky to connect Saffron's house to the cliffs on the mainland, allowing for travel on the path between the Northern Realm and the Western Realm. That bridge would be guarded, according to Saffron, but she would not divulge what type of guard. The small bridge over the creek already housed a clutch of water dragons and coterie of nymphs. Valiant had to give her credit. Saffron had planned much better than he would have.

*****

"Are you moving here?" Layton cut through the undergrowth, improving the seldom-used trail to Kavi's home. Improving the path would not make it more noticeable. Kavi's land was shielded with magic preventing unwelcome visitors from seeing the trail. If the rumors were true, humans and magic folk became ill if they were too close to the border of her land, unless she had invited them. Layton didn't know how the magic worked or who had crafted such a spell.

Valiant stiffened but didn't look up from his task. "Why would you think that?"

"You come to the Seen more than any of your siblings, and your attachment to Carwen is obvious."

"How obvious?" Valiant stopped in mid-swing and stared at Layton.

Layton grinned. "Very, to those of us who have seen you with her. Of your younger siblings, Saffron commented, but only to me. Clarity knows, but only cares about Tempest's actions, and I doubt she has spared a thought for your attachment to a shifter. Fauna is very private and provides the same courtesy of privacy to others. As far as Mother and Temperance are concerned, you would know better than I."

Relief etched Valiant's face. They returned to their task in silence until he said, "You and Saffron are close. Do you know all of her talents?"

"If Saffron had shared such knowledge with me, Uncle, it would not be something I would share without her spoken permission."

Valiant nodded, pleased that his nephew knew how to guard a secret, but still, he wondered how strong Saffron was. He had been unable to find additional information.

They reached an outcropping and looked over the valley. Layton pointed to the wild horses. "When last I traveled to the west, the humans were training the horses to pull carts. One man was attempting to ride them."

"How did he fare?"

"Not well, but not as bad as when the fae tried to tame the unicorns." Layton watched the horses.

"Think you to train a horse?"

"It would be grand, but I doubt I have the time." Layton watched the horses and repeated, "It would be grand."

*****

Layton walked toward Grandfather's receiving rooms. This would not be pleasant, but the deed was done. He walked up to Ash and said, "I await Lord Ellwood's pleasure."

"Enter. He is expecting you." Ash threw open the door.

Inclining his head to Ash, Layton entered. The rooms were a bit more crowded than he wished, but that could work in his favor. Or not. The outcome depended entirely on Ellwood's mood.

Prized

Ellwood leaned back and laughed at something one of his guards said. Spying Layton, he said, "Here comes my grandson now. What news have you?"

Layton bowed. "Lord Ellwood, I come to take my leave of you."

"Are you off to the Central Realm again?" Amusement greeted Lord Ellwood's question. The realm waited daily for word that Lady Nolween and Layton had exchanged vows. Lord Quest of the Central Realm had already given his blessing.

"Yes. Lady Nolween and I have exchanged vows. We tell her family tonight."

"I see. Do you wish rooms here so that Lady Nolween will have the comforts of court, or shall you remain with your father?"

"Neither of us desire life in court. I have procured land on the Kaveri River south of the Western Realm Residence."

The court stilled. While a short stay in the Central Realm would have been expected, it was typically the female who moved to the realm where the male lived. It was not common for members of two courts to exchange vows and move to different realm all together.

Layton watched anger flash across Ellwood's face. It was replaced quickly with a tight smile. Layton doubted anyone else noticed, but he had been waiting for it.

"Have you told Lady Tempest of your plans?"

"No, Lord Ellwood. I have come to tell you first." Layton had learned his lessons well. When delivering bad news to Ellwood, always make sure he had something to soften the blow. That he was told before Tempest would amuse the Forest Lord.

"Then I suggest you tell her before she hears the news from someone else. Good hunting, Grandson."

"Good hunting, Lord Ellwood." Layton bowed and left. That had gone much better than he had hoped. Knowing Ellwood would send someone to tell Tempest, Layton took his time meandering through the gardens on his way to his mother's rooms.

He arrived at his mother's treehouse just as Lady Fennel left. She bowed with an apologetic smile and passed without speaking. Layton grinned. Everything had gone according to plan. He opened the door and entered to find Temperance sitting on the balcony with his mother.

Tempest arched her eyebrow. "You told the court before you told your own mother?"

Temperance giggled.

246

Rolling her eyes, Tempest said, "How can I make my son feel guilty when you break down and laugh."

Layton kissed his mother on the cheek. "You are the one who taught me how to maneuver through court. Why make me feel guilty for following your instructions?"

"Sorry, sister mine." Temperance wiped the tears of laughter from her eyes. "But it was hard enough to feign shock when Lady Fennel was sent here to make sure you knew Father was told first. I couldn't keep up the pretense any longer."

"Fair enough." Tempest hugged her son. "How did you come by land in the Western Realm? It was a masterstroke. Had you settled in the Central Realm, it would have caused problems eventually."

"Let's just say, I owe a couple of boons to people." Layton grinned. "I do hope you're happy for us."

"Thrilled. You will make an excellent team. I couldn't have picked a better wife for you."

A quick knock was heard at the door, but before an invitation was extended, Valiant walked in. "Congratulations, nephew. Vows with Lady Nolween and a residence of your own. I'm jealous."

"Then get a wife of your own, preferably one of your choosing, not Grandfather's. I must leave, or I'll be late. We tell her court this evening." Layton clapped Valiant's shoulder and left.

Prized

Beginning of the End

3723 BCE – 3257 BCE

Chapter 21 – 3723 BCE

Valiant moved quickly down the living bridge and into the Northern Realm residence, ignoring all who tried to claim his attention. Valiant knocked on the private office of the Northern Realm's representative to the High Court, entering when he received permission. Temperance sat behind the desk.

"It is true?" Valiant asked. The question was redundant. She was sitting in the chair.

Temperance smiled. "Yes. I was selected as the Northern Realm representative to the High Court."

"Er, are you happy?"

"I would say relieved. Now I have a proper mission, something to fill my days." Temperance continued to make notes on the parchment.

Valiant harrumphed.

Sighing, she sat back and looked up at her brother. "I am well suited to the task. I have found that I can temper Father's reactions better than most, excluding Ridge, of course."

"But... do you enjoy the work?"

"You, brother mine, would chafe under the endless meetings and protocol, as would Tempest. I find it soothing to both my temperament and my ego. I can do good on the High Council."

"But the other council members? How will you go on with them?"

"Cloud of the Central Realm has been most helpful."

Valiant narrowed his eyes on Temperance. "Cloud has only been on the council for six months. How much could he know?"

"Stop. Cloud has been helpful in that he has shown me around and explained how the council works. Please, brother mine. I must finish reviewing this tome before the council gathers this day."

Prized

Valiant bowed and left. As he walked down the hall, he felt a weight lift from his shoulders. If Temperance was pleased with her new position, he could finally devote time to his own pursuits.

"Valiant, Lord Ellwood requests you attend him in the receiving hall."

Nodding to Ash, Valiant turned, and the two men walked toward the hall. "Any idea what this is about?"

"Not I. Lord Ellwood asked for you after Pinus entered the hall."

Valiant frowned. Had he injured Pinus in some way recently? He didn't think so, but Pinus was such a fool it was hard to say.

Ash announced him, and Valiant walked into the hall. Bowing, he said, "Lord Ellwood, you sent for me?"

"Yes, my son. I have heard from numerous sources that Lady Talmai holds your interest, yet you have not sought my permission to address her."

Valiant shot Pinus a look that promised retribution in the near future. "I do not take such steps lightly, Father. I will seek your approval when the time is right."

"You grew up together. Surely a thousand years is ample time to know your mind. You are not leading a daughter of my court astray, are you?"

Most of the assembled suspected that Valiant had led many daughters of the five courts astray, excepting only Lady Talmai. Amid snickering, Valiant said, "Of course not."

"Good. When you finally ask, you may be assured that you will be greeted with my approval."

Valiant's mouth dropped open. The Forest Lord had just said – in front of the court – that he would approve a union with Talmai. The noon repast was in an hour. She, and the entire court, would know before then. He bowed and left. His search for Talmai failed. Deciding his best bet was to find her and confess that he loved another, he arrived for the noon repast.

Generally, the noon repast was a casual affair with few in attendance. Most grabbed food and continued on with their day. Today, the feasting hall was packed.

Elm came to stand by his side. "Everyone knows."

"Everyone?"

"I think a couple of pixies who clean the private rooms may not have heard." Elm's smile was apologetic. "If you want, I'll throw the first punch. We could both end up needing healers."

"As fun as that sounds," Lady Talmai said, "I desire a word with Valiant."

Elm bowed and backed away.

Valiant opened his mouth to speak but was stopped by gentle fingers placed over his mouth.

Talmai spoke softly but pitched her voice so that the tables nearest them would hear her words. "If circumstances were different, I would welcome your address, but I find we will not suit. Please do not utter words that might cause embarrassment for both of us."

Valiant's mouth dropped open for the second time that day.

Talmai leaned in and hugged him. When he returned the hug, she whispered so that only his shifter hearing could hear. "You love another. I have long known that. I wish both of you very happy. Do not allow Lord Ellwood to determine your future mate."

Talmai turned to Elm. "Have you seen Lady Temperance? I wish to speak with her."

Elm held out his arm and moved her through the silent crowd.

"Couldn't hold her interest?" Pinus asked.

"He held her interest for centuries. How long have you held the interest of a female?" Ciam asked.

*****

Looking around, he realized the contents of the room were not needed. Valiant finished packing his bag and turned to leave. Tempest blocked his path. He didn't want to have this discussion again. "It's done. I told Mother. I'm going to wed Carwen, and we will set up a clan north of the Alpha Clan near one of the large bodies of water. Grandmother offered me the land."

"You're really leaving. Why not bring Carwen here?"

Valiant dropped his bags and glared at Tempest. "Do you think I would bring her here where she would be without her family or friends, surrounded by fae who consider her less than them? And let's not forget Father. Can you imagine how he would treat her? She is not the wife he picked for me."

"I'll miss you."

"And I, you, but you don't need my protection. You never have." Valiant placed a kiss on his sister's forehead. A wicked grin crossed his face. "Although the realms might need protection from you. Try not to castrate potential suitors."

Tempest rolled her eyes. The bards had worked hard to include that phrase in the songs sung of her break with Ridge. "I heard some of the shifters living near the Alpha Clan are moving with you."

"Yes, and Cwenhild is not happy about it. I guess most of the younger shifters want to get away from the Alpha Clan."

"It's her own fault. She is a tyrant and was vocal about wanting you to lead a clan of her choosing. I'm not surprised they chose you." Tempest grinned.

"Yet, somehow, she'll blame me for her loss of workers. She really is a lot like Father."

"I've noticed that, as well." Tempest pulled Valiant into a tight hug. "Visit often."

"Doubtful, but you may visit me anytime. You will always be welcome in my home and the clan I, no doubt, will end up leading."

Opening a way, he left the Farseen and exited in a clearing in the Seen where he had told Carwen to wait for him. He had planned to slip away without speaking to anyone. Just a little time together before they were joined. Taren had scouted the site with Valiant and would be able to lead the others to the new clan.   Obviously, that wasn't going to happen. He looked at the group gathered in the field. She was joined by at least thirty other shifters, mostly families with children, ready to travel with their belongings and supplies. They had even copied the small two wheels on the back of their carts. The same ones he had made for Carwen's cart. Although humans didn't yet have a wheel, the Farseen had used them for some time. Hopefully, this small gift to the Seen would go unnoticed by the fae. Ever since the Atlantis incident, the realm queens disapproved gifting the Seen with knowledge from the Farseen. Valiant stuffed down his groan and, even though he knew the answer, asked, "What's this?"

Taren placed his youngest on his cart and walked over. "We told you we wanted to move. You will be a strong clan leader. We've chosen to follow you."

Valiant looked around as the assembled crowd nodded as one. When his eyes fell on Carwen, she smiled. Not knowing what else to do, he admitted, "I'm not sure I want a clan."

"Well, we're following you, so you have one. Better decide how you're gonna rule."

Frustration welled up in Valiant. "Why don't you lead the clan and take them somewhere?"

"Look at this group. We both know you're the leader, and I'm your second. I've found I like being second."

"You mean you don't want the headaches from leading."

"That too," Taren said. Lowering his voice so that only the two of them would hear, he added, "We both know you won't follow anyone, except Tempest and even her you are known to ignore. You will eventually lead a clan, regardless of your desires. This one wants you, and you already know all of us. If you go off with Carwen alone, she will be happy for a while, but she's always been surrounded by kith and kin. She will miss her friends, and you know it. This way, she will have friends with her from the beginning, even though her father chooses to stay with the Alpha Clan."

Valiant sighed. He liked being alone but had been concerned that Carwen would tire of the solitude. Alone meant no one would jest at his expense. But Carwen was much more outgoing than he. Raising his voice, he said, "The journey is difficult. It took six days of hard walking, including crossing two mountain passes, to scout the land that Cwenhild gifted me."

"Aren't you opening a way?" A couple of men called out the question.

"Can anyone else open a way?" When no one spoke, Valiant said, "I will not be able to always transport you back south when needed. You must know the best route to take. The only way to do that is to walk it."

"Told you." Taren grinned. "He may have been raised in the Farseen, but he knows how to lead successfully in the Seen."

Ignoring Taren, Valiant said, "If you wish to go back to the Alpha Clan, you should do so now. I will not transport you back if you decide the journey is too rough."

"At least with you, we can be ranked in the clan, right? We will have the privileges that being a member of a clan brings. I no longer wish to work for the Alpha Clan without knowing why I'm doing whatever I'm told to do."

"Yes, any adult who makes it to my destination will be ranked."

"I'm in."

"Me too."

Prized

When no one left, Taren whispered, "We want to have a say in how we live. The Alphas issue orders without our input."

Valiant nodded. It was why he wouldn't live with the Alpha Clan as well. "Taren will lead as he helped me scout the area a while back. I'll bring up the rear. Everyone else in between us. There will be no stragglers. If there is an injury, we all stay until the injured can move again."

Murmurs of agreement met his announcement.

Valiant tossed his bag on the cart Carwen had prepared for them and watched the clan move out. His clan. Now he was responsible for these shifters. He glanced at Carwen, and her smile lit up his heart. He would do anything to keep that smile on her face.

The first couple of days were pleasant enough. Shifters stayed human to carry their supplies. Those pulling the carts were well pleased with the efficiency of the wheel. The children thought they were on a grand journey, but by day two they realized that adventure was hard work. On day three, when Rhun, Taren's eldest, sprinted toward Valiant, he knew there was a problem.

Stopping to take a deep breath, Rhun said, "Sickness. Mama needs Carwen."

"Go. I'll set up camp." Valiant whistled. When the adults turned toward him, he pointed to an opening that would make a good camp and headed that way. He was surprised and gratified that the others followed him without argument, even though it was only midday.

Cadel stopped his cart next to Valiant. "Problem?"

"Sickness. Help the others get settled and see if anyone else is showing symptoms of any kind."

Cadel nodded and issued orders to his twins who would shift in the next few months and be ranked in the clan.

Valiant joined Carwen, who was with Taren and two other families.

"They ate something while foraging for food as they walked. We don't know what, and they're too sick to tell us."

Valiant noticed the sick were the same age as Rhun. He caught Rhun's eye and asked, "Did you walk with them earlier?"

Rhun winced, but said, "They picked berries. I didn't know what they were, so I didn't eat any."

"Go find me the plant."

"Wait." Carwen handed Rhun a piece of cloth. "If it's what I think it is, even touching it is poisonous. Pick it using this."

Feeling useless, as he always did around sickness, Valiant walked back to the camp.

"What is it?"

"Who's sick?"

"Is it contagious?"

The questions came from women huddled together, holding their young children.

"It appears to be something they ate," Valiant said.

"They ate the berries of the adder's root." Carwen joined the crowd. "It's a good thing the symptoms appear so quickly. They hadn't eaten much, but Vala had an uncommon reaction to the berries, and she's very sick.

The sickness delayed the journey by three days. There was some grumbling when Valiant said they would wait a third day. After Valient asked who would carry the nearly grown children when they became weak and tired, everyone agreed another day in an agreeable camp would be acceptable.

The last part of the trip was as challenging as Valiant had promised, but none of his new clan gave up. He found that by the time they entered the valley next to the loch where they would make their home, he had already noted which clan members would be good at various tasks. When he saw movement near the loch, Valiant called a halt and told his clan to wait. He shifted to his bird form and flew to the camp to see who waited for them. He landed and shifted, not bothering to hide his anger. "What are you doing here?"

Standing over a pot of food, Cwenhild looked up in surprise. "Why are you angry? I simply thought to provide you and your clan with a good meal after a long journey."

"Hello, brother mine." Tempest walked out of the woods with fish in a basket. "Growl all you want. I came to see how you're treating my new sister. We planned to arrive a couple of days after your journey. What trouble befell you?"

Without answering, he shifted and returned to his clan. Shifting back to human form once again, Valiant grabbed the cart and headed for his new home contemplating options for removing his grandmother and sister from his world.

"Who's there?" Cadel asked, falling in line behind Valiant.

Prized

Taren motioned for the others to pass so that he could take the rear and watch for stragglers. No need to get lax now. "Only Cwenhild or Tempest can make him that mad, that fast."

"Right on both counts," Valiant growled.

"Does this mean the Alpha Clan and the fae will visit often?" Cadel asked.

"Not if I can help it." Valiant tightened his hold on the cart, and they moved into the valley that would become their home.

Carwen touched his shoulder, and Valiant wasn't surprised that her touch relaxed him. It had happened often enough. She whispered, "You are our Alpha. You have never felt the push to obey Cwenhild. Give her this. Allow her to say goodbye to those who came with us on her terms."

Valiant didn't respond, but he knew she was right. The smell of frying fish greeted the clan as they finished their journey. Even he admitted, if only to himself, that fresh fish he didn't have to work for would be good this evening. An open sitting area around the cooking pot had been laid out. He ignored both his grandmother and sister, working first on his own tent, and then helping his clan with theirs.

While the shifters set up their tents, Cwenhild laid out a basket with fruit leather.

"I didn't know there was any left." Carwen looked over the dried fruit made from the pulp of the hawthorn berry.

"I put some aside for your trip. It's not yet warm enough for berry picking and suspected the children would enjoy a treat after their long journey."

"So will we all. Thank you, Sovereign." Gwynne, Cadel's wife, shooed the kids away. "You may have the excellent treat the sovereign brought after tents are raised, and water is fetched."

Tempest joined Carwen and said, "Walk with me."

They walked through the field, picking early herbs for a while. Finally, Carwen asked, "Is there a reason for this walk?"

Tempest smiled and handed Carwen a bracelet.

Looking at the bracelet, Carwen tried to hide her surprise. Her father was the most praised jewelry worker in both dimensions. It was not his design. What did she need with another bracelet?

"Lord Ellwood is not a kind and benevolent leader. He is not happy that Valiant left and that he has taken a shifter to wife." Tempest sighed. "Father will do nothing so low as to attack, but he won't object if another fae does. If something happens and you are not safe, even if you simply feel you are not safe, take the bracelet off. It will call to me, no matter what dimension I'm in and I will come. Once you put it on, only you will be able to see or feel it. At least, that's my hope."

"You don't know?"

"I know that no one else will see it, but magic behaves oddly around Valiant. I am unsure if he will see it or not. If he does, simply say it was my welcome to the family gift."

Carwen shook her head. "I have never lied to Valiant. I won't start now. If he asks, I will tell him the truth."

"The decision is, of course, yours. I think you should know that Valiant has never been as happy anywhere as he is when he's with you. I wish you blessings in your new life." Having said her peace, Tempest opened a way and left.

Carwen returned to camp with a basket full of herbs and a bracelet on her arm.

*****

A few days later, descaling fish, Carwen watched the bracelet reflect the sun. Tempest's craftsmanship was nearly as good as Adair's. She had waited to see if anyone noticed it, but they didn't. Tempest was full of surprises. So engrossed in her thoughts, Carwen didn't notice his approach until Valiant pulled her into his arms for a kiss.

"My love, you must take care to watch your surroundings. If the bracelet Tempest gave you is so distracting, perhaps you should put it up."

"You can see it?"

"Of course."

She grimaced. Would Valiant be angry that his sister was watching out for his wife? "Why didn't you say anything?"

"Why didn't you," he countered. When Carwen frowned, Valiant raised her chin and looked into her eyes. "It's okay. I'm not mad. In fact, I'm relieved. I know she can work a spell to make jewelry invisible to others. Jewelry that will call to her if there is danger. The fae expression is a Bracelet of Honor, and few have the talent to create such an item. It is not surprising that Tempest is able. I do worry about you and now the entire clan. I'm glad she has given you such a gift."

"I was afraid you would be angry."

Prized

"Years ago, I would have been, but I've learned a few things. Father takes a long view, and he might attack when I'm away or if I let down my guard. Tempest is an excellent fighter and a powerful ally."

Chapter 22 – 3720 BCE

Tempest marched through the residence, a weapon in each hand. Blood dripped from her sais and her clothing, evidence that the battle with unaligned fae was the worst she had experienced. She had lost three worthy warriors, one respectable arbitrator, and her temper. When Tempest lost her temper, she killed every unaligned fae in the Dark Woods using a combination of fire and spells. Fools to think they could take on the Forest Lord in his own territory, especially with Tempest guarding his lands. It was not the first time she had proved herself since Valiant moved to the Seen, but it was the bloodiest.

She walked into the receiving hall and bowed to Ash. "Tell Father I am here. Now."

Ash took in her appearance, clenched his teeth, and left. When he returned, Ash said, "Lady Tempest, the Forest Lord will see you." He held the door open, and she walked in.

Tempest ignored Temperance, who stood at the left hand of their father, her mother standing on his left, and Tempest gave the slightest of bows to him. "The Dark Woods no longer provide cover for your enemies."

"Very well, daughter mine. Why did they attack?"

"I know not." Tempest gritted her teeth, but admitted, "I killed them all before questioning them."

Lord Ellwood laughed. "I always thought Valiant was the one with the temper. It appears I was wrong about that."

Tempest's eyes flashed, but she didn't speak.

"Ellwood, do not provoke your eldest when she's in a mood." Lady Rayna said.

Prized

Ridge cleared his throat. "Lord Ellwood, perhaps Milady should clean up before her blood stains your floors."

"It's not my blood," Tempest said.

"All the more reason to clean up," Ridge retorted.

"Regardless of whose blood it is, I do not want it in my hall." Ellwood's decree would have been more impressive if he weren't smiling.

Tempest snarled. "You demanded my presence immediately to provide a status. Immediately does not leave room for cleaning up."

Before Tempest let blood fly in the hall, Rayna grabbed her daughter's arm, ignoring the blood, and they left by the private entrance.

"How do you put up with that, that…"

"Tempest. He is your father and the Lord of the Realm. If you tire of his orders, move to the Seen as Valiant has done."

Tempest raised a single eyebrow. "Do you wish me gone?"

"I wish me happy. You will never be happy here. Perhaps in the Seen, you will find a male who holds your attention." Rayna pressed her lips together for a second before she said, "I, too, tire of the Farseen. The time is not far off when my children will have to choose to remain under Lord Ellwood's rule or return to the Alpha Clan with me."

Tempest stopped moving and stared at her mother. "Finally."

"What do you mean?"

"Whatever you may have felt for Father has been over for some time. I, for one, feel only relief." When Rayna glared at her eldest, Tempest laughed. "Kyan and I had a bet that you would leave before the end of winter last year. I lost that bet."

"I worry about the younger girls."

"What's to worry about? I think they all will wish to stay here."

"Even Clarity?"

"She, more than the rest of us, enjoys being a daughter of the court."

"But she shifts."

"You know as well as I that she craves power. She will never pass you or me in a clan. Even she realizes that."

*****

"Are you leaving?" Fauna asked while braiding Clarity's hair.

262

"I have no trips planned" Clarity looked at her reflection. Tempest wore her hair higher. "Shouldn't the braid start higher?"

Fauna nodded and brushed out her sister's hair to start over. "Valiant's gone. Tempest will leave soon, or she'll wait and leave with Mother. Mother and Father will break their vows before another winter solstice, and Mother will leave. Layton will stay because he married a fae and lives outside of Lord Ellwood's influence. Saffron has already moved to her own residence, and I suspect will stay there. You shift so you have the option. If I shifted, I would move to the Seen, where it is serene."

"You would give this up for life in the dirty temporary camps the shifters set up?" Clarity raised an eyebrow in surprise before laughing. "You would. Now that Gilmer moved to Valiant's camp, you could be with him. He admires you as you admire him."

Fauna looked around. When she didn't see any pixies, she whispered, "I would give this up to get away from Father, and perhaps to be with Gilmer, but it doesn't matter. I don't shift. I would never be accepted there. All would consider me Father's spy. I will remain in the Farseen where my dominant abilities may yet work for me."

Clarity snorted. Fauna was the weakest of Lord Ellwood's offspring with very little power of her own. She had no dominant abilities. Many thought Fauna was touched as she never spoke a harsh word or engaged in court intrigue. Fauna was the only family member Clarity cared for.

Hair perfectly braided, dressed in a lovely gown displaying the Northern Realm colors, Clarity walked in the family gardens upset by Fauna's words. She never wanted to leave the Northern Realm. There was nothing in the Seen to draw her there. Unfortunately, there was nothing in the Farseen to keep her here.

"Daughter mine, how pleasant to see you."

Clarity whipped her head around to stare at Lord Ellwood. He rarely entered the gardens as they had become Mother's domain. The two were rarely in the same area of the residence, and, while there was no official division, everyone in the court knew which areas were used by whom.

"Lord Ellwood." Clarity stood and bowed.

Ellwood took her hand and guided her to her favorite bench. Wondering if he knew, she sat, waiting for him to speak.

Prized

"I hope you know that the strain between Lady Rayna and I has nothing to do with you."

Clarity bit back her scoff. The only child that had ever interested Father was Tempest. Nothing Clarity ever did had not already been done by his firstborn, who was superior to all. Only Tempest could cause a strain between their parents because only Tempest was loved by both.

Ellwood smiled sadly. "I see a future where your mother will return to the Seen. She is no longer happy living amongst the fae. I cannot go with her for I must live where I rule. I wish there were some way for me to protect Lady Rayna."

This time Clarity did scoff out loud.

He nodded. "I know Lady Tempest will go with her, if for no other reason than to be closer to Valiant, but my firstborn is not given to speaking with me. I need someone with Lady Rayna who will help me protect her."

Clarity watched the water dragons playing in the Kaveri River. Was Father asking her to spy on Mother? Or did he sincerely want to protect her from afar? It didn't seem likely, but Clarity wanted to be his chosen. Not just one of his offspring, but the one he depended on. Trusted. Loved.

Valiant and Tempest openly disliked Father. Temperance was a dutiful daughter of the court, and, while she was faithful to Father, she would never be in a position to move to the Seen. Saffron didn't like anyone, and she hid in her tree castle as it was commonly called. Fauna was Fauna. Sweet and caring, but lacking the power to protect herself, much less anyone else. Like Saffron, Fauna didn't shift.

Clarity turned a smiling face on her father. "What can I do to help protect Mother?"

Ellwood kissed his daughter on the forehead. They sat together for some time talking.

*****

When Corentin, the largest of the Farseen's moons, was waxing, Lady Rayna and Lord Ellwood stood in front of the stone into which their vows were carved. The stone had been placed on a recessed wall niche beside the entrance to the family treehouses.

The dispute was simply another in a long line of arguments. It was not a matter of great importance, but that no longer mattered. Rayna looked up at the male she thought she would spend forever with. She no longer saw her husband, but a ruthless lord who only cared for his schemes. Oh, he cared for his court, but only because his court was the source of his supremacy. He was the most powerful of the realm lords, and he would not allow anyone or anything to change that. For the first time, Rayna saw Ellwood for what he was, a bloodthirsty tyrant.

Her voice was steady when she said, "I will no longer attend your needs, shield your heart from harm, or honor you."

"Nor will I address your needs, cherish your heart, or honor you," Ellwood retorted.

The stone crumbled and fell to the floor.

Rayna's eyebrows raised at the hurt she heard in his voice. She wondered if it was because she was the first to break their vows, or if he still felt something for her. She suspected it was the former. She turned and walked through the way. Clarity nodded to her father and followed her mother.

Tempest inclined her head to Lord Ellwood, followed Rayna and Clarity into the way, and closed it behind them.

The rubble from the shattered stone remained where it was for centuries. Ellwood forbade the pixies to clean it up.

*****

Kyan opened a way to Ralliner's lair for their scheduled meeting. As he approached the entrance to her lair, the guard on the right twisted his neck and lowered his head until he was eye level with Kyan. "Enter in peace. Congregate in peace. Leave in peace."

Kyan finished the quote, saying, "Or make the blood price so high, your enemies will desire peace."

"Just so," the other dragon said. "Tread carefully, but if you make a mess, please clean it up."

Both dragons laughed.

Shaking his head, Kyan walked into the cave. As he wondered what he was supposed to tread carefully over, Kyan heard someone walking before he saw them. When Kyan saw who had just left Ralliner's, he growled. "I told you if you ever hurt my sister, we would have a problem."

Ellwood's lip curved up into a snarl. "She broke our vows first."

"What did you do to cause her to take such an action?"

"Ask her." Ellwood moved to walk past, and Kyan threw a punch. Ellwood blocked the punch and twisted to kick Kyan into the wall.

Prized

Kyan bounced off the wall and dropped into a fighting stance. "I'll remove your head from your body."

"If you think you can." Ellwood stood poised and ready.

The fight lasted a good while, but in the end, they were both leaning on the cave wall to give the appearance of being upright. Both men were bloodied. Blood flowed into Ellwood's eyes from a gash on his forehead, blocking his vision. Kyan was pleased to note that Ellwood couldn't stand straight. As for himself, he could put no weight on his left leg.

"Gentlemen, if either of you can be called thus, I will not allow my lair to be the location of the start of a war between the shifters and the fae." Ralliner's voice slid into each man's head, though her body could not be seen.

Kyan knew a moment of dizziness and then found himself in the meadow next to the sovereign's hut. Forgetting about his left leg, he stepped forward and promptly fell to the ground. He lay there for a minute, wondering if it was worth the effort to crawl to his hut. He groaned when Tempest came into his field of view.

"What happened?"

Tempest's expression was so bland that Kyan knew she was trying not to laugh.

Rather than explain he had fought with her father, Kyan said, "I fell."

Now Tempest did grin. "Looks to me like you fell into someone's fist... more than once."

Valiant leaned over and nodded. "Yep. That's what it looks like."

"Keep your opinions to yourself and help me into my hut."

Tempest grabbed the fish Valiant had slung over his shoulder. "I'll get the healing herbs and meet you in Kyan's tent."

"Don't tell Rayna," Kyan said.

As soon as Tempest was gone, Valiant helped Kyan to stand, forcing his uncle to lean on him. "Don't put any weight on that leg. Consider me your left leg until we get to your hut." As they slowly moved through the meadow, Valiant asked, "At least tell me Father is in worse shape than you."

Grunting from the pain, Kyan retorted, "How did you know?"

"You said, 'Don't tell Rayna.' The only reason you wouldn't want her to know is that you came to blows with Lord Ellwood. Besides, who else would you fight within the Farseen?"

"What makes you think I was in the Farseen?"

"The way you were tossed through was opened by a dragon."

Kyan sighed and surrendered. "We were fairly even until Ralliner intervened."

"Too bad."

Kyan cursed when Valiant lifted him to carry him over the stream. Guess Valiant was tired of their slow progress.

Chapter 23 – 3490 BCE

"You've been watching the herd for days." Valiant stopped beside his nephew. Layton and Nolween had come to visit. Nolween enjoyed learning to cook and clean without the aid of pixies. At the same time, Layton helped Valiant with some business in the east. Once they returned to Valiant's clan, Layton had taken to watching the wild horses nearby. "What are you planning?"

"The horses in the Botai Settlement are not just beasts of burden now. They are riding them."

"I know. I've worked a trade with a shifter in Esen's clan, and he is coming here to train my clan to work with horses."

"I've always wanted to ride one."

Valiant laughed. "You've spoken of that since you were a child. Do you remember watching the fae try to ride unicorns? Their injuries were severe."

"Horses don't have magic. No horn that lightning can spew forth from."

"They can still throw you and trample you."

"Perhaps, or perhaps I'll ride."

"If the humans see us, they will think us nuts."

"Us?" Layton raised an eyebrow.

"I can't let you undertake such a foolish activity without supervision. Tempest would never forgive me."

Layton laughed. "You want to ride one as well."

"Yes, I do."

Layton walked toward the herd. "We should do this before Carwen and Nolween discover our plan."

268

"I agree. Our wives will not approve of such silliness." Valiant clapped his nephew on the shoulder.

Three days later, Valiant opened a way and carried Layton into the settlement.

Nolween looked up and shook her head. "You finally did it. Managed to hurt yourself in your silly quest."

"It was an accident." Valiant walked past the women and into his home, where he laid Layton on a mat.

"Accident?" Carwen pushed Valiant out of the way and dropped down beside Layton. "You fools were trying to ride a horse."

"Actually," Layton hissed when she placed her hand on the break, "we were trying to tame one first."

"How did you know?" Valiant asked.

Nolween looked up from mixing an herbal pain reliever. "Taren's young have been following you. They found it amusing that their Alpha couldn't control a horse."

"Valiant, be useful and get Telyn unless you want me to set his leg."

Valiant opened a way and did as Carwen asked. When he returned with the Alpha Clan's healer arrived, she adjusted his leg in practiced moves and healed it.

"Drink this." Nolween handed Layton the mixture she had just made. "It will help relax you and aid in healing."

Carwen tapped her foot on the floor, glaring at her husband. "No more horseplay until Esen's man comes to train you properly."

"Yes, dear." Valiant kissed her cheek.

Prized

Fae/Shifter War

3267 – 3257 BCE

Chapter 24 – 3267 BCE

Valiant stopped in mid-swing and dropped to his knees.

"What happened?" Taren had been around his Alpha enough to know when someone in the Alpha Clan was talking directly into his mind.

"Cwenhild, under attack. Protect our clan." Leaving Taren in charge of his clan, Valiant ran through the way on four furry legs. Kavi had sent the location straight into his brain. He had forgotten how painful that was. He slowed when he saw the carnage. It was considerable, and he had arrived too late to be of use.

Fae mercenaries, unaligned to any realm, had been crushed, probably by wind. As with Tempest, it was the sovereign's favored element for brute force. Shifters loyal to the Alpha Clan were dead, mostly burned, and formed a circle around the sovereign. Afon, Cwenhild's consort, the fae would say, had been run through with a fae blade and beheaded. Beside Afon, Cwenhild's body had been crushed and run through with multiple swords. The necklace Kyan made and presented to the sovereign as a symbol of her rule, had fallen to the ground and was surrounded by the bright colors of the fall leaves.

Surprised the fae didn't take it as a symbol of victory, Valiant shifted and reached down to pick it up so that Rayna could claim her birthright. It didn't move, but his fingers burned when he touched it. He pulled his fingers back. Though they felt burnt, the skin was not harmed. Valiant stared at his grandmother's body while rubbing his fingers. He had never truly loved her, but he had respected her, a respect that came only after he was the leader of his own clan. Her guidance had been invaluable over the five hundred years since he had moved to the Seen and become Alpha of his own clan.

Clarity reached for the stone and pulled her hand away quickly.

"Only the next sovereign can pick it up." Kyan walked through a way with many of the family and stopped beside Valiant.

Tempest walked out of a different way in time to see Clarity's actions. "You know Rayna is the next sovereign. Only she can pick it up."

"Never hurts to check." Clarity gave Tempest an appraising look. "Are you going to try?"

"No need, Rayna is our sovereign."

"Try." Clarity's challenge was not a surprise to anyone.

Tempest reached down and touched the stone. Valiant looked at the assassin's ring that Kyan had turned over to her only a few weeks ago, glad it wasn't on his finger. Valiant didn't mind killing, but he didn't want to spend as much time traveling for the sovereign as Tempest did. At first, he thought the necklace moved, but Tempest pulled her empty hand back. "As I said, no need to try."

Clarity's lip turned up in a snarl. "Where is Rayna?"

Tempest pointed to the way she had left open. Rayna walked through. "Tempest suggested that I wait until she verified the area was secure."

Valiant barked a laugh before he realized his mother was serious. That was a surprise. Rayna didn't follow suggestions. She gave orders. Always had. Perhaps the shock of knowing she was now the sovereign had tempered her domineering nature, at least for the moment.

"Well?"

Clarity's impatient question was so typical, it irritated Valiant, and he said, "Rayna is now our sovereign. She will do as she sees fit in her own time."

"How logical you are," Clarity said.

"Enough." Rayna leaned down to pick up the symbol of a sovereign's rule. Her hand rested on the stone. She neither picked it up or let it go.

Tempest's whisper was heard by everyone in the clearing. "Pick it up, Mother. We have a species to unify and a war to wage."

"War?" Clarity raised an eyebrow.

"Of course, war." Rayna grabbed the necklace, placed it around her neck, and turned to the core of her family. All who could gathered when they felt Cwenhild die or Kavi told them, depending on their individual gifts. Standing tall, Rayna looked each person in the eye. "The fae killed the shifter sovereign. They declared war. Line up for a dominance push. We must be a united Alpha Clan. A blending of Cwenhild's line and my line."

Rona, Katell's daughter, and the only granddaughter of Cwenhild lined up with the others. Her first shift was only last spring.

"No," Katell said.

"Yes." Rayna laid a hand on Katell's shoulder for silence. "She is needed."

No other words were spoken. The already ranked members of the Alpha Clan lined up in order. Rayna, Tempest, Kavi, Katell, Loane, and Jocosa.

Valiant watched in surprise when Tempest joined them. He hadn't known that she had already been ranked in the Alpha Clan. Made sense. She had taken over the duties of the sovereign's enforcer from Kyan a while back. He bit back a smile at Clarity's responding snarl to Tempest's rank.

"I have removed Kyan from the clan ranking as he now serves as the sovereign's protector."

"And he's done a great job." The snide remark from Clarity carried.

Rayna turned a withering stare on her daughter. "Cwenhild ordered him to protect me on my scouting trip. Not even Kyan can be in two places at once."

Fire flashed in Clarity's eyes, but she remained silent. Clarity was older than Rona, so she walked up to start the dominance push with Jocosa.

"No." Rayna pointed to her son. "Valiant is older. He goes first."

"He's already Alpha of his own clan!" Clarity protested.

"And he will also be ranked in the Alpha Clan." Rayna's voice left no room for discussion.

Valiant grinned and walked up to Jocosa. He breezed through the push until he reached Tempest. After they had stared at each other for some time, Rayna tapped them both on the shoulder. "Since they are obviously an even match, Tempest, as my enforcer, will remain second. Valiant will be third."

Valiant hid his irritation that once again, Tempest was the chosen one. After he thought about it, Valiant found he was okay with that. Tempest was forever traveling on the sovereign's business. Internal shifter issues had never interested him unless it was within his own clan.

Clarity went next and ended up between Katell and Loane.

Rona's ranking surprised everyone. She passed her mother but was stopped by Kavi.

Prized

Rona smiled, obviously pleased with herself.

"Rona will remain with the clan when we fight," Rayna said.

The smile that had lit up Rona's face turned angry. "I am an adult."

"Yes, an adult who is a member of the Alpha Clan," Rayna agreed. "As such, you will obey my commands. When we are engaged in battle elsewhere, you will protect the clan. Lead them in combat if necessary. Someone must protect those who are weaker than the fae."

*****

Tempest walked out of the way and stopped in front of Valiant. "You didn't have to scream. What's so urgent?"

"Carwen."

"Is she sick? Shall I call for a healer?"

"No, not sick exactly."

"Well, if she's not… oh." Tempest grabbed her brother in a hug. "I'm so happy for you."

"But, we're at war. We can't have a baby now."

"The babies disagree."

"Babies? Plural? You sure?"

"When have I ever been wrong about a birth?"

Valiant nodded. Alpha females and their birthing bonds were odd but useful. "I'm just stressed. We're at war."

"I'm hoping to avoid that."

"How? The fae attacked, we retaliated. They're gonna retaliate. It's how war works."

"If we can come to an agreement before the death toll climbs higher, we might end it."

"I think it's too late for that."

"In that, Clarity agrees with you."

Valiant shook his head. "That may be the first time I've agreed with Clarity."

"I'm pretty sure you're right. Come, let's check on Carwen."

"Will you hold the birthing bond?"

"No, I'll send for Telyn. I can't fight if I'm holding a bond."

*****

"You were warned." Tempest stood at the head of the shifter fighting force, fire in her left hand, a sword in her right. Two sais sheathed on her back and a dagger sheathed on each hip. And those were just the visible weapons. She glared at the unaligned fae. "Leave or die."

276

"'Tis the sovereign's assassin." A warrior laughed. "I do not think even you can defeat all of us."

"I suspect you are wrong, but, as it is, we stand with Tempest," Adair said.

"Look. It's the maker of baubles. He would fetch a fair price as a slave."

Adair moved to attack. Tempest stretched out her hand and used the flat end of the sword to block his path.

The warrior cast an amused eye over the shifters. "Assassin. These pitiful shifters are not strong enough to hold back our numbers. We are the superior fighting force."

"Superior in arrogance, perhaps. Superior in combat, I think not." Valiant walked out of the tree line with the majority of the warriors from his clan. "Stop talking and let us battle like warriors." Valiant jumped and used wind to propel himself forward. He landed in front of the fae, drawing first blood by beheading the arrogant fool.

Tempest sighed. She had hoped to prevent another battle. Truth be told, she had hoped to stop the war before too many lives were lost, but it was not meant to be. The ground would flow red with blood this day. She yelled a battle cry and joined her brother in the fray. The shifters and fae fought.

Once the battle was over, Tempest looked at Valiant. "That seemed too easy."

"I was thinking the same. Even unaligned, the fae weren't as well trained as I would expect." Valiant used a cloth to wipe the blood off his weapon.

Tempest grabbed her head and dropped to one knee. Carwen's bracelet called to her. "Carwen."

Valiant didn't wait. He opened a way and ran into it without further information.

Tempest growled and followed him, as did the rest of Valiant's clan. The clan scattered, searching for their families.

Everyone in Valiant's camp, which was everyone who had not gone to protect the new sovereign, lay dead or wounded. The attack on Rayna had been a distraction. The goal had been the destruction of Val's clan.

There was no one to fight. As soon as Valiant and Tempest arrived, the fae left, leaving fire in their wake to prevent anyone from following. Tempest watched Valiant run for his house. She knew what he would find. Carwen on the ground, clutching her stomach in a vain attempt to protect their unborn twins. Tempest opened a way and called for Jocosa, a healer in the Alpha Clan.

She walked over and checked Gilmer, Fauna's friend, but Tempest knew he was already dead. Gilmer had remained behind to guard the clan. No one had expected the fae to attack Valiant's clan, but she should have. Destroy Valiant's clan, and he would lose his fighting edge. It was precisely the type of attack Ellwood was known for and one of the reasons the other realm lords feared him.

Taren returned, holding his youngest, a six-month-old girl. "Wynne is dead. She hid Aylwen. My older children require healing."

Another of the warriors returned carrying his dead wife. "Why? Why did the fae attack our clan?"

"You know. We discussed it when we left the Alpha Clan to follow Valiant. The fae were bound to attack him if war broke out between our people. This is the risk we took." Taren turned to face Tempest. "This was your father, yes?"

"I can't prove anything." When Taren growled, she said only, "I grieve with thee." Turning to the others, she said, "Help Jocosa search for the wounded. Gather the wounded, bury the dead. I'll patrol."

"Jocosa, come with me." Taren walked toward the wounded, still carrying his youngest."

Tempest pointed to two of the single men from Valiant's camp. "You two with me."

Valiant's cry of anguish silenced the camp.

"Adair, join Valiant in his home." She didn't bother to tell Adair Carwen was dead. Valiant's scream said that plain enough.

Once she had secured the area, Tempest stood guard over the entrance to Valiant's home, knowing both men wanted to be alone with Carwen while they grieved.

A short time later, Taren — still holding Aylwen — handed a small basket to Tempest.

"What's this?"

"Eat."

She didn't take the basket. "Give it to the wounded. They need it more."

"You need your strength in case we're attacked again." He shoved the basket at Tempest at the same time he handed his daughter over to her. "Watch Vala. Tell Valiant we need him."

Tempest was forced to take the basket with the child.

"I trust Aylwen is safe with you." Taren walked away.

Tempest looked down at the child, who smiled up at her and grabbed one of her braids. Tempest winced and gently loosened the child's grip.

"What are you doing with Aylwen?" Valiant stood at the entrance to his hut, wearing more weapons than Tempest ever remembered seeing draped across his body.

"Do you think you are the only one to suffer? I'm watching the only member of Taren's family who isn't dead or wounded while he helps look for survivors."

"I will kill Lord Ellwood." Valiant's vow was spoken more to himself than his sister as he went to check on his clan.

"Well, Aylwen, it looks like I have work to do."

*****

"What are we waiting for? When do we attack?" Valiant paced. He hadn't been able to be still since Carwen's death.

"Whom shall we attack?" Rayna stared at her son.

"Ellwood."

"Have you proof of his involvement?" Rayna turned her focus on her eldest. "Tempest, what did you find?"

"All attackers were unaligned fae." When Valiant harrumphed, she sighed. "Yes, I agree. Lord Ellwood was behind the attack, but there is no proof. Father did not get to where he is by making foolish mistakes. Nothing ties back to him. Not people, not weapons. Nothing. However, the fact remains that no other fae, but Father, has a reason to go after Valiant's clan."

Valiant jumped down from the rock, saying, "I will — "

"Do nothing." Rayna's response was soft, but her face was set in granite. "You will do nothing at this time. You and Tempest are our best defense against a fae attack force. I need you close."

"Following your orders is what cost me the life of my wife and unborn children."

"Valiant!"

"Quiet, Clarity. I will not hear platitudes from you of all people." Valiant jumped back on the rock and started pacing again.

Clarity snarled but, when Tempest shook her head, remained silent.

Prized

Loane stood. "While I know Lord Ellwood was behind this, I cannot prove it outside of what I saw in the minds of the fae you killed." When Valiant growled, she joined him on the rock. "Do not snarl at me, nephew. We cannot approach the Tetrad with only my word. No telepath is given such power."

Valiant balled his hands into fists. "I need to hit something."

"Shift. Run," Loane said.

When he left, Tempest raised a single eyebrow. "Was that wise?"

"Better that he releases his anger now. Rayna will have a plan of attack before he returns."

*****

In wolf form, Valiant ran. At first, he had no clear direction. What was the sovereign thinking? They should take the fight to the fae, not wait for the fae to come here. He had left Taren in charge of his clan, a clan he had failed to protect. No way would Valiant return to the Alpha Clan, but he no longer felt qualified to protect his clan. Taren had done more to help the clan rebuild than Valiant, but then Taren lost his wife, but his children live. Valiant shook his head. That wasn't fair. Valiant ran until he reached the cliffs overlooking the enormous expanse of water. He dropped to his belly and watched the waves for a while. The salt air tickled his nose as he plotted.

A smile slowly took over his face, showing his very sharp teeth. He knew what to do.

The next morning, Valiant opened a way and entered the Northern Realm. He, better than most, knew how supplies traveled between the realms, and he doubted if anyone would think to change the process. Finding a comfortable position on the overlook, he settled in to wait.

It didn't take long before his target arrived.

Nymphs carried supplies from the Western Realm to the Northern Realm. Perfect. Valiant stood and focused his fire on the supplies. Just the supplies. He wanted to scare the workers, not kill them. When the supplies burned, the nymphs screamed and jumped away from the sudden fire. Valiant grinned. It wouldn't stop trade. Too many fae could open ways. However, the disruption would irritate Ellwood, and that was the goal.

Next, he attacked unaligned fae in the Northern Realm. He knew his father allowed them to remain in his woods as long as they performed duplicitous tasks that benefited the Forest Lord. He watched and attacked only if he found one alone. This process of attacking supplies and unaligned fae continued for days. The only change was that Valiant left messages that would confuse everyone except Lord Ellwood. Valiant wanted his sire to know who was causing him pain.

One day, Valiant waited at yet another location. He was surprised when he saw Harden walking with the nymphs. Apparently, Lord Ellwood decided to change tactics. Valiant frowned. He wished no ill to his childhood friend, but Harden served Lord Ellwood. Valiant's anger returned. Anyone who stood with Lord Ellwood stood against Valiant.

Setting the supplies ablaze, once again, Valiant watched in surprise as the fire cooled. Harden opened a way and sent the nymphs through with the supplies. Setting his stance, Valiant switched to water. Unlike fire, Harden had no control over water. Just to be sure, Valiant moved the ground under Harden, and his childhood friend tumbled into the mud.

"Starless night, Valiant." Harden, now wet and covered in mud, stood. "I know you can hear me. Talk to me."

Valiant appeared in front of Harden. "There is nothing to talk about. Ellwood killed my wife and unborn children."

"I grieve with thee."

"Do you? Do you really? Has Ellwood killed your family? Oh wait, you aren't mated yet, are you? Exactly how do you feel my pain?" Valiant threw another fireball at Harden.

Harden absorbed the fireball. "Real mature. Can't we talk?"

"No." Valiant doused Harden with water.

"Fine. Next time, Lord Ellwood will give orders to kill you. I had hoped to talk you down." Harden opened a way and left.

Valiant sighed. He couldn't talk. If he did, he was afraid he would kill everyone. Carwen was not just his wife. She was his center. The anger he had felt all of his life would fade away in Carwen's presence. Now, he would never find his calm again. Never had he felt so alone.

*****

Tempest tracked Loane down in a village, where she was healing sick children in a human settlement. The work was delicate as she had to slowly heal them to prevent the humans from discovering her magic. Loane was the only member of the Alpha Clan to even attempt such delicate work. "Do you still believe it was wise to send him hunting?"

"Not wise, simply the best option."

Prized

"He sneaks into the Farseen, attacks realm warriors and unaligned fae, leaving ridiculous messages for Ellwood before he returns to the Seen." Tempest dropped to the ground and leaned back on a tree. "How is that better?"

"He is not attacking Rayna."

"What?"

"That was his intent before I suggested he leave. He was so angry he was going to attack his mother, our sovereign. Do you think that would have been better?"

Tempest sighed. "No. Has he calmed at all?"

"Don't you know?"

"His pain was too much. I…" Tempest's voice trailed off. After a minute, she admitted, "I couldn't take his pain."

"So, you closed down completely. Did it occur to you that if you shared your pain over the loss of Carwen and the twins, it might help him?"

Tempest's mouth dropped open. "Of course not."

"Think about it. Now go. The sick requires my attention."

Tempest left Loane and opened a way to the sanctuary in the West that she and Valiant still used. She flew through in bird form as her human form was too different from the humans who lived there. After verifying no other humans were nearby, Tempest shifted and meditated. Eventually, she opened her mind and then opened a way to Valiant's location. At least he was currently in the Seen.

*****

Valiant shook his head and eyed the way that opened right in front of him. It held Tempest's signature. He choked at the pain he felt, but the pain that flowed through him was not his own. He listened for a moment and verified it was Tempest. Her sorrow at the loss of Carwen and the twins. He walked through the way in human form.

"It's a good thing we are high in these mountains, brother mine. Have you forgotten what the humans in this area look like?"

"If you opened a way, it was safe."

"I'm sorry I closed my mind to you. I could not deal with your pain, as well as my own. I failed Carwen."

"How did you fail her?"

"Her initial call came while we battled the unaligned fae. Her death blow came just as we defeated them."

282

"What could you have done?" Valiant's voice lost some of its anger. "Neither of us could leave the shifters to face the fae alone. And you know if you left, I would have followed. You didn't do this. The Forest Lord did."

Tempest grabbed her brother and hugged him tightly. High in the mountains, above the tree line, brother and sister grieved.

*****

How did you do that? Tempest's voice echoed in Valiant's head. He ignored her.

Having surprised even himself, Valiant looked at the carnage. When he had returned with Tempest to the Alpha Clan, Rayna revealed her plan for revenge on the fae. Although she didn't call it that. Rayna took the fight to the fae realms, keeping the fighting out of the Seen to protect the shifters who weren't so able to care for themselves. It had the side benefit of protecting humans as well.

The shifters fought alone. The witches and wizards of the Seen were not powerful enough to fight against the fae, although they were getting stronger as they learned their craft. Vampires and demons weren't even a consideration. The blood-sucking demons thought only of their food, while the underground demons wanted nothing to do with anyone not of their race. The remaining preternaturals of the Seen were not powerful enough to be of use in a war where elemental powers were the weapon of choice.

For that reason, Valiant stood alone on the highest sand dune of the Southern Realm. Using the knowledge his grandfather had given him, Valiant had gathered the elements thrown at the shifters by the fae, condensed it into a ball, and returned it to the center of the fae fighting force. The explosion flattened the majority of the fae. The remainder attempted to reform, but Tempest used wind to knock them into the mountain.

Tempest must have heard his confusion that she hadn't killed them outright, because she spoke into his head once more. *Those who remained are too inexperienced to kill.*

Valiant nodded. Both of them disliked attacking those who couldn't protect themselves.

Clashes of this nature became normal. Sometimes Valiant and Tempest fought alone, and sometimes other members of the Alpha and other clans joined them. But the results rarely wavered as they fought the fae. Together, the brother and sister duo had always been powerful.

Chapter 25 – 3258 BCE

"Now? We're at war! You can't have a baby now." Layton ran his fingers through his hair.

When the contraction finished, Nolween smiled at her husband. "We've been at war with the shifters for nine years. Did you expect the fighting to stop because of our child's birth?"

"No, of course not," Layton muttered. When Nolween giggled, he rolled his eyes. "Maybe I did. Who shall I send for?" Although he wanted his mother at the birth, Layton knew that no fae realm would allow Lady Tempest to visit. Honestly, he couldn't blame them. Tempest and Valiant had done a lot of damage to all five realms. It had been hard enough to convince the fae that he was his father's son and not his mother's spy. If Tempest ever showed up in his territory, his family would be in grave danger from all five realms.

Lady Z breezed into the room. "I have come for the birth and brought Lady Hero."

Layton looked up in relief. If his mother couldn't be here, Lady Z was a good substitute. And Lady Hero was the most sought-after midwife in the realms. Still. "How did you know?"

Lady Z raised a single eyebrow.

Layton nodded. "Elementals." How convenient for his aunt that all elementals talked to her. The things she must know.

The labor continued into the night. The women evicted Layton from his own bedchamber while they tended his wife. Just before the sun rose, Layton heard the soft cry of a baby, then another. He sat up and smiled. His kid had a set of lungs on him. He stood and approached the door. It opened before he got there.

Prized

Smiling, Lady Z held back the door and allowed him to enter. Layton looked at the two babies and then his wife.

"Surprise," Nolween said. "Orton is our firstborn and Kelton our second."

Tenderly, Layton hugged his wife and sons. When Nolween became tired, he carried the twins into the other room to let her sleep.

"Twins." Lady Z took a baby and handed him a cup of tea. "You didn't tell us your wife was gifting you twins."

"We didn't know. Normally, I would have asked Mother to attend…" his voice trailed off.

Lady Z smiled sadly. "This silly war must end."

"Then you stop it. I know of no one else who can."

"Your faith in my abilities is misplaced. I can no more stop this war than you can." She placed one twin in the only bassinette and said, "I will tell Tempest of the birth." With those words, Lady Z left.

For a long while, Layton looked back and forth between the bundle he held and the other in the bassinette. "Twins. I need to double everything."

Lady Hero stuck her head out the door. "She's awake and ready to feed them."

When he came out of the bedchamber, his father and Nolween's parents were waiting for him.

*****

Tempest stuffed down her dominance and opened a way. Never had she been so glad for her ability to hide what she was. No fae would know the sovereign's assassin was in the Farseen. She wouldn't disturb her son or his family, but she had to see the twins. She had not even known Nolween was expecting. Her first grandchildren would never know her unless the war ended, and maybe not even then. She had done some despicable things in this war.

She flew toward Layton's home in her bird form, careful to remain in the shadows. The flying form she took was a predator, and there was none like it in the Farseen. The shutters of Layton's home were not closed completely. She found a perch and peaked in to see Ridge holding both boys. The smile on his face said more than words. Nolween's parents were also in the room. After a few seconds, Ridge handed a boy to each of them.

She knew a flash of anger that he got to enter Layton's home without putting the family in danger, but she pushed it away. That was war. She couldn't blame any one person for it. Although in her more uncharitable moments, she wondered if the war could have been prevented if Valiant had not gone on the attack; but if the roles had been reversed, and the fae had killed her mate and children, she would have done worse. Tempest had always had the more dangerous temper. Hearing the door open, Tempest flew to the underside of the roof to be further in the shadows.

Ridge closed his eyes for a moment and took a deep breath. When he released it, he opened his eyes and turned toward the exact spot where Tempest hid. Speaking so low that only a shifter could hear, he said, "You forget how well I know you. Wait here. I'll bring them out."

Tempest didn't shift or speak. She considered leaving but knew that she could defend herself — even from Ridge — and this might be her only chance to hold them. She was surprised when, a few minutes later, Layton and Ridge came out, each holding a bundle in his arms. They walked past the house to a sitting area hidden from view by rocks.

After a few seconds, Tempest flew into the woods and shifted, taking a form that none would associate with the Sovereign's Assassin. She walked into the sitting area and said nothing. There were ears everywhere. A twin was placed in each arm, and the men stood guard as she cooed to each child. A few minutes later, she handed the children back to their fae family, walked back into the woods, shifted, and flew into the night so she could open a way far from Layton's home. No one could trace ways, but why take the chance. She didn't speak to Layton or Ridge.

*****

While Tempest met her grandsons, Valiant moved through the Northern Realm with his grandfather.

"I still don't know why we're here." Valiant showed Ilar the cave where he and his sisters had played.

"I have never seen the Farseen."

"Wartime is not a good time for traveling."

"Mayhap you're right. Mayhap you're wrong." Ilar moved around the cave and nodded. "This will do nicely. You may leave, Grandson."

"How will you return? You can't open a way."

"True, but I'm not here to leave. I wish to stay for a while."

Valiant stared at his grandfather. "What are you planning?"

"Nothing for you to concern yourself over. Now go. Return in two weeks, but not before."

Prized

"No wonder you didn't stay with Cwenhild. You're both too bossy. The Forest Lord has many spies in these woods."

"Go."

Valiant bowed and left. He was under no illusion as to what Ilar wanted. As he got to know his shifter grandfather, it became obvious that, though Ilar couldn't live with the sovereign, he still loved her. Knowing it would do no good to argue, Valiant left his grandfather to his vengeance.

*****

Ilar was gifted in many ways. One was the ability to take multiple forms. He had three forms that no one else had ever seen. The fly was, by far, the most convenient for a spy. He watched the Forest Lord's home with no one the wiser for many days. When the time was right, Ilar flew into Ellwood's chambers, shifted to his human form, and waited. He sat on the windowsill so that when Ellwood opened the door, he would see Ilar.

Ellwood threw open his door, saw an unknown shifter, and threw fire. The fire curved around the shifter and set the drapes on fire. The Forest Lord put out the flame and looked at Ilar as if working on a puzzle.

"Don't you want to know who I am?" Ilar stood and braced for a fight.

"You are a shifter. I don't need any other information."

Ilar grinned. "I am the grandfather of your children."

Ellwood tilted his head for a moment. "You were Cwenhild's consort?"

"I am, was, her mate."

"I bid thee welcome to my residence, Father mine. Curious. In all my time in the Seen, I never once met you."

"I didn't bow well to the sovereign."

"I understand." Ellwood tossed his overcoat on a chair. "Are we to fight?"

"Yes"

"To what end?"

"Your death."

Ellwood laughed. "We would have been friends in another time."

The shifter smiled grimly but didn't move. Although Ellwood commanded water, air, earth, and fire, those elements had no impact on Ilar. He didn't even bother to move. When Ellwood lost his temper and swung his sword in a wide arc, Ilar moved quickly out of the way.

A light came into Ellwood's eyes and the shifter knew he was in trouble. Ellwood pulled metal fireplace implements from their stand and threw them with a precision Ilar would have appreciated if he wasn't so busy dodging the weapons.

The battle lasted longer than expected. The shifter had considerable skill, but in the end, the Forest Lord's physical strength was superior. Ellwood looked down and asked, "Who are you, really?"

Ilar grinned but didn't speak. Taking one final breath, the light went out of his eyes.

Ellwood gathered up the warrior, opened a way, and sent him back to Rayna's site.

*****

"Who is that?" Clarity asked, pushing the body off her. The dead body had come through a way and dropped on her.

"Grandfather." Valiant dropped by Ilar's body. He glared at Rayna. "This is Ellwood's work."

"It was certainly Ellwood's signature on the way. But how? Ilar could not have gotten to the Farseen without help, and Ellwood didn't know Ilar." Unshed tears filled Rayna's eyes. "How do you know who Ilar is?"

Valiant ignored the question. He had known what his grandfather intended. He shouldn't have taken Ilar to the Farseen. The problem was Ilar and Valiant agreed that Ellwood needed to die, and Valiant thought Ilar would be the victor because of his immunity.

Tempest used wind to move a couple of fallen trees to create a funeral pyre before she raised Ilar's body and placed it on top. While Tempest worked, Ilar's children gathered. When Rayna nodded, Tempest ignited the fire, and Valiant sang a song to aid a warrior into the afterlife. Valiant remained long after the others had left. Neither Rayna nor Tempest said anything to him, but Valiant was sure they both knew it was his fault.

"It wasn't." Kavi laid a hand on Valiant's shoulder.

Valiant turned surprised eyes on Kavi. "I thought everyone had left."

"Ilar could be difficult, but he was very persuasive. He would have managed to get to the Farseen without your help. He wouldn't want you to blame yourself for his choices."

Chapter 26 – 3257 BCE

"I cannot stay." Kulvir's tone was apologetic. "The supreme matriarchs have decreed the battle between the shifters and fae outside the preview of dragons.

"As expected," Valiant said. He waved as Kulvir flew away. He had been surprised that Tulvir had not recalled her son to the tribe long before this. Smiling grimly, Valiant set a shield around the odd combination of ruling fae from all five realms. The shield prevented the fae from leaving this location, but they were also safe inside. Nothing he or Tempest could do would harm them. He felt Tempest layer a containment spell over his shield as if his shield weren't strong enough. Valiant growled. He could still hear his mother's voice in his head.

"Keep the fae occupied. If all goes well, I will sign a treaty with the High Court this day. Clarity, you will lead the shifter force on an attack in the sand dunes of the Southern Realm. Tempest and Valiant will contain the foolishly named Death Squad in the Western Realm near Chrysocolla Falls."

Valiant managed a grin, remembering Clarity's pleasure at being in charge of the troops until she realized she was just a diversion. Her jealousy of Tempest was so obvious he wondered why Rayna didn't put a stop to it. One day, Clarity would do something horrific if she continued down her current path.

Valiant frowned when Lord Ellwood and Lord Leaf arrived. Ellwood had not spoken to Valiant since he moved to the Seen. Not even with all the pointed messages he had left for his father.

"Still hiding behind your sister?" Ellwood's soft words carried to Valiant's shifter hearing. "As a son, you are a disappointment."

"Surely I've disappointed you as more than just a son." Valiant allowed his voice to carry for all to hear. "I seem to recall that you were disappointed in my fighting skills, both hand-to-hand and with weapons when I was young. As an adult, every decision I made was a disappointment to you, from my choice in living accommodations to my chosen wife."

Ellwood seemed to consider Valiant's words. "True. Your every action, as a son and a member of my court, has been a disappointment to me."

"Ignore him. Father doesn't matter." Tempest grinned at Valiant. "He never did."

Valiant's eyes lit up, and he nodded. "At one time, I thought he did. I was wrong about that, too."

"Then come, Valiant the Bold. Let us battle for control of the Northern Realm."

Tempest screamed both inside Valiant's head and aloud. "No. Do not —"

"Sorry, sister mine. The challenge is made, and I accept." Valiant bowed to his father. "See you on the killing field."

Ellwood disappeared. Before Valiant followed his father, he heard Lord Leaf say to Tempest, "Will you go after them or shall we battle?"

Valiant didn't wait to hear her answer. Valiant knew Tempest held honor high, and she had sworn to Mother that she would keep the Death Squad occupied.

Valiant arrived to find only his father in the arena. No observers. He approached slowly, looking for traps.

Ellwood turned to face him with a ball of fire in hand. "You are truly a disappointment." As he finished the sentence, Ellwood threw the fire.

The fire swerved away from Valiant, and he laughed. "You never understood my powers, did you?"

"Your powers are nothing." Ellwood threw balls of fire in a continuous motion. The balls swerved away before touching Valiant.

"They are subtle. That is true." Valiant didn't move, and he knew that most people thought he wasn't doing anything when elemental powers appeared to twist and turn, always missing him. Valiant didn't have to do much, but he did need to pay attention to his opponent's movements. He wasn't even sure Tempest understood. She had not attended his training with Ilar.

Angered by his son's seemingly unconcerned demeanor, Ellwood uprooted trees and sent them flying at Valiant, who dove out of the way. Elements couldn't harm him, but physical items could.

An evil grin lit Ellwood's face. Pleased that he had found something Valiant was afraid of, he sent tree after tree at his son. Valiant was quick, dodging this way and that. Tiring of the game, the Forest Lord gathered a grove of trees and buried Valiant. Before he thought better of it, Ellwood used wind to press the trees into the ground. Ellwood laughed and waited for Valiant to push the trees away.

Nothing happened.

The grin fell from Ellwood's lips. After a few minutes, when nothing happened, Ellwood used wind to remove the trees. Valiant had been crushed. The fool didn't even protect himself. That boy had always been a disappointment. More interested in music than fighting, shifters instead of fae, doing as Tempest wished and not as his father decreed. How could that boy have been his?

Ellwood's anger dissipated as he realized that he had a new problem. Tempest had devoted herself to Valiant since his wife died. Now she would have time to focus on her own anger.

*****

Kyan opened a way to the Southern Realm. The Shetaffire Treaty had been signed, and he had come ahead to verify there was a secure place for the High Court and Rayna to appear. He looked at the devastation. Why had Rayna left Clarity in charge? The most bloodthirsty of the Alpha Clan, Clarity needed supervision at all times. He followed Clarity's eyes and saw Tempest, standing over Fauna's dead body.

It was then that Kyan saw the change in Tempest. Her sorrow at Fauna's death gave way as anger took over. Tempest turned her eyes on the fae, called wind, and flattened nine squadrons of fae warriors and their commanders. Fighters on both sides stopped to see the devastation. As a result, the combat zone was strangely silent when the fae high court and the shifter sovereign walked through the way behind Kyan.

Terra, Eastern Realm envoy to the High Court, did not appear to notice the odd silence as she opened a scroll. "The High Court and

shifter sovereign have signed the Shetaffire Treaty. It reads as follows."
Her clear voice sang the words.

> "Shifters and fae reside in peace.
> No longer shall they fight
> Transgressions by their own designs
> To spare us further plight.
>
> No harm between the two shall cause
> A war to break anew.
> But cooler heads will rule the day
> To keep us calm and true.
>
> Use the Treaty of Harmony
> To organize with grace
> A discourse between kith and kin
> So we can meet someplace."

Terra closed the scroll, and the shifter sovereign joined the five High Court Envoys to respond, "So must it be." The treaty was in place, and the fighting stopped.

Tempest opened a way and left.

Kyan and Saffron ran to Fauna's body, and that was when Clarity saw Fauna's charred body. She screamed. "She killed Fauna. Tempest killed Fauna."

"You know that was not her intention. Where is Tempest?" Saffron asked.

"With Valiant, of course." Even though tears fell down her face, Clarity's eyes were black as night.

Temperance clutched Cloud's arm for support. Before she fainted, she said one word. "Valiant..." Cloud caught her before she hit the ground.

Lord Elros held out his hands in a symbol for peace. "Lord Ellwood challenged Valiant to a duel. They left together. Lady Tempest stayed to keep the Death Squad from joining the fight here."

"And then she came here, killed Lady Fauna, and destroyed nine squadrons of warriors, killing my sons." Lord River gathered water, but Lord Sky and Lord Elros stopped him before the fighting started anew.

Prized

"She did so before the treaty was proclaimed," Elros said.

"Who knew that she had such power? What spell was it?" Sky asked.

Rayna stepped forward. "I don't think it was a spell. Wind has always been her best element. If she was angry at being tricked into killing her sister and worried about Valiant and Lord Ellwood fighting, her emotions fueled her wind. She has never displayed that much power before."

Kyan looked up in surprise but said nothing.

*****

Tempest exited the way into the Northern Realm's killing field. Valiant's bloodied and broken body lay in the center of the field, recognized only by his clothing. Both his head and heart had been crushed. She didn't need to identify the body. She had felt his death before she saw him. The field had been compacted as if a heavy weight had pressed into it, causing a crater. Ellwood was nowhere to be seen. The Patron's Sword was missing, but she saw Kulvir flying away with something in his talon.

Tempest screamed and dropped to the ground beside her brother. He had always been her other half. Although they were born triplets, Tempest and Valiant had considered themselves twins. Even as children, Temperance was on the outside, never fully understanding her more volatile siblings. Never joining in their pranks. Never shifting.

Tempest felt the way open but didn't turn around. "Leave me."

"You are not the only one here to mourn our brother," Temperance said.

Tempest looked up to see silent tears falling down Temperance's face. "Did Father announce his victory?"

"I have not seen him. I heard your scream."

"You don't have the power to hear my mind."

"Everyone heard you scream. The ruling fae of the five realms, the lesser fae, and even the realm queens. Grandmother sent me to suggest that you might want to close your mind, else everyone will know your weakness."

"Valiant has always been my weakness. Even Father knew that truth."

"Yes. I suspect Valiant goaded Father into displaying his temper, and the death was an accident."

Tempest stood and turned to face her sister. "You dare to blame Valiant?"

"No, but Father's temper is well known to us all, as was Valiant's sarcastic retorts."

Turning back to Valiant's lifeless body, Tempest asked, "Are we to duel now?"

"There is no need. We signed a treaty with the sovereign."

"Who?"

"The Fae High Court and the Shifter Sovereign. The Shetaffire Treaty by name. Do you wish me to sing it for you?"

Tempest's eyes turned black as night. "Mother dared to sign a treaty?"

"She didn't know about Valiant at the time."

"Or Fauna." Saffron appeared directly in Tempest's line of sight. "The treaty prevents revenge killings, and your mind is still open for all to hear, sister mine."

Tempest narrowed her eyes on Saffron.

Saffron didn't move, but a sad smile played across her lips. "If you attack, you are in for a surprise."

Glancing at Valiant, Tempest said, "I do not wish for any more family to die. One day Father and I will meet again, and he is the one who will be surprised." Tempest opened a way. Before she walked through it, she said, "It was not my intention to kill Fauna, the gentlest of us all, but I cannot deny that is what I did. Peace be with you, sisters mine. I doubt I will ever have peace again." Tempest walked into the way and closed it before they could respond.

*****

Kyan marched toward Tulvir's cave in long, sure strides. He stopped before the dragon guards.

The guard on the right twisted his neck and lowered his head until he was eye level with Kyan. "You are not scheduled to see Tulvir this day."

"But, nevertheless, she expects him," the dragon on the left said, "Enter in peace. Congregate in peace. Leave in peace."

Kyan finished the quote, saying the words all dragons exchanged before a formal meeting. "Or make the blood price so high, your enemies will desire peace."

The dragons moved, and he entered the cave. He had been so many times that he knew the way, which was good. No young dragons marked the path he was to take. When Kyan reached Tulvir's den, he yelled, "How high did the blood price need to go?"

"Blame you me for the fae/shifter war?"

"Of course not, but you knew. That's why you had me make jewelry, and you provided the spells. To help protect my family. Why didn't you tell me the details? I could have protected everyone." Kyan paced around the room. He knew it wasn't wise to question a dragon.

"No one lives forever. Not even dragons." Tulvir stretched out and waited.

Kyan sighed. Dragons were the most patient of creatures, waiting long periods of time to exact revenge, but they could also be short-tempered, destroying everything in their path. He stopped moving and waited for Tulvir to speak.

Tulvir huffed, and a bit of smoke came out her nose. "Some events must occur within a specified time. Some events can be altered slightly. Some events can be stopped completely. My assistance prevented the ruling fae from taking over the Seen, but there was no way to remove all loss from the equation."

"Then we are done?" Kyan asked.

"Only if you wish it so. There is more to do, and more I can teach you. The danger to the Seen is not over. I will see you at our next scheduled gathering." Tulvir slowly disappeared from Kyan's sight.

He stared at the empty space for a while. They had been friends for over three thousand years, and he had not known she could fade from sight.

*****

"Don't." Layton stood before Tempest on the bridge to the Western Realm residence.

"Don't what, son mine?"

"Coy doesn't suit you, Mother." Layton stretched his neck. "You have made yourself unwelcome in every court except this one. Why? And before you say anything, remember, I loved Valiant, too. We are not the only to mourn, but you are the only one preventing both sides from healing. If numbers are counted, I'm fairly certain you and Valiant killed more fae than all fae of the five realms combined have killed shifters, witches, and humans. Yet, after the treaty, no one has tried to antagonize you."

"Let them try." Tempest leveled her eyes on her son. "Your count is flawed. You only counted those who died in battle. The fae killed many in the Seen before we went to war."

"Go home. If you want to fight, go fight Lord Ellwood. Of course, if you kill him, you will become the Forest Lord, and a war between the realms will break out. Because of your recent actions, no fae will trust you."

"Who sent you out here on the bridge?"

"No one. Lord River does not know I'm here."

"My son, the entire court knows you're on this bridge with me. They watch."

Layton turned and saw that every balcony was full of spectators. He turned back to Tempest. "I don't want to fight you, Mother, but do not mistake my intention. If you go before the Lord of the Western Realm and act as you have in other courts, I will defend my realm." Layton looked at his powerful mother and added, "If we fight, Ridge will learn of it. Regardless of who kills whom, Father will arrive and kill the victor."

"Think you that your father can kill me?"

"If you were to kill me, you would be too distraught to fight with a clear head. Ridge always fights with a clear head. That you know is truth."

Eyeing him with interest, Tempest changed topics. "Why this realm? Why protect them and not the others?"

Layton bit his lip to keep from smiling. Tempest was ruthless, but if she were calm enough that her curiosity was piqued, she would not fight. "The Western Realm provided me a safe place to raise my family. I will not desert them. You taught me to protect those who deserved protection. We both know you have no fight with this realm."

"I find myself wishing to see my grandchildren upon occasion. Ask Lady Nolween to inform me of an acceptable time to visit. If you both prefer, you may bring them to visit me in the Seen. Lady Saffron will surely open a way for you." Without another word, Tempest opened a way and left.

As soon as the way closed, Lord River appeared before Layton. "What boon do you desire for calming Lady Tempest?"

Layton bowed to his realm lord. "As I said when I first petitioned you for land in this realm, I desire a quiet life away from court."

"If that ever changes, notify me." Lord River teleported away.

Prized

Layton took a deep breath, walked away from the residence, toward his family and home. In truth, he understood Tempest, just as he had understood Valiant. Had someone killed his wife and children — his heart — he would kill all in his path, proving to everyone that he was his mother's son.

A New Era
1901 - 1961 CE

Prized

Chapter 27 — 1901 CE

"Why does she marry every single one of them?" Clarity stood in front of the full-length mirror wearing yet another bridesmaid dress. "And for goodness sake, remember I'm going by Clare now."

"At least we don't have to wear the same dress Rayna is wearing. That's a fashion I'm glad to see gone." Tempest frowned and adjusted her dress to better hide her weapons.

Bliss laughed. "Are you telling me her dress is worse than this pale-yellow train wreck of lace and layers?"

"Probably not, but I haven't seen the dress," Tempest grinned at one of her younger sisters.

"Rayna's dress is lovely, and at least it's white. Unlike you, Tempest, I almost miss the tradition where the bridesmaids wear the same thing as the bride." Serenity came to stand beside her sisters and looked at their reflections. "We are all too pale to wear this yellow color. What was Mother thinking?"

"That she would look more beautiful by comparison." Clare rubbed her arms. "The lace itches."

"Yes, it does. Come, sisters mine. 'Tis time to get our mother wed. Again. Maybe this one will stick." Tempest walked out of the room, followed by Clarity (Clare), Integrity (Rita), Serenity, Pleasance (Lea), Bliss, Patience (Pat), and Charity (Char). When Rayna married, her bridesmaids were always her living daughters. Tempest, as the oldest, was the maid of honor, and the remaining girls lined up in order of birth. It was the only time they didn't line up in their rank order in the Alpha Clan.

"It just might," Serenity said. "Wesley calms Mother."

"About time someone did." Tranquility (Quill), Serenity's twin brother, leaned on the wall, smoking a cigarette.

Prized

"Mother hates it when we smoke," Clare hissed.

"Hush. Have a drag." Quill handed Clare the joint. After she inhaled deeply and handed back the cigarette, he asked, "All better now?"

"Much," Clare admitted, though she didn't smile.

Quill held out his arm to Serenity as their other brothers joined them.

Those brothers who had a sister with whom they shared a father held out their left arm as Quill had. Reliability (Eli) took Pat's arm, and Majesty (Jes) took Char's arm.

Rita walked over to Benevolence (Ben), Pat joined Restraint (Rain), and Bliss took the arm of Eloquence (Quin).

"If Rayna has children with Wesley, I hope she doesn't name them after virtues," Rita said.

"I don't think there are many virtue names left, unless she reuses some names from those who have died." Tempest looked around. "At least we're a handsome group of siblings."

"Yes, you are." Wesley's eldest brother held out his arm to Tempest while Wesley's younger brother offered Clare his arm "Come, let's get those two wed."

"Excellent suggestion." Tempest led them down the path to the tree where the wedding would take place.

Chapter 28 – 1961 CE

Phoenix stomped out of the house, slamming the door behind him.

"Problem?" Kyan didn't look up from his task. Sitting in the gazebo with his stones and tools spread out on the table, he added another gem to Rayna's necklace. She couldn't possibly wear a mother's ring. With today's birth, Rayna was now the mother of thirty-three children, thirteen of whom had died over the centuries.

Curling his lip, Phoenix said, "Why does this kid have a normal name? Sam, of all things. A nice, average name."

Kyan grinned. It was a valid question. Rayna had a habit of naming her children after virtues, and most of them had expressed displeasure with their names at some point, except for the two sets of triplets born and raised in the Farseen. Ellwood's children had always accepted their names, but then, the fae tended to have names that were unconventional by Seen standards. Since she married Wesley Griffin, Rayna chose to name her children after birds. "To be honest, she named your newborn brother, Sparrow. Wesley went to the town hall and told them the name on the birth certificate was to be changed to Samuel Kyan Griffin."

"After you, how sweet."

"I think he used my name to soften the blow to her ego when your mother found out what he had done."

"Dad could have done the same for me," Phoenix muttered.

"Probably not. Rayna has mellowed of late. When you were born, she would not have reacted well to a name switch."

Phoenix would have continued to complain, but Tempest walked toward them. "Later." Phoenix jumped, shifted into a falcon, and flew away.

When Tempest dropped into a chair beside Kyan, he said, "You need to do something about Phoenix's attitude toward you."

Tempest shrugged. She had long ago accepted her role as enforcer, for both the shifter community and her family. Better they hate her, refer to her as the assassin, than the sovereign. "He's entitled to his anger towards me." Tempest verified no one was around, in human or shifter form, and added, "Jes is going to offer Phoenix a job at his hunting lodge in upper New York State."

"Good. At least Phoenix listens to Jes most of the time. At some point, he's going to figure out he has gifts, and he wasn't told."

"I know." Tempest balled her hands into fists and slowly unclenched them. "You've seen how he is. Phoenix won't listen to Mother or me. Like Ilar, and Valiant, he doesn't have to obey anyone. I will keep that information from him as long as I can. I won't watch another brother die because of those gifts."

Kyan watched Tempest walk away. He didn't need any mind powers to know that, nearly four thousand years after the fact, she still mourned Valiant's death and somehow blamed herself.

Farseen Chronicles

Deceived
Enthralled
Betrayed
Revealed
Destined
Vowed
Prized

Finding Earth

Drifters Rising
The Maiden Voyage of the Okar Lane

More information about the worlds of N. R. Tucker's mind – including flash fiction, character lists, glossaries, and maps – can be found at

NRTucker.com

www.ingramcontent.com/pod-product-compliance
Lightning Source LLC
Chambersburg PA
CBHW062120170626
46813CB00002B/518